OMEGA

TRICKED

By S.C. Wynne

The World That I've Created

Dear Reader,

You needn't have read my Bodyguard and Babies series to enjoy this book. However, I've written this small guide to fill you in on a few things about my world just to make it easier on your little gray cells.

My realm exists within the modern, contemporary world. There are omegas and alphas that are wolves, but they appear human, and no longer shift. However, their inner wolf instincts do still affect them very profoundly. The female omegas have the babies and it's the role of the alpha to take care of them when in a relationship.

There are special omegas called solar eclipse omegas. These are male omegas that can have babies. They came about hundreds of years ago when a mystery illness affected the female wolves and they were unable to carry babies. No one knows where the solar eclipse omegas came from, but the why is obvious since they ended up saving the alpha omega world because the sickness didn't affect them.

There is a mysterious group of wise alpha elders called the Ancients who watch over the alphas and omegas, recording history. They mostly stay apart from the regular alpha and omegas, but they do get involved on occasion when they deem it fitting to protect the solar eclipse omegas. No one really knows the extent of the Ancients powers.

The Ancients insist the solar eclipse omegas remain a secret and so most of these special omegas don't even know they are unique, until they become pregnant. Originally, only ten solar eclipse omegas were born per generation, but that seems to be changing and they are becoming more common. No one knows why.

Solar eclipse omegas are born fertile, and have a hidden omega pouch. They do not have a birth canal, and that makes the pregnancies high risk. The solar eclipse omega has a three-month gestational period, and when it's time to give birth they go to a compound in the mountains where there is a special medical facility and community just for them.

Hope this helps you understand my world, and enjoy the book!

S.C.

Chapter One

Dylan

Was it normal to think about ending my life on a daily basis?

Probably not. Of course not.

But life held nothing for me anymore. Nothing inspired me. Nothing excited me. Day after day, I helped pregnant solar eclipse omegas through their pregnancies. I weighed them. Counseled them. Held their hands during their C-sections. Yet inside, I was dead. I was a dried-up twig of the omega I'd once been. I didn't care. Not about the babies. Not about the omegas. Certainly not about the alphas. The last alpha I could tolerate, besides Dr. Peters, was Jack, and he'd gone weeks ago. He and Carter had left the compound with their son, Paul, embarking on a complicated but hopefully bright future.

And here I was, trying to think of a reason to go on.

"Dylan." Dr. Peters's sharp voice cut through my mental fog. "I need a hand here."

I jolted into action, rushing to his side to help him, as he tugged the wiggling infant from the omega pouch. I held the squirming child while he clipped the umbilical cord efficiently. The omega's alpha hovered at the head of the bed, having already expressed no desire to cut the cord. He seemed squeamish about the birth process, like most alphas.

"Is it a girl?" the omega asked, lifting his head, his cheeks flushed pink.

"Yep. She's perfect." I forced myself to sound cheerful.

I took the baby to the area where we cleaned and weighed the newborns. The baby wiggled and whimpered, and I had to stuff down memories of my late son, Ayden. Memories didn't help. They made it worse. It was probably a horrible idea to work as a labor delivery nurse after losing my own child. But that was really all I knew how to do. If I was going to keep breathing, I needed to eat, and that meant I needed to work.

I was definitely disconnected, but I didn't want anything bad to happen to the omegas or the babies. I held on to the hope that by doing something useful like bringing babies into the world, my life still had *some* meaning. I needed to believe there was a reason for me to keep living. A reason other than the obvious reason: breeding. Omegas were made to breed, but I wouldn't go down that road. Never again. I'd done my duty once. I'd bonded with Jacob and had a child by surrogate. Then Jacob had taken everything from me. Everything worth living for. I couldn't imagine ever having another child. I couldn't take that chance. Alphas couldn't be trusted. It was that simple. I'd never put myself in the position of relying on an alpha again. They could so easily tell you what you wanted to hear, even as they did the complete opposite behind your back.

Once Dr. Peters had sewn the omega's abdomen closed, I plastered on a smile and carried the now clean infant to the omega. "She's hungry."

The omega nodded. "Okay. Will you help me? I've never breastfed before."

I set the child on his chest. "Of course. We need to be mindful of your stitches."

"Okay. I can't feel anything now because I'm still numb."

"You'll be sore for about a week, but then the incision should start healing. Ready to breastfeed?" I asked.

The omega nodded, looking anxious. "As ready as I'll ever be."

I met the gaze of the alpha, trying to keep resentment from my gaze. "Did you want to go grab some coffee?"

The alpha frowned. "No." He put his hand on his omega's shoulder." I want to be here for support."

That was surprising; most alphas couldn't wait for a reason to bolt when the subject of breastfeeding came up. "Sure. Whatever you want."

The omega smiled gratefully at his alpha, and the alpha kissed him.

My gut tensed, but I focused on my job. I opened the upper flap on the front of the omega's gown. "Hold the baby up to the nipple. She should instinctively latch on, but sometimes they need a little nudging."

"Okay." The omega did as instructed, and the baby sniffed and fussed. "She's not doing anything."

"Lift her higher," I said softly. "She'll get there."

He frowned, a sheen of sweat on his forehead. "You sure?"

"Yes." I smiled. "It's your first time. Just relax."

He blew out a shaky breath. "Okay." He adjusted the position of the baby, and she suddenly latched on. "Whoa!" The omega winced and laughed. "That feels… weird."

I patted the omega's shoulder. "Good job."

"You did it." The alpha watched with a wondrous expression. "You're a natural, love."

I studied the alpha, wondering why he was so attentive to his omega. It was a nice change, but unusual. Maybe these two really were in love. Just because my alpha had been an asshole, that didn't mean they all were.

Just most of them.

Dr. Peters walked up and addressed the omega. "Looks like you're a pro already."

"Hardly." The omega laughed but looked flattered.

Turning to me, Dr. Peters said, "Hey, Dylan, can I have a word?"

I tensed but nodded. "Of course." Dr. Peters was very easygoing, but I could tell from his serious expression something was bothering him.

Dr. Peters led the way to his office, and I followed, feeling nervous. He had me sit and went around the big oak desk to sit. His leather chair creaked beneath his weight, and he clasped his hands on the desk, leaning forward. "Are you doing okay?"

"Yes," I said automatically.

His expression was skeptical. "You sure?"

I swallowed. "Of course."

He sighed. "I think you need to leave the compound."

Panic jolted through me. "What?" I widened my eyes. "But… I don't want to leave. This is my home."

He grimaced. "Wait. Sorry." He held out his hand in a placating manner. "I just mean, I'd like you to leave once a week to go do something fun."

Relief flooded me, and I slumped in my chair. "Shit. You scared me. I thought you were kicking me out."

"God, no. I need you." He laughed gruffly. "I'd be lost without you. But you're really in your head lately."

I avoided his gaze. "Sorry."

He sighed. "You don't have to be sorry. But, obviously, I need you engaged."

I winced. "I'll do better." I couldn't exactly argue with him since I knew he was right. I was going through the motions and apparently not hiding it as well as I'd thought.

"I think going into town once a week might help you… relax."

"Why would it?"

He looked uncomfortable. "Well, you're young and you must have… needs."

Heat spread up my throat to my cheeks. "Not really."

He cleared his throat. "We all have physical needs, Dylan. There's nothing wrong with that."

I kept my face blank, but inside I was cringing. I had zero desire to go into town to mingle socially with other alphas and omegas. I simply wanted to stay here in the compound and work as many hours as possible. "I'm not good at meeting new people."

"There are singles groups in town. They often have lots of fun activities. Sharing common interests is a great way to get to know someone and make a romantic connection."

I clenched my jaw. "I'm not joining a singles club."

"Why not?"

"I have no interest in making a romantic connection."

He leaned back, looking frustrated. "Dylan, it's not healthy for you to be alone."

"That's old-fashioned thinking."

He narrowed his eyes. "No. Omegas aren't made to be alone."

"Says who? Busybody alphas?"

He looked annoyed, but he kept his voice even. "Says all the research."

"I'm fine alone."

"You're most definitely not fine." His tone was stern. "You've been here six months. You should be getting better, but you actually seem worse lately."

I met his gaze directly. "I lost a child. I can't just go on dates and pretend that didn't happen."

"Of course not. But you can't judge all alphas by Jacob. Most alphas are good. They'd never harm their own child."

I stood, feeling sick. "I don't want to talk about that," I growled.

He held out his hand. "I'm sorry. We don't have to talk about what Jacob did."

"Then why do you always bring it up?"

"Because you frustrate me. You have such potential, but you won't deal with your demons." He scowled. "There's no excuse for Jacob's behavior. But he was unusual. Unstable."

I stared at him feeling nauseous and angry. "Joining a singles group won't bring back my baby. I can't be well because you want me to be."

"I know. But you have to try."

"I don't actually. I just have to do my job better."

His exasperation was obvious. "Which I don't think you will be able to do, unless you deal with your pain and loss."

"I can't be around alphas I don't know." My legs were shaking so bad, I had to sit again. "I can't stand it."

"There are so many quality alphas. I think you'd benefit from spending time with some good alphas."

"No." I shook my head sharply. "I'll go into town. I'll join a damn book club if that will make you happy. But don't expect me to date or find a mate. That will never happen again. *Never*."

His shoulders bowed, and his eyes darkened with empathy. "Okay. I guess it's still too soon."

"Yeah." *A million years would be too soon.* I curled my hand into a fist, trying to control my resentment. What right did he have to butt into my personal life? I worked for him, that was all. Typical alpha, trying to control all omegas they came into contact with. Even the good ones couldn't seem to help that impulse.

"I want you to take tomorrow off."

"But... tomorrow isn't my usual day off."

"I know that, Dylan." His voice was firm. "But I want you to take the day off regardless."

I scowled. "This is ridiculous."

Ignoring my peevish comment, he continued. "Go online tonight and see what local groups interest you. Then take a trip into town tomorrow, and meet some new people. I know you hate the idea of that, but it will be good for you. I'm sure of it."

I exhaled roughly. "Fine." I couldn't even imagine doing any of that, but I didn't want to piss Dr. Peters off. I needed to at least pretend to do what he wanted so he'd let me stay at the compound.

He looked pleased when I acquiesced. "Good. I know you don't agree with me yet, but you'll end up thanking me in the long run. No omega should be alone and cooped up at the compound day in day out. Omegas need companionship, and I think you'll come to see that I'm right."

I stood, my mouth a hard line. "I'll go into town, but I have no intention of dating."

He sighed. "Just try not to be too prickly. If an alpha wants to talk to you, be nice."

I pressed my lips together. "May I be excused?"

His mouth drooped with disappointment. "I care about you, Dylan. I'm not trying to be mean."

"I know."

He sighed. "You can go. I'll see you Wednesday."

"Yep." I stood and left his office, resentment rolling through me. I did realize he meant well; he simply didn't understand what I was going through. Losing a child wasn't something I could just shake off. Learning to trust again wasn't something I had in me. I'd never trust another alpha. *Never.*

Chapter Two

Lex

"You can't just stick your head in the sand, Lex," Gabriele said, raking a hand through his black hair. "The men are looking to you for answers."

I set my watercolor brush down and pulled my painting smock off over my head. I tossed it over a chair carelessly and gave him a hard look. "As I've told you a dozen times, I have no interest in running the Sabine crime syndicate."

"Jesus, Lex. You're the only Sabine left. Who the hell else is going to step up?"

Frustration rolled through me. "Anyone who wants to do it is fine by me."

He widened his eyes. "It doesn't work like that. It's your rightful position as the last of your line."

I scowled and moved to pour myself a glass of whiskey. "You know more about the inner workings of the organization than I do. You should be in charge."

"First off all, I'm not a Sabine. Secondly, I prefer taking orders, not giving them. I'm not cut out to be the head honcho."

I leaned toward him and said pointedly, "Neither am I."

"You don't give yourself enough credit. You're a natural leader."

I grimaced. "But I don't enjoy all the violence and conniving that Dad thrived on."

He twisted his lips. "You're no angel, Lex."

I narrowed my eyes. "I never said I was an angel. But I'm trying to change."

"You've certainly enjoyed the power and privilege your dad's violence and conniving have afforded you."

"Like I said, I'm no angel. But I have tried to distance myself from Dad the last year. I've started a legitimate business, and I want to focus on that."

"You mean the art gallery that you funded using your dad's dirty money?"

My face warmed. "I paid him back every penny. The gallery is making a nice profit now, without Dad's help."

"Lex, you're a fool if you don't think half of your success is because you're the son of Corbin Sabine."

His words hit on my insecurities. Of course I worried that people only supported me because of who my dad was. I longed to stand on my own two feet, apart from my dad, but his shadow was always there over me. I had no idea who liked me for me or who was using me. It was impossible to trust people because the second they knew I was a Sabine, they treated me differently. But I didn't want to live my life as a thug, conning and extorting money. Of course, growing up like I had,

I could be violent if needed, but I liked to believe that wasn't my true nature.

"For all we know Dad is just testing us," I grumbled. "It would be just like him to pretend to disappear to see what we all do."

Gabriele looked unconvinced. "Do you seriously believe that?"

If Dad had only been gone a few weeks, perhaps I would have believed that, but a month away from his beloved empire seemed hard to swallow. He lived and breathed this smarmy business. It was hard to imagine him turning his back on all he'd built just to yank my chain. "I don't know what to think."

"He wouldn't be away this long. His absence has created instability. He wouldn't want that."

"I suppose not."

"Something has happened to him. I'm sure of it. As his only living son, it's your duty to find out what that is. You can't just let someone take him out and not retaliate."

"Retaliate against who exactly?" I arched one brow. "No one has any information. No one is claiming responsibility. No one is asking for money. It's like he just disappeared off the face of the earth. What am I supposed to do about that?"

"You have contacts. You know people."

I scowled and then threw back my whiskey, swallowing it in one gulp. My eyes teared as the liquid seared a trail down my throat. Once I felt I could speak without coughing, I said, "He went up to the mountains, and no one has seen or heard from him since. That's not a lot to go on."

"You haven't even gone up there. Don't you think you should?"

"And do what exactly?"

"Ask questions. At least pretend you give a damn."

Guilt nudged me. "I do give a damn. Maybe I didn't get along with him very well, but he was still my dad."

"Exactly. If someone fucked him over, you need to get revenge. You need to defend the Sabine name, or God knows what will happen. You might be next. If someone is making a power move, we all might be in danger simply because we stand beside you, Lex. None of us have run. Even though there is uneasiness in the ranks because we don't understand what has happened, we haven't deserted your side, Lex. We're still here in case someone comes after you too. We'll defend you to our last breath. You know that, right?"

His words were so fiercely loyal, it was hard not to be moved. I met his passionate gaze. "I appreciate that, Gabriele. I do. I've always respected how loyal you are to my family."

He gave a sharp nod. "Thank you." He shifted uneasily. "It would make me and the men feel better if you took *some* sort of action."

Feeling resigned, I nodded. "What do you think I should do?"

Tension left his shoulders, and he said, "The last phone conversation I had with your dad, he was sniffing around that weird compound in the mountains, trying to locate Jack and Carter. If he found them, maybe Jack killed him just like he did Nick."

I grimaced. "Do you really think Jack would murder Dad? He felt guilty enough about killing Nick."

"Yes, but let's not forget, he killed Nick to protect Carter. Maybe he felt forced to do that again with your dad."

I frowned. "If that was true, I think Jack would come to me, like he did when he killed Nick."

Gabriele chewed his bottom lip. "Perhaps. But unless you go up there to poke around, we'll never know."

"I don't know why Dad couldn't just drop it with Jack. Jack loved Carter. Of course he'd kill to protect him. Nick was an asshole for even threatening to kill the kid. Who of us wouldn't protect those we love?"

"Isn't that what your Dad is doing by going after Jack?"

"No. Dad barely had the time of day for Nick. This is all about pride for him. I'd bet money on that. Jack did what he had to do because Nick was being an asshole. He even risked his life to come to Dad and tell him what he'd done. Dad should have dropped it. When Jack and Carter went off the map, Dad should have let it go."

"Your dad never let anything go."

"Yeah, and now he's disappeared and probably dead because of that."

"If that's true, we need to know that. We can't just go on with no leader, Lex. You must know that."

I exhaled roughly, feeling as if I had no choice. Gabriele had shown loyalty to me, and he and the others were looking to me to lead them. I hated the idea of taking that role, but they had put their trust in me. As much as I wanted to brush my father's disappearance under the rug, that wasn't possible. I was a Sabine, whether I wanted that or not. I couldn't just allow someone to vanish Dad without at least trying to figure out what had happened. Whether I'd been close to Dad or not, I owed him this.

"Fine. I'll go up to the mountains and see if I can figure anything out."

"I'll go with you. Me and one other guy should be good. We don't want to draw too much attention, but I don't want you to go alone."

"Okay." I poured myself another whiskey. "If we discover Dad is dead, that doesn't mean I'll take over the organization. I want you to know that. Yes, I'll do this because I owe it to Dad, but this doesn't mean I'm accepting that my fate is running the Sabine mob."

His expression was empathetic. "I understand."

I lifted my glass and peered at the amber liquid. "If nothing else, going up to the compound should bring us some clarity."

"And hopefully, some closure."

"Amen." I swallowed the whiskey and left the room to pack.

S.C. Wynne

Chapter Three

Dylan

"We're going to start off with something easy that should help chase away the panic I see on some of your faces." A few people laughed as Tom, the omega running the cooking class, smiled at us. "Also, I see we have a few new faces today. Would you like to introduce yourselves?"

I froze as the class turned to stare at me. Sweat broke out on my upper lip as I struggled to think of what to say about myself. I hadn't expected to have to talk and had no interest in sharing anything about myself with this group of strangers. Before I could speak, a deep voice behind me spoke first.

"Well, I guess there isn't much to tell. My name is Lex. I'm in Yellow Springs on business but figured I've always loved cooking, so why not take a class?"

I turned to find a stunningly good-looking alpha in the seat behind me. He must have come in after me because there was no way I wouldn't have noticed him. Our eyes met, and a shiver of awareness passed through me. Startled, I turned back around so my back was to him. I hadn't felt any kind of physical reaction toward any alpha in years. I didn't like that it was happening now. It was unsettling and made me feel like quitting the class immediately.

"Have you ever taken a cooking class before?" Tom asked, smiling at Lex.

"Nope. But I cook for myself a lot. I'm not a big fan of fast food, and I actually enjoy cooking."

Tom nodded, looking pleased. "Excellent." His gaze fell on me. "And what about you? Do you enjoy cooking?"

I squirmed in my seat, feeling annoyed that the teacher was making us introduce ourselves. What was the point? I didn't plan on being besties with any of these people. "I don't cook much," I said quietly.

"That must be nice," a female omega said with a snicker. "I have to do all the cooking at my house. My alpha probably doesn't even know what a grater looks like."

Everybody laughed, and I started to relax a bit, but then Tom focused on me again.

"I don't think you said your name." Tom looked at me expectantly.

I swallowed. "Dylan."

"Do you live here in town, Dylan? Or are you just visiting on business like Lex?"

I grimaced. "I live at the compound."

There was a bit of murmuring from the class. Everyone in town knew about the compound, but what we did there a mystery to most people. The compound did sometimes hire people from town, but they were sworn to secrecy and had to sign an NDA. Solar eclipse omegas were a closely guarded secret. The Ancients didn't want the general population knowing about us, and that was fine by me. The last thing I wanted was to try and explain to people that I could get pregnant just like a female omega.

"Well, welcome," Tom said, his gaze curious now. "We don't get many students from the compound."

I held his gaze in silence and was relieved when another student piped up.

"What are we going to cook today?" she asked cheerfully.

Tom seemed to shake himself. "Uh… pasta puttanesca. It's simple but very flavorful."

Everyone seemed to be pleased with his choice, and I was just happy the attention was off me. Tom explained that we'd break into groups of three to cook. He gave a big spiel on safety using the stoves and knives but quickly reassured us that his speech was mostly just for liability reasons.

Since I'd missed the first class, I didn't know anyone. When everyone began to break off into groups, I felt like I was in grammar school all over again. It was odd to be twenty-two years old but reduced to the awkwardness of childhood simply because of splitting into groups.

Someone tapped my shoulder, and when I turned, there was an omega about my age standing there. His expression was friendly and his green eyes bright. "Want to be in our group?" He gestured to the alpha named Lex, who stood beside him. "I always take the newbs under my wing."

I frowned, not thrilled about the idea of being in a group with an alpha. What was this guy Lex even doing here? Alphas didn't need to cook; that was their omega's job. "Um…"

The omega stuck out his hand. "I'm Tucker by the way. Sorry, I should have introduced myself."

I shook Tucker's hand, unsure of how to respond. I warily eyed Lex again, feeling uneasy. Lex seemed to notice, and he frowned but didn't say anything. Once again, I was struck by how attractive he was, and my pulse raised as our eyes met.

"I don't bite," Lex said softly.

"That's what they all say," I muttered.

Tucker laughed. "Come on, it'll be fun. I know my stuff, and there isn't anyone else for you to team up with anyway."

I glanced around and found he was right. Everyone had already split into threes. I forced a smile at Tucker, carefully avoiding Lex's gaze. "I guess I don't have much choice."

"Not really." Tucker looked pleased. "Follow me. Our cooking area is at the back." He walked away, and I was left with Lex.

Lex studied me. "Have I offended you somehow?" He looked a bit perplexed. "I don't think we've met, right?"

"No. We've never met."

He pushed his hands into his expensive suit jacket. "Then why do I get the distinct impression you don't like me?"

I shrugged. "I'm not a fan of most alphas."

"Ahhhh." He nodded. "I see." He didn't seem offended, which was surprising. "I don't blame you. Most alphas are overbearing and arrogant. I can't stand most of us either."

A gruff laugh broke from my tight throat. "That's a surprising reaction."

"Is it? There's so much chest puffing and macho bullshit among alphas; I find it tedious."

I thought maybe he was pulling my leg, but he didn't seem to be. "I guess we have our dislike of alphas in common."

"Exactly. We might as well be cooking partners." His lips twitched.

His easygoing attitude actually relaxed me. "I guess we can do that. Tucker will be there too, so you're out numbered."

He smirked. "I can hold my own."

"We'll see."

Lex laughed softly under his breath, and I headed in Tucker's direction. Lex followed me, and we listened to Tucker explain how the stove worked and where the cooking supplies were. I had to stifle a few yawns during Tucker's speech. I was tired, and still resentful that Dr. Peters had forced me to do this, but if it kept him off my back, I'd stick with it for a few classes.

"There aren't many alphas who join these cooking classes." Tucker pulled a can opener from the drawer as he spoke.

"Like I said, I like cooking." Lex shrugged.

I eyed his fancy suit. "You plan on cooking in that?"

Tucker laughed. "Yeah, you should at least take off your jacket. That suit looks pricey."

Lex glanced down at his black suit. "Oh, yeah. You're right." He shrugged out of the jacket and went to hang it over the back of his chair.

I didn't want to notice how nice his body was, or the firm strength of his thighs, but I did. He was sexy, and I was obviously sexually frustrated. Why else was I so aware of how good he smelled and unable to keep my eyes off his body? When he returned to us, I made a point of ignoring him. Regardless of Dr. Peters's wish that I'd get romantically involved, that wasn't *my* wish. Besides, Lex was probably straight.

It doesn't matter. Straight or gay, I have no interest in any alpha.

Tom raised his voice to get our attention. "Okay, a little background about this dish. Puttanesca translates roughly into 'Lady of the night,' although not everyone agrees. It's rumored during WWII many Italian women were forced to work as prostitutes, since there weren't a lot of jobs for women back then. Some say prostitutes cooked this meal between clients because they needed a quick dish—I personally find that hard to believe.

I mean, if I have a hot date, I don't eat anchovies, right?"

Everybody else laughed at Tom's joke, but I leaned against the counter wishing he'd just get on with the damn cooking lesson. I didn't want to spend my entire day in town. I simply wanted to do my duty and then head home. When Lex leaned on the counter next to me, I was surprised. I gave him an uneasy glance, but he seemed focused on what the instructor was saying. His shoulder brushed mine, sending warm tingles down my arm, and I stiffened and moved away. Was he completely unaware of how close he was to me, or did he simply not care? I decided he probably just didn't realize how near he was standing. It wasn't like he'd shown any interest in me; in fact, he seemed much more interested in talking to Tucker.

"Okay, first thing we're going to do is chop four cloves of garlic and saute them in olive oil." Tom began to walk down the narrow aisle that separated the cooking stations. "We'll cook the garlic about a minute, just until it smells fragrant."

Lex chuffed. "Garlic is always fragrant."

The class laughed, and Tom grinned. "Good point."

I studied Lex, puzzled by how he could look so sophisticated yet be so seemingly down to earth. I still couldn't understand what he was doing in this class. He was the only alpha, but he seemed completely at ease. Most alphas preferred to hang with their own kind, unless they were on the prowl. But Lex didn't give off a predatory vibe; he actually appeared to be interested in the cooking lesson. I had to grudgingly admit, he piqued my curiosity. If he was here on business, why was he taking a cooking class in the afternoon, instead of working? And what was his business? He looked like a high-roller type. Yellow Springs was a small, quaint town, not really the place slick business types frequented.

I pulled my gaze from Lex and began to chop anchovies as instructed by Tucker, trying not to gag. I wasn't a big fan of stinky fish products to begin with, and cutting these smelly fish wasn't sitting well with my stomach. I swallowed and held my breath, pressing my lips tight to stop myself from heaving.

Lex was dicing tomatoes and seemed to notice I was struggling. He moved closer and said quietly, "Why don't you finish the tomatoes, and I'll chop the anchovies?"

I appreciated him keeping his voice low and not drawing attention to me. "That's okay." Why I said that when I truly wanted to take him up on his offer, I wasn't sure. Pride maybe? I didn't want to look like a wuss?

He frowned. "I'm serious. I like anchovies, but judging from the nauseated expression on your face, you don't."

I paused what I was doing, my stomach rolling from the scent of fish. "Yeah. I'm not really a fan."

He surprised me when he took the knife from my hand and held out his. "Come on, switch with me."

When our fingers brushed, my stomach twittered with awareness. What the hell was wrong with me? Why did he affect me so strongly, when I was trying so hard to ignore him? "Fine," I said brusquely, taking his knife and moving to the cutting board he'd been working at. I didn't like admitting defeat, but I also didn't want to humiliate myself by puking the first day of class.

"It's nothing to be ashamed of," he whispered. "I get that same look on my face when I have to eat ochre."

I didn't respond, baffled by how empathetic he seemed. Since when did alphas give a crap about small things like an omega's feelings? Jacob had been the type to mock me if I showed any weakness.

Tom stopped at our station. "Nicely chopped tomatoes, Dylan. You must have some good knife skills."

Since I hadn't chopped 99 percent of the tomatoes, I grimaced, but before I could come clean, Lex interjected. "Should I toss the anchovies in the pan with the garlic now?" he asked.

Tom nodded and moved over to him. "Yes. Then we'll add the tomatoes, olives, and capers."

"Sounds good." Lex smiled at Tom, and the omega seemed to beam. I couldn't really blame him; alphas could often excite us when they focused their attention on us. If we were open to being claimed, we couldn't help but react to their alpha energy. Tom was obviously open to Lex, but I still couldn't tell if Lex was straight or not. It was possible Lex was just a friendly type of guy.

Tom moved on to the next station, and I addressed Lex. "You should have told him you chopped the tomatoes."

He laughed. "Why? Is there some tomato chopping award I'm not aware of?"

I frowned. "But you did the work."

"So?"

"Alphas usually love the attention and praise." Hell, half the time they took the praise when it wasn't even owed to them.

"I'm here to learn to cook better, not stroke my ego," Lex said, his light blue eyes fixed on me. "Why are you here? You don't seem interested in cooking."

My cheeks warmed, and I looked away. "It's none of your business why I'm here."

"True." He smirked. "But since you won't tell me, now I simply have to find out your story."

Scowling, I gave him an irritated look. "I hope you're joking."

"Maybe."

Thankfully, Tucker came up at that moment, so the conversation died. But it wasn't lost on me that the rest of the lesson Lex seemed to watch me, as if studying for a test. By the time the cooking class was over, I couldn't escape from his inquisitive gaze fast enough.

S.C. Wynne

Chapter Four

Lex

It wasn't easy pumping the good citizens of Yellow Springs for information. While they loved to talk, they had very little to say about the compound nestled in the mountains above the city. It was as if there was some unspoken rule about not discussing what went on there. The secrecy surrounding the fortress only made me more curious. Had my dad stumbled on something going on in the compound and he'd been silenced? I didn't want to be a conspiracy theory type of person, but the unwillingness of anyone to divulge information pertaining to the compound seemed odd.

My one hope was that kid Dylan. I'd taken that local cooking class on a whim, in hopes of breaking the monotony of small-town living. When Dylan had announced he lived at the compound, I'd been floored by my luck. Then when Tucker had picked me and Dylan to be his cooking partners, I'd almost laughed at how fortune was shining on me. I'd spent days hanging out at the local bars and restaurants, trying to get information about the compound, and then miraculously, Dylan had fallen in my lap.

Of course, getting anything out of Dylan had its challenges. He wasn't an easy person to talk to. He was guarded and wary of alphas. There was also a bit of a time crunch. The class was only six sessions long. That meant I'd have to work fast to figure out a way to get close to Dylan before the semester ended. We'd had two classes so far, and I was on my way to the third. Dylan hadn't said much to me during the first two classes, but I held out hope I could charm him. I could sense his unwilling attraction to me. While I was straight, I was usually quite adept at getting omegas of both genders to like me.

When I arrived at the culinary school, I took my usual seat behind Dylan. While he didn't turn around and greet me, I could sense he was aware of me. Tucker came in a few minutes behind me, and he of course was happy to chat. As I talked with Tucker about what the next recipe might be, I noticed Dylan turning his head slightly, as if listening to our conversation. I smiled inwardly, hoping that was a sign he wanted to be friends.

The instructor Tom arrived with a small stack of recipe books. "I thought I'd let you guys choose what recipe you want to cook." He held up three book. "I have Chinese, Mexican, and French cookbooks. I'm going to pass them around, and I want you to discuss with your cooking partners what to make."

Tucker moved to kneel beside us, and Dylan turned in his chair to face the other omega.

"What are you two leaning towards?" Tucker asked, his eyes bright. "I'm open to any cuisine."

Dylan flicked his wary gaze to mine. "I don't really care," he mumbled.

"You sure?" I nudged. "You must have some preference."

I pulled his brows together. "I guess if I had to choose one... I'd probably pick Mexican."

"That's fine by me," Tucker said. "How about you, Lex?"

"Whatever you guys want." I spoke softly, watching Dylan. I wanted him to look at me. It was hard to charm someone who never met your eyes.

"Then when the Mexican recipe book comes around, we'll pick a dish." Tucker stood.

Dylan turned his back on me again, and I stuffed down my irritation. I didn't know what his beef was with alphas, but it was deeply ingrained. I'd been nothing but nice to him since we met, and yet, he didn't trust me. It was obvious.

"Hey, I was thinking, the three of us should grab a drink after class tonight." Tucker had his hand on his hips, and his gaze was direct. He was a confident, warm omega, and it was hard not to like him. He'd been patient with the two of us from day one. I admired his air of serenity. "Would you guys want to do that?"

"Absolutely." I had no reason to rush back to the hotel, and spending more time around Dylan was a great opportunity. Having Tucker along too might be the best way to get Dylan to open up about life at the compound. Dylan wasn't exactly relaxed with Tucker, but he was more so than with me.

Dylan's shoulders tensed and his jaw clenched. "I can't."

Tucker frowned. "Really?"

Dylan kept his gaze down. "I have to get back to the compound right after the class."

"You *have* to get back? Or you want to get back?" Tucker narrowed his eyes.

"I have to."

I didn't know Dylan at all, but I was still fairly certain he was lying. "What's the rush?" I asked, trying to keep my expression pleasant.

He slid his sky-blue eyes in my direction and shrugged. "I just have to get back."

"That's too bad. I'd have liked to spend some time with you out of class." I watched Dylan as I spoke, observing that he looked skeptical.

"Not sure why," he said softly.

"What do you mean? You seem like an interesting guy."

He looked at me as if he thought I was mocking him, which seemed odd. But then the recipe books arrived at our desk, and the conversation switched over to that instead. It was frustrating that Tucker had handed me the perfect opportunity to talk more with Dylan, but he'd shot the idea down. It wasn't like we could force Dylan. If he had no interest in socializing with us, that was that.

We picked the recipe we wanted to cook, enchilada suiza, and Tucker gathered all the ingredients from the pantry. We were halfway through preparing the dish when Tucker got a phone call.

He answered, and then he grimaced. "Shit. Really?" He spoke on the phone a few more moments, then hung up and pulled off his apron.

I paused grating cheese. "Everything okay?"

He winced. "That was my roommate. I'm afraid I have to go. A water pipe busted in the ceiling of my apartment and it's flooding everything."

"Oh, crap." Dylan widened his eyes.

"Damn," I said.

Tucker met my gaze. "I'm sorry. We'll have to grab that drink another time."

"Of course." I smiled. "No problem."

Tucker patted Dylan's back distractedly, and then he took off toward the teacher, no doubt to explain why he had to leave early.

Once he was gone, Dylan seemed even more uptight than usual. He said nothing and just continued to shred chicken with his back to me. I studied the back of his auburn head, wondering what the best way was to connect to the prickly little bastard. With Tucker gone, this was the perfect time to try and bond more with him.

I cleared my throat. "So… what do you like to do in your free time?"

He glanced at me as if surprised I was addressing him. "Me?"

I laughed. "Yeah. You."

He shifted uneasily. "I work a lot."

"What do you do?"

He took so long to answer, I thought he wasn't going to. But then he said, "I'm a labor delivery nurse."

I lifted my brows in surprise. "Really? You deliver babies?"

"Yes."

He looked like he didn't want to keep talking, but I didn't care. I had to make some progress or I'd never get anything out of him. "Do you like it?"

He hesitated. "Yes. Mostly."

"What don't you like about it?"

A gleam of suspicion suddenly appeared in his eyes. "Why do you care?"

"Why?" I asked, taken aback.

"Yeah. Why do you care about my life?"

Irritation nipped at me, but I swallowed my angry retort. "I'm making conversation, Dylan. It's what people do."

"You're asking a lot of questions."

"How else do I get to know you?" I hoped I sounded reasonable. It wasn't easy stomping down my irritation. I never had to work this hard to get someone to like me. His dislike of me was puzzling, especially since I'd been nothing but kind.

He set the piece of chicken he held down and faced me. "But that's just it. Why are you trying to get to know me?"

"Why not get to know you?"

Running his gaze over me, he said, "It doesn't take a genius to see we're very different from each other. You obviously have money. I don't."

"So? I like all kinds of omegas."

"Is that right?"

"I liked Tucker's idea of spending time outside of the class. We should definitely do that."

He narrowed his eyes. "You're not hitting on me, right?"

"*What*?" I sputtered. "Hitting on you?" I laughed gruffly. "No. I'm not hitting on you. I... I date women."

"Oh."

What was that in his expression? Relief? Disappointment? Both? I couldn't tell. "I'm simply trying to get to know you because we're in a class together. My motives aren't salacious." I was flustered he'd thought I was hitting on him. Had I been giving off some sort of lecherous vibe I wasn't aware of?

He watched me as if he wasn't sure he believed me. I kind of had to admire his mistrustful instincts. I *was* simply trying to get information about the compound and had no real interest in his life. Maybe he could sense that. Or, perhaps I wasn't as good at charming omegas as I'd thought I was.

"I don't see why a guy like you would be here in Yellow Springs." He continued to watch me with that piercing gaze of his. "You say you're here for work, but you never talk about your work."

Intuitive little prick.

I tried to think quickly. "That's because I took this class to forget about work."

"Hmmm." He went back to shredding chicken, his shoulders stiff.

I didn't want the conversation to end on that awkward note. "You know, you don't talk about your job either."

He stopped what he was doing, but he didn't turn around. "True."

"But even so, I don't make you feel bad."

He faced me, his expression conflicted. "I'm… I'm not trying to make you feel bad."

I shrugged, making sure my expression had the perfect hint of hurt. "Well, it certainly isn't a good feeling when I'm just being friendly and you shoot me down."

He twisted his lips, studying me intently. "I'm not allowed to talk about my job."

"That's fine. But you don't have to act like just because I'm interested, I'm a bad person."

He frowned. "Sorry.

I sighed. "It's okay."

He met my gaze. "I guess you get me a little flustered."

"I do?" Okay, maybe I did still have it after all. "Why?"

"It doesn't matter." He went back to the chicken. I assumed he'd withdraw into his shell again, but then he said, "So… what is it you do?"

I smirked inwardly. My little guilt trip had worked. "I sell medical equipment." Now that I knew what he did for a living, I figured telling him I was in a somewhat connected field might help form a bond. The more things in common you had with a mark, the easier it was to get close. People who wouldn't give you the time of day often opened up if you shared the same job or knew mutual friends. It was as if you were suddenly welcomed into a secret club.

He perked up. "You do?"

"Yep." I really hoped he wouldn't ask me any detailed questions. My knowledge of medical equipment was limited.

He eyed my slacks. "So you're a salesman? That's why you're always so dressed up?"

I smiled. "Need to look my best."

He nodded, running his gaze over my body. He sucked in a breath and looked away. "I guess."

"My company decided we needed to spread out more on this side of the country."

"Huh." He chewed his lower lip. "It is hard to find reliable companies who'll deliver to Yellow

Springs. They always promise the moon but seldom deliver."

"God, right?" I forced a laugh. "My company strives to be better than that."

"The clinic I work for is always looking for reputable companies. Do you have a business card?"

I froze. *Shit.* "Uh… not on me. I can bring one next time if you want."

He frowned. "You don't have one on you?"

I tried to look sincere. "Like I said, this class is to forget about work."

"Oh yeah."

I layered the shredded cheese over the corn tortillas according to the recipe, all the while thinking of ways to get Dylan to talk to me about himself some more. If I pushed too hard, he'd clam up. That was obvious. But having all this time alone with him was a godsend, and I hated wasting it.

"I have to admit, I find the compound intriguing," I said.

He glanced at me. "Is that right?"

"Yeah. Probably because everyone is so secretive about the place."

"It's a special place, but the less people know the better."

That was an interesting statement. "Is it like an actual city in there?"

He hesitated, and then he said, "It's more like a very large neighborhood. Everybody knows everybody."

"Sounds nice."

"It is." His tone was emotionless. "There are a ton of happy couples."

I laughed. "You don't sound thrilled."

He gave a grudging smile over his shoulder. "It's a wonderful place, but when it comes to happiness, sometimes it's not just about where you live."

I was intrigued by his statement. "What do you mean?"

He shook his head. "Never mind. It's not important."

I sighed. "You know, Dylan, you don't have to be so guarded with me. I'd like us to be friends." I hoped I sounded sincere. Approachable.

His expression was enigmatic, and for a split second he seemed to soften. Then his mouth tightened, and he went back to his chore. "We should focus on this recipe. It's hard to concentrate when I'm talking."

After that comment, I couldn't get anything out of him but grunts. I'd felt like we were making progress, but he was closed off again. He was a tough nut, that was for sure. If I was going to crack his shell, it wasn't going to be easy. If he barely talked to me in class, and he refused to socialize with me and Tucker outside of class, I was at a loss as how to connect to him. I wasn't ready to give up though. He was the one person I'd met in town who worked at the compound. I was determined to figure out a way to get inside that damn fortress and solve the mystery of what had happened to Dad.

Chapter Five

Dylan

I was unsettled to find myself thinking about Lex during the week. He was different from most alphas I'd known, and he was a bit of a mystery. There was no denying I was physically attracted to him. Not that that really mattered. I definitely wasn't in the market for an alpha, and he'd admitted he was straight. But his confidence did turn me on. I didn't want to find him attractive, but it was hard not to. He was one of the most beautiful alphas I'd ever seen. Meeting him had awakened a sexual yearning I'd worked hard to suppress. The moment I'd seen him and caught his scent, I'd felt drawn to him physically. It was unsettling to say the least.

I wiped the sweat from my brow and focused on the paperwork in front of me. Maybe Dr. Peters had a point about how unnatural it was for an omega to keep themselves from all personal interaction. Omegas were social by nature. Maybe because being alone went against our sole purpose for existing. But while I could grudgingly admit I was sexually attracted to Lex, I had zero interest in forming any actual kind of relationship with him or any other alpha. But judging by the warmth of my cock at the thought of Lex, maybe it was time I sought out at least some physical release.

I blew out a shaky breath at the idea of pursuing something physical with someone in town. There weren't really any available alphas at the compound. The only reason alphas were here usually was to accompany their solar eclipse omega. That meant if I wanted to find someone to sleep with, they would have to be in town. That also meant I'd have to put myself out there if I was going to hook up with anyone. I hated the very idea of that, but meeting Lex had reminded me that I had sexual needs.

I couldn't help but blame Dr. Peters for the reawakening of my libido. If he'd never insisted I go into town, I'd never have met Lex. These lusty thoughts only started when I ran into him. I'd been perfectly happy being celibate up to that point. Now, my need was a scratch that definitely needed itching. I'd been distracted enough before, but now I was twice as muddled because thoughts of sex occupied my mind *along* with my grief.

The phone rang beside me, and I jumped. "Hello?"

"This is Sam from Yellow Springs Medical Company. How are you today?"

"Fine." I tapped my pencil on the desk. "What can I do for you?"

"We have your speculum and amniotic hook order. Usually we'd deliver it, but our truck is broken down. I'm sorry, but we won't be able to make it up the mountain for a few days."

I frowned, knowing we were low on those items at the clinic. "Do you want us to come and get them?"

"Well, if you need them, I think you'll have to. We're hoping the truck will be fixed in a few days, but who the heck knows with trucks, right?" He laughed gruffly.

I glanced at my watch. It was almost five, and I'd be off soon. "How late are you open?"

"Six."

I frowned. "I guess I can come to town and get the stuff before then."

"Awesome. I'll even throw in a case of forceps, since I feel bad about this."

"Oh, well, that's kind of you."

"We want to keep your business."

I stood. "I'll be there in about a half hour."

"Sounds good." He hung up.

He hadn't given me the address of his business, so I had to look it up. Grumbling, I texted Dr. Peters to let him know where I was going, and that I was borrowing the clinic's van. I left the compound feeling irritable. As I drove into town, it occurred to me that there was no rush to get back to the compound. If I was serious about trying to hook up with someone, maybe this was the perfect time. My dick throbbed at the thought of that, even as my gut churned. I was nervous about letting an alpha touch me, but I needed relief. Resisting my urges was becoming painful, and I craved the touch of another man's hands on my body. Jerking off was fine up to a point, but there was nothing like the feeling of a thick cock buried deep inside me. I wanted that rush of endorphins that real sex gave me.

Dr. Peters had wanted me to join singles groups so that I could meet someone and actually have a relationship. But I didn't want that. Lust was something I could deal with without forming any sort of romantic connection. Whether Dr. Peters thought I should have an alpha or not was a moot point. I had no desire for that. He couldn't force me to date or take an alpha. The only reason I was considering sleeping with someone was because *I* wanted that. Or at least, I thought maybe I did. I decided I'd play it by ear once I was in town.

The road into town was steep and winding. I had the window rolled down, and I inhaled the tangy scent of spruce pines. The sun felt nice on my shoulder, and the sky was cloudless and deep azure. It was beautiful up in the hills. I enjoyed living away from the bustle of the city. I hoped there never came a time when Dr. Peters asked me to leave the compound. I couldn't imagine where I'd go, and even though I mostly isolated myself from the others at the compound, I did like the people I worked with. They were kind and truly seemed to care about the solar eclipse omegas they helped.

When I arrived in town, I squinted at the addresses on the buildings, looking for the Yellow Springs Medical Company. I eventually found the large whitewashed building on the south side of town. When I pulled through the big gates and into the cramped parking lot, an alpha came out of the building. He was probably in his fifties with gray eyes and a dusting of silver at his temples.

"You must be from the compound. I'm Sam." He held out his hand, and we shook.

I shielded my eyes against the late-afternoon sun. "Nice to meet you. I'm Dylan."

"Again, I'm really sorry about this. That truck has been giving us lots of trouble lately. Probably time to buy a new one, but they're expensive, so the boss has been putting it off."

"It's fine. Things happen." I opened the back of the van as I spoke.

"Appreciate you being so understanding." He smiled and then went back inside the building. He opened the big double doors and began wheeling boxes to the van. Once he had them stacked beside the vehicle, he started loading cases into the back of my van.

I helped him toss some cases into the van, trying to decide if I actually wanted to stop at a bar and have a drink or not. I was definitely tempted, and my pulse raced at the idea of actually having sex. It had been so long—would I even remember what the hell to do? I studied Sam out of the corner of my eye. He had a nice calm energy about him. His hands were calloused and tanned, and he had an easy smile. It would be nice if I could find someone like him to fuck. He didn't seem threatening, and sometimes older alphas were excellent lovers.

Once all the boxes were in the van, Sam brushed his palms off on his jeans and then shook my hand once more. His grip was warm and firm. "Thanks again for coming into town. You saved my ass. The boss was about ready to tie these cases to my back and make me hump them up the mountain myself."

"It's not your fault the truck broke down."

He smiled. "Since when does that ever matter to the boss, right?"

My pulse bumped at his warm smile. "That's the truth."

"But, they have all the power, so what can we do?" He sighed.

"Good point." I hesitated but then forced myself to speak. "Uh… I was thinking about maybe grabbing a beer while I was in town. Know any good places?" I'd barely left the compound the six months I'd been there, so I was clueless about what Yellow Springs had to offer.

He hesitated. "Oh, well, there are a few good ones. You looking for cheap booze or atmosphere?"

I grimaced at my jeans and rumpled T-shirt. "Nothing fancy, that's for sure."

He nodded. "Well, there's the Purple Pooch a few doors down. It's kind of a dive, but the beer is cheap and ice-cold."

"Sounds perfect." I laughed nervously. I was trying to drum up the courage to ask him if he'd care to join me, when I noticed he had a golden band on his ring finger.

Damn.

"There's also Leo's about a half mile away. It's a nicer clientele but pricier." He gave me a good-natured smile.

I pushed down my disappointment that he was obviously taken and moved to the van. "Thanks. Maybe I'll give the Purple Pooch a try. The name is intriguing."

He chuckled and headed toward the building. "Thanks again for being so cool about everything."

I climbed in the van. "No problem." I started the engine and backed out of the parking lot. It would have been nice to have someone like Sam with me when I went to the Purple Pooch. Walking into a bar alone was always daunting, and I was nervous as hell and still uncertain I wanted to do this. I decided I'd go to the Purple Pooch and just play it by ear. I'd have a drink and see if anyone caught my eye. If not, I'd just leave; no harm done.

I parked the van in the back parking lot of the Purple Pooch and sat in the van as anxiety ate at me. My hands that gripped the wheel were sweaty, and my heart banged my ribs. It had been so long since I'd tried to flirt and put myself out there, I felt like I'd forgotten how. It would have been a lot easier if I could just get drunk, but I still needed to drive the van back to the compound. No, two beers would be my limit. Dr. Peters wouldn't be too thrilled with me if I ended up crashing the van because I was drunk.

Opening the vehicle door, I got out slowly. As I approached the building, I could hear music coming from inside the bar, and it reminded me of when I'd been younger. Before Jacob. The dating scene hadn't scared me back then. The prospect of meeting an alpha of my own had excited me. I'd yearned for a personal connection in those days. I'd been a completely different person back; hopeful and willing to trust.

And that trust had almost killed me.

The back door opened and a buff, balding alpha came out, tugging a pack of cigarettes from his back pocket. When he saw me, he ran his eyes over my body. I had to stifle my natural reaction to scowl at him. I needed to try to be nice. Approachable. I was here to be ogled. That was how this all worked. I needed to put my surly, pissed-off attitude away for the night if I wanted to get laid.

"Hey," I said stiffly as we passed each other.

The guy didn't speak, but he craned his neck to check out my ass. I smirked and opened the door to the club. It took my eyes a minute to adjust to the darkness, and I winced as the loud music seemed to rattle my internal organs. The smell of booze and sweat took me back a few years, but I sucked in a calming breath and made my way toward the long oak bar.

The bartender was an older woman with a nose piercing and tattoos covering her arms. "Hey, cutie. What can I get you?" She smiled, which made her look years younger.

"Any beers on tap?"

She snorted. "Baby, we have eight beers on tap. What do you like? I'm sure I can match you up to something."

"Uh… I like Stella Artois."

"You're in luck. That's one we actually have on tap."

"Oh, great." I sat on the nearest stool, trying to relax my tense muscles. I could feel eyes on me, and it just made me more nervous. How had I ever been okay with this meat market scene? But I did remember enjoying it back in the day. I'd liked the chase, and the anticipation. Unfortunately, at the moment, the anticipation was making me light-headed and slightly nauseous.

The bartender turned her back on me as she got my beer. I used the mirror behind the bar to scan the room. There was a dance floor, but no one was dancing. Tables and chairs lined the dance floor, and there were a few booths toward the corners of the room. There were no actual gay bars in Yellow Springs, so omegas and alphas of my sexual persuasion just had to weed through all the straight guys. That wasn't too hard for me because if an alpha was interested, he'd approach me. It was much harder on the gay alphas because they probably got shot down a lot.

The bartender set my beer in front of me. "Running a tab?"

"Uh… I guess." I nodded and slid my credit card across the counter. "Seems pretty deserted in here."

"It'll get busy later. We have a dollar drink special running from seven to midnight. All the cheapskates flood in for that." Her smile took the bite out of her words.

"Hopefully I'll be long gone before midnight."

She nodded. "Uh, yeah. You're gonna be popular. You're adorable and you're fresh meat."

Uneasiness slid down my spine at her words.

That's why you're here stupid—to get laid.

Was this a horrible mistake? Now that I was here, I was definitely second-guessing myself. Yes, I was horny. Yes, Lex had sparked something inside of me that had made me want sex. But what had made me think I was emotionally ready for sex? I was physically ready, but letting someone inside me, well, that was pretty fucking intimate. Suddenly the thought of allowing a stranger to take me felt alarming. Why I'd let it get this far I wasn't sure, but I was definitely freaking out now that I was in the moment.

"Come here often, beautiful?" a gruff voice mumbled near my ear.

I turned to find an alpha sitting beside me. I'd been so deep in thought I hadn't even noticed him sit down. I tried to think of what to say. His line was so cheesy, I could have laughed. Except I also felt like crying at the predicament I'd put myself in. The past few years I'd barely been able to make eye contact with alphas; how the hell was I supposed to let one fuck me? I'd definitely been thinking with my dick when I'd come here this evening. But now, all my bravery had drained away, and I was simply riddled with insecurities and my usual resentment. All I wanted to do was slink out of the bar and pretend this had never happened.

"Shy?" he asked when I didn't respond.

I swallowed hard. "I uh… I think I made a mistake."

He lifted one thick brow. "How so?"

My stomach churned as I held his lecherous gaze. I could smell his arousal, and it made me sick. Lex's natural scent had been clean and grassy, and his cologne expensive. His eyes had been so beautiful it had almost been impossible to look away. This alpha looked rough, and I didn't find him appealing at all. I had no idea why I'd been so instantly attracted to Lex, but I wasn't even the slightest bit attracted to this alpha.

"I shouldn't have come in here."

He frowned. "You just wandered in by mistake?"

"No… but I don't think this is my kind of place."

The guy snorted a humorless laugh. "What are you, some kind of tease?"

"What?" I wrinkled my brow.

"You walked in reeking of arousal, and now you're going to pretend you don't want to get laid?" The guy's mouth was a hard line.

My face warmed because it hadn't occurred to me I'd have been giving off a scent. God, I really had forgotten how this worked. Of course I'd been wafting pheromones. I'd been thinking about sex for days, and that scent would have been obvious to any nearby alpha with a halfway decent sense of smell.

"I'm not obligated to have sex," I said, my voice wobbling. "I'm allowed to come in and have a drink."

The guy hesitated, and then he gave a slow smile. "Sure you are."

Relieved he'd backed down, I drank a big gulp of my beer and stood. "I'm going to use the restroom." I needed to clear my head and figure out if I was staying or going.

"I'll save your seat, beautiful."

I shivered as his voice washed over me, and headed straight for the bathroom. Once inside the small room, I splashed my face with cold water and stared at myself in the mirror. "You're a fucking idiot," I hissed at my reflection. My auburn hair was mussed and my blue eyes bright against my pale skin. "What are you *doing*?"

Someone walked in, and I pretended to wash my hands. I was confused as hell about what to do next. A part of me felt I was overreacting, and a part of me wanted out of this bar immediately. But I didn't want to act like a coward. Maybe I wasn't ready to fuck anybody tonight, but I could still sit and finish my beer. The only way I'd ever get over my antisocial behavior was if I forced myself to be around other people. Dr. Peters was probably right about that.

I exhaled and made myself return to my seat. The alpha who'd been talking to me earlier was still there. I slid onto my barstool and noticed there was a second pint next to the one I'd bought. "What's this?"

"I bought you a drink." He studied me, his muddy brown eyes scanning my face.

"I wasn't sure I wanted another drink."

He shrugged. "Well, I already paid for it."

Irritation rolled through at his arrogant assumption I'd want him to buy me a drink. His smug expression brought back all my resentments against alphas and their controlling behavior. Just because he'd sat next to me and bought me a drink, that didn't mean he owned me or that I owed him anything. But knowing how alphas thought, he probably disagreed.

I signaled to the bartender. "You know what? I think I'm ready to cash out."

She raised her brows. "So soon?"

S.C. Wynne

"Yeah. This isn't really my scene." I had to squelch the desire to give the alpha next to me a dirty look. I wasn't ready for this yet. I still had way too many angry emotions against alphas swirling around inside of me.

"Whatever you want." She went to the cash register.

The alpha gave me an assessing look. "I didn't mean to offend you. You just seemed really uptight, and I thought another drink might help loosen you up."

He was saying the right words, but something about his tone didn't feel sincere. "I'm not looking for sex. I just want to finish my drink in peace, and then I'll be on my way."

He shrugged. "Suit yourself."

I picked up the drink I'd bought and finished it off quickly. I eyed the beer he'd bought uneasily. I didn't want to feel obligated to him.

He gave a gruff laugh. "It's just a drink. No need to overreact."

I didn't respond.

He gestured to the drink he'd bought me. "Look, I get you don't want to hang out with me, but don't waste the beer."

"Why don't you drink it? Then it won't go to waste."

He held up his glass. "I'm more of a rum and Coke kind of guy."

"Oh." I frowned. Maybe he really had just been making a nice gesture by buying me another drink. Anytime I'd ever gone out drinking in the past, alphas had always bought me drinks. I probably was making too much of this. It was just a beer for goodness' sake. I sighed and picked up the second pint. "Thanks."

"Don't mention it." He shifted to face me. "What's your name?"

I figured it couldn't hurt to tell him. "Dylan."

"I'm Hank." His smile didn't reach his eyes.

"You live in Yellow Springs?"

"Passing through." He sipped his drink. "Been here a few weeks, not sure when I'll be leaving. That's up to the boss."

"I see." I sipped the beer, trying to will myself to relax. The music was still so loud it was giving me a headache. In the mirror, I noticed other alphas would sometimes start to approach me, but one look from Hank and they'd turn around. He was definitely acting territorial, which annoyed me, but I figured alphas couldn't help but be that way.

As I sipped the beer Hank had bought me, he asked me questions about Yellow Springs. I didn't really have much information for him since I rarely came into town. When my drink was half-gone, I began to feel a bit woozy. I was surprised since I could usually hold my booze well. But I was definitely feeling the effects.

"Shit. I think that last drink really hit me." I pressed my hands to my throbbing temple, noticing the air in the room seemed stifling.

"Is that right?" Hank stared at me with a blank expression.

I slid off my stool, and my legs were like spaghetti. Hank grabbed my arm, and I fell against him.

"Sorry," I mumbled, trying to stand up straight but finding it impossible.

What the fuck is wrong with me?

"You okay?" the bartender asked.

"He's fine." Hank waved her away. "I'll look after him."

"I god-a go," I rasped. My tongue was sluggish, and I found it difficult to form words. The lights seemed too bright, and the room was spinning. "What's habbening?"

"Just relax, kid. Everything will be fine." Hank's hot breath wafted across my cheek.

He sounded way too calm and unconcerned. I knew suddenly that he'd drugged my drink. There was no other explanation for why I was ready to fall on my ass from a beer and a half. I could drink way more than that. I tried to pull away from him, and he held on tight, digging his fingers into my arm.

"You *fucker*," I hissed. "You roofied me?"

His chuckle was malevolent. "I'm gonna enjoy fucking your uptight little ass."

Fear shot through me, and I started struggling harder. If he got me outside and alone, I was in real trouble. I figured I needed to make my stand now, while I was in public. My vision was so blurry now, I wasn't sure if people could see what was happening. I probably just looked like I'd had too much to drink and Hank was trying to help me. I opened my mouth, trying to call for help, but nothing came out but gibberish.

Hank half carried and half dragged me toward the door. I tried to kick him, but he was too quick, and I was too uncoordinated. He shoved the door open, and the scent of the damp night mixed with tobacco reached my nostrils. I tried to grab the doorjamb to stop him from pulling me outside, but he was way stronger than me.

"Please." I managed to force that word from my tight throat.

He just gave that unpleasant laugh again and continued to drag me out into the parking lot. My heart banged so loudly, I was sure he could hear it. I tried again to kick and punch at him, but I missed.

"What the fuck are you doing, Hank?" A familiar male voice came from behind me.

I couldn't quite place the voice, but I had a glimmer of hope because the person didn't sound pleased with how Hank was behaving.

"Help me," I whispered.

"Let him go," the familiar voice barked.

Hank let go of me immediately, and without Hank holding me up, I crumpled to the ground with a groan.

"He's a snobby prick," Hank grumbled. "He needs to be taught a lesson."

The asphalt was rough against my cheek, and I forced my lids open. Through blurry eyes, I watched a pair of expensive Italian loafers approaching, and then Lex's blurry face appeared as he knelt over me.

Lex studied me like I was a science experiment, and his expression was perplexing. He didn't look concerned; he mostly looked pissed. "What did you do to him?"

"I gave him some circles. What's the big deal?"

"Jesus. What part of keep a low profile did you not grasp?" Lex gave a snort of disgust, and he grabbed me under my arms. With a grunt he pulled me to my feet, and I leaned on Lex in a haze of confusion.

While it seemed Lex might be helping me, he also seemed really annoyed. I could feel impatience radiating off him in waves. The two men bickered as I clung to Lex, trying not to black out. I had no idea what they said, but at one point I was dragged to a black car. The door opened, and I was dumped, none too gently, into the back seat.

I wasn't sure whose car I was in, but I prayed it wasn't Hank's. I wanted to ask what was happening, but my throat was so dry, I couldn't speak. I heard the engine start, and I closed my eyes as everything went black.

S.C. Wynne

Chapter Six

Lex

"What the fuck were you thinking?" I yelled at Hank.

Hank wilted under my anger and dropped his gaze. "What's the big deal?"

"What's the big deal?" I asked, my voice raising with incredulity. "You roofied the one person in town who could get me into that fucking compound!"

"He's out of it. He has no idea what's happening." He gestured to the bathroom, where we'd dumped Dylan in the tub.

"He could wake up any second."

"He won't. He'll be out a while." Hank smirked.

I narrowed my eyes. "Seriously, Hank. What was your plan? You were going to rape the kid, and then what? Was I supposed to try and befriend him after that? He'd be in the hospital or talking to the cops, and they'd all be looking for you."

"Okay, maybe I didn't think it through."

"Ya think?"

Hank shrugged. "You didn't hear how snooty he was. He pissed me off."

I laughed harshly. "I didn't hear how snooty he was? Are you serious? I've put up with his attitude for weeks. But you know what I didn't do, Hank? I didn't drug him and try to rape him."

He winced. "Why are you so protective of him? It's not like I've never done this kind of shit before. Your dad didn't care."

I widened my eyes. "My dad didn't care if you raped people?" I felt sick to my stomach. "I don't believe you."

"You don't have to believe me. So long as I did what he wanted, he didn't care what I did in my spare time."

I had a bad taste in my mouth as I watched him. Was that true? Dad hadn't cared if this Neanderthal sexually assaulted people? How was that possible?

Gabriele came through the door, looking rattled. "Shit. What are we going to do with that kid?"

"I don't know yet," I snapped.

"If he wakes up, we're in even deeper shit." Gabriele scowled. "Why did you bring him here?"

"I couldn't just leave him unconscious in the parking lot." I raked a shaky hand through my hair, looking around the hotel suite. "Don't worry. Nobody saw us bring him up here."

"So now what do we do with him?" Gabriele asked breathlessly. "If he wakes up, he might start yelling."

"Maybe we can find his car and dump him in it," Hank said. "What kind of car does he drive?"

I gave him an irritable look. "I don't know. Some kind of white van."

"There can't be that many of those in the parking lot of the Purple Pooch." Hank met my gaze, dropping his after a few seconds. "Look, I fucked up. But we can still salvage this."

"What if he recognized my voice?" I asked angrily. "All those weeks of kissing his ass and trying to get him to trust me will mean nothing."

"He probably won't remember anything," Hank said with a snide laugh. "Rohypnol seems to give people a kind of amnesia. They never remember shit."

"You have no idea how disturbing I find it that you would know that." I gave him a hard look.

He shrugged.

"Maybe Hank is right. Let's just put a blindfold on him in case he wakes up and dump him in his car," Gabriele said.

"I'm so pissed right now." I glared at Hank. "You've fucked everything up." I held my fingers up. "I was *this* close to getting him to trust me. Now, he won't trust anyone. He'll be twice as freaked-out about talking to strangers."

"Sorry," muttered Hank. "How was I supposed to know he was the same kid you were wooing? I mean, what are the fucking odds?"

I shook my head. "You're unreal." I was a hair from firing his ass. The only reason I hesitated was he was useful when it came to the dirty work. He had no qualms about burying bodies, no questions asked. He'd been with my dad a long time, and even though he was obviously a disgusting person, he was loyal. I needed loyalty right now. When we got back home, I'd figure out what to do about Hank. I wasn't going to have a fucking rapist working for me. Maybe Dad really hadn't cared, but I did. Just looking at Hank made my skin crawl now.

Gabriele's scowl suddenly changed, and he snapped his fingers. "Boss, shit. I think I have a brilliant idea."

"What?" I asked.

"Maybe there's a way to get closer to the kid. I mean, that's the whole point, right? To get into the compound through that kid?"

"Yeah."

He hesitated, and then he nodded. "Yeah, I think this might work." He rubbed his hands together. "What if we tie him up and make him think he's been kidnapped? But we fake that you've been grabbed too?"

"What the fuck?" I looked at him like he was nuts. "Why would we do that?"

"Because then you can both escape together." He laughed. "It's the perfect plan."

I frowned. "So… we keep him instead of dropping him off at his van?"

"Yes." Gabriele nodded. "We'll make it like you were both grabbed together. That way, if he does remember seeing you in the parking lot, you can spin it as if you were trying to help him."

"You think he'll buy that?"

"I do." He laughed. "He already knows you. He's more likely to believe you tried to help him."

"Huh." I frowned.

"We'll make it look good too. Might have to mess up your pretty face a bit."

I didn't love the idea of that, but I had to admit, Gabriele's plan was a stroke of genius. "Shit. That might actually work. He'll bond to me quicker than he would have on the outside."

"Exactly. You'll be best buddies within hours."

"Maybe." I chuffed. "He's pretty stubborn about opening up."

"Yeah, but you'll both be *victims*. He'd already be drawn to you because you're an alpha, and he'll naturally seek your protection. But with you both in the same predicament, it will be you two against the bad guys."

"God." I laughed. "I think this could work."

"So you're cool with the idea?" Gabriele looked flattered.

I nodded slowly. "My only concern is he'll want to go to the cops. That could be a problem."

"Why?" Hank asked.

"Because the cops will want to know who I am. They're not going to be fine with me just saying I'm a salesman from out of town. I can snow the average person with that shit, but the cops will want details. That means Dylan will find out I'm not a salesman, which means Dylan will know I lied to him."

"Hmmm." Gabriele frowned. "That's true."

"Maybe you could convince him that going to the cops isn't a good idea." Hank rubbed his jaw.

I grimaced. "But why wouldn't we go to the cops? If we were kidnapped, that would be the normal reaction. Maybe it's just easier to drop him off at his van after all. It's less complicated."

Gabriele shook his head. "I don't agree. Think about it, Lex. Jesus, you would be close to him instantly. Otherwise, like you said, he's going to wake up in his van ten times more guarded than before."

I sat on the end of the bed, feeling unsure of what to do. "Okay, but I need a good reason not to go to the cops."

"You could say you heard the bad guys talking about how they have the cops in their pocket?" Hank said. "There are plenty of dirty cops. He'd probably believe you."

Excitement rippled through me. "Shit, he might even take me straight to the compound." I met Gabriele's gaze. "If this works, I owe you a fucking big bonus."

Gabriele grinned. "I won't turn that down."

"Hey, what about me?" Hank grumbled.

I gave him a disgusted look. "You almost derailed our whole trip. Are you serious?"

"The kid was asking for it," Hank muttered, giving me a surly glance. "Your dad wasn't so uptight."

Anger boiled in my gut. "Watch it, Hank."

He pressed his lips together, his skin mottled. "I'm just saying, the Sabines break the law all the time. What's the big deal with that kid?"

"We don't *rape* people."

He chuffed. "Your dad has killed plenty of people. Don't start acting like the Sabines are innocent."

"That was Dad. Not me."

Sneering, Hank said, "Keep this up and I'm gonna start thinking you're soft like your dad always said."

"You want me to show you how not weak I am, just keep talking," I growled.

He clenched his jaw but didn't speak.

I straightened and moved away from him before I did something I might regret. I blew out a tired breath. "Okay, we need to be sure housekeeping doesn't come in this room. Also, we should gag the kid and tie his hands and legs ASAP. We don't need him calling for help or making a run for it."

"I'm on it," Gabriele said. "I have rope in my room. Be right back."

Hank stood. "What should I do?"

I studied him. "Stay out of my sight for the night."

His mouth hardened. "Yes, sir." He moved to the door and shot me a resentful glance over his shoulder as he left my room.

My stomach churned because I knew he was going to be a problem. I couldn't have a man like him around. My family did plenty of bad shit, but rape was a line I wasn't crossing. Illogically, it almost felt worse than murder. I couldn't believe Hank's behavior would have been cool with Dad. But something had made Hank think his behavior was acceptable. I was beginning to think maybe I'd known my dad even less than I'd realized.

Chapter Seven

Dylan

I opened my eyes, bewildered to find I was lying in a tub. My temples pounded and I was nauseated. My hands and ankles were bound, and there was a gag in my mouth. I started to panic, feeling as if I couldn't breathe. Sweat ran down my face as I struggled against the tie wraps cutting into my wrists and ankles.

What the hell was happening?

The last thing I remembered was picking up the supplies at the Yellow Spring Medical Company. Had I gone somewhere after that? Had someone jumped me? Terror jolted through me as I realized I couldn't break free from the tie wraps. I was trapped and close to hyperventilating from fear. I tried to slow my breathing because I was on the verge of passing out again. I pressed my face against the cool fiberglass of the tub, willing myself to relax.

It took a while, but eventually my pulse slowed, and the nausea started to subside. I looked nervously around the bathroom where I was being held. There was a pedestal sink, toilet, and the tub I was in. The floor was a tan ceramic tile, and there were no personal items of any kind on the counter. I trained my eyes on the small bottles of shampoo and body scrub in a basket on the sink. They had the bright yellow logo of a local hotel on them. So, I was in a hotel and not someone's house? Was that better or worse? How had I ended up here? No matter how many times I searched my memory, I couldn't remember what had brought me here. If someone had kidnapped me, I couldn't imagine why. I had no money. No connections. I was the last person anyone would bother with.

I strained my ears, trying to hear if there was anyone in the main room. I thought maybe I heard the rumble of voices, but it could have been a TV. I was terrified. How long had I been here? Judging by how numb my legs and arms felt, it had been at least a few hours, maybe more. Since I wasn't a wealthy person, I was afraid maybe I'd just been grabbed by some random psycho. If that was true, what would this person want?

I searched my fuzzy memory for anything that would help me put the pieces together. I'd been at the medical company, and I remembered thinking Sam was a nice guy. Had I gone somewhere with Sam? I vaguely recalled being attracted to him, but I seemed to remember driving away. Why hadn't I gone straight home? Had I been pulled over by someone on my way to the compound?

Closing my eyes, I fought the desire to sleep. I needed to try and think of a way out of this nightmare. I couldn't afford to just sleep and hope for the best. I had to come up with some sort of plan to escape. I shifted my position so that the blood could get to the numb parts of my body. I was thankful my hands were tied in front and not behind my back. That position would have been agony.

When the door suddenly opened, panic shot through me. A tall, slender alpha walked in with a ski mask covering his face. He wore dress slacks, which immediately made me think of Lex. But this wasn't Lex. This alpha wasn't as muscled as Lex, and he didn't have the same air of confidence. He carried what looked like a fast food hamburger and a soft drink.

He moved closer, his eyes emotionless. "Are you hungry?"

I wasn't even close to hungry. I was petrified. I shook my head since talking while gagged was no easy task.

He crouched beside the tub, studying me. "Boss wants you to eat."

I swallowed hard and held his gaze.

He reached for me, and I flinched. He sighed in exasperation. "I'm just lowering the gag."

I continued to stare at him in fear.

"But I should warn you, if you yell, you'll regret it." His tone was cold.

I gave a sharp nod to show I understood.

He tugged the gag from my mouth, and I breathed a sigh of relief as I sucked in air. He unwrapped half of the burger and held it to my lips. When I turned my head away, he grunted.

"Just take a few bites so I can tell the boss you ate something."

My throat was parched, and I eyed the soda. "I'm thirsty, not hungry."

He frowned but put the straw to my lips. I sucked greedily at the sweet, syrupy liquid, feeling as if I couldn't get enough. How long had it been since I'd had anything to drink? It must have been a while because when the straw made loud sounds, signaling I'd drained the cup, I still craved more. He tossed the empty cup into the bathroom trash can and put the burger back up to my lips.

The scent of charred meat and onions made my stomach roll, and I once again turned my face away. "I can't. I'll puke."

He scowled. "He's not going to be happy if you don't eat anything."

I pressed my lips tight, holding his frustrated gaze. I wasn't trying to be obstinate; I truly just didn't want to vomit all over myself.

He stood and tore off half of the burger, then tossed it in the toilet and flushed. "There. You ate half."

Surprised he'd gone that route instead of trying to force-feed the burger down my throat, relief flooded me. I wasn't sure if he'd done that to cover my ass or his, but it didn't matter.

"Why am I here?" I asked, my voice trembling.

He watched me in silence, then bent down and roughly tugged the gag back into place. "I don't have any information for you. Sorry."

Resentment ate at me, but I tried not to show it. What would it hurt to at least tell me why I was being held captive? I averted my face so he couldn't see how angry I was, and I heard the sound of the door opening and closing. When I glanced over, he was gone.

While he hadn't told me anything useful on purpose, the few things he'd said and done had clued me in to a few things: he had a boss directing things, and they wanted me to eat and drink. Apparently, they didn't want me dead. At least, not yet. The guy also hadn't looked or acted like a crazy psycho. He'd seemed cold and deliberate. It definitely hadn't been his first time in this sort of situation. He hadn't been the least bit nervous. But why would professional thugs be holding me? I'd never been involved in anything illegal or run with a shady crowd. I had no rich family to extort for cash, or gambling debts. This entire situation would have made much more sense if I'd been taken by a random sicko.

I sighed and leaned back against the tub. I was so fucking tired. Fear was exhausting, and I was still suffering from the effects of some kind of drug. How someone had managed to drug me was still a mystery. I did have the nagging feeling I'd gone somewhere after visiting the medical company, but I couldn't remember where.

I squeezed my eyes closed, wanting to sleep. Trying to figure this all out was too much. It didn't help any that I felt hopeless. I wasn't sure anyone would even notice I was missing, or if they did, they probably wouldn't be alarmed. Dr. Peters had made no secret about wanting me to go into town to find an alpha. If I didn't show up for a few days, it wouldn't worry anyone. I was a grown person. I wasn't obligated to tell people what I was doing, or spend all my time at the compound.

As fear ate at me, Lex drifted into my mind. My attraction to him was what got me into this predicament. If I hadn't started having lusty urges because of him, I'd most likely be safely at the compound right now. I'd never have gone into that fucking bar— My eyes flew open. *The Purple Pooch*. I'd gone into the Purple Pooch, and there had been an alpha there. I shivered, remembering the guy's bland brown eyes and creepy vibe. Had something happened with him? He'd bought me a drink... but then what?

Think. Think. Did something happen?

My head pounded as I tried to dig up buried memories. Unfortunately, it was as if those foggy recollections were hidden behind a filmy curtain. I could almost grab them, but they fluttered just out of reach. I comforted myself with the knowledge that if that memory had returned, perhaps others would.

Whether those memories would help me get out of this terrifying situation, I had no way of knowing. But I had to believe I would escape. I hadn't gone through all I had the past year just to end up murdered in a bathtub. I'd spent months and months trying to put myself back together after losing Ayden. I'd wanted to die more than anything after my son perished. But I hadn't taken my life. I'd somehow managed to forge ahead, crippled emotionally but trying to heal. I'd had to take it day by day, but I hadn't given in to the desire to end everything.

A strangled laugh stuck in my throat, muffled by the gag. This twisted situation made one thing clear: I didn't want to die. I wanted to escape to safety. After a year of toying with the notion of ending my life, I now realized I didn't want to die. I wanted to live.

My sudden epiphany was shocking, but it also filled me with a strange calm. I'd watch and wait for a chance to escape. I'd act submissive until the moment was right, and then I'd run. I'd run from these monsters who held me. I'd run with everything in me.

I'd run for my life.

S.C. Wynne

Chapter Eight

Lex

"I'm sorry, boss," Gabriele said, right before he punched me in the face.

His fist smashed against my cheekbone, and I gritted my teeth to stifle my cry of pain. My face throbbed, and I glared at him. It wasn't fair to be mad; this was all just part of preparing me for my big acting debut. We'd had Dylan trapped in the bathroom for two days, and it was time for me to play the other victim.

I was going to pretend that I too had been grabbed at the Purple Pooch while trying to save him. I'd say I'd tried to stop Hank from grabbing him and had been taken too. That made me his instant hero. I'd say Hank had kept us separate at first because he'd been working me over, furious that I'd interrupted his kidnapping of Dylan. I hoped Dylan would buy my story and accept that now we'd have to fight together to survive.

I straightened and met Gabriele's apologetic gaze. "Smack my bottom lip. Make it bleed."

"You sure?" He looked uneasy. "Swear you're not going to beat my ass when this is all over?"

I laughed grimly. "While at the moment I'd love to do exactly that, if this plan works, I'll forgive you the bloody lip."

"And the bruised cheek." He winced as he stared at my face. "Shit, it's already swelling."

I touched my cheek and cringed at how tender it felt. "That will just make it more believable."

Gabriele sighed. "Maybe you should have had Hank do this part. I have a feeling he'd enjoy it."

I scowled. "Yeah, a little too much. No, thanks."

"Where is Hank?" Gabriele frowned.

"I sent him to work out in the hotel gym. The guys got too much pent-up aggression." I braced myself. "Okay, I'm read. Hit me."

His face tensed. "Okay." He swung his arm and hit me hard.

I fell backward on the bed, my head ringing. When I licked my lower lip, I tasted blood, and I nodded approvingly. I sat up, and the room spun around a little. "Shit. You clocked me good."

"Sorry." Gabriele truly looked repentant.

I stood slowly and resisted the instinctive urge to punch him back. "Okay. When you throw me in the bathroom, you gotta make it look good. Shove me hard. I'm gonna fight back, so be ready."

"Okay." He clenched his jaw. "I hope this works."

"Me too." I had high hopes. Gabriele said that Dylan seemed more and more demoralized as time went on. Two days of not knowing what was happening had him cowed. "Remember, tomorrow after you bring us food, you're going to accidentally forget to lock the door." I smirked. "Then I'll play the hero and lead us to freedom."

"You've got it." Gabriele sounded confident, but the twitch in his cheek gave him away.

We walked to the bathroom door. "Okay, here we go," I whispered. I had to admit, I was anxious. Dylan had been so difficult to connect to before, a small part of me worried he'd see through this ruse. If so, this whole charade wouldn't work, and we'd have to figure out what to do with him. I didn't like the idea of hurting the kid, but I also had no desire to go to prison for kidnapping. As much as I hated violence, if it was him or me… it'd be him. "Remember, make it believable."

Nodding, Gabriele unlatched the slide lock we'd installed on the outside of the bathroom door. He yanked the door open and growled, "Get in there, asshole."

He shoved me hard, and I went flying onto the ceramic tile. I almost hit my head on the toilet but managed to miss at the last second. I jumped to my feet and lunged toward the door, taking a swing at Gabriele's head. He ducked and kicked me backward, and I fell on my ass with a grunt. I almost laughed because he wasn't playing around. But instead, I plastered an angry expression on my face and tried for the door again. Out of the corner of my eye, I noticed Dylan sitting up, looking startled.

"You'll pay for this, fucker!" I growled, winking at Gabriele.

He didn't respond; instead he slammed the door in my face. I pounded on it, yelling for him to let me out, which of course, he ignored. Breathing hard, I turned around when Dylan started mumbling loudly, his words muffled by the gag in his mouth. When I faced him, I did my best to look shocked.

"*Dylan*?" I hurried to him, hoping I looked convincing. "Jesus, are you okay?" I made my hands tremble as I pulled the gag from his mouth. "I was so worried."

His eyes were wide, and he looked like he was in shock. "You're bleeding."

I touched my lip, looking at the glistening blood on my fingertips. "The bastard punched me." I was relieved he didn't seem suspicious of me; he simply looked bewildered. "I saw the other guy trying to kidnap you. I... I tried to stop him, but he knocked me out and took me too."

"Oh, God. I'm so sorry."

"Don't blame yourself. I couldn't just stand by and not try to help you."

"I can't believe you're here." His face was flushed, his eyes glittering. "I'm... I'm not hallucinating, am I?"

I shook my head. "No. Are you okay? Did they hurt you?"

"I'm fine. I mean..." He wrinkled his brow and glanced at his tied wrists and ankles.

"Shit. Let's get you out of those." I fiddled with the little plastic locking mechanism of the tie wraps, feeling a nudge of guilt when I noticed they had cut into his pale skin. Once I had his wrists free, I went to work on his ankles.

He rubbed the tender flesh of his wrists, wincing when he touched the bruises and cuts. "Fuck, feels so good to move." He groaned and bit his bottom lip. "I can barely feel my arms."

Guilt again hit me, and I started rubbing his biceps and forearms. A weird feeling came over me as I smoothed my hands over his skin; it was a mixture of protectiveness and something else I couldn't put my finger on. "How's that? Better?"

He shivered and avoided my gaze. "Uh… yeah." He clenched his jaw. "That's good. You can stop."

I wasn't sure if he didn't like me touching him or if he really was fine. "You sure?"

"Yes." He swallowed, his face flushed.

Once he was free, I helped him stand and climb from the tub. His legs were obviously weak after days of not using them for anything other than bathroom breaks. He leaned on me, and that strange protective feeling came over me again as his slender, warm body pressed against me. I had the oddest urge to put my arms around him and comfort him. It freaked me out a little, and I had to stop myself from pushing him away.

"I'm sorry," he whispered, pressing his face against my chest. "I'm so fucking weak."

"It's okay." I hooked one arm around his waist and met his wide-eyed stare. My chest squeezed at the gratitude and raw emotion. He'd obviously been terrified, and I felt like a fucking asshole. But he wasn't my friend; he was someone I was using for information. I had to remember that. Dad had disappeared near the compound, and Dylan might know more than he was letting on.

"I'm so happy you're here," he whispered. "I was so scared."

A lump formed in my throat because I'd never seen him so unguarded. Certainly not with me. "It's fine." I patted his back awkwardly and let him go.

He swayed, and I thought he might fall, but he grabbed the towel holder and stayed upright. "You say they beat you?" he asked.

"The big guy was pissed off at me for interfering." I sat on the side of the tub.

He hesitated, and then he sat beside me. "Thank you for trying to help me."

"God. Of course. I had to help."

I'm going to hell for sure.

He shivered. "I think the bigger guy drugged me. He bought me a drink, and then I started feeling groggy."

"What a pig."

He watched me with bloodshot eyes. "I can't believe you're here."

Now that I was seeing him up close and personal, his thrashed condition was getting to me more than I'd expected. He had a couple of days' growth on his chin, and he looked even thinner than I remembered. His delicate cheekbones jutted even more than usual. It had only been two days, but he looked like he'd aged ten years. I'd been so caught up in my plan to use him for information, I'd kind of forgotten he was a real person, and that this experience was probably the worst thing that had ever happened to him.

I forced myself to stop obsessing about how exhausted he looked and focused on the plan. "Did they try to rough you up too?" I asked.

"No. Not yet." He was looking at me like I was Sir Lancelot come to save the day.

"If we get a chance, we have to try and make a break for it," I said softly.

He paled and swallowed hard. "Really?"

"We can't just give up, Dylan. We have to fight. God knows what they have in store for us."

He glanced at the door, his breathing picking up speed. "How many of them are there?"

"I only saw two."

He glanced down at my hands. "I wonder why they didn't tie you up?"

Oops.

I winced inwardly and tried to think of a reason. "They did. I got loose." I rubbed my wrists, pretending they were sore.

"Oh." He nodded, glancing down at his own bruised wrists. "I was out of it. The drug that guy gave me hit me hard. I kept hoping someone would come to help me… but no one did."

I cleared my throat. "Well, I'm here now. You're not alone."

"Yes." A muscle worked in his cheek.

"Do you think you could identify the alpha from the bar if you had to?" I needed to know just how much he remembered about Hank.

He grimaced. "I'm not sure. It was dark in the bar. Maybe?"

I stood and paced, as if agitated with the situation. "How often do they check on you?"

"Twice a day." His cheeks pinkened. "They… they let me use the toilet, and they try to feed me. But I haven't been able to eat."

"No?" My guilt returned at the nervous shake of his head.

"I just can't."

Irritation nipped at me. Gabriele had said he was eating a little. He must have lied. "Well, you need your strength. If we have an opportunity to bolt, you'll need to be able to run."

His gaze was bright. "Now that you're here, maybe I'll feel better. Maybe I'll be able to eat."

I'd expected him to take longer to trust me. But from the grateful expression and the way he kept inching closer, I knew he already felt a bond with me. That made me feel odd. Almost protective. Strange emotions rippled through me as I held his guileless gaze. He'd always been so guarded, his sudden rush of faith in me was a bit heady. I'd have been lying if I didn't admit a part of me liked being his hero. It was nice to have him look at me the way he was doing. My heart squeezed when he gave me a weak smile.

"I'm sorry I was such a jerk to you in our cooking class." He lowered his lashes. "I have trust issues."

"That's all right."

He wrinkled his brow. "I can't believe we're both in this situation together."

I didn't want him to ponder on that point too hard. "We'll get away. I'm confident of that."

He gave a weak smile. "I feel so much better with you here. I was so scared." His shoulders slumped, and he suddenly looked exhausted. "I'm so tired."

"Maybe you should rest," I said.

"I feel like that's all I do."

"You're not eating or sleeping. You've been through a traumatic experience. Why don't you try to sleep?" I put my hand on his shoulder, glad to see he didn't stiffen. "I'll watch over you."

He gave a jagged laugh. "You're being so kind, but you're in as bad a situation as me."

I studied him, taking in his smooth white skin and pretty blue eyes. I seemed so aware of him physically, when I usually didn't notice a guy's looks. "I'm an alpha. I have to be strong."

"I guess."

I grabbed the towels off the towel rack and tossed them on the bottom of the tub. "Use those as a cushion. That will make you more comfortable." I forced a smile. "Sleep."

He looked ready to doze off just sitting there. "Okay. Maybe I will."

I helped him back into the tub, since it was really the only halfway comfortable place to sleep. Once he was settled, I sat beside the tub, bracing my back against the wall.

"I feel bad that you're on the floor," he mumbled.

"I'm fine. Don't worry about me." I shrugged. "I've slept in far worse places." As the words left my mouth, I realized that probably wasn't a very normal thing to say. But I truly had slept in worse places. When I'd been younger, I'd wanted nothing more than to impress Dad. He'd had me sleep in rat-infested warehouses and grimy hotels, telling me it built character. As I'd gotten older, I'd realized he'd probably just found it funny to put me through that shit. Maybe a part of him had believed it would toughen me up, but it didn't seem like something a loving father should put his son through. But then, Corbin Sabine had always been an enigma to me and everyone else.

He frowned. "You have?"

I laughed. "Depending on the city, Motel 6 can be pretty sketchy."

He didn't smile; he simply watched me in silence. I hated it when he went quiet because I had no idea what he was thinking. I relaxed a little when he slumped into the tub and closed his eyes.

"I'm so glad I'm not alone anymore," he whispered.

My stomach clenched, and some strange instinct made me reach out to brush the hair off his forehead. He opened his eyes at my touch, looking surprised. I pulled my hand back. "Sorry."

He blinked at me, but then the tension left his face. "It's okay. It felt kind of nice. Reassuring."

Reassuring. I'm the reassuring kidnapper. Fuck. I'm an asshole.

"I'm glad you feel better with me here." Oddly enough, I wasn't actually lying. I *was* getting a sort of pleasure out of comforting him. Was this what people with Munchausen syndrome experienced? Was I some sick fuck who thought breaking someone down to their lowest point was fine, so long as I then brought them back to a happy place? I'd done many bad things in my life, but this was a new low, even for me.

He closed his eyes again, and soon his breathing became slow and even. I studied him, taking in the beauty of his relaxed features. His lashes were dark compared to the soft auburn hair on his head. His lips were full and his nose perfect. I found myself fascinated with staring at him, and it puzzled me. I almost felt… *attracted* to him. But that made no sense because I wasn't into men. I was into women. Always had been.

I pulled my gaze away and shook my head. It was no doubt just my alpha instincts kicking in. I couldn't help feeling protective of an omega in need. He was vulnerable, and I would have had to be a heartless bastard not to feel remorse for how I'd treated him.

I am a heartless bastard, so why do I care?

He'd be fine once we made our big break for freedom. There was no permanent damage done. Once we escaped, hopefully he'd take me to the compound. There, he could lick his wounds, and I could sniff out information about whether or not Dad had been inside those walls. People didn't disappear into thin air, and Dad especially wasn't someone who you could get the drop on easily. He was a mean, tough son of a bitch, and if he was missing for this long, something bad had happened. I didn't want to think the worst, but I was a realist. I could see Dad walking away from me before he'd walk away from his beloved crooked empire.

But something told me Dad hadn't walked away at all. Not willingly.

Chapter Nine

Dylan

I snapped my eyes open, panicked as I sensed someone else in the dark bathroom. I sat up and recognized the outline of Lex next to the tub. Relief flooded me as I remembered that Lex had been kidnapped too. There wasn't a thug sneaking up on me; it was simply Lex. By some miracle, I wasn't facing this nightmare alone anymore.

"You okay?" he asked softly.

"Yes." I rubbed my face, wincing as the movement stretched the cuts on my wrists. "I forgot you were here."

He didn't respond. What could he say? That he was happy to be here? My bones ached, and I shifted my position. "We should switch off. You take the tub for a while."

"No." His voice was firm.

"Why not?"

"Because I'm not tired."

I sighed and sat up cross-legged in the large tub. "How long did I sleep?"

"Not sure exactly, but it seemed like hours?"

"Really?" I bugged my eyes, shocked I'd been out that long.

"You needed it."

"I guess." I watched the crack of light under the door, noticing moving shadows now and then, as if someone was walking past. Did our captors listen at the door? A shiver ran down my spine. "I wish I knew what they wanted."

"Who knows the mind of a criminal?"

"Another criminal?"

He grunted a response.

"Do you think we'll get out of this alive?" I hated that my voice wobbled, but I was terrified we both might die. That fear had rolled around in my head for days, constantly keeping me on edge.

"Yes." He sounded confident.

I rested my arms on the edge of the tub. "I wish I had your certainty."

"There's no reason to hurt us."

I frowned. "There's no reason to grab us in the first place other than to hurt us."

"Well, you may have a point there."

"God." I shivered. "I don't want to think of what that Hank guy wanted to do to me. Or… still might do to me."

"No. I won't let him." He surprised me when he put his hand on mine. His skin was firm and warm, and I instantly felt better. I knew that was because he was an alpha. It was difficult not to respond to his calming touch. Although, only days ago I hadn't found it hard to resist him at all. Things had changed the minute he walked into my nightmare.

I inhaled his familiar clean scent, wanting to invite him into the tub with me. It would have been so nice to have him hold me. Not in a sexual way, but in a comforting way. I'd been so scared before he came, I'd felt hopeless. I'd wanted to be strong, but being alone for days had eaten away at my resolve. Of course, I didn't bother asking him to join me in the tub. He'd feel awkward doing that. He was straight, and most straight guys didn't hug each other for comfort.

"Do they check on you during the night?" he asked.

"Not usually."

"But they bring food?"

"Yes."

"Is it at least good food? They didn't bother feeding me."

"I think it's fast food? I've been so out of it, I'm not sure what they offered me."

"Don't suppose they offered you an espresso?" he asked wryly.

"Not that I recall." I grimaced. "I didn't dare put in a special order."

He laughed. "No. I wouldn't think so." He removed his hand from mine.

I studied his dark silhouette. "You're taking this situation well."

"What choice do I have?"

"You're an alpha. Shouldn't you try and kick the door down?" I was mostly kidding, but I was a bit surprised at how serene he appeared.

"I'd rather not get shot."

My stomach dropped. "Do they have guns?"

He hesitated. "I definitely saw guns."

"Shit." My pulse sped up. "God, this is so confusing, and... and terrifying."

"Yes." He shifted so that he faced me. "I overheard something when they first grabbed me. I'm trying to decide if I should tell you."

"What is it?"

"It might upset you more to hear."

Fear rippled through me. "Oh, God. What? What did you hear? Are they going to torture us?"

"No. No. Nothing like that." He leaned toward me and said softly, "They said they have the local cops in their pocket."

My eyes widened. "Seriously?" Was that true? Did they have the police on their side? "All of them?"

He shrugged. "Well, I don't know. But if there are dirty cops involved, how would we know who to trust?"

"Right." I closed my eyes, attempting to control the panic trying to take root. "So, if we do escape, we can't go to the police?"

"I wouldn't risk it."

I frowned. "I'd go to the compound… but where would you go?"

"I'd have to try and get out of town."

"But if they have the cops on their side, they might grab you again." Uneasiness ate at me. "I wish I knew what they wanted. If we get away, I have no idea if dirty cops would search for us or if you'd be safe leaving town."

"Me neither."

I studied his still form. "Maybe you could come to the compound… with me. Just until we're sure you're safe."

His head turned toward me, but the darkness hid his expression. "Not sure about that. From what I've heard, the compound doesn't like outsiders."

He was right. We weren't supposed to bring strangers into the compound. The solar eclipse omega's safety was a top priority, and there were protocols that had to be followed. Anybody who worked at the compound, or entered even, had to go through background checks and interviews. Especially after what had happened when Jack and Carter had been here. One of the guards had betrayed the trust of the compound and taken a bribe. Jack and Carter had almost been murdered by some mobster. I didn't know all the details; it had been very hush-hush. But because of that breech in security, the regulations were now even tougher. But surely under these extreme circumstances, an exception would be made? Lex's life would be in danger as much as mine. I couldn't just leave him vulnerable, while seeking refuge myself.

"If we escape, I'll bring you with me. I'm sure I can convince them to let you in."

"I don't know, Dylan. I don't want to go where I'm not welcome." He sighed. "I don't know anything about the compound. It all sounds very secretive."

I frowned. "Yeah, it is. But trust me when I say there are reasons for that." If I did take him inside the compound, what would be his reaction if he found out about the solar eclipse omegas—if he found out about me? Would he be repulsed by us? Fascinated? Could he be trusted with that information when he finally returned home?

"It might be best if I just try to get home."

I frowned. "Well, I can't force you to come with me. But I do think it would be safer for you."

"Hmmm." He didn't sound convinced.

"What's your hesitation?"

"I guess… the compound is an unknown for me. It's hard to feel safe about going somewhere I know nothing about."

"I understand. But *if* we're lucky enough to escape, and if there are dirty cops looking for us, I think it might be the smartest move. Just temporarily."

"Perhaps."

I touched his shoulder. "If we get out of here, it will be your turn to trust me."

I saw his nod in the dim light. "Okay. If we make it out alive, I'll go with you to the compound. But just for a little while, just until we're sure it's safe to leave town."

Relief filled me. "Good." I grimaced. "Now all we have to do is escape."

"Yeah, just that one small detail."

It was bizarre to think that only days ago, I hadn't trusted Lex. I'd found him attractive but hadn't had any desire to get to know him better. He'd seemed too slick, too confident. He'd watched me a lot, and that had made me uneasy. But now we were in a situation together that forced me to rely on him. If we were going to survive this, we needed to depend on each other.

"Why were you at the Purple Pooch?" I asked softly.

He gave a gruff laugh. "Promise you won't judge me?"

"Yes."

"I was looking to get laid."

My face flushed, and I swallowed loudly. "Oh."

"There weren't many women there though. It was almost all guys."

"Don't knock it till you've tried it," I said weakly.

He gave a hard laugh. "Yeah, not interested."

"I know. You made that clear in class." I grimaced.

"Oh, yeah. When you thought I was hitting on you."

Heat deepened in my cheeks. "In my defense, you were asking a lot of personal questions. Most guys don't do that just because."

"I'm in sales, remember? It's my job to ask questions. That's how I make a sale. The more I know about someone, the easier it is to sell to them. I guess it's become a habit to ask questions, whether I'm working or not."

"I see."

"Hey, why were you at the Purple Pooch?" he asked suddenly.

"Oh, well… my memory's a little fuzzy, but I think I wanted a beer."

"That's all?" He sounded skeptical.

"It is a bar."

"True." I could feel his gaze on me. He leaned his head back against the wall. "I wonder what time it is."

I studied the strip of light beneath the door. "I think it's almost morning."

"I hope they feed us. I'm starving."

I wrinkled my face in distaste. "I'm too nervous to eat."

He stood and stretched, then flipped on the bathroom light. I winced and shielded my eyes.

He must have noticed my reaction, because he said, "Sorry." He looked tired, and his suit jacket was rumpled. I'd never seen him anything but perfectly groomed. "That was a long night."

"Yes." I stood slowly, holding on to the tile wall to steady myself. I was still weak from not eating, but I did feel better after having some sleep. "I need to pee. Can you turn your back?"

"Of course," he said, turning to face the door.

Feeling self-conscious, I unzipped my jeans and did my business. Then I redid my pants and washed my hands. "Okay, it's safe to look."

"My turn."

I took his spot, leaning on the door for support. Even though I was weak, it felt good to walk around and get the blood pumping again. He relieved himself and alerted me when he was done. I brushed my teeth with my finger and warm water, and he did the same. We fell into a natural rhythm, moving around each other silently. At one point, he took his shirt off and washed his armpits with the shower gel from the basket on the sink. I couldn't help but check out his bare torso when he stripped off his shirt. He was perfect—muscles in all the right places and tanned, smooth skin.

I was distracted from staring when there was a rattling of the doorknob, and Lex and I locked eyes.

"Get away from the door," a male voice commanded from the other side of the door. "Stand in the tub."

We backed away and did as instructed. I was breathless with fear because maybe they were feeding us, and maybe they were going to murder us. I had no idea which. The door swung slowly open, and the same alpha with the ski mask who'd fed me the last two days entered, holding a tray with two fast-food breakfast sandwiches and two small paper coffee cups.

The guy watched us warily, his eyes glittering from behind the ski mask. I could feel Lex's tension beside me and really hoped he didn't do anything stupid. I didn't want him to get hurt, and I wasn't confident in my ability to back him up, given my exhausted state.

The guy set the cups on the sink counter and tossed the sandwiches at us. Lex caught them both with one hand, which was good because I was so out of it, they probably would have smacked me in the face.

"Breakfast is served," the guy said snidely, and then he backed out of the small room, closing the door with a bang.

I slumped with relief and shook my head when Lex tried to hand me one of the sandwiches.

"Dylan, you need to eat." He frowned.

"I can't." I rubbed my empty stomach.

He ignored me and unwrapped one of the sandwiches. The enticing scent of warm English muffin, Canadian bacon, and butter filled my nose. "Come on. Just take a few bites." He held the sandwich to my lips.

I turned my head. "You eat it."

"Dylan." His voice was stern.

Something inside of me responded to his alpha energy, and I took the sandwich from him. Our fingers brushed, but he didn't seem to notice. I did though, and as tingles spiraled through my hand, I turned away. I definitely didn't want him to pick up on the fact he affected me physically. That would be embarrassing.

He peeled the wrapper off the other sandwich and bit into it with gusto. Kidnapping didn't seem to dampen his appetite any. When he glanced up and noticed I hadn't started eating, he pulled his dark brows together. "Eat."

I sighed and forced myself to bite into the sandwich. It was still warm, and it tasted delicious. I took another bite, suddenly feeling ravenous. He watched me with a little smile hovering on his lips. As hungry as I was, I couldn't make it past four bites. When I held the rest of the food out to him, he frowned, looking disappointed. But he took it.

"No point in wasting it. Not if you want it," I said, giving him a conciliatory look.

"You need food."

I grabbed my coffee and sat on the edge of the tub. "I had food."

"That wouldn't satiate a bird."

I shrugged and dropped my gaze to the floor as I sipped my coffee. After a few minutes, he finished off my sandwich too. I tried not to watch him eat my leftovers. There was something oddly sensual about him putting his mouth where mine had been, and the last thing I needed was to get some random hard-on.

Once the food and coffee was consumed, we tossed the cups and wrappers in the trash. Lex moved to the door, and he pressed his ear against the wood.

"What are you doing?" I whispered.

"Trying to hear what they're talking about." He adjusted his position and kept listening. "It sounds like they're going out," he said softly.

"Really?" I perked up.

He nodded and continued to eavesdrop. "One of them wants to go drink and play pool, and the other guy doesn't want him to do that."

"Seriously?"

"Yes."

"I wish they'd tell us why we're here instead of playing pool."

"Me too." He kept listening. "I think I heard the door."

"Do you think they're gone?" My heart pounded as I stood and approached him.

"I don't know. I think so." He glanced down at the knob, and he twisted it slowly.

"It's no use. They have a lock on the outside of the door." I sighed.

He hesitated. "I know, but… people get sloppy sometimes."

Leaning against the wall, I said, "Sure, but… the odds are slim."

He met my gaze, and his expression was inscrutable. "Dylan, when the guy left, I didn't hear him lock the door."

"Wh… what?"

He nodded slowly. "When he locked me in yesterday, there was a lot of noise when he slid the lock into position." He licked his lips, looking nervous. "But this morning… I didn't hear the lock slide closed."

"Maybe we were just distracted by the food, so we didn't notice."

He turned back to the door, listening. "I'm going to try the door."

"Oh, God, Lex." My pulse spiked alarmingly.

"I know what I heard… or didn't hear." He sounded so convinced, it was hard not to believe him. He slowly turned the knob and pulled on the door. When it moved inward, he looked as shocked as me. "Shit. Shit. I… I don't think it's locked."

I was light-headed with fear. "If there out there, and you open the door…" My voice shook with fear. "They might kill us."

He hesitated. "You don't want me to try?"

I swallowed hard. "I'm just scared."

He nodded. "I know. Me too. But I don't hear them. I think they're gone."

"But if you're wrong?" I whispered, holding his gaze.

He clenched his jaw. "We have to try. We have to."

As terrified as I was, he was an alpha, and I could feel myself responding to the authority in his voice. "Okay. If you really think they're gone." I hugged myself, trying to calm down.

He gave me a curt nod. "You ready?"

No. I'm not even a little ready.

"Yes," I lied, bracing myself for whatever came next.

He slowly tugged on the door and it opened. No lock jangled. Nothing held it in place. It simply opened freely. Lex's mouth fell open in surprise, and I grabbed his arm when the hinges squeaked softly.

"Be careful." My eyes were wide.

He held up a shushing hand, and we listened. There were no sounds from the front room. Of course, that didn't mean no one was there. It just meant they weren't making any noise.

He opened the door wider, and he grabbed my wrist. "Come on."

Now that the door was open, nothing could have kept me there. When he moved forward, I followed, pressing close to him. As we rounded the small hallway that led into the main room of the suite, I saw a master bedroom off to the right. There was no movement though. No one popped their head out to demand we stop. No one thrust a gun in our face. No one did anything at all because the suite was deserted, except for us.

"Thank God," Lex hissed, and he bolted toward the front door. "Hurry."

He still had a death grip on my arm, and he practically dragged me across the wide suite. My heart pounded so hard, I could barely catch my breath. We weren't home free yet. They could still walk in any second and grab us. But I didn't want to think about that. Instead, I pushed away all thoughts of failure and clung to Lex as if he were my lifeline.

Because he was.

S.C. Wynne

Chapter Ten

Lex

The fear in Dylan's eyes when I'd gone to open the door had been so palpable, I'd thought he might pass out. For one annoying second, I'd assumed I was going to have to abort the escape. But by some miracle, he'd trusted me. Shaking with trepidation, he'd followed me. I felt a bit guilty about fooling him, a tad flattered he'd actually listened to me, and *mostly*, relieved we were finally out of that cramped, vile bathroom.

Once we were out of the hotel room, I led Dylan down toward the bottom floor. We passed no one in the hallways or stairwell. From the hotel lobby, I rushed Dylan past the front desk, making sure not to make eye contact with the hotel clerks. The last thing I needed was them asking us questions that might derail my entire plan. Once outside on the sidewalk, we made our way out to the busy street. It was early morning, so there was lots of traffic as people rushed to work. I tried to think like someone running for their life. If I simply strolled along unconcerned, Dylan might begin to suspect why I was so nonchalant about escaping.

"Where should we go?" Dylan asked, glancing around uneasily.

"Should we try to get back to our cars at the Purple Pooch?"

What little color he had in his face drained away. "God, I don't want to go anywhere near that place. Don't you think that would be a bad idea? For all we know the kidnappers are there right now."

He truly *was* thinking like someone fleeing for their life. "So, how do we get to the compound?"

Chewing his bottom lip, he said, "I'll call Dr. Peters. He'll send someone." He tucked into the doorway of the Waterford Realty office. "Mrs. Waterford knows me. She'll let me use the phone. I'll tell her my van broke down or something."

"Okay." I glanced around, as if nervous we were being followed. Truth was, Gabriele and Hank were in the hotel bar. They had strict orders not to leave the hotel until I was able to contact them and give them the all clear. So far, everything had gone like clockwork. Now I just needed to see if Dylan could get me into the compound.

I stayed outside while Dylan slipped into the Realtor's office. I watched through the glass window on the door as he spoke to her. If she wondered why he looked so exhausted and scruffy, it wasn't apparent on her face. Once Dylan made his call, he returned to me.

"They'll pick us up in half an hour." His voice wobbled, and his eyes slid nervously around the area. "Do you think it's safe to wait here?"

"Yes. We're quite a ways from the hotel, and there are a lot of people around."

"I'd feel so much better if we could go to the police."

Without thinking, I put my arm around his shoulders. "It's okay, Dylan. I think we'll be safe now."

He leaned into me, and that odd protectiveness came over me again. What was it about the kid that tapped into my alpha instincts so much? He wasn't the first person I'd ever conned, and he wouldn't be the last. But he had a fragile vulnerability that made me yearn to comfort him. That seemed pretty twisted, considering I was the one orchestrating this whole thing.

He sank down to sit on the redbrick steps, and I joined him. His shoulder pushed into mine, and I didn't really mind. I liked that I could comfort him. I'd never had an omega respond to me so intensely before. Male or female. It was kind of nice to tap into my alpha side and give him the reassurance he obviously needed. It was easy enough to do too. Just a pat on the back here and a kind word there, and he beamed. I'd pull back once we were inside the compound. I wouldn't need to keep him so close to me then, not once I had my objective accomplished.

"If you hadn't been kidnapped too, I'd still be up there in that room." He glanced up at me, his eyes haunted.

"No. You'd have gotten out."

He shook his head. "I was too scared. I told myself I'd wait for the right moment to escape, but the truth is, I was way too petrified to try anything."

I patted his hand. "Well, we're out now. No need to beat yourself up about it."

He stared at my hand resting on his. "True."

I half expected him to pull his hand away from mine. But he didn't. Instead he sighed and rested his head against my shoulder. I glanced around uneasily. I hoped he wasn't mistaking my kindness for anything else. While I enjoyed soothing him, I wasn't interested in anything more intimate with him. But he had to know that since I'd been clear about my sexuality. He was probably just doing what anyone would do under duress: cling to the one other person who understood what you were going through.

"Did you tell Dr. Peters you had someone with you?" I asked.

"Yes." He lifted his head. "He said he'd talk to Charles Pederson, the head of security, to get you an emergency clearance."

"Okay." *Hot damn.* That had been pretty fucking easy.

"You'll probably be restricted to certain areas." He grimaced.

"Really?" I frowned. "Why?"

He shrugged. "Just because."

There it was again, that secretive vibe about the compound. What the hell did they do in there? Was it actually some sort of military base? I decided not to push for details. Once I was inside, I'd find a way to go where I needed to go. If they thought I was Dylan's friend, odds were they wouldn't watch me twenty-four seven. I wondered if Dylan knew anything about Dad's disappearance. I still wasn't sure Dad had actually made it inside the fortress.

"Do you have crime inside the compound?" I asked casually.

"Crime?"

"Yeah, like thefts or murders."

He bugged his eyes, looking horrified. "God, no."

I laughed at his expression. "It's not impossible. Wherever alphas and omegas mingle, there can be trouble."

"We've never had a robbery or murder while I've been there." He wrinkled his brow. "The worst thing that's ever happened was an animal attack at the back gates. But that was a month ago."

"An animal attack?"

He shivered. "Yeah."

"What kind of animal?"

"No one knows," he said quietly.

Uneasiness shifted through me. "Who was attacked?"

Before he could answer, a white van pulled up on the street in front of us.

"Oh, they were quicker than I thought." Dylan stood, looking pleased.

An alpha with dark hair tinged with silver climbed from the passenger side and approached. He wore an olive-green uniform that had some sort of gold insignia on it. I didn't recognize the uniform, but the alpha had a distinctly military air about him. He nodded at Dylan. "How are you, Dylan?"

"I've been better." Dylan gave a dry laugh, but then he gestured toward the older alpha. "This is Charles Pederson, head of security."

"Nice to meet you." I held out my hand, but the older alpha didn't take it. I shoved it in my pocket awkwardly.

"We don't usually allow people into the compound without extensive screening." His expression said he didn't think they should let me in without that now. "But apparently you're in trouble, so I've decided to allow you entrance."

Bingo.

Dylan bumped my elbow with his. "Told you so. I knew they wouldn't hang you out to dry."

I smiled at him. "I appreciate it. It's been a traumatic few days."

"Hmmm. I'm sure it has been." Charles eyed me without emotion. "Well, follow me." He led us to the van, throwing open the side door for us. "Watch your head."

I let Dylan go first, and then I followed, none too gracefully. Once seated, Dylan gave me a reassuring smile. I guess it was his turn to comfort me. I was excited that my plan had worked, but nervous about what came next. Yes, I was going to get inside, but then what? I wanted to ask Dylan more about the animal attack he'd mentioned, but now wasn't the time.

Nobody spoke on the drive up into the mountains. Dylan's head kept bobbing, as if he was falling asleep, and I stared out the window at the thick pines. I wasn't much of an outdoorsman, preferring city life to roughing it. Hopefully they had indoor plumbing and running water inside the compound. God only knew what I was getting myself into, and all because Dad had run off and not told us what he was up to. A simple text telling us what his plans were would have been appreciated, but then, nobody told Dad what to do.

I didn't miss him. I didn't even feel guilty about that to be honest. I'd idolized him growing up, but when I entered my teens, we'd drifted apart. The brutality of his business began to bother me, and Dad changed. He'd been more fair and balanced when I was younger. As the years passed, he got harder and colder. He became consumed by grabbing all the power and money he could. No matter who it hurt. I couldn't respect that. I too could be hard. Maybe even cruel. But everything I did had a reason. I wasn't cruel simply to be cruel.

I glanced over at Dylan. His thick lashes made half-moons on his pale cheeks, and his breathing was steady. He was asleep. His head hung down in an awkward, probably uncomfortable position, especially considering how slender his neck was.

Poor kid.

I had to fight the urge to pull him over and let him rest his head on me. I clenched my jaw against that impulse. What was going on with me?

I was old enough to be Dylan's father, but I wasn't his father. Now that we were safe, I'd expected these protective, nurturing impulses to fade away. But I still felt the need to shield Dylan. Maybe I was simply sleep deprived and not myself. This entire trip had been stressful. Trying to find Dad when the trail had gone completely cold wasn't easy. There was a lot riding on this trip, and if I couldn't find Dad, the pressure to take over for him was going to increase tenfold.

I watched Dylan some more, envying his ability to fall asleep in the van. I couldn't relax. It didn't help any that I kept catching suspicious looks from Charles in the rearview mirror. He definitely didn't trust me. *Good instincts, Charlie.* Hopefully, once I was inside the compound, Charles would forget all about me. I certainly didn't need him breathing down my neck.

The van continued to wind up and up into the steep mountains. The scent of pine was strong, and wild roses' purple blooms poked through the greenery, greedily reaching for the sun. Just when I didn't think I could take the endless winding another minute, the van slowed and turned onto a dirt road. Charles jumped out and opened a metal gate, and the driver steered the vehicle through. Charles climbed back in the van, and we continued on down the dusty road.

Dylan woke up, looking confused about where he was. I patted his leg, and he gave me a grateful smile. "I fell asleep?"

"You did. I envy you."

He rubbed his neck. "You wouldn't envy the crick in my neck."

I laughed. "Next time, use my shoulder."

Looking uneasy, he said, "Hopefully there will be no next time."

The van stopped suddenly and the seat belt cut into my neck. Instinctively, I held out my arm to keep Dylan from flying forward. Of course, he had his belt on too, so it was unnecessary, but he gave me a warm smile anyway. My chest squeezed as his light blue eyes held mine.

"Home sweet home," he said softly.

I peered out the windows and got my first glimpse of the compound. The walls were higher than I'd expected, and barbed wire curled along the top. There was a guard post above the gates, but I couldn't see into it. Were there armed guards? Probably. Charles Pederson didn't look like he'd waste his time running an operation that didn't use guns.

"There didn't used to be barbed wire or guard posts," Dylan said. "Not in the beginning."

"But that changed?" I met his gaze.

He nodded. "Over the years, it's become more obvious that the world is too violent of a place. We can't protect the solar—" He stopped. "People who live here, if we aren't truly prepared to fight."

"It doesn't look like it would be easy to break in."

"It isn't," rumbled Charles. "Not unless you want a bullet between the eyes."

A chill went through me at his cold tone. "That's good to know. Makes me feel safe."

He grunted and opened his door. "Let's go."

We climbed from the van and followed him to a gray building with no windows. When we entered the building, the chill of air-conditioning made me sigh. Dylan seemed to notice, and he smiled.

"Did you think we lived like barbarians?" he asked.

"I didn't know what to expect." I laughed. "This is all new to me."

Charles stopped us as we entered the building. "I need to pat you two down."

Dylan scowled. "What?"

"Need to check for weapons." Charles's hard expression was unapologetic.

"We don't have weapons," Dylan said impatiently.

Charles slid his gaze to me. "Have to be careful."

"This is ridiculous." Dylan shook his head.

"Dylan, I'm already bending the rules hugely letting your buddy in without the usual background checks. How about you show a little respect for the process?" Charles's eyes glittered.

Sighing, Dylan held his arms out, giving me an apologetic glance. "Sorry. I'm sure you feel super welcome now."

"It's fine." I smiled at him. "It's best to be careful. I understand." I was really hoping old Charlie wasn't going to take my fingerprints so he could run them. That would be a major problem because I had a record—and my record wasn't for salesman of the year.

I stood stiffly as Charles ran his hands over me. I stared up at the ceiling, resisting the urge to knee the older alpha in the groin. Once he'd patted down me, and Dylan, he straightened. "You said the guys who grabbed you implied they have the local police in their pocket?" he asked.

I nodded. "Yes."

He narrowed his eyes. "I find that hard to believe."

"Why?" I asked.

"Because I know most of the cops in the Yellow Springs Police Department, and they're not the type to take a bribe."

Dylan shifted uneasily. "You know as well as I do, Charles, that sometimes people fool you." His tone was pointed.

I had no idea what Dylan was getting at, but his comment seemed to have an effect on Charles. He hardened his jaw, and he nodded. "True enough." He rubbed his chin. "There could be a few rotten apples, but no way do I buy the entire department is crooked."

"Will you look into it?" Dylan glanced toward me. "I'm not sure it's safe for Lex to try and go home until we're sure he won't be in danger."

"I'll look into it." Charles's slate-colored eyes rested on me. "I understand you've both had a very traumatic experience and you'll need to rest. But tomorrow, I'd like you to come in and give me some more personal details about yourself, Lex. We can only be so relaxed when it comes to the safety of our residents."

Damn.

If he insisted on fingerprinting me or getting my full name, I was fucked. I was inside the compound, thanks to Dylan, but unless I had a chance to poke my nose around and ask questions, being inside wasn't going to do any good. If Charles kicked me out after the first day, that would screw everything up.

"Sure. I'm happy to talk to you." I made sure I sounded agreeable, but I was going to have to come up with some reason why I couldn't make it in tomorrow. I needed at least a couple of days to sniff out information.

Charles nodded. "Good. I'm glad we see eye to eye on this."

"If we didn't, what would you do? Put bamboo under my fingernails?" I smirked.

He didn't look amused. "I don't find the safety of our residents to be a laughing matter."

"Oh, lighten up, Charles." Dylan sounded annoyed. "Geez."

Giving Dylan an impatient glance, Charles said, "Lex is going to stay with you, Dylan. The only available cabins I have are in the restricted areas."

Dylan looked surprised but not displeased. "That's fine. I have room."

I wasn't sure if I was glad to stay with Dylan or if that would hamper my movements too much. If I'd been staying alone, I'd have had much more freedom. That was no doubt why Charles was making me room with Dylan. Asshole.

"I don't want you going near the clinic," Charles addressed me. "I don't want you roaming the compound. You're to stay close to Dylan's cabin for now."

I frowned. "Feels like I'm still being held captive."

"Not at all." Charles forced a smile, but it wasn't warm by any means. "Just until we know more about you."

"Of course."

"You do realize the only reason we escaped was *because* of Lex, right?" Dylan's cheeks were flushed, and he looked angry now.

Charles appeared unmoved. "Nobody is forcing Lex to stay here. If he's uncomfortable with the rules, I can arrange a ride back to town for him."

"You know that would be dangerous for him," snapped Dylan.

Shrugging, Charles moved toward a door at the back of the long room. "My priority is, and always will be, the residents. It's my job to think this way, Dylan. I'm sorry if that's a problem for you."

Dylan shook his head. "Come on, Lex. Let's get out of here."

Charles stood aside, and Dylan pushed open the door looking pissed.

I was flattered at how defensive Dylan was of me, especially considering how little he'd cared for me when we first met. He'd definitely fallen for my innocent act hook, line and sinker. I patted his back as we walked out into the bright sun.

"It's okay. He's just doing his job." I kept my tone light.

His jaw clenched. "He's always been a hard-ass. You'd think he'd be kinder right now, considering all we've been through."

"Let's forget about him. I'm looking forward to a hot shower and some rest."

He sighed. "Yeah. You're right. Why waste energy thinking about Charles."

Dylan led me along a paved path that spilled into a street. I trailed along behind him as he strode in the middle of the road. There were cabins on either side of the street, painted in bright colors. Abandoned bicycles and children's toys were on the lawns, but there was no sign of any kids.

"It's so quiet," I commented, glancing at the houses that all had their shades drawn. It was as silent as a ghost town.

"I'm sure Charles has issued a lockdown order," grumbled Dylan.

I frowned. "Lockdown?"

"Yes."

"Why?" I laughed. "Are the residents not allowed to see outsiders?"

He paused and then said softly, "It's more about what you're allowed to see."

I had no idea what that meant. "Okay."

He grimaced. "I can't really elaborate. Sorry."

"It's fine. I understand," I lied. I felt a bit like I was in an episode of *The Twilight Zone*. Were there three-headed children living here or something?

After about a ten-minute hike, we stopped in front of a cabin with a trim green lawn. "This is me." Dylan went up the driveway.

I followed him to the front door of the cabin. "This is cute."

He snorted. "Thanks."

"I mean cute in a super manly way." I laughed.

"Of course." He pushed open the door, and I followed him inside.

It was cool and dark. He opened the blinds at the front of the room, and I took in the space.

Bookcases at the far end of the room and one blue couch occupied the living room. Other than that, the room was empty. There were no photos, or artwork on the walls. I stayed silent because I couldn't really bring myself to compliment his decor. There wasn't any real decor.

"I know," he said, giving a sheepish laugh. "There are prison cells that have more atmosphere."

I grinned, grateful I didn't have to lie. "You have a couch and books. What else do you need?"

"Plenty, actually." He grimaced. "I've been at the compound six months, but I've never really bothered to make this a home. It's just where I sleep and eat."

Not sure how to respond, I didn't.

He glanced at me, running his eyes over my body. "You're taller than me, and more muscular."

"Thank you?"

He laughed. "No, I just mean, I don't have any clothes I can loan you. They'd be too small."

I hadn't thought about that. I hated the idea of showering and then putting on the same dirty clothes.

He brightened. "Hold on. My neighbor Jim is about your size. I'll go see if he has anything he'd loan you."

I winced. "Oh, no. I don't want you bothering some strange guy for me. That would be weird."

"He won't mind. He's actually really nice." He moved to the door. "I'll be right back."

Before I could object again, he was gone.

I stood alone in his house, feeling guilty about using Dylan, and relieved I was finally in the compound. It had been touch and go for a few seconds there with Charles. But I was inside, and when night fell, I'd snoop around a little on the grounds. In the meantime, I'd try and pump Dylan for any information I could. He'd probably be much easier to get stuff out of now that he trusted me.

My gaze fell on two small golden picture frames on the bookcase. I hadn't noticed them at first. I moved closer and stopped in front of the photos. They were both of a young child. I wasn't great with kids' ages, but I'd guess the child was no more than a year old. He had auburn hair and the same eyes as Dylan. I knew instantly the child was Dylan's son, and an uneasy feeling came over me. Dylan never talked about having a child. He never really talked about anything personal. Was that because it was too painful? Or was he simply detached?

I picked up the photo and studied it. The kid was cute. Did Dylan have an alpha? If so, why wasn't he living with his alpha? I was surprised at how distasteful I found the idea of Dylan having an alpha. What sense did that make? It was always best for omegas to have an alpha. Dylan was a good kid; he deserved to have an alpha to watch over him.

When the front door opened and Dylan walked in, I set the photo down quickly. Unfortunately, I wasn't fast enough and Dylan saw what I'd been doing. His face tensed, and he closed the door quietly behind him. He held some clothing in his arms, and he approached me slowly.

"Sorry. I was just curious." I gestured toward the photos of the child.

He didn't speak, just kept coming closer, wearing a weird expression.

"I see you were successful in getting me clothes."

"Yes," he said sharply, his stare still focused and borderline accusing.

"I wasn't snooping." I grimaced. "I just saw the photos and wondered who it was."

His mouth was a grim line, and he held out the clothes to me. I took them, and he stood where he was, watching me. I'd never had an omega make me feel small before. I was an alpha after all. We were generally the ones with power in a relationship. Omegas were the more submissive partner. They lived to serve alphas. But the look on his face had me wilting inside. It bothered me that he was upset with me. I'd never felt anything like it.

I gestured to the photo, trying to regain my composure. "Is that your son?"

His cheeks flushed and his eyes glittered. "I don't want to talk about it."

Surprised at the harshness of his voice, I held up my hands. "That's fine. I didn't realize it was a sensitive subject."

"Don't touch my stuff."

"No problem." I studied his angry face, ten times more curious about him than before. What the hell was his deal? He looked ready to stab me for simply touching the photo of his son. His fury intrigued me. He'd seemed so mild mannered, but obviously there was much more simmering beneath the surface. Where had this aggressive energy been when he'd been held captive? There'd been no glimpse of it.

He turned and walked away. "I'll show you to the guest room."

A spark of excitement pulsed through me. I liked this edgier side of him. I liked the angry flame that had ignited in his blue eyes. I felt breathless, and vaguely turned on, as I followed him to the guest room. That last part shocked the shit out of me. I couldn't remember ever being attracted to men, but there was something about Dylan that did seem to affect me oddly. I'd always been drawn to omegas who were troubled. Perhaps that was all this was. I was tired, and my libido probably didn't know the difference right now between a male omega and a female omega. It was simply turned on by the spark I'd seen in him. It was a challenge, and I liked challenges.

Especially in bed.

That thought brought me up short. I had no desire to fuck a guy. None. Jesus, I was obviously exhausted from the last week of trying to find out information about Dad. In fact, the last few months had been very stressful, and draining, with Dad missing. No wonder I wasn't myself.

Dylan stopped at a door and opened it. "There are clean sheets on the bed, and you have your own bathroom."

I stood in the doorway, making sure my face gave away none of the bizarre emotions running through me. "I appreciate this, Dylan. You didn't have to go to bat for me."

His gaze softened ever so slightly. "I owe you my life."

Shame ate at my gut as I held his gaze. I'd rescued him from nothing. I'd helped him escape a trap of my own making. As he watched me, I felt lower than I'd ever felt in my life. If he ever found out what a fucking liar I was, he'd hate me. He'd *loathe* me.

And rightfully so.

Chapter Eleven

Dylan

Lex showered in his bathroom, and I showered in the master bath. As I worked shampoo through my hair, I grappled with the anger I'd felt when Lex discovered Ayden's photos. He hadn't done anything wrong by looking at them, but I'd been mad. I wasn't even sure why. He'd known I was upset, and, surprisingly, he hadn't pushed back. He'd taken my anger gracefully and hadn't tried to put me in my place.

That was rare. Most alphas like him didn't let omegas speak to them the way I had. He was a powerful alpha too. I knew instinctively he didn't take shit from anyone. But he'd been kind. Patient. Jacob would have smacked me across the face for daring to speak angrily. Jacob had been aggressive and weak-willed. He'd been a fucking coward, and I hated him so much it made me shake. It was so unfair that I couldn't hurt him back. I couldn't get revenge on him for all he'd taken from me. I was left to simply seethe, and grieve, without any way to truly heal.

I'd apologize. Lex deserved an apology for sure. I sighed and rinsed my hair. I climbed from the shower, dried off, and dressed quickly. It was nice having Lex in my home. After the harrowing experience I'd gone through the last few days, being alone would have been stressful. But I felt safe with Lex here. I knew logically that nothing could hurt me here inside the compound, but my fear was still there.

I went into the living room and found Lex in the kitchen. He stood with the fridge door open, and he looked guilty when I came into the room.

"I'm sorry. I'm being nosy because I'm hungry." He laughed sheepishly.

He looked sexy with his damp hair combed back. Even his bruised face and cut lip couldn't detract from how good-looking he was. The clothes I'd borrowed for him fit perfectly. He had a much nicer body than my neighbor Jim. The shirt hugged his sinewy biceps, and the jeans showed off his muscular thighs. He smelled like coconut shower gel and that familiar clean grassy scent that was all his own.

His gaze ran over my bare legs, and his eyes flickered strangely. If I hadn't known better, I'd have said I'd glimpsed attraction, but that was impossible. He liked women. Unfortunately.

"Help yourself." I moved closer.

"How about I make us omelets?" he asked.

I frowned. "Oh, I don't want to make you do that."

"I like cooking. Remember?" He grabbed eggs and cheddar cheese. "Do you like omelets?"

"Yes." I leaned against the sink.

He raised one dark brow. "Will you eat if I cook you something?"

My stomach growled as if on cue. I clamped my hand over my flat belly. "I will. Now that I'm not being held captive, I'm happy to eat."

He nodded, his expression serious. "Do you feel better now? Safer?"

"Of course." I didn't bother to elaborate that it was partly because of his presence.

"Good." His gaze was searching. "I'm sorry you had to go through that."

"It's not your fault."

He turned his back on me. "No. I know. But still, I hate that you were terrified."

"We're safe now. That's what matters." I ran my gaze down his broad back, trying not to fixate on his body. "I wish the bastards who did that to us would be arrested. But I know that won't happen."

"No. They're probably long gone from that hotel by now."

While he cracked eggs and heated butter in a sauté pan, I grabbed two beers from the fridge. "Do you drink beer?"

"I do." He took the cold bottle from me. "Thanks."

"I think I'm gonna have more than one." I smirked, popping the lid off the beverage.

He didn't say anything, just sipped his beer.

I set the small table and then sat down to watch him cook. He moved with ease around the space, obviously at home in the kitchen. "You don't look like you needed a cooking class."

He glanced at me over his shoulder. "I was bored."

"Ahhh. I see." I swallowed half of my beer. "You never did get me a business card."

He stilled. "They're back at my hotel. But I'm not sure I want to go anywhere near there right now."

"I don't blame you. I have no desire to go near town period. Not until we know if the local police are truly dirty."

"Yeah."

"What's the name of your company? I can just look it up online to get the phone number. If your prices are good, I'll make sure we throw you guys some business."

He hesitated. "Uh… yeah. That would be great."

I laughed. "So… what's the name of the company?"

He suddenly hissed and dropped the spatula. "Shit. I burned myself."

I jumped up quickly and grabbed ice from the freezer. "Where?"

"My arm."

"Here, let me see."

He held out his arm, and I took hold of his wrist. There was a red welt on the inside of his arm, and I pressed the ice to it. "If you can get ice on the skin fast enough, it may not blister."

He winced at the touch of ice. "Ouch."

I smiled. "I know, but you'll thank me if it doesn't blister."

"True."

I was very aware of his scent and the heat of his body near mine. My cock warmed as my fingers pressed his skin. It would have been so perfect if he liked guys. How convenient would that have been? We could have fucked in celebration of escaping our captors. Nothing made you feel more alive than hot sex.

I felt his gaze on me, and when I looked up, he looked away, his expression confused. "You okay?" I asked.

"Yep." He licked his lips.

I tried not to fixate on his full, wet mouth, but it wasn't easy. I really wanted him. I was surprised at the intensity of my need. We'd just escaped a very traumatic experience, and I didn't chase straight guys. That wasn't my thing. But something about Lex had me buzzing with lust. I didn't want him to catch on, so I kept my gaze down. "Just a few minutes more."

"All right."

I let go of him long enough to grab the first aid kit from under the sink. I smeared burn ointment on his wound and blew on it. "There."

He shivered, and I felt his gaze on me again.

"I uh… I need to flip the omelets or they'll burn," he said gruffly.

"Oh, okay. Let me just bandage it." I did that quickly and released his hand. "That should be good enough. I don't think it will blister."

He wiggled his fingers, grimacing a bit. "It's sore, but I think I can finish."

"You don't have to. I'm sure I can figure out how to flip an omelet."

His lips twitched. "You just stick to saving lives. I'll handle our food needs."

I laughed and went back to the table. "I deliver babies. I'm not saving lives."

"Sure you are. If someone who knows their shit isn't there, things can go wrong." He flipped the omelets onto the plates I'd set beside him earlier.

"Dr. Peters does all the hard stuff. I just assist."

"He wouldn't want just anyone in there with him. He obviously values you, right?" He carried the plates to the table.

"I guess."

"Babies could die if it wasn't for you." He sat as he spoke.

I stiffened and didn't respond.

He must have noticed because he said gently, "I'm sorry. Did I say something wrong?"

I shook my head and picked up my fork, but my hand shook.

"Shit. I obviously did. I'm sorry." He sighed. "I keep upsetting you."

I glanced at him, surprised to find he looked worried. "You didn't do anything. It's just…"

A thick silence fell.

"Look, Dylan, I know something bad happened in your past. It's none of my business, but if you want to talk, I don't mind listening." He sounded sincere, and he touched my arm.

I was horrified when my eyes stung. The lump in my throat was painful as I struggled to keep my emotions in check. I didn't understand why I felt so emotional at the sound of his voice, but something tugged at me. "I never talk about it," I whispered.

"Maybe you should," he said softly.

Why did I want to tell him? I barely knew Lex. Was I simply shell-shocked from the kidnapping? Why would being held hostage make me want to bare my soul to him? But I did want to tell him things. I wanted him to understand why I'd been such a prick to him from the first moment we'd met. I wanted him to know why I'd bit his head off earlier when he'd looked at Ayden's photos. I wanted him to understand that I wasn't just a jerk, I had a reason for how I was. Jacob had turned me into this bitter asshole who stumbled through life afraid to feel again.

He surprised me when he stood and pulled me up too. His strong arms went around me, and a few hot tears spilled down my cheeks. It felt so nice to be held as he stroked my back, telling me he understood. Of course, he didn't. He probably thought I was unhinged. Maybe I was. I felt like I'd gone insane the day Ayden died. I hadn't been myself since. I hadn't been able to find comfort in anything. Nothing. Everything left me cold.

But I did feel a sense of comfort as Lex held me. The heat of his body against mine and the sound of his soothing, husky voice sank right into me. His touch was like a shot of Oxycontin, blurring away the pain that usually ravaged me. I buried my face against his chest. Any second I expected him to push me away, pat my head, and remind me he liked women. But he didn't.

I straightened and wiped roughly at my wet eyes. "Jesus. You must think I'm the biggest wimp."

"No." He shook his head.

I blew out a shaky breath and sat down again, staring at the food. "We should eat before it gets cold."

"Right." He settled in his seat and picked up his fork. He started to eat, keeping his eyes on the food.

I grabbed my fork too and cut into the cheesy omelet with the side of the utensil. I was hungry from days of not eating, but I barely tasted the food. Not because it wasn't delicious—it was. But I was aware of tension between us. I knew he wanted me to talk to him. He wanted me to share what it was that made me lose my shit with him simply because he looked at a photo. I couldn't blame him. He was staying with me. He was probably uneasy about what harmless thing he said or did that could next set me off.

I set my fork down and finished my beer. I stood and grabbed another from the fridge and returned to my chair. After I'd polished off half of my second ale, I wiped my mouth and met his curious gaze. "That photograph is of my son, Ayden."

He nodded but didn't speak.

"He was eighteen months old when that photo was taken." I swallowed, trying not to think about the sweet scent of my son's skin and his husky little laugh that had melted my heart.

Lex pulled his brows together. "But he doesn't live with you." It wasn't a question.

I shook my head.

"I assume you used a surrogate because he looks just like you."

"Yes," I said quietly. Of course, he had no idea I was a solar eclipse omega and able to have babies. But I could only get pregnant with my fated mate, and Jacob hadn't been my fated mate. We'd also used my sperm because Jacob's sperm count had been too low. Maybe that had been the universe trying to prevent someone as defective as Jacob from reproducing.

"Do you have an alpha?" He studied me intently.

That was a very logical question. Few omegas would try and raise a family without an alpha in their life. There was a stigma about single omegas raising children without the presence of an alpha in the home. If you asked me, it was antiquated thinking, but it was how our society functioned.

I cleared my throat, trying to force the words from my tight throat. "I had an alpha. Jacob was his name."

"I see." He stopped eating and set his fork down slowly. "Did he leave and take your child from you?"

I dropped my gaze to the table, fixating on the little scratches in the wood. "He did take my child away."

"Damn."

When I looked up, the empathy in his eyes was obvious. I knew he thought Jacob had simply left me and gotten custody of our son. I clenched my hands, trying to make myself tell him the rest of the story. But I hated saying it out loud. It made it more real when I said the words.

"Do you at least get to see your son?" he asked quietly.

I opened my mouth, but no words came out.

"That's bullshit if he won't let you see Ayden." Anger flashed through his eyes. "Listen, Dylan, I know a lot of lawyers. Great lawyers. Let me hook you up with a good divorce attorney. We might be able to change the terms of your visitation arrangement."

"That won't do any good," I whispered.

"You don't know these lawyers. They're beasts in the courtroom." He sounded confident, and I knew he liked the idea of helping me.

I winced. "No, you don't understand. Of course you don't...."

He tilted his head, his expression puzzled. "What don't I understand?"

"I can't ever see Ayden again."

"But why?"

"Because he's gone."

"Gone?"

I closed my eyes, feeling light-headed. "Jacob and I had major problems. He was... violent. When I finally stood up to him and told him I'd had enough, he... he took Ayden." I opened my eyes, and I was sure the pain in my eyes was obvious because he stilled. "He went to a hotel and he... he." I couldn't keep talking because my throat closed up.

His eyes widened, and horror swept over his features. "Oh, God."

I stared at my clenched fists. "He gave Ayden an overdose of sleeping pills, and he hung himself."

"No," he groaned, reaching out to touch my chilled hands. "God, no. Why? *Why* would he do that?"

I shook my head, holding back my tears. "To hurt me? To punish me? I've asked myself that same question a thousand times. I'll never know exactly what he was thinking, but I know I *hate* him. I hate him so much I can't stand it sometimes."

His touch tightened on my fingers. "No wonder you don't trust alphas. Fuck, no wonder, Dylan."

I exhaled roughly. "Who knows what's inside a person's mind? How can I ever trust anyone again? I'd never have thought Jacob would do that. I knew he was an asshole. I knew he could be cruel. But…" I shook my head. "I never saw that evil in him. If I didn't see it in him… I could so easily miss it in someone else."

His expression was tense. "I don't blame you." Something flickered in his gaze. "I wouldn't blame you if you never trusted anyone ever again."

I was emotionally drained from telling him the truth, but it also felt good. He seemed to truly understand my anguish, and he hadn't tried to give me meaningless platitudes. He'd simply been horrified, and shaken. "I don't like to talk about it." I pressed a hand to my aching heart. "It's painful, and it makes people uncomfortable. They don't know what to do or say."

"Yeah." He pulled his hand away from mine. "I don't know what to say. But… it helps me understand you better. It makes some of the harsh things you've said to me in the past feel less personal. If that makes sense?"

"Good. I'm glad. I don't actually want to be mean. It's just that I find it difficult to trust. I think I always will."

"Of course you will. I would too." He shook his head, still looking shell-shocked.

"You might be the only alpha I truly *almost* trust."

His brows rose. "Me?"

"Yes. After what we went through together, you've pretty much proved yourself."

Red spears appeared on his high cheekbones, and he avoided my gaze. "I'm... flattered."

"I'm glad I told you. It's hard to get to know someone when you're hiding a major chunk of yourself." I smiled tentatively.

"True."

I studied his handsome face, taking in his strong jaw and the upward curve of his mouth. While I couldn't tell him about what I was, or that I could bear children, I'd shared the most important part of myself with him: Ayden. Lex was a good alpha. I was sure of it. I hoped we'd always be close. He'd never see me romantically, but Lex would probably always be special to me. I hoped when he finally left the compound and went home, he'd remember me. It'd be nice to think I meant something to him too.

S.C. Wynne

Chapter Twelve

Lex

After my heart-to-heart with Dylan, we washed the dishes and sat out on the back porch. At first, our conversation was superficial, as if neither of us wanted to return to the emotional mood of earlier. I was still in shock about the story Dylan had shared with me. I couldn't begin to fathom the level of betrayal and heartbreak he'd endured during his young life. Losing a child under any circumstances would be devastating, but to be betrayed by his alpha like that would have done immeasurable damage. No wonder he'd looked at me like I was trying to trick him.

Aren't you?

I winced inwardly, feeling guilt over how I'd fooled him myself. I hoped he'd never need to know how I'd played him. If I could just get some info about Dad, I'd be on my way, and he never had to find out that I'd used him to get inside the compound.

"I'm surprised I like it up here in the mountains," I said, looking out over the thick carpet of spruce pines that covered the hills surrounding the compound. "I'm a city boy through and through, but it is beautiful up here."

"It's so quiet." He sipped his third beer and then sighed. "Sometimes a little too quiet."

I smiled. "Where did you live before?"

"Bartholomew, Arizona."

"Never heard of it."

"It's a fairly large city. Lots of noise, traffic, crime."

I studied his profile, taking in his perfect nose and long lashes. "Do you plan on going back there?"

He frowned. "I haven't thought that far ahead."

"Can you stay here as long as you want?" I asked. "Or will Commander Charlie make you leave?"

He laughed. "He won't make me leave. Charles is all right. He's just a stickler for rules."

"Hmmm."

He laughed again, turning his amused gaze on me. "Really. He's an okay guy."

"He doesn't like me."

"No. He doesn't." He grinned.

It was nice to see him smile. Most of my time with Dylan he'd been either terrified or emotionally in pain. I liked seeing his eyes bright and his mood playful. "I'll probably win him over. I can get most people to like me."

He snorted. "You have quite an ego."

I shrugged. "It's the truth. People usually warm up to me."

He rolled his eyes. "I didn't."

"You did eventually." I smirked.

"We were kidnapped." He chuffed. "I'd have bonded to *anyone* who was thrown in with me."

I was surprised when his heartfelt statement bothered me. "Oh, really?"

"Yes."

"That's not a very flattering thing to say to the alpha who saved your ass." What did I care if he had no real connection to me? I wasn't here to form a bond with him or anyone. I was here to find out info about Dad's disappearance.

He studied me. "I was happy to see you though. Not gonna lie. When they threw you into that bathroom with me…" He laughed gruffly. "I thought I was dreaming."

"See, now you get it. Most omegas think I'm a dream."

"Like I said, you have quite the ego." He sighed and sipped his beer.

We sat in companionable silence, watching the pink and lavender sky darken as the sun lowered in the sky. Once Dylan went to bed, I planned on sneaking out of the cabin. I hoped there would be some moonlight tonight. I didn't have a flashlight, but if I did, I'd probably have been reticent to use it. No doubt Charles and his minions would notice any unauthorized flashlight usage.

"Is there anyone waiting anxiously for you to return home?" he asked casually.

"No one in particular." I shot him a glance, wondering why he was asking. "Why?"

"Curiosity." He avoided my gaze. "I don't know much about your personal life. I know you like women, and that you can cook."

"And that I'm a hero."

He laughed, and shook his head. "Well, you're my hero."

Oddly enough, pleasure washed through me at his soft words. "I'm gathering you don't get a lot of visitors here?"

"Why do you say that?"

"Because Charles didn't seem happy to have me arrive on his doorstep."

"We get visitors. They don't usually stay long."

I frowned. "I still don't get what the point of this place is. It doesn't have a vacation vibe."

"No. This isn't a vacation resort. I know you have a million questions." He sighed. "I'm afraid I can't enlighten you."

"Why not? Is it a military thing?"

"No."

I drummed my fingers on the arm of my chair. "You never finished telling me about that animal attack."

He stilled. "I don't know much."

"Who was attacked?"

"They don't know."

I frowned. "Wait. What?"

He pulled his lips tight across his teeth in a grimace. "I don't know all the details. I know one of the guards took a bribe and almost got some guests killed. But I don't know who wanted to hurt them."

"How does that tie in with an animal attack?"

"Apparently it all happened at the same time." He gave a raspy laugh. "I seriously have no idea what actually happened. I just know that the crooked guard was fired, and later it was discovered that there was blood and some ripped clothing behind the compound. Charles said he found tracks, and that it was an animal attack of some kind, but the blood was too contaminated for any reliable DNA to be gathered."

An uneasy feeling came over me as he spoke. Was it possible Dad had bribed that guard? That was exactly the kind of thing he'd do, and he'd been hanging around the compound. He'd been hell-bent on finding Jack and Carter, and according to Gabriele, their trail had led him here. Had Dad been up here at the time of the animal attack?

Dylan was watching me. "Are you okay? You look a little pale."

I shook myself. "Sure. It's just a bit unsettling to think some animal attacked someone right outside of the compound."

"I agree. It shook everyone up for a while. But no body was ever found, and there were tire tracks driving away from the scene. Maybe whoever it was drove away."

"And never reported being attacked?" I frowned. "That seems weird."

"I guess."

"If there's a wild animal attacking people, wouldn't you think that person would have come forward? If only to warn others?"

He nodded. "I know what you mean. The whole incident seemed odd. But it was obvious Charles didn't really want anyone asking questions, so no one pushed."

"Is that how it is around here? If Charles tells you to drop it, you drop it?" I scowled.

"Pretty much. He works closely with the Ancients."

The Ancients.

I laughed. "God, I haven't thought about them since I was a kid." My mom had told me stories of the Ancients, when I was a child. But Dad hadn't had any interest in what he called "Fairy Tales." After Mom passed, he hadn't ever mentioned the Ancients.

Dylan didn't say anything. He finished off his beer and set the empty bottle next to his chair. Then he put his feet up on the porch railing and let out a long sigh.

"Have you ever seen the Ancients?"

"No." He frowned.

"But you believe in them?"

"Well, yes. Charles talks to them. He wouldn't lie about that."

"How do you know?"

"Because Charles may be a hard-ass, but he's honorable and scrupulously honest." He gave me an irritable look. "I know you don't like him any more than he likes you, but he's a good alpha. He keeps us safe."

I laughed. "From what? Other than that one supposed animal attack, you say there's no crime here. What exactly is he protecting you from?"

He leaned toward me, his expression dead serious. "The outside."

I raised my brows. "Wow. That's... wow."

He clenched his jaw. "You don't understand because you only have half the story."

"So tell me the whole story."

He shook his head sharply. "Hell no."

His unwillingness to talk annoyed me. But I tried to push down my frustrations. If I got him pissed off at me, he wouldn't want me around, and at the moment, he was my only ally. Without him championing me, Charles would toss my ass out of the compound immediately.

"Suit yourself." I stood, faking a yawn. "If it's okay with you, I think I'd like to hit the hay early. I'm exhausted."

"Of course." He looked up at me, his expression inscrutable. "I'll be joining you soon." He grimaced. "I don't mean I'll be *joining* you... I mean, I'll be going to bed too. Soon."

I laughed. "Yeah, I didn't think you planned on sleeping with me."

He smirked, and his eyes had a flirty gleam. "I mean, I'm game if you are."

"Uh, yeah. We've been over this." I was surprised to find his flirting didn't bother me. I almost liked the fact that he found me attractive. Maybe it was my ego. After all, it was flattering when someone found you attractive, of either sex. "Nothing personal. I'm sure you're amazing in bed. But I like boobs."

He laughed and glanced down at his chest. "Well, damn."

Chuckling, I headed toward the french doors that led into the house. "I'll see you in the morning, Dylan."

"Night, Lex." He gave a careless wave.

Once I was in my room, I closed the door and lay on the bed. I stayed in my clothes, ready for my night of snooping. I thought about my conversation with Dylan concerning the supposed animal attack. Dad had been up here searching for Jack and Carter. But even if Dad had been up here during the time of the animal attack, I couldn't imagine *any* animal getting the drop on him. Not to mention his driver, Sal, who was a mean son of a bitch. But the fact that neither man had bothered to contact anyone for an entire month was mystifying. Worrisome.

I stared out the window at the inky black sky, watching the stars twinkle like tiny candles.

An hour passed, and then another. My eyes grew heavy, and I had to fight the desire to sleep. Since Dad had disappeared, I'd been on edge. I needed closure, one way or the other. Until I had that, I wouldn't be able to rest. I wanted things to go back to the way they'd been: Dad running his evil empire, and me forging a new, mostly law-abiding, life on my own.

When the light under the door went out, I sat up. Hopefully, Dylan had finally gone to bed. Forcing myself to be patient, I waited another hour after the cabin went dark, just to be sure he was actually asleep. When I felt certain he probably was snoozing, I got off the bed slowly. I opened my door and waited, listening for any sign Dylan was still awake. But the cabin was silent.

I crept across the floor slowly, hoping to avoid any creaking floorboards. I went into the kitchen and grabbed a knife from the holder on the counter, and a pair of latex gloves I'd seen under the sink, when Dylan had grabbed the first aid kit. I slipped out of the cabin quietly, closing the door behind me. I stood on the porch, trying to figure out which direction I should take. I'd have loved a chance to rifle through Charles's office but didn't think I had the nerve to do that just yet. Charles was so anal, he probably slept in his office. I decided to go toward the back of the compound, away from the residential part. I stayed in the shadows, moving slowly and deliberately in the opposite direction of where I'd entered the compound. I passed a row of unlocked storage sheds, and I went through them one by one, not even sure what I hoped to find. When they yielded nothing, I continued on. At one point I came upon a large building with the word AUTO BODY painted on the front of the building.

This looks promising.

I moved toward it and peeked in the grimy windows. Some things could be easily hidden, but a car wasn't one of those things. If Dad's car was in that building, that would be pretty damning evidence that someone was trying to conceal the fact that Dad had been in the compound. Maybe Dylan trusted Charles, but I had no such faith in that man. He struck me as the type who would do anything to achieve his goals. He was power hungry and liked running this place like his personal kingdom.

There were several vehicles inside the building, but it was hard to get a really good look from the outside. I tried the door and found it locked. I was more than capable of picking a lock, but unsure if I should go that route. I didn't know if they used alarm systems inside the compound, and if I accidentally set one off, that could be the end of my visit.

I moved around the building, looking for an alarm box. I found one on the south side of the structure, and I examined it carefully. I could simply cut the power line to the box, but odds were there was a backup battery. I decided my best bet would be to find the phone line and cut that. That way, even if an alarm went off, the signal wouldn't be sent, and that would give me time to look around. What I didn't know was whether there were people patrolling the grounds. If an alarm sounded, I didn't think that would be heard as far as the security building at the front. But if anyone was close by, they'd probably hear it.

I felt a bit frozen, and uneasy about taking action. But the sole reason for getting inside the compound was to snoop. If I was too afraid to do anything in case I got caught, I might as well have stayed in town. I hadn't gone to all the trouble of kidnapping Dylan just so I could chicken out now. I had to figure out if my dad had been inside the compound or somehow involved in that bizarre animal-attack story. If it were even true. Dylan had said Charles didn't like questions about the animal attack, and that right there seemed suspicious to me. If Charles had had something to do with Dad's disappearance, I'd have someone to blame. Someone to punish. I needed that. The men needed that. Because not knowing what had happened to Dad had us all in a demoralizing limbo.

Sucking in a calming breath, I moved slowly along the building, searching for a phone line. Without a flashlight, it was slow going. Eventually I stumbled upon the line running from underground and up the wall toward the roof. I sliced it with my knife and went to find a window to climb through. I chose a smaller window on the back of the building, shielded from the street. Once I knew where I'd enter from, I returned to the alarm box and opened it up. It looked like a fairly basic setup. Holding my breath, I sliced through the power line and waited to see if the battery backup went off. It took a few seconds, but inside the big building, a horn started blaring.

Fuck.

Well, at least I hoped the signal wasn't getting out. I was screwed if they had a cell phone signal backup, or if anyone was nearby. I ran to the back and broke the window with my elbow. I scrambled through, taking care not to slice myself on the broken glass. Once inside, I was really wishing I had a flashlight. The screeching horn had my nerves on edge, but I focused on the job at hand. I strode quickly through the vehicles, searching for my dad's car. There were about ten automobiles in the building, some on lifts, some missing tires. I almost slipped and fell on my ass a few times because of oil on the floor. I didn't see Dad's black BMW anywhere, and I wasn't sure if that was the better or worse scenario.

Sweat beaded on my forehead as I searched the dark building. Every second that passed meant Charles and his crew could be closing in. I was frustrated when none of the vehicles were Dad's. My gut had told me his car might actually be in here. But it wasn't. Raking a hand through my hair, I moved toward the back window. I was out of time. I had to go or I risked being caught. As I passed a big dumpster against a wall, I gave a cursory glance inside. It was packed with bumpers and rims, and I started to move past. But then something caught my eye.

I leaned over the edge, trying to focus on a rectangular piece of metal. My heart began to pound as I stared in shock. A white license plate was wedged toward the bottom of the bin. The word CRUSHER was engraved on the plate. CRUSHER had been Dad's nickname. He'd had a reputation because he could break a man's ribs with a single punch. The name had stuck with him as he worked his way up the ranks of the organization, and he'd found it amusing to keep that nickname, even once he was the boss.

I started shaking as I stared at the license. I'd been right; Dad's car had been inside the compound. That meant *he'd* been inside. Was he being held somewhere? Was Charles the sort of man who'd kidnap someone? It seemed unlikely Charles would be able to hold two men captive for an entire month, without discovery. Charles was obviously a tight-ass, but Dylan had said he was honorable and scrupulously honest. Yet, there was my dad's license plate, tossed in the garbage. I could think of no logical reason why it would be there for non-nefarious reasons.

I jumped onto the side of the dumpster, balancing on my stomach. I reached down as far as I could, my shoulder muscles burning as I tried to lengthen them so I could grab the license. I wasn't leaving it here. Hell no. That was the only piece of evidence I had that Dad had actually made it inside the compound. I wasn't going to go to the cops. That wasn't why I was grabbing it. No, I wanted the license to remind me that this wasn't my imagination or a trick of the light. Dad had been here, and I was on the right track. If Charles had killed Dad, he'd have to pay.

I almost fell in but grabbed the side just in time. My fingers brushed the metal, and with a grunt, I managed to clamp onto the license. I yanked it free from the other debris and jumped off the bin. Breathing hard, I tucked it under my shirt, in the waistband of my jeans. I ran for the window, well aware I should have been gone five minutes ago. I slipped out of the window but managed to slice my elbow in the process.

"Shit," I hissed, wiping the glass with the hem of my shirt. I didn't need to leave my DNA all over the place. I jumped down onto the hard ground and bolted for the bushes that ran along the back of the structure. From there I made my way in the direction of Dylan's house, avoiding the road. At one point, two guys went running past with flashlights, and one of them was yelling into a radio.

I'd cut it close. Too close. One minute longer and they might have grabbed me as I left the building. The metal of the license plate was cold against my skin, and I felt a bit in shock. I didn't have a good feeling in the pit of my stomach. While Dad and I had had a dysfunctional relationship, the idea of him dead was still stunning. And I felt in my soul that he was indeed dead. The second I'd seen that license plate buried in the trash, I'd known. It was hard to believe that a man as vibrant and alive as Corbin Sabine could be gone, but I knew he was.

Once I was close to Dylan's house, I started to run. I feared the second Charles discovered a break-in on the grounds, he'd suspect me. After all, Dylan said there was no crime here. No way a guy like Charles wouldn't immediately conclude I was the common denominator. I hurried up the steps of Dylan's cabin and slipped into the house. I went to the kitchen and returned the gloves and the knife to where they belonged.

When I got in my room, I went into the bathroom, locking the door. I pulled the license plate from my waistband. It wasn't bent or damaged in any way. It was mostly pristine, not counting dust and a bit of oil. I stared at it until my eyes watered. Then I set it on the counter and washed up in the sink. I didn't dare run the shower because that would be a bit suspicious if Dylan woke up and heard that. I also washed the dirt from the bottom of my shoes, and I put a Band-Aid on my cut.

Once I had all the oil and grime off me, I stripped down to my underwear. I needed to hide the license plate. If Charles somehow found I had it, and he was responsible for getting rid of my dad, that would be the end of me. I didn't know if Dylan had been involved in any of that stuff. I couldn't picture Dylan being involved in killing anyone, but people could fool you. I'd certainly fooled Dylan.

The hiding spot I chose couldn't be anything obvious, like under the mattress. My gaze fell on a nondescript seascape that hung on the wall over the bed. That hiding spot wouldn't withstand a thorough toss of the room, but it would do fine for a cursory search. I climbed on the bed and removed the painting from the wall. I unscrewed the backing and tucked the license plate behind the print. I then reassembled the frame and rehung the painting, taking care not to leave it crooked. I climbed in bed, feeling numb and unable to process what I'd experienced.

I closed my eyes and then jerked them open again when there was a loud banging on the front door of the house. My pulse sped as I sat up. A strip of light appeared under the door as a lamp was flicked on somewhere in the cabin. I heard voices. I recognized Dylan's soft voice and the deep rumble of another voice. There was a sharp rap on my door, and I heard Dylan protesting.

"Come in," I called out.

The door swung open quickly, and the light turned on. Charles stood in the doorway, looking grim. Dylan was behind him, anger simmering in his eyes.

"I'm sorry, Lex. He just barged in," Dylan grumbled.

Shielding my eyes, I asked, "What's going on?" I tried my best to appear groggy and confused. I really hoped I could carry it off because Charles looked ready to strangle someone.

Charles didn't speak; he just walked into the room, making a beeline for my shoes. He turned them over and grunted. He faced me. "Have you been here all night?"

"What?" Again, I did my best to look like an innocent angel.

"Have you been here all night?" snapped Charles.

"Yes. Why?" I met Dylan's gaze. "What's going on?"

Dylan said, "Someone broke into the auto body shop."

I frowned. "Really?"

"Yeah." Charles watched me, his stare frigid. "Funny how we never have any trouble until you show up."

I tried to look indignant. "I was sound asleep. You can ask Dylan—I've been here all night."

"He was. He was here with me." Dylan nodded.

Charles didn't look convinced. "Just so you know, Lex, my guys now have orders to shoot first, ask questions later."

I widened my eyes. "Jesus. Is this a prison camp?"

Dylan looked flustered. "I think you should go, Charles. You're overreacting. You can see he just woke up."

Clenching his jaw, Charles gave me a frustrated look. "You should watch yourself, Dylan. I know people, and this guy is no good."

"Fuck you, Charles. I haven't done a damn thing," I lied. I was thanking my lucky stars it had occurred to me to rinse the bottom of my shoes. Dylan might have been swayed if they'd been covered in mud and oil.

"I still expect you to come down to the security building tomorrow," Charles said gruffly.

"I know that. I fully intend to."

Charles turned and walked to the door of my bedroom. "Sorry about disturbing your night." He didn't sound the least bit sorry.

Dylan gave me an apologetic look and followed Charles out of the room.

I collapsed on the bed, heart banging my ribs. Crap, I'd barely gotten back in time. I'd known Charles would be suspicious of me, but I'd assumed he'd be subtler about his feelings. He'd come in like a sledgehammer. Well, it was probably best that I knew exactly how he felt. There was no doubt he'd be watching every single move I made. Odds were he'd even watch the cabin now. That was going to definitely cramp my ability to continue snooping. But I guess I had the proof I needed that Dad had at least been in the compound. Now I needed to decide what to do about that. Charles ran this place, and there was no way someone had disassembled my dad's car into parts without him knowing. He was in charge, and that meant he was to blame by default.

My guys needed a scapegoat. They needed closure. The best way to give them that was to find someone to punish. While the idea of punishing Charles was welcome, doing it myself was not. I wasn't a hugely violent person. I could do what needed doing, but that didn't mean I looked forward to it. Hank would be perfect for the job. Problem was, there was no way in hell I was going to be able to get him inside the compound. There was also no way I could grab Charles and get him *out* of the compound. Not to mention, this all would have to happen immediately because if Charles took my prints and dug deeper, he'd know the truth about me, and he'd throw me out of the compound.

I needed time. I had to avoid going to meet with Charles tomorrow. I'd feign illness and hopefully stall the interview. I hoped Charles wasn't such a hard-ass he'd come to me and try to force the interview. I didn't think Dylan would be cool with that. He'd looked pretty angry tonight when Charles had barged in. I'd have to hide behind Dylan a bit longer, just until I could figure out how to get the drop on Charles.

I really hoped Dylan never discovered what a monster I could be. I liked the kid. I hadn't wanted to like him, but his vulnerability had somehow gotten through to me. It would be a shame if he knew I'd used him. He'd been through so much already, I hated the idea of contributing to him never trusting anyone ever again. But this was survival time. I had to bring someone's head on a stick, if only so the men could relax and choose a new leader.

I'd do this for them, and Gabriele. I'd give them all closure. But there was no fucking way I'd take over the Sabine empire. Just this short stint had reminded me how much I hated the deceit and violence of this world. I clenched my jaw, steeling myself for what was to come. I'd figure out a way to get Charles all to myself. Once I knew the truth, I'd do what had to be done.

Chapter Thirteen

Dylan

Charles really hated Lex. He couldn't even hide it, which was surprising. I'd never seen Charles take such an instant dislike to someone. The way he'd charged into my house last night, accusing Lex of breaking into the auto body shop, had been disconcerting. I had the distinct impression that if I hadn't been there, he'd have hauled Lex off to his security building and done God knew what to him.

I looked up as Lex entered the room. He moved slowly, and he looked tired. He sat on the couch, resting his head against the back pillows. There was the gleam of sweat on his face, and he closed his eyes and shivered.

"Are you okay?" I stood and moved to him.

He didn't respond immediately, but then he spoke with great effort. "I think I have the flu."

"Really?" I perched on the arm of the couch, studying his pale features. "You do look a little gray."

He opened his eyes, and they looked bloodshot. "It must be all the stress. Now that we're safe, I guess my body just decided to shut down."

"You should go back to bed."

He sighed. "I don't want to be a baby."

"Lex, if you're sick, you have to rest."

"I have to go talk to Charles." He tried to push up off the couch but then sank back down. "Shit, I'm so dizzy."

I frowned. "You're not going anywhere. I'll call Charles and tell him we have to postpone the interview."

"He won't like that," he said weakly.

"Tough shit. You're sick. What will it matter if he waits a few days to talk to you?" I touched his arm. "Come on, let's get you back in bed."

He hesitated, but then he let me help him off the couch and into his room. He practically fell onto the bed, moaning. I started to feel his forehead to see if he had a fever, but he pushed my hand away. "Don't get too close or you might get sick too."

I frowned but didn't argue. "Undress and get under the covers. I'll handle Charles."

"I'm not your problem, Dylan."

"You're being silly. I'm happy to take care of you," I said softly. "I owe you my life, Lex. Let me do this."

He met my gaze, and shame seemed to wash through his eyes. I knew how prideful alphas were, and assumed he didn't like feeling weak. "You're a good omega," he said. "I'm sorry."

I gave a stiff laugh. "Sorry for what? Being sick? You can't help that."

He dropped his gaze. "I suppose."

"Come on. Get your clothes off."

He slowly unzipped his jeans, and I averted my eyes. There was the swish of clothing, and then he moved under the blankets. When I looked back, his cheeks were flushed, and his shoulders were bare. That familiar nudge of lust went thorough me at the sight of his muscled torso, but I made sure not to show my feelings. What kind of a jerk lusted after someone who was sick?

"I'm going to call Charles, and then I'll make you some chicken broth."

He rolled over onto his side, his blue eyes darker than usual. "I don't want you to go to a bunch of trouble for me."

"Stop." I pulled the covers up higher on his shoulders, feeling a need to comfort him.

He closed his eyes and whispered, "Thank you, Dylan."

I patted his hip and moved to the door. I glanced back at him and found him watching me. I smiled and left the room, closing the door behind me. It had been such a long time since I had anyone to take care of. I'd almost forgotten how nice it felt to care about someone. And I was beginning to truly care about Lex. I had to be careful though. I didn't want to fall for him because he'd be going soon, and he'd never return my feelings. But it was a relief to realize I actually might be capable of falling for someone again someday. Lex was reminding me that there were good alphas in the world too. Alphas you could depend on, who would protect you, not hurt you.

My hands shook as I dialed Charles's number.

"Charles Pederson here," he said curtly as he answered.

My stomach clenched, but I forced myself to speak. "Uh… hey… Charles. It's Dylan."

There was a short silence and then, "Yes?"

"I'm afraid we'll have to postpone your interview with Lex."

"Why?" he demanded.

"He's sick."

There was a gruff, unpleasant laugh on the other end of the line. "What kind of bullshit is this?"

"It's not bullshit. He's sick, and he needs to rest."

"Dylan." He sounded tired. "He's faking. I'd bet my left nut on that."

Anger rose inside me. "He's not. You're just too suspicious for your own good."

"And you're gullible," he snapped.

"No. He's sick, and you'll have to wait to grill him."

He exhaled roughly. "Fine. But if he tries to stall longer than a day, it better be because he's on his death bed."

"God, you're a hard man." I scowled.

"I don't want him hurting you or anyone else in the compound. He's a dangerous man, Dylan. I'm not sure why you're so attached to him, but it's a mistake. I can see him clearer than you can. You have rose-colored glasses on."

"He saved my life!" I growled. "He's the reason I'm not still kidnapped. You weren't there. You have no idea how awful and terrifying that was. He got me out of there, and I'm grateful to him. You should be too. But instead, you've been a dick to him from the moment you met him."

He didn't speak immediately, but when he did, his tone was patient, almost indulgent. "I'm just worried for you, Dylan. I know what you've been through, and I don't want you hurt again. Lex is the kind of man who will use people to get what he wants. I know his type on sight. You'll see. When I finally have the chance to get his actual information, I have little doubt I'll find a treasure trove of deceit and lies that will make your head spin."

"You're wrong." I gripped the phone so tight, my fingers hurt.

He sighed. "I hope you're right. I truly do. I'd give anything to be wrong so that you won't be disappointed yet again in an alpha. But I know I'm not wrong. Watch your back, kid. Or you might end up with a knife in it."

A chill went through me, and I hung up abruptly. He was wrong. He didn't even know Lex. I knew way more about Lex than Charles did. He'd barely said two words to Lex. He'd made his mind up the second he laid eyes on him, and that was unfair. But even though I didn't agree with Charles's summation of Lex, an uneasy feeling settled in my gut as I went about making chicken broth for him.

Even I had to admit, Lex's illness was conveniently timed. But he truly had looked awful, and he'd seemed so weak and pale. People did get sick, and it wasn't always good timing. I mean, how many times had I gotten sick right before a vacation or an important event? It happened. Just because Lex was sick and had to cancel his interview with Charles, that didn't mean he was faking. Charles was just extremely paranoid because of his job. It was his job to be suspicious of anyone who tried to enter the compound.

I couldn't accept what Charles was saying about Lex. Lex had helped me. He'd comforted me; even once we'd been here in my cabin, he'd been kind. I couldn't believe he was faking that. His eyes had been filled with true empathy yesterday when he'd heard my story about Jacob and Ayden. His touch had been warm and affectionate. You couldn't fake that shit. Could you?

I did my best to push away Charles's negative words. I finished the broth and ladled the steaming soup into a bowl. Then I set the food on a tray with some saltine crackers. I carried the tray to Lex's room, and when I entered, I found him still awake.

"You're supposed to be asleep," I scolded gently.

"I dozed a few times." He watched me, his expression difficult to read.

I set the tray on the nightstand next to the bed. "Can you sit up?"

He nodded and struggled into an upright position.

The covers slid down, revealing his rippled abs, and my mouth went dry. I'd never had such a visceral reaction to an alpha before. I'd experienced lust many a time, but what I felt for Lex was raw and primal. My dick warmed, and my face flushed as need clawed at me. I was embarrassed, of course. I was supposed to be taking care of him, not lusting after him. I tried to ignore the desire to touch him and pulled up a chair.

"Shall I feed you?" I smiled.

He shook his head. "No." He reached for the tray, and I helped him put it on his lap.

"Your color is still awful."

He sipped the broth off the spoon he held. His hand shook slightly, and he grimaced. Once he'd swallowed, he said, "I feel like crap. I don't think I can eat very much."

"That's okay. Anything is better than nothing."

He nodded and took another spoonful. Then he set it down, as if holding the spoon was exhausting. "How did Charles take the news?"

I winced. "He was as big an asshole as you'd expect."

"I'm sure."

I studied him. "He thinks you're faking just so you won't have to talk to him."

"Is that a surprise?" He met my gaze. "He doesn't like me."

"Understatement of the year."

"Yeah." He cleared his throat. "Can I use your phone later? I need to call work and let them know I'm alive."

"Of course."

"Unless phone calls aren't allowed by You Know Who."

"As far as I know, Charles isn't controlling things like that."

"Okay, good." He took another mouthful of soup and then another. I was glad he seemed to have some appetite. I'd been worried he wouldn't get anything down. He ate half the broth and one saltine, and then he set the spoon down. "That's the best I can do."

"You did great." I smiled.

He studied me, his blue eyes wary. "Do you believe what he's saying about me?"

"Charles?" I shook my head. "No."

He dropped his gaze. "I'm not an angel. I've done… bad things."

Surprised at his confession, I frowned. "What kind of bad things?"

A muscle worked in his jaw. "I'd rather not say."

I narrowed my eyes. "Illegal things?"

His cheeks seemed pink as he met my gaze with an almost defiant expression. "Sometimes."

I was shocked at his response, but curious about why he was being so open. "Why are you telling me this?"

"Because I like you." He shrugged. "I don't want you to think I'm a saint, when, in fact, I'm not."

"I've never met a saint. I'm not a saint."

"You are compared to me," he muttered, frowning.

"What exactly are you trying to say, Lex?" I felt breathless as I held his gaze. Was Charles right? Was Lex trying to tell me that Charles was right about him?

His face changed suddenly, and he gave a weak smile. "Ignore me. I'm being silly because I don't feel well."

Relief filled me at his return to the Lex I knew. "You don't have to be perfect. We all make mistakes."

"Yes." He nodded, a funny look on his face. "I suppose that's true."

I reached out and touched his hand. The feel of his warm, firm skin under mine was wonderful. He didn't move away, and that pleased me. "All you need to think about is getting well. Charles can be mad all he wants, but I like who you are. Nothing he says will change that."

He swallowed. "Okay."

He looked so worried, I hated it. "I'm serious. Charles needed a scapegoat last night, and you were convenient."

"I do understand why he's suspicious of me. If you truly never have crime here, and suddenly someone does something just as I show up, he's right to be concerned."

"He needs to be logical though. You were in bed, obviously asleep. I think I'd have noticed if you sneaked in and out of the cabin. I'm a light sleeper."

"I guess he's just doing his job. You should feel pleased he cares so much."

"You're mighty nice about all of this."

He shrugged. "I understand the need to protect what you care about."

His gaze was so intent, I felt a warm flush. I'd have given anything to have him care about me. He'd be a good alpha, I was sure of it. He'd be protective and warm. He'd be everything Jacob hadn't been. I'd chosen so poorly the first time around. I'd been young, and Jacob had been persuasive. Our relationship had been rocky from the beginning, but once we had a child, Jacob became even worse. He was jealous and insanely possessive. But he'd never made an aggressive move toward Ayden, and so it hadn't occurred to me he'd hurt him. That had been a catastrophic mistake on my part. One I'd never forgive myself for making. Never.

"Are you okay?" Lex asked, watching me with a gentle expression.

I nodded. "Just thinking about the past. Thinking how *I* didn't protect what I cared about."

"No, Dylan. That wasn't what I was getting at."

"But it's true." I met his gaze. "You know it is."

He shook his head. "We can't read minds. We're forced to trust people and pray they don't screw us over."

"Maybe." I stood and grabbed the tray. "You should rest. I'll check on you later."

"Dylan." His voice was urgent. "It's not your fault if someone tricks you. You need to understand that."

I wasn't sure why any of this mattered so much to him, but I knew he was trying to soothe me. "I'm not sure I agree with you. But I appreciate that you care."

He wrinkled his brow, looking almost flustered. "Yes. I… I do actually care."

I smiled, pleased at his heartfelt words. "Me too. Which is why I'm nagging you to rest."

He slid down in the bed, his expression still muddled. "I hate the idea of ever hurting you, Dylan."

I frowned. "Then don't."

He closed his eyes, and his mouth hardened. "Easier said than done sometimes."

I had no idea what was eating at him, but it didn't exactly comfort me, especially after all the things Charles had said. But he looked like he was about to fall asleep, so I left the room with my stomach churning.

Chapter Fourteen

Lex

It was a dream. I realized that it was a dream. Dylan was crawling into bed with me. He had a funny look in his eyes, and I knew he wanted me. My heart pounded with a mix of uneasiness and anticipation. In that weird way dreams fast-forward, we were both suddenly naked. I could smell his arousal, and my cock was shockingly hard. As he pressed his naked body against mine, my arm went around him. Why wasn't I pushing him off? Why didn't I reject him and warn him away? No, instead, in the dream, I rolled over on top of him, and he smiled as if in victory.

He opened his thighs. "Fuck me," he whispered. "I want it."

I'd never fucked a guy, nor had I wanted to. I'd never even had anal with a girl. But instead of being freaked-out, my cock hardened painfully. I was aroused and there was no denying it. My fingers dug into his hips, and I searched his face. His lips were beautiful—plump and cherry red. I lowered my head and kissed him. I kissed him gently at first, but when he opened his mouth, I pushed my tongue in aggressively.

He groaned into my mouth and began rubbing against me. Oh, fuck, the friction of his cock on mine was too good. Too fucking good. I didn't care that he was a male. I didn't care about anything but getting inside his body. I wanted to fuck him. It was shocking but exciting. I wanted to enter his body and spill my seed. I wanted to mark him. Breed him. But what sense did that make? Breed a male? Why did that not seem crazy?

His expression changed. "You don't want me."

My throat was tight, but I forced out the words. "I do want you."

"No. You don't like men."

"I like you." As if to make my point, I kissed him again, and he moaned and rolled his hips. "I *want* you."

He spread his legs wider and started stroking himself. "Show me."

My heart pounded, but I rose up onto my knees and stared down between his legs. His cock was ruddy and thick, seeping a creamy trail over his stomach. My dick was straight and achingly hard. I touched his fuzzy balls, and he sighed. My fingers trailed to the base of his cock, and I stroked lightly up his length. Curious to see his reaction, I watched him. He arched his back, begging me breathlessly to take what I wanted.

What I wanted.

Fuck. *He* was what I wanted. I feathered a finger over his pink hole, mesmerized by how he shuddered with pleasure. How would I even fit inside that puckered velvety opening? "I don't want to hurt you."

His expression was odd. "But you will. You know you will."

"I have to do this." My voice sounded strange. "I'm supposed to do this."

"Yes. It has to happen."

I wasn't sure if we were talking about sex anymore. Maybe my subconscious was working through the guilt I felt about using him. But when he touched my cock, sliding his hand up and down my length, I focused once again on my carnal need. I'd never wanted anyone like I wanted Dylan in the dream. I felt like I'd die if I didn't bury myself inside him.

"I don't want you to regret this," I whispered.

He simply shrugged, confusing me more.

But I couldn't stop. There was no way I had that sort of control. Instead, I leaned down and spit on his hole, and he jerked. I smeared the saliva over his hole, and I pushed the tip of my thumb into him. He cried out and arched his spine, panting with pleasure. His obvious delight encouraged me, and I added another finger. He was so fucking tight and hot, I almost came just from the sensation of his hole squeezing my thumb. But I held off. I wanted to be inside him when I let loose.

Jesus. Am I actually going to fuck him? I'm going to fuck a man?

I hesitated, as my subconscious warred with dream me. Perhaps my sanity was trying to return to remind me that I didn't fuck men. I fucked women. But all I could think about was sinking deep inside him. I knew that wasn't what I normally wanted, but I craved it now.

I began stroking myself lazily, and I crouched over Dylan. His eyes glittered up at me, and his breathing came fast. I nudged my knee between his legs, opening him wider for me. Then I lowered myself on him, and I pressed my cock to his entrance. He trembled beneath me, his lips parted with anticipation. I pushed in slowly, sliding past the tense muscles of his anus. I was light-headed with pleasure as his body squeezed me tight. I almost came but somehow held off, shivering with ecstasy as he shuddered and groaned at the intrusion.

He cried out and wound his arms around me, whimpering against my chest. I pulled him close and whispered words of comfort. The dream felt so real. I could almost smell and taste him. I started moving my hips in long, slow strokes. He groaned and wrapped his legs around me, and I started to thrust harder. Why hadn't I ever done this before? Nothing had ever felt as good as fucking this man beneath me. His musky scent drove me nuts. I wanted to fuck him through the mattress, fill him full, and do it again. I wanted him screaming with pleasure. I wanted... I wanted...

I started coming. My eyes rolled up in my head as seed flooded out of me. "Oh *fuck*," I mumbled, fucking him harder in my dream. I jerked my hips as sleep began to lift, and my lids rose slowly. I woke to find myself covered in sweat, my abdomen slick with my own release.

Shock rolled through me, even as tremors of pleasure continued to assault me. My bones and muscles were like mush, and I almost felt drunk. My hand was covered with sticky cum, and my dick slowly softened in my grip.

I couldn't move. That had been the best wet dream I'd ever had. In fact, that dream had been better than any *actual* sex I'd ever had. I was embarrassed, and surprised, that Dylan had been at the heart of my fantasy. I didn't understand the feelings he drummed up in me, but as I lay there with my cum-soaked cock in my hand, it was obvious denying I was attracted to him was a bit silly. I didn't understand why he got to me, but he did. I had sexual *and* emotional feelings for Dylan, and that was ridiculous. Foolish.

Sitting up, I grabbed some tissues from the nightstand and cleaned myself off. He'd shared too much with me, and it had gotten into my heart. I should never have allowed myself to think about him as anything but a mark. I wasn't sure why Dylan was able to affect me when usually no one did. Maybe because I'd seen his vulnerability firsthand. He'd looked to me as if I was a hero, and it had felt nice. I didn't want him hurt. I really, really didn't want anything to hurt him.

But I knew I would.

Just my leaving would hurt him. He was bonding to me. We were growing closer and closer each day, whether that was smart or not. Dylan was even ignoring Charles's warnings about me. He'd known Charles way longer than me, so why wasn't he listening to the other alpha? Why couldn't either of us pull back? Just his scent had begun to drive me nuts. The way his hair curled at the nape of his neck, and the brilliant blue of his eyes with that dark ring made my pulse spike. Maybe I hadn't acted on anything except in a dream, but I was horribly aware the dream was simply allowing me to experience what I wanted to happen with Dylan in real life.

How was this possible?

I closed my eyes as the truth of that rolled through me. I wanted to fuck Dylan. I wanted to be around him so I could protect him and take care of him. I felt a little crazy as that realization hit me. Those feelings were irrational, and there was no way that could happen. I was here on a mission. I was using Dylan to get what I wanted, just like I'd used dozens of people over my lifetime. He couldn't mean anything to me. That wouldn't work. Besides, if he knew the real me, he'd be horrified that he'd ever even trusted me. There was no way this was turning into a relationship. The very idea of that was hysterical, and yet, I didn't feel like laughing.

There was a soft knock on my bedroom door, and it opened slowly. The object of my dirty dream appeared, looking fresh and young. I pulled the covers up, feeling embarrassed about what I'd been up to.

"I wanted to know if you were hungry for dinner?"

I stared at him, taking in how good he looked. I was seventeen years older than him. He was just beginning his life, and I was old and jaded by comparison. He'd had a traumatic beginning to his life, but if he could heal, he'd find another alpha to love him. Maybe they could even try for another child through a surrogate again. Why did my stomach crawl at the idea of him finding happiness with another alpha? What the hell was *wrong* with me?

"Lex? Did you hear me?"

I shook myself. "Yeah. Sorry." I avoided his gaze. "I don't think I'm hungry."

"No?" He looked worried, and he came closer. "Do you feel worse?"

I felt like such a dick pretending to be sick. It shouldn't have mattered, but I hated lying to his face over and over again. None of this should have bothered me because he was just supposed to be a means to an end. "I'm not worse."

He slumped with relief. "You scared me."

"You shouldn't worry about me so much."

"I can't help it." He moved closer and sat on the edge of my bed. His hip bumped my leg, and I scooted away slightly. He must have noticed and misinterpreted my movement. "Don't worry. Being gay isn't contagious."

My face warmed. "I was just making room for you to sit."

"Oh." He smiled. "Sometimes people are weird." He reached out before I realized what he was doing, and he pressed his palm to my forehead. I stiffened, and he nodded approvingly. "You don't have a fever."

"Oh, uh… good."

He watched me in silence, and I squirmed a bit. He smiled. "Sorry. Am I making you uncomfortable?"

"No, I love it when people stare at me."

He laughed. "I was just thinking how weird it is that I like you now."

I just blinked at him, not knowing what to say.

"I mean, because I didn't trust you before. In our cooking class."

"Oh, I see."

He sighed. "You've given me hope."

Shame ate at me as I held his trusting gaze. I'd never planned for things to go like this. When I first set my sights on him, I'd had no idea what he'd gone through, or that I could affect him so profoundly. I'd needed to use him to get inside the compound, but I'd never intended to destroy the poor kid. I had to find a way to do what I needed to, while still keeping the truth from him.

"I'm flattered," I said weakly.

"Things would be perfect if you were gay." He grinned.

My face warmed as I thought about my dream. "Even if I was, I'm not staying here. It wouldn't work anyway."

"I know. I'm just saying we could have had some fun times together."

"I see." I avoided his gaze. "Well, it's a moot point because... you know... I'm straight."

I'm a straight alpha who fantasizes about fucking men. Right.

"I know." He grimaced. "I got off track. I was simply trying to say thank you for reminding me there are good alphas too. It feels nice to trust and respect an alpha again."

I didn't respond. What could I say? Instead, I simply closed my eyes as shame washed through me.

The mattress moved and he stood. "I'll check on you later."

I nodded, keeping my eyes shut. I heard the door close softly, and when I opened my eyes he was gone. I rolled over and punched the pillow, feeling frustrated. I needed to harden myself. I had shit to do, and thinking warm fuzzy feelings about Dylan was the last thing I needed. His feelings weren't the priority. I had to remember that. Dylan was, and had always been, a means to an end.

S.C. Wynne

Chapter Fifteen

Dylan

I'd taken the day off work to care for Lex. I already had tomorrow off too, so if he was still sick, I'd be here to help him. I was surprised how reticent I was to leave him alone. I liked being around him. His energy calmed me and made me happy. I hadn't felt that in so long, it was a nice change to wake up not dreading the day.

I worried Lex might not be well enough to meet with Charles tomorrow. The other alpha wasn't going to be patient about putting his interview off again. I could only run interference for so long before Charles would have his way. He was stubborn and not easily swayed from his task.

I sat out on the back porch, sipping some green tea. My earlier conversation with Lex was on my mind. He'd been giving off some mixed signals today. He'd been so adamant about being straight at first, and I didn't want to read into things. But the last day, I'd caught certain looks that confused me. I'd have sworn there was a hint of lust in his gaze when I'd entered his bedroom earlier. But if he was bisexual, I wasn't sure why he'd lie. Maybe he wasn't aware of it? Was that possible? I didn't know his exact age, but I guessed he was in his thirties. Could you get to be that old and not know you were bisexual? I had no idea. I'd always known I was gay.

It did seem Lex was hiding other things too. That whole conversation about him not being a good person had made me wonder what he was trying to say. No one was perfect, but he'd seemed like he was warning me off. He didn't need to. Even if he had been open to sleeping with me, I was well aware he wasn't staying here. He had a life back where he lived.

I frowned as it occurred to me I still really didn't know anything about him. I hadn't even gotten the name of his company out of him yet. Uneasiness gnawed at me as I mulled that over. He hadn't refused to tell me; he'd burned his arm, and I'd gotten distracted. I laughed at my suspicious mind. He wouldn't have burned himself just to avoid giving me the name of his company. That was silly.

Later tonight, if he seemed up to talking, I'd revisit the name of his company. If he brushed me off again, that would be troubling. But he wouldn't. I was sure of that. I was letting Charles's dire warning get to me too much. I mean, yes, it was a bit odd I knew nothing about Lex's personal life. He knew way more about mine. He'd admitted he didn't have anyone at home waiting for him. But I'd had to ask. He never volunteered anything. That didn't mean he was a liar—that could just be he was private. Lots of people were. I usually was.

There was a knock on the front door, and I went to answer it, praying it wasn't Charles. When I opened it, I found Dr. Peters standing there.

"What are you doing here?" I asked, surprised but stepping aside to let him enter.

He grimaced as he brushed past. "Charles wanted me to come and check on your visitor."

I closed the door and faced him. "What?"

He looked uncomfortable. "Charles asked if I'd examine the outsider."

"His name is Lex." I bristled.

"Right. Sorry." He opened the black bag he carried and pulled out a thermometer and his stethoscope. "Charles just wants to make sure he doesn't have anything contagious."

Anger roiled in my stomach. "He's just trying to prove Lex is faking, isn't he?"

Dr. Peters's face pinked. "I have no idea what his motivation is; he simply called me and asked if I'd check Lex out."

"He's better already. He doesn't have anything contagious."

He frowned. "Is there some reason I can't examine him? It's not unusual to have a doctor check a sick person over."

I scowled. "It's unusual to have a doctor appear on your doorstep when you didn't call one."

He sighed. "Dylan, I'm between a rock and a hard place. I can't refuse Charles, but I can see my visit is making you uncomfortable."

I felt bad for him. I knew Dr. Peters was a good person. He wasn't the type to snoop, but Charles had authority, and he couldn't ignore a request from the head of security easily. "Charles is just paranoid."

"I'm sure he is. But I don't want to defy him, and I'm not going to lie and say I examined Lex if I didn't."

I bit my bottom lip. "He's probably sleeping. He's very tired."

"He can go back to sleep when I'm done with the examination. It will only take a few minutes. I don't plan on taking blood or urine. I just need to give him a cursory exam so that I can tell Charles I did."

Frustrated, I moved toward Lex's room. "This is ridiculous."

"I'll be quick." He followed me.

I knocked softly on Lex's door and opened it. Lex was sitting up, looking amiable. His expression changed when he noticed Dr. Peters and the stethoscope in his hand. "This is my boss, Dr. Peters."

Lex frowned. "Okay."

"Charles wants him to check you over. To be sure what you have isn't contagious." I grimaced, well aware he knew exactly what Charles was up to, as I did.

"Sorry to intrude." Dr. Peters gave an uneasy laugh. "Charles is a hard man to refuse."

Pressing his lips tight, Lex met my gaze. "You're cool with this?"

"I don't really have any say." I scowled. "Charles runs the show."

Irritation was plain on Lex's face, but then he said, "I guess it wouldn't hurt anything to have a checkup."

"I'm sorry. Charles is being a jerk." I sighed.

"It's fine." Lex threw back the covers.

I turned away and left the room, giving them privacy. I went into the kitchen and began peeling potatoes for dinner. I wasn't much of a cook, but I was able to make a pretty good beef stew. I tried not to think about how annoyed I was with Charles. I understood that his job was to keep us all safe, but his fixation on Lex was definitely getting ridiculous. Lex hadn't done anything suspicious that I was aware of. He'd only used the phone once, to call his office, to let them know he was taking a few sick days. If he was a criminal mastermind, surely he'd have done something other than lie in bed all day.

I had the potatoes boiling and the beef defrosted by the time Dr. Peters came out of Lex's room. He tucked his equipment away in his bag, and he joined me in the kitchen.

"How'd it go?" I asked.

He leaned against the counter. "No fever. His throat isn't red or irritated. He said he had a touch of intestinal issues, but whatever he had seems to have passed."

"Good." I faced him, crossing my arms. "He wasn't faking. He looked horrible this morning."

"Sure. I believe you. You both went through a lot. His sickness could have been stress related even." He hesitated. "How are you feeling?"

"Fine."

His lips curved in a smile. "You'd say that no matter what."

I frowned. "If I was sick, I'd say so."

His smile faded. "I hope you know I'm not taking sides with Charles against you."

I didn't respond because I wasn't sure what he thought about Lex.

He sighed. "What do you really know about this Lex fella?"

"I know that he saved my life." I tried to keep my impatience out of my voice. "I know that he hasn't done anything to deserve Charles's suspicion."

"Charles means well."

"Does he?" I scowled. "To me, it seems more like he needs someone to fixate on, and Lex is the lucky candidate."

"Come on, Dylan. Charles isn't like that. He has good instincts."

I raised my brows. "So then you *are* on his side."

He frowned. "No. But I do trust him. Don't you?"

I blew out an impatient breath. "I trust Lex."

"Even though you don't know him?" He rubbed his jaw, looking uneasy. "I mean, he seems like a charming guy, but I do get the feeling he's hiding something."

"Would you have felt that way though if Charles hadn't put that in your head? I don't think so." I moved away and grabbed a carton of beef stock from the pantry. "Charles has his mind made up."

He moved closer. "Listen, all I'm saying is, be careful. Maybe Charles is blinded by suspicion, but you're blinded too because you like Lex. Keep your eyes open."

"My eyes are wide open," I muttered, pouring the stock into the pot.

"I hope so."

I shook my head and tossed the empty beef stock carton into the trash. "You're the one who wanted me to go out and meet someone."

He pulled his brows together. "Are you and Lex romantically involved?"

"No." I winced. "I just mean, I'm made a connection with someone, and you're still not happy."

He grimaced and seemed to choose his words carefully. "I'm glad you like Lex. I'm happy you seem to really admire him. All I want is for you to be careful until we know more about him."

"I know that he's brave and he helped me. That's enough for now." Dr. Peters's overprotectiveness was annoying. He knew nothing about Lex, but I could sense his uneasiness at the very idea of me having feelings toward the other alpha. It was none of his business. That went for Charles too. They needed to butt out.

"Just take it slowly."

"Message received," I growled.

His phone rang, and he answered it. I knew from the uptight expression he got that it was Charles. He went into the living room, and he spoke softly for a few minutes. Then he returned. "That was Charles."

"I figured." I scowled. "What did you tell him?"

"I told him that I believed Lex actually did have a touch of the flu, and that he could do with another day's rest."

I widened my eyes. "What?"

"I said Lex needed an extra day to recuperate before Charles interviews him."

I was so surprised, I had no idea what to say. I stared at him, speechless.

He smiled. "Lex truly does seem worn-out, and I have no doubt Charles will be hard on him. He deserves to be at his best when he faces Charles."

My heart squeezed with affection for my boss. "Thank you. I… I don't know what to say."

He shrugged. "What's the difference if he interviews him tomorrow or the next day? The answers won't change."

"Wow. Thank you, Dr. Peters."

He smiled kindly. "I expect you bright and early on Wednesday." He moved toward the front door.

"Absolutely. I'll be there." I followed him, feeling a bit guilty he'd gotten the brunt of my frustrations with Charles.

"Good." He opened the door and then paused. "Lex knows not to wander around, right? Charles isn't playing games."

My stomach tensed. "Yes. He knows. Charles made sure he knew."

"Okay, good." He stepped out onto the porch. "I hope you're not mad at me."

"Not at all." I forced myself to speak with a lightness I was far from feeling. "I'm pissed at Charles, not you."

"I understand your frustration." He studied me. "Well, I'll see you Wednesday." He looked past me, as if making sure Lex was nowhere around eavesdropping. "We have two omegas scheduled to deliver."

"I'll be there."

He smiled. "Excellent. See you then." He strode down the short path to the street.

I watched him until he was out of sight, and then I closed the door, feeling uneasy. That had been a kind gesture by Dr. Peters, allowing Lex an extra day to heal. But I still could tell he didn't trust Lex. Charles was suspicious by nature, but Dr. Peters really wasn't. Yet he too seemed wary of

Lex. Was I right that Charles had poisoned his opinion, or was he really sensing something in Lex that I was missing? After what I'd been through with Jacob, I didn't trust my own instincts a hundred percent.

I went back to the kitchen and stirred the pot of broth while I tried to think things through. I needed to make more of an effort to get things out of Lex. It did make me uncomfortable that I had no idea about his life. I didn't even know where he was from, or if he had siblings. I'd trusted him based solely on the fact we'd shared a traumatic experience together. But it was time to dig deeper. If Lex was on the up-and-up, there was no reason he shouldn't be okay with talking about himself.

The rest of the afternoon was spent with me finishing the stew and cleaning the cabin. I liked to clean when I was stressed. I felt more relaxed with everything in its place. I scrubbed my bathroom, the whole time thinking about every moment I'd ever spent with Lex. During the cooking classes, I myself hadn't really trusted him. Why? What had it been about him that made me leery to get to know him? Tucker hadn't had any such reservations, but Tucker was like that. He was open and friendly to everyone. What had bothered me about Lex was he'd seemed too good to be true. Too slick. Too sophisticated to be in Yellow Springs, let alone taking a rec center cooking class.

I hated thinking I couldn't trust Lex. He'd saved me. Even once we'd returned to the compound, he'd been so kind to me, and comforting when I told him about Jacob and Ayden. He'd been genuinely horrified to hear my story, and that hadn't been fake. I was sure of it. But there were a lot of gaps with Lex. The fact I'd spent at least two days with him and knew nothing about him was a red flag. I couldn't imagine why he'd bother trying to trick me though. What would be his endgame? Being inside the compound was extremely restrictive. If he had ulterior motives, he'd have stayed on the outside. Of course, he couldn't have known what life was like in here. He'd have had no idea how suspicious Charles was, or that he'd have been watched the moment he entered.

I tried to remember every conversation I'd ever had with Lex. One thing that had put my back up about Lex in the beginning was that he'd asked a lot of questions about the compound. He'd been super interested in the animal attack too. But wouldn't anyone be? While I felt Lex was hiding things, I was too. He had no idea that I was a solar eclipse omega, or that they even existed. Lots of people had secrets, but that didn't mean they were evil. Maybe Lex had things in his life he was embarrassed about, and so he didn't volunteer them. That didn't make him a bad person.

The rest of the day went by with those confusing thoughts spinning around inside my head. I trusted Lex and I trusted Dr. Peters. Because of that, it was impossible to come to a satisfactory conclusion about what to think. When dinnertime approached, I ladled a hearty serving of soup for Lex and put some warm bread on a plate.

I carried the tray into his bedroom, and he looked excited to see the food.

"Looks like your appetite is back." I smiled and set the tray on his lap.

He inhaled the warm yeasty scent of the bread and then the soup with a sigh. "This smells delicious."

"I hope it is. It's about the only thing I really know how to cook." I pulled up a chair and sat beside the bed.

He picked up the spoon and glanced at me. "Aren't you eating?"

"I'll eat later. I had a big lunch," I lied. Truth was, I had no appetite. I was too stressed out about things.

He nodded and dug into the steaming stew. He groaned at the first bite and licked his lips. "This is amazing."

"Really?" I beamed. "It's a family recipe."

"It's fantastic." He continued eating.

I watched him for a few moments, feeling an inordinate amount of satisfaction at how much he seemed to enjoy the food. I hadn't had anyone to cook for in so long. Taking care of Lex fed my need as an omega to nurture. "There's more if you want seconds."

He shook his head, scraping the bottom of the bowl with his spoon. "No. This was perfect." He finished off his bread, and then he closed his eyes. "I've never enjoyed a meal more."

I laughed. "I find that hard to believe. You probably dine at fancy restaurants all the time. All foodies do."

He opened his eyes and smiled. "Still, there's nothing like a home-cooked meal."

"Okay. I'll give you that." I cleared my throat. "I have some good news."

He looked at me expectantly.

"You have an extra day's reprieve before you have to talk to Charles."

He looked shocked. "I do?"

"Yes. Dr. Peters told him you needed one extra day to rest." I smiled at how nonplussed he appeared.

"Really?"

"Yep."

He laughed weakly. "That's great. I was dreading tomorrow."

"I can imagine."

He sighed. "Without that hanging over my head, maybe I can actually sleep tonight."

"I hope so. Nothing heals you like sleep." I took the tray from his lap and put it on the nightstand. Then I settled back in my chair. "Um... I was thinking... I feel like I don't know anything about you."

His expression changed immediately, and his smile faded. "Does Charles want you to pump me for info?"

I widened my eyes. "What? No."

"You sure?" He definitely looked guarded now.

"Lex, I just want to know more about you."

A sheepish expression moved across his features. "Sorry. Charles has me paranoid."

"I don't work for him. I'm simply curious about you."

He sighed. "Okay."

I relaxed slightly. "Let's start with the name of the company you work for." I laughed. "I still have no idea."

"Heaton Industries," he said immediately, as if he'd been waiting for the question.

"I think I might have heard of them."

"You probably have. They're definitely making a big push for new business this year."

"Yes, I'm sure I've seen their ads."

He nodded but didn't speak.

"I'll steer Dr. Peters toward them." I smiled. "Providing your prices are good."

He winked at me. "I'll take care of you."

Little tingles radiated through me at his flirty tone. "Sounds great."

He dropped his gaze, a flush sweeping across his cheeks. He looked almost bashful, which was not something I expected from Lex.

I cleared my throat. "How about family? Any brothers or sisters?" I asked.

His face tensed. "I had one brother, but he's gone."

"I'm sorry." I grimaced.

He shrugged. "We weren't close."

"Still," I said softly. "Family is family."

He nodded, his expression hard to read. "What about you?"

"I'm an only child." I met his curious gaze. "My parents both died two years ago."

"Oh, I'm sorry. Was it a car accident or something?"

"No. My father had a heart attack, and my mother couldn't live without him. Two weeks later, I swear she died of a broken heart." I met his sympathetic gaze. "I miss her, but I'm oddly glad she died too. So that they can be together."

"You're a romantic I see."

"Not really." I frowned. "I mean, I wouldn't have thought so."

"You believe in a love that transcends even death." He smirked. "I'd say that's something a romantic would do."

I met his amused gaze. "I think there are certain instances where I can believe in that sort of love. My parents were fated mates."

He narrowed his eyes. "You think that stuff is real?"

I nodded. "Of course."

"Oh, that's right. You believe the Ancients exist." He twisted his lips. "I keep forgetting how young and gullible you are."

Heat rose in my cheeks. "I'm not gullible."

"I'd bet money Charles thinks you are." His gaze was intent.

"Charles is wrong."

"Maybe."

"I've seen true love with my own eyes. My parents were devoted to each other. Why wouldn't I believe in that?" I tried not to sound too defensive, but I did feel a bit self-conscious. He, of course, didn't know what I knew about fated mates. I expected he'd come back with some other cynical comment, but he didn't.

His gaze softened, and he smiled gently. "It's a nice thought. I wish I had your ability to believe in something so whimsical."

"You say that as if it's all in my mind."

"I can see that you believe it a hundred percent."

"I do." I stood, and picking up the tray, I met his gaze. "I didn't find true love myself, but I do believe it can happen for others."

"And I like that about you," he said in a velvety voice. "I like that you believe in things that I find fantastical. It's charming."

I laughed. "I'm glad I can keep you amused."

His lips twitched.

I moved to the door and hesitated. "Are you sure you don't need any more food? I don't want you going hungry."

"Yes." He looked away. "You don't have to worry about me, Dylan. I know how to watch out for myself."

"Okay. Well, have a good night." I left his room, but I found it difficult to shake the feeling his comment hadn't had anything to do with food.

S.C. Wynne

Chapter Sixteen

Lex

As night fell outside the cabin, the cloudless sky became a deep Prussian blue. The stars were so bright, it caught me by surprise. Living in the city, it was hard to see the stars most nights. The window was cracked open, and the sound of crickets and the breeze rustling the tree leaves was soothing. I was surprised I didn't miss the sounds of the city. I'd assumed I would because I was so used to it, but I was enjoying the serenity of the mountains.

I'd been thinking all day about what I needed to do, now that I knew something had happened to Dad. I assumed he was dead. However, the only way I'd know that for sure was if I could question the one man who knew everything that went on around here: Charles Pederson. I had to find out what he knew but realized he wouldn't tell me anything willingly. That had brought me to the conclusion I'd have to take him hostage somehow and interrogate him none too gently.

But that wasn't going to happen easily. I'd need outside help to make that happen. That was why I was waiting for Dylan to go to sleep so that I could use the phone to call Gabriele. I'd called earlier to let him know where I was, but I hadn't been able to talk much. Not with Dylan in the kitchen just a few feet away. Once Dylan was asleep, I'd take the phone out on the front porch so I could talk freely.

It took a few hours until Dylan went to bed, but eventually the light under the door disappeared. I waited longer, to be sure he had time to fall asleep. Then I got out of bed slowly and opened my door, listening. The cabin was silent, so I padded on bare feet to the cordless phone in the main room. I sincerely hoped Charles wasn't loony enough to tap Dylan's phone line, in hopes of exposing me as the fraud he thought I was. And actually was.

I opened the front door and crept out onto the wooden porch. After closing the door with care, I sat on the step. I then pressed a button on the receiver, listening for any telltale clicks that might clue me in to fact my call was being monitored. I didn't hear anything, so I dialed Gabriele's number.

"Hello?" He sounded groggy, but he answered on the first ring.

"It's me."

He cleared his throat, and I heard rustling sounds. "Hey, boss. Have you found out anything useful?"

"I have."

"Oh, yeah?" He sounded breathless.

I hesitated. "I... I found the license plate to Dad's car on the grounds of the compound."

There was a thick silence, and then he rasped, "Seriously?" He sounded shocked.

"Yes."

"Shit. So… you were right. Your dad did get inside."

"Looks like it."

"Did you find anything else?"

I stamped down my frustration. "No. I assume they chopped the car up into parts to hide its existence."

"Probably."

I exhaled roughly. "I… I think he's dead, Gabriele."

"Aww, hell." Just two soft words, but they had a lot of passion behind them. "I'm sorry."

I shrugged, even though he couldn't see me. "I just don't see him being alive after a month."

"You sure he's not just tied up somewhere on the compound?"

I winced. "My gut says no. Plus, the odds of someone holding Dad and Sal for over a month? Why bother? No one is asking for money, or anything. What would be the point of holding them? They couldn't hold them forever."

"True."

"Knowing Dad, he wouldn't have gone down without a fight."

"Also true."

"The guy in charge of security here, he's a colossal asshole. His name is Charles Pederson." I gripped the phone tight. "He knows everything that happens around here. If someone killed Dad, he either did it, or he knows who did."

"Okay. So what do you want me and Hank to do?"

"I have a plan. I'll need you two to help me grab this Charles guy."

"Grab him?" He sounded uncertain. "How do we get inside? You said the place is like a fortress."

"It is. There's no way you could get in here." I laughed stiffly. "But I don't want you to break in."

"I'm not following."

I chuffed. "Instead of breaking in, we're going to get Charles to come outside of the compound, and then we're going to grab the asshole."

He was quiet. "Do you really think that will work?"

I smirked. "I think it will. The guy detests me. He's been trying like hell to get me in to his office so he can interrogate me. I've been spending all my time avoiding that. But I've decided I've been going about that all wrong."

"You have?" He sounded thoroughly confused.

"Yeah. I'm going to confess to Charles that I'm not who I said I was, and that I had a hand in Dylan's kidnapping. He's going to take pleasure in throwing me out of the compound." I laughed harshly. "Then we grab him and take him to a prearranged spot and question him. Forcefully."

"You think this will work?"

"I couldn't do it alone, but with you and Hank? Yeah, it will work." I glanced around and lowered my voice. "Listen, I want you to rent a place outside of town. It has to be a house, and it can't have any neighbors for miles."

"Uh… okay. I'll start looking first thing tomorrow."

"Good."

"You sure it's safe for you to stay there?"

"Yeah. Dylan is in my corner. He's not going to stand by and let Charles murder me without making a fuss." I smiled grimly.

"You sure that Charles guy is responsible for your dad's disappearance?"

I chuffed. "What I do know is people don't do shit around here without Charles's permission. If he didn't do it, I want him to tell me who did. I want to know what the fuck happened to Dad. He didn't just disappear off the face of the earth, and finding the license plate proves he was here."

"True."

"Charles is the guy in charge, and to me, that means he's the guy who's going to pay."

Gabriele blew out a long, tired-sounding breath. "Whatever you say, boss."

I frowned at his reticent tone. "You said the men needed closure. I'm trying to give them that."

"Right. I understand."

"You don't sound like you approve."

"No. I do. I just wish there was a way to know for sure what happened to Corbin."

"We can ask Charles all the questions we want once we have him at our mercy." I was going to enjoy watching that smug expression leave Charles's face when he realized he wasn't in control anymore.

"How do you know Charles won't just throw you out and we can't get near him?"

I laughed. "Because the guy *loathes* me. I can pretty much guarantee he'll escort me out through the gates personally, just so he can gloat."

"And we'll be waiting."

"Yes. I'm going to march myself down to his office Wednesday morning for my big confession at 9:00 a.m. sharp. You and Hank need to be up on the mountain before then. It's a long drive." I gave him detailed directions about the side road and gate. "Don't park too near the compound until it's go time. One of you can stay with the car, and one of you can help me subdue Charles. Once we grab him, whoever is driving can tear up quick, and we'll get out of there as fast as possible."

"What if someone notices us beforehand?"

"I don't know. Bring a picnic basket or something, and say you were going to have lunch in the great outdoors. Use your imagination."

"Supposing he just kicks you out and slams the door in your face?"

I twisted my lips. "Then I'll have to wait until he comes out of the compound for some other reason. He has to leave sometime."

"Why are we waiting till Wednesday? Frankly, I'm getting a little tired of this town. The charm has worn off. Maybe it's hanging out with just Hank that is making it so unpleasant, but I'd love to get the hell out of here. Can't you just march down to his office tomorrow?"

I could easily do that. But I didn't want to. I'd rationalized all day about how waiting was a better idea because it gave Gabriele time to rent a house and for me to plan things out more carefully. But the stupid truth was, I wanted to spend tomorrow with Dylan. This was the last time I'd ever see the kid, and for whatever reason, I wanted to spend the day with him. After the dream I'd had, and talking more with him this evening, I wanted to explore my feelings with him a little bit. He'd awakened something inside of me that I was having trouble ignoring. Accepting even. If I was ever going to explore these feelings, I wanted it to be with Dylan.

"Wednesday will be fine," I said firmly. "Remember, you guys need to be up near the compound slightly before 9:00 a.m. I don't think I can handle Charles alone. He's a tough bastard."

Gabriele chuckled. "And you're out of practice roughing guys up."

I frowned. "You'll understand when you meet him. Even you wouldn't be able to subdue this guy without help."

"Sounds intriguing," he said softly.

"Focus, Gabriele." The irony of me lecturing him about keeping his mind on the job was not lost on me. I'd have been lying if I didn't admit all I could think about was spending my last day here with Dylan. I'd never see him again after tomorrow, and oddly enough that bothered me.

"I'll fill Hank in on the plan."

"How's he been behaving?"

Gabriele's voice lowered. "He's gone out a few times at night. I have no idea what he's doing, and I don't even want to know."

"The guy's a pig," I hissed.

I still needed to deal with Hank when we got back to our home base in the city of Turbin. He wasn't the kind of person I wanted around. I'd probably have to give him a nice chunk of change to make him go away. Hopefully he'd take it. I didn't want him around anymore. Not after how he'd treated Dylan. If I hadn't stumbled on him that day in the parking lot of the Purple Pooch, God knew what he'd have done to Dylan. My blood boiled just thinking about that.

"How's the kid?" Gabriele asked. "Recovered from his ordeal?"

"He's good."

Maybe there was something in my tone because he laughed. "You have a soft spot for him. I can tell."

"He's a nice kid."

"Yeah, but it's more than that."

I hardened my jaw. "He's a means to an end."

He chuckled. "Yeah, you keep telling yourself that, boss."

My face warmed. "I have to go."

"Sure you do. The conversation is just getting interesting."

"You have an overactive imagination."

He chuffed. "I'm not surprised you're in denial. You don't want to care about anyone. You think that makes you weak."

"Thanks for the psychoanalysis, but I'm not really in the mood."

He sighed. "Your dad really did a number on you, Lex."

"I suggest you focus on what we need to do the day after tomorrow. You're the one who told me the men needed closure. Once Charles admits to killing Dad and he pays the price, we can all move on."

"Have you given any more thought to taking over for your dad?"

"My thoughts on that haven't changed."

He sighed. "I wish you'd rethink that."

"I said I'd step in and find out what happened to Dad. If anything, this has just reminded me how much I hate this world. I don't like the deceit."

"This is because of Dylan, isn't it?"

I hesitated. "He's a part of it of course. He's the main person I've had to lie to. I don't like it. He doesn't deserve to be used like I'm doing. I'm hoping I can leave here and do what we need to do without him ever realizing the extent of my deceit."

"How's that work?

"I'm telling Charles the truth right before we take him. It's not like he'll have a chance to tell Dylan anything I say. Dylan never has to know the kidnapping was faked."

"True."

"Dylan has had some terrible things happen to him. I'd prefer not to be one of those things."

"And you're still going to deny that you have actual feelings toward Dylan?" His tone was dubious.

I exhaled roughly, confusion nipping at me. "I don't know why I feel protective over him. It makes no sense."

"He obviously hit a cord inside of you. It's nothing to be ashamed of."

"I've never had any attraction to a guy before."

"If you are you are. It's no big deal."

"I don't understand why I'd feel that now. If I was going to be attracted to a guy, surely it would have happened a long time ago. Also, I'd think it would be some aggressive type around my age. Not a gentle kid, seventeen years my junior."

"I guess none of that matters because the day after tomorrow, you'll never see him again."

My heart squeezed. "Yes."

"You could tell him how you feel."

"Why bother?"

"I don't know. Maybe he'd be a good first experience."

"God. This is nuts." I raked a hand through my hair, half-relieved to be discussing this with someone, and half-embarrassed. But Gabriele was a good friend, and we'd known each other since we were in our teens.

"I say go for it. See if it's something you like. Maybe you'll be turned off when push comes to shove." He laughed. "Or maybe you'll discover a part of you you've kept repressed."

"But that's just it: I haven't repressed anything that I'm aware of. I've just never been attracted to a man before."

"To be honest, you've barely been attracted to women."

I frowned. "What are you talking about? I've been with lots of women."

"You've fucked. You've never fallen in love. I can't think of one chick you were with more than a few weeks tops."

I searched my memory, running through the women I'd dated over the years. "Surely I stayed with some of them longer than that."

"Nope. You've never been serious about anyone."

"Well, it wasn't because I secretly yearned for dick." I laughed gruffly.

"I'm not saying it was, but maybe you're into this kid Dylan because you've finally managed to connect with someone emotionally."

"I connect with you emotionally."

He chuffed. "Yeah, but we're like brothers."

"True." I sighed wearily and then shook myself. "This is all a distraction. I need to focus on what we're going to do to Charles. I can't be worrying about whether I have the hots for Dylan or not."

"Right."

"I won't be able to talk to you before Wednesday. Remember, rent that house, and be up on the mountain before 9:00 a.m." I sounded gruffer than I intended because I felt foolish about having feelings of any kind toward Dylan. I didn't want Gabriele thinking I was weak.

"Will do, boss."

I hung up and stood to go in the house. I crept into the cabin, listening for any sign that Dylan was awake. It was quiet though, so I hung up the phone and went back to my room. I got in bed thinking about my conversation with Gabriele. I wasn't surprised that he'd been supportive about my odd, and sudden, interest in Dylan. Gabriele was like that. He had a kind heart, and he always had my back. He'd always known he was gay, so maybe that was why it was no big deal to him if I suddenly discovered I was bisexual.

It would have mattered to Dad though. He'd been a homophobe for as long as I could remember. Had I maybe suppressed sexual feelings because I didn't want him judging me? I didn't think that was it. I'd just never noticed guys in a sexual way before. In fact, I hadn't even had an immediate response to Dylan. It had taken a little time, and slowly I'd started to notice little things about him, like his scent and his lips. Even now, just the thought of his mouth made me hard.

Jesus, I did feel compelled to explore these feelings with him. He'd definitely dropped little hints here and there about being attracted to me. If he was interested in fooling around with me, was I brave enough to go through with it? My heart beat faster thinking about getting intimate with him. The dream I'd had about him was burned in my memory. I wanted that. I wanted to touch and taste him for real. It was crazy to think that could be true, but the hunger I had wasn't fading.

If we did fool around, he'd have to understand it wasn't ever going to lead to anything. Obviously he had no idea I was disappearing from his life in a few days. But I knew, and I didn't want to pretend things were more than they were. He'd be confused when I vanished, but odds were everything would be chaotic when Charles disappeared too. I'd be lost in the shuffle, and he'd get over me fast.

I closed my eyes, a tiny thrill shooting through me at what tomorrow might bring. I'd drop hints to Dylan, and if he picked them up, I'd let him lead. I wasn't forcing anything on him. I only wanted him if he truly wanted me. I smiled and rolled over onto my side. By this time tomorrow, if all went well, I'd have had a taste of Dylan. I couldn't think of anything I'd wanted that bad in decades.

Chapter Seventeen

Dylan

Something was different about Lex when he came into the kitchen the next morning. Something seemed to buzz beneath the surface, and he watched me more. I could feel his eyes on me as I put dishes in the dishwasher.

"How are you feeling?" I asked, glancing up to meet his intent gaze.

"Way better." He smiled and then looked away.

I closed the door of the machine. "Can I make you something to eat?"

"I'm fine with cereal."

I frowned. "Cereal? You should have something more substantial than that."

"Why? I don't plan on doing anything taxing today." He laughed.

"But you're just getting over being sick. You need protein and fat." I opened the fridge. "Let me make you some eggs."

"I thought you didn't cook?"

"I don't." I grinned, grabbing eggs and butter. "But I can try."

He chuckled and came closer. When he took the eggs from me, our fingers brushed. He didn't seem to notice, but I sure did. A spark worked its way through my hand and up my arm. I did my best not to react, but it wasn't easy. The effect he had on me was startling sometimes. I couldn't remember an alpha giving me goose bumps before, not like he did. Sometimes when our eyes met, my mouth went dry. Usually I could hide my reactions easier because he kept his distance, but today he was definitely more in my personal space.

"Do you want anything," he asked softly.

I swallowed. "Wh-what?"

A slow smile spread across his face. "To eat."

"Oh." I laughed a bit too loudly. "No. I already ate." I grabbed a saute pan for him from the cupboard.

He took it and moved to the stove. Once he had butter melting, he cracked three eggs, and they dropped into the pan, sizzling loudly.

"Would you like some bacon?"

"Nah."

"Toast?"

He smiled. "Sure."

I grabbed a bag of sourdough bread I had on the counter. "One slice or two?"

"One, please." He flipped the eggs as he spoke.

I dropped the bread in the toaster and leaned against the counter to watch him work. My gaze ran down his long, lean legs, and my pulse picked up when he glanced at me over his shoulder.

Our eyes met, and I'd have sworn I saw arousal in the blue depths of his eyes. "It's nice to see you feeling good again."

"I'm back to my old self."

"You probably can't wait to get home," I said.

"Uh... yeah. Of course, I still need Charles to give me the all clear."

"True. I hope he's actually checking into dirty-cop theory like he said he would."

He frowned. "Why wouldn't he?"

I shrugged. "He probably didn't believe it was true, and if he doesn't think it's true, it must not be true."

"God, how can you guys stand living with an alpha like him in control?" he grumbled. "If I lived here, I'd probably punch him in the face."

I laughed. "He means well."

"So you say."

"Anyway, I'll be sorry to see you go." I hadn't actually planned on saying that, but it slipped out. "I mean, I know you have to go."

"Yeah." He slid the eggs onto the plate just as the toaster popped.

I buttered his toast and carried it to where he'd taken a seat at the kitchen table. I sat across from him, folding my arms. He dug into his food as if he was starving, and I smiled. I'd never seen anyone's appetite recover so quickly after the flu.

"Are your parents still alive?" I asked.

His fork froze midway between the plate and his mouth. But then he shoved the eggs into his mouth and shook his head. "No."

"So no parents, and your brother is gone?" I frowned. "I'm sorry."

"You're in the same boat." He sounded offhand, as if he didn't want my sympathy.

"I guess I am."

He mopped up the yolk on his plate with the toast, and once he'd inhaled that too, he stood and went to rinse his plate. I kind of got the feeling he did that on purpose to stop me asking questions. He really didn't seem to enjoy talking about himself. I found that odd, seeing as alphas usually loved to brag about themselves.

Once his plate was rinsed, he faced me, looking uncertain. "I don't mean to cramp your style. If there's something you need to do, feel free. You don't have to babysit me."

"It's my day off. I don't have anything to do."

He nodded, his blue eyes enigmatic.

"Do you feel up to taking a walk?" I asked.

He frowned. "Am I allowed to walk around?"

"We can keep to the public areas." I smiled weakly. "Sorry. I know this is all really annoying to you."

"For now, I'm on Charles's turf. I have to do what he says." His lips twisted, and he had a funny look. "God save him when he's on my turf though."

A chill shivered through me at his malicious tone. "What?" I laughed.

He forced a smile. "Oh, I just have fantasies of making him as miserable as he's made me."

"Ahhh." I couldn't tell if he was joking or not. "So, would you want to go for a walk? Get some fresh air?"

"Sure. Sounds great."

"We have a clothing store here. We could stop there and grab a few essentials like underwear, or shirts?"

Looking down at his body, he laughed. "I guess we can't raid your neighbor's closet again?"

I smiled. "We could try."

He shook his head. "No, it's okay. I won't be here long enough to need anything."

I frowned. "But… you don't really know how long you'll be here."

His face tensed. "True… Let's play it by ear." He avoided my gaze. "Did you want to walk now?"

"Uh, yeah." He was definitely being a bit cagey, and I wasn't sure why. He had to know it wasn't safe to go into town until we were sure the local cops weren't dirty. "I'm sure Charles will have it figured out soon. He's not one to let dust settle under his feet."

We headed toward the front door, and once outside, he sighed. "I was beginning to feel a little like a vampire." He inhaled the crisp air, looking serene. "The air is so pure here."

"It takes some getting used to." I smiled.

"I remember when I was a kid, a friend of mine invited me on a church retreat in the mountains." He laughed. "My dad didn't let me go because he said the air was too thin and it wouldn't be good for me."

"Why wouldn't it be good for you?"

He grimaced. "I had a touch of asthma when I was younger."

"Really?" That was surprising because he seemed so fit—a perfect specimen of an alpha.

"Yeah. It seems to have gone away as I matured, but I always had it stuck in my head the mountain air would be bad for me." He shook his head. "My dad had all kinds of dumb theories like that."

"We don't choose our family." I studied his profile.

His mouth hardened. "Yes. I wonder what I'd have been like if I'd had a different father."

"I think you turned out all right."

"You don't really know me though."

He was hinting again. Hinting that he wasn't a good person. "You think your dad warped you somehow?"

"Probably." He studied the ground as we walked. "My dad was a hard man to please. We were very different."

"In what way?"

He frowned and seemed to pick his words carefully. "He wanted me to... uh... take over the family business. But, I have no desire to do that. I want to be independent."

"I can understand that." I patted his back, and he gave me a grateful smile. "So, do you enjoy selling medical equipment instead?" I couldn't imagine he'd be intellectually stimulated doing that; he seemed too vibrant to find sales satisfying, but who was I to judge? Perhaps it was more stimulating than I realized.

"Uh... what I'd really like to do is run an art gallery one day."

I grinned. "Now *that* I can see you doing."

"You don't think sales suits me?" He frowned.

"Well—" I twisted my lips to keep from smiling. "—you're slick enough to carry it off."

"Slick, huh?"

"Slick as oil." I hopped over a puddle in the middle of the trail.

He chuckled. "Yeah, I do run on autopilot a lot. It's dull work. I don't know, for some reason catheters just don't give me a hard-on."

A flush went through me at his flippant comment. "Gee, now I'm curious what does."

He stopped walking, and he laughed gruffly. "I shouldn't have said that."

I shrugged. "No, it's fine. Just because I'm super turned on now, don't worry about it."

His expression was impossible to read, but he seemed breathless. "I'm not wrong that you find me attractive, right?" He sounded so uncertain, it was a bit endearing.

"I haven't exactly hidden that from you."

"No. But maybe your feelings changed now that we've spent more time together." His blue eyes were brilliant in the morning sun.

My cheeks felt warm, but I continued to hold his gaze. "They haven't." My heart was beating quicker because this conversation was intriguing, and not one I'd ever expected to have with him. "Is that important? Does it matter if they've changed or not?"

He started walking again, his expression muddled. "Perhaps it's the mountain air messing with my head."

"Messing with you how?"

He pushed his hands into his jean pockets. "Oh, I've just been having strange dreams."

"You have?" I kept my eyes on the gravelly road. "What... what kind of dreams?"

A muscle worked in his cheek. "Promise you won't laugh?"

"I promise."

"I had a dream about you." He gave a strangled laugh. "A… a sex dream."

I had to stop walking then, and he did too. I stared at him with my mouth hanging open. "You had a… *sex* dream about *me*?"

He winced and looked around. "Shhh."

I laughed. "When?"

His cheeks were flushed. "Night before last."

"Wow." I bit my bottom lip, arousal flaring inside me. "That's surprising."

"Tell me about it."

After his revelation, I wasn't quite sure where to go with the conversation. "Well, did the dream upset you?"

He frowned. "Upset me?"

"Yeah, you know, did you feel dirty afterwards?" I grimaced. "Maybe freaked-out?"

He didn't speak right away, but then he said quietly, "I didn't feel dirty. I did feel pretty… rattled."

Trying to keep the conversation on lighter ground, I said, "I'd feel the same way if I had a dream about having sex with Dr. Peters."

Laughing, the tension seemed to leave him. "I'm glad we can laugh about this."

"Yep. Nothing is better for my ego than people laughing about the idea of having sex with me." I spoke flippantly, but there was a part of me that wished he was taking this more seriously.

His smile faded. "I wasn't laughing in the dream." He kept his gaze away from mine. "It was… hot. Surprisingly so."

"It's even more fun in real life."

We fell into an uneasy silence. Finally, he broke it.

"Can I ask you something?"

"Yes." I cast him a curious glance.

"Did you always know you liked guys? I mean, was there ever any doubt in your mind?" His expression was serious, and I realized he truly wanted my honest answer.

"I always knew."

"Never wavered?" He frowned.

"No." I grimaced. "Well, maybe in kindergarten. I think I did have a brief thing for my teacher, Mrs. Brown. But then her husband would come in to help out sometimes, and I quickly realized I had an even bigger thing for him."

His smile was rueful. "I can't understand how I'd get to the age of thirty-nine and not have any idea I might be curious about…" His voice trailed off, and he avoided my gaze.

"Does it really matter when you figure it out? So long as you do?"

He nodded. "Maybe not. Although, it makes it more awkward when everyone thinks you're one thing, but you might be another."

"Fuck what other people think," I growled.

He widened his eyes. "Whoa."

"Sorry." I kicked at a stone in the road. "The thing is, worrying about what society wanted is how I got involved with Jacob. I was a good little omega, and I went in search of an alpha." My voice sounded bitter. "I'd have been better off alone."

He surprised me when he put his arm around my shoulders. "No way you could know anything that would happen. You can't beat yourself up for not seeing the future." His jaw hardened and he gave me a funny look. "I mean that. Things happen sometimes, and you can't control them."

"I just feel like I should have seen that evil in Jacob. How could I miss it?"

He dropped his arm from my shoulder. "You probably used to look for the best in people. A lot of omegas do."

"Now I expect the worst."

"That's not good either. Somewhere in the middle is best."

"I guess." I glanced at him. "I meant what I said though; you can't worry about what everyone thinks. If you decide you're attracted to men, that's your business. No one else's."

He sighed and gestured toward a crop of boulders nestled in the shade of a grove of pines. "Mind if we sit for a bit?"

"Not at all."

We climbed up on the rocks, and he stared up into the clear blue sky. "Am I the kind of man you're usually attracted to?" he asked.

"I don't really have a specific type. I just go by whether or not I feel aroused." My face warmed. "This is weird to talk about out loud."

His lips twitched. "Yes. I agree." He cleared his throat. "I'm a lot older than you."

"You don't look it though." I ran my gaze over his lanky body. "You're gorgeous. I suspect you know that."

He grimaced. "I know that women like me."

"Of course they do." I laughed. "And I don't care about your age."

His gaze slid to mine. "I find myself not caring about yours either."

"Well, I guess if you can overlook the fact I'm a dude, my age should be nothing." I grinned.

"Good point."

I felt his gaze on me again, and my pulse sped up. Was he actually considering being with me? I felt breathless at the idea. Was I ready? Could I be with an alpha? Could I be with Lex? I kept my eyes averted, listening to the sound of kids playing in the distance. For the longest time I hadn't been able to be around children. It had hurt too much. But gradually, I'd been able desensitize myself so that I didn't unravel every time a child giggled. My life would have been so different if I'd met an alpha like Lex, instead of Jacob. But I couldn't turn back time, and what had happened would forever be a scar on my heart.

"You know I won't be here long," he said softly.

"I know."

"I'm not proposing we start a relationship."

"I know that too." I met his assessing gaze. "You're curious, and I'm willing. That's all this would be."

He nodded. "Yes."

I appreciated he wasn't sugarcoating his proposal. He was surprised by his attraction to me, and inquisitive. A part of him probably expected to be turned off, and might even hope for that. Then he could go back to what he was familiar with. Didn't we all prefer sticking with what we knew? I knew I had. I'd stayed away from all alphas because being alone had become my default. I'd felt safest on my own. But then Lex had come into my life and saved me. Saved me from the bad guys. Saved me from the lonely mental prison I'd lived in. I wanted to help him figure this out. Mostly because I yearned to have him, but also because it was something I could actually give him.

"What do you say we walk back?" I asked quietly.

He gave me a sharp look. "Yeah?"

I lifted one shoulder. "We can play it by ear. We don't have to do anything if you don't want."

"I want it all."

"Oh." My heart skipped a beat. "Okay."

He watched me, an almost predatory look in his eyes. He slid off the rock, and his eyes never left me. He held out his hand for me, and I took it. Once on the ground, his palm on the small of my back was warm, firm, commanding. A thrill went through me, and we headed back in the direction of my cabin.

When we reached my home, we went inside without a word. I headed to my room, and he followed. No hesitation. I'd expected maybe he'd need a bit of coaxing, but I'd been wrong. He seemed almost impatient as we stripped our clothing off. He held my gaze, and my heart pounded at the need I saw there. He wasn't afraid. He was hungry.

I grabbed lube and a condom and climbed on the bed, and he did the same. I couldn't believe we were really going to do this. But it felt right. We hadn't known each other that long, but the idea of giving myself to him seemed perfect.

I lay on my back, and he took the spot beside me. His cock was hard, an obvious indication he was turned on. It was no surprise I was hard; I'd wanted him for a while now. He ran his gaze over my naked body, and he licked his lips.

"Can I touch you?" he asked softly.

"Yes."

He smoothed his palm slowly over my chest, brushing my already beaded nipple. "I like touching you."

I smiled, sighing because his exploring hand felt nice. I jumped a little when his hand went lower, skirting over my abdomen, circling my belly button. He leaned over and his mouth hovered above mine. His breath was warm on my lips, and I could feel his uncertainty. Whether that was from shyness, or something else, I didn't know, but then he took my mouth in a warm, achingly delicious kiss. I moaned into his mouth, and he sucked my tongue, searching and seeking urgently.

I wrapped my hand around the back of his neck, deepening the kiss. He didn't pull back; instead he moved to cover my body with his, pressing me into the mattress with his weight. The assertiveness of that move took me by surprise, but his movements were gentle, and so I relaxed back into his kiss. His hands roamed my body, and he moved from kissing my mouth, to my jaw, and then my neck. He worked a hot trail down to my nipple, and he sucked and licked until I moaned and moved against him sensually.

My lust grew so quickly, I was startled by how much I needed him inside me. I rolled my hips and our cocks dragged together, warm, hard, and slick from precum. My ass throbbed with the need to be filled. I couldn't remember ever having such an animalistic craving to be taken.

"You taste good," he said softly. "I wasn't sure if I'd like the taste of a man."

I ran my hands down his spine, cupping his firm buttocks and rocking against his lithe body. "I love everything about men."

S.C. Wynne

He didn't smile. He looked very serious as he cupped my face. "I don't want you to regret this."

"I won't."

He kissed me, softly, and when he lifted his head, he said, "This moment is real. No matter what else happens, this was real."

I frowned, unsure of what he meant. But then he kissed me again, and all rational thought evaporated.

Chapter Eighteen

Lex

It was like my dream only better. His scent, his moans, the way he kissed me as if my mouth on his gave him life. I always enjoyed sex, but this was different. Maybe it was because I liked Dylan so much. I wanted to please him almost more than myself, and that definitely wasn't like me.

He was so giving, in and out of bed, nothing like the prickly omega I'd first met. The minute I touched him, he was open to me. His body was young and beautiful, lean but muscled. His lips were soft and urgent as they opened under mine. I'd expected to be freaked-out touching him, kissing him. But I wasn't. I wanted more.

As we continued to move against each other, he trembled beneath me, our kisses becoming more desperate. The hard planes of his body felt so different from that of a female, but just as good. I liked the scratch of his leg hairs, and the rasp of stubble on his chin. I liked that he was strong and yet pliable. He allowed me the illusion of control, when in reality he was holding back. Letting me lead.

He ran his fingers through my hair, kissing my throat. He licked the sweat from my skin and smiled against my shoulder. "I can't believe this is happening."

"Me neither," I whispered, nudging his thighs open. My attraction to him made no sense.

But I wasn't dealing with logic right now. He was so beautiful in my eyes. I couldn't resist him. I had to have him. I felt territorial, even though that was crazy. I'd never felt the desire to claim an omega. I knew it was expected of me, eventually. Had to carry on the family name after all. Ironic, considering I spent most of my time running from my name.

He opened his legs wider, holding my gaze. "You'll need to prep me."

I nodded, for the first time feeling a bit nervous. "What do I do?"

"Slick your cock and a couple of fingers." He licked his lips. "You still want to do this?"

"Yeah," I rumbled. "I want to do this, Dylan."

"Okay." He smiled. "Just making sure."

I took the lube and did as he'd instructed, making sure my cock and fingers were slippery. Then I began to stroke over his hole, watching the pleasure wash across his features. He moaned and lifted his hips, as if trying to entice me to move quicker. I pressed one fingertip to his puckered entrance, and his lips parted with anticipation. I pushed in gently, and he hissed.

"Fuck," he moaned.

I slid my finger in deeper, watching with fascination at the pleasure in his frantic gaze. "You like that, don't you?"

He nodded, tugging at my hips. "Give me more fingers."

I obliged, excitement ramping inside of me as I pushed two more fingers into his tight heat. I loved making him feel good, and it was obvious from the way he clamped his thighs on my arm and rutted against me that what I was doing to him felt amazing. I couldn't imagine enjoying a guy's fingers in my ass, but he was loving it and begging for more.

My dick was so hard it ached, and all I wanted was to ram inside him and let loose, but I held back. I'd never get to touch him again. This was my one and only chance to pleasure him; I wanted him to always remember our moment together. I wanted to ruin him for other alphas. I knew that was silly, and selfish, but I didn't like the idea of him ever wanting any other alpha. I didn't want him looking at anyone else the way he was looking at me. The moment felt too intimate. Too personal. He shouldn't allow anyone this close again. Just me. Just me.

He jerked and gasped when my finger slid in a different direction. "Oh, fuck," he yelped. "Yeah, right there. Fuck."

I studied him, fascinated that he got such joy out of my fingers inside of him. "Prostate?" I asked softly.

He nodded. "So good."

I'd never had my prostate stimulated, but watching his reaction, it was hard not to envy him. I rubbed my finger in that same spot and he came unglued, humping against me with a desperation that made my heart hammer. "Don't come yet, Dylan," I ordered.

He nodded, sweat beading on his upper lip. "Fuck me. I can't wait much longer."

I pulled my hand from him and knelt between his thighs. This was it. But it wasn't a dream this time. I was actually going to fuck him. I was going to push inside another male and thrust until we both came. I could barely pull in a breath I was so excited. My cock seeped as I rubbed it over his hole, and he held my gaze, moaning. I didn't want to wear the condom. I wanted warm flesh on warm flesh. I wanted nothing between us. I wanted our only time together to be perfect.

Maybe he read something in my expression because he whispered, "Don't wear it."

The jolt of excitement that rocked through me almost made me come. "What?"

"I haven't been with anyone since…"

I hesitated. "But I have."

A line appeared between his brows, but he didn't say anything.

"It will still be good. Even with a condom." I kissed him and he responded hungrily.

When the kiss ended, he whispered, "Please. Give me what I want."

His pleading words seemed to sink into my soul and wind around my heart. I didn't seem to have the strength to deny him, even though logically I knew I was being irresponsible by not wearing a condom. I hadn't had sex ever without a rubber, and the thought of barebacking Dylan was so exciting, I had to squeeze beneath the head of my cock where it met the shaft to stop myself from coming.

Jesus.

Watching my face, he gave a funny smile. "That turns you on even more, doesn't it? The idea of coming inside me bare."

I swallowed hard, unable to speak.

"Do it." As he spoke, he began to rock against me, opening his legs as my cock slid down the crack of his ass. Like a ship finding safe harbor, the tip settled comfortably against his hole. "Just do it," he begged.

My cockhead pressed the tense muscles of his anus, and instinct screamed for me to do what he wanted. What I wanted. He was begging for it, and I felt out of control as words spun around in my brain: *Take him. Take him. Take him.* His desperate gaze and words seeped in and woke something primal inside of me. Logic flew out of my head as pure lust raged through me. I wanted to bite his neck as I took him. I wanted to mark him as mine, like we'd have done in ancient times. I wanted all other alphas to know that Dylan was my omega. My omega.

He moved so quickly, I barely had time to register what he was doing. He twisted and rolled so that he was on top of me. My hands instinctively went to rest on his hips, balancing him. Without speaking, he began sliding his hips back and forth, dragging our cocks together. The friction was delicious, and I dug my fingers into his skin, watching him.

He smiled and slowing began inching up the length of my dick, until his anus was at the tip. Then he reached behind and guided it into himself. The first squeeze of him had my brain short-circuiting. He slid all the way onto my cock with a hiss, and I cried out because it felt so fucking good. He threw his head back, and his hips began to roll, up and down, back and forth. His body shuddered as he slid up and down on my shaft, and I began to thrust upward, meeting him.

"Yeah," he whimpered. "That's it. That's it."

I felt insane with the need to pound into him. My hips seemed to jerk uncontrollably as I pumped into his tight heat. I couldn't catch my breath, but I just kept going. I had to. I had to. I fucking had to. I didn't care that we hadn't used a condom. I didn't care that we were being loud. All I cared about was the slick friction and the drive to come inside him. I had to give him my release. I had no idea why it was so important, but everything in me said it had to happen. He had to be filled full of my seed. There was no turning back. This had to happen, or I felt like I'd die.

He began stroking himself, his mouth open, his eyes the bluest I'd ever seen. "Oh, God," he whispered, his hips moving faster. "Oh, God. I'm coming. I'm coming."

My balls buzzed and throbbed as his hole clenched on my cock. A thick stream of cum splattered my abdomen, and then another. My dick jerked and spilled a flood of seed inside his tight channel. Ecstasy swamped me, and my eyes rolled up in my head. "Fuck," I cried out, as my muscles quaked and shuddered. I came so hard my vision blurred, and I clenched my teeth. The pleasure was so intense, it bordered on painful.

Dylan collapsed on me, with my twitching cock still buried inside of him. The insane drive to fuck had quieted, and after a few moments, I carefully pulled out of him. He slumped beside me on the bed, a happy grin on his face.

"Jesus. You're an animal in bed." He laughed weakly.

I wiped my sweaty brow, feeling shaky. "You too." I blew out a breath. "That was wild."

He rolled on his side to face me. "How do you feel? Any weird emotions?"

"No." I frowned. "I'm... I'm good." I'd expected to feel *some* regret, or confusion, but I just felt good. It had felt so perfect to be inside him, I couldn't lie and say I felt anything but amazing.

"Nothing seemed off for you?" His gaze was searching.

I raised one brow. "Did I seem like I wasn't enjoying myself?" There was no way that was possible. I'd practically brought the house down expressing how good it felt.

He smirked. "You seemed happy."

"To put it mildly," I said softly, tracing my finger along his hip. "I really thought maybe I'd get halfway in and chicken out."

"I loved it." He licked his lips. "All of it."

I frowned. "I planned on wearing the condom."

He grimaced. "Yeah. I'll be honest, I kind of lost control."

"I didn't have the willpower to force the issue."

He sat up on his elbow. "I truly haven't been with anyone."

"Yeah, but like I said, I have been. I've always used protection, so I'm sure I'm fine." I frowned. "But it was reckless, Dylan. I hope you won't do that again… with anyone else." The very idea of him with anyone else made my skin crawl, but I attempted to hide that bizarre reaction.

His lashes were thick on his cheeks as he avoided my gaze. "I've never wanted that with anyone else," he said quietly. "It felt right with you."

I was flattered but still worried for him. "Just promise me you'll use protection from now on."

"I will." He grabbed some tissues from the nightstand, and we cleaned off.

I rolled onto my back and stared up at the ceiling. "Shouldn't I be traumatized or something?"

He laughed. "You mean because you had sex with a man?"

"Yeah. It seems like I should be at least a little… weirded out." How could I so easily switch to fucking a guy and not feel the least bit odd?

"I don't really know. I'm no expert."

It surprised me that, even now, I could hardly look away from his full lips. I still wanted him. I'd hoped maybe being with him would work it out of my system, but I still craved him. That was a problem, seeing as I was leaving tomorrow. I certainly hoped I could go back to enjoying women again. But when I thought of sex, it was only Dylan who came to mind. Not women, and not any other man I could think of.

I was distracted from my thoughts when Dylan gave a soft groan. I flicked my gaze to him and found him rubbing his stomach. "You okay?"

He nodded, but he was white as a ghost, and there was a sheen of sweat on his face.

I frowned, moving closer. "Was I too rough?"

"No. You didn't do anything. I'm just a bit nauseated." He shivered.

My stomach churned, and I wanted to pull him into my arms to comfort him. But I wasn't sure he'd appreciate that gesture. After all, he wasn't actually my omega. I brushed hair from his forehead, and when he met my gaze, I was startled by how blue his eyes were. I blinked at the brilliance of his irises. Was it just the lighting in the room that made them stand out so much? I was about to say something, but he jumped from the bed suddenly and rushed into his bathroom.

I sat up, concerned to hear him retching in the bathroom. I rose and dressed quickly, then went to the door. "Can I get you anything?"

"No," he mumbled weakly. "I'll be fine in a minute."

I wanted to give him privacy but couldn't force myself to leave him. After a few minutes, I heard water running, and he came out. He looked surprised to see me hovering, and he sighed and fell onto the bed. "I think stress is getting to me."

I sat on the foot of the bed. "You're sure I didn't do anything? I *was* kind of rough." My dick twitched at the memory of pounding into him, but I shoved those feelings down. Now was not the time to lust after him.

"Lex, you didn't hurt me." He curled into a ball and hugged his knees to his chest. I pulled the blankets over him, and he whispered, "Thank you."

Maybe I should have left him alone to sleep, but I couldn't seem to. I stayed where I was, anxiety bubbling in my gut as I listened to his slow breathing. I knew he fell asleep at some point, and he whimpered and moved around, dreaming. I hadn't ever felt so protective about anyone before; it was an odd sensation, and not entirely pleasant.

When he finally woke, hours later, he seemed better. He sat up, wiping his eyes. "Shit. I slept?"

"Yes. You obviously needed it."

He watched me, his expression puzzled. "You stayed here the whole time?"

I nodded. "I didn't feel right leaving you."

He gave a funny laugh. "I guess it's becoming a habit for you to take care of me."

Guilt nipped at me because the first time had all been an act. This time it wasn't though. I'd been unable to walk away from him as he slept. I didn't know why, but the pull to stay close had been powerful. Now that he seemed more like himself, the tension drained from me.

I stood. "I'm going to shower."

"I'd offer to join you, but I'm still a little weak."

My body warmed at the idea of him wet and needy in the shower. I had to stop myself from taking him up on his offer. "You should rest some more. I'll cook dinner."

"Really?" He sounded pleased. "That would be wonderful."

I smiled. "My pleasure." I left his room, ignoring the desire to stay. He was fine now. Whatever had bothered him earlier seemed to have passed. He wasn't my omega, and I had no right to hover around him as if I was his alpha.

I thought about tomorrow and the fact I'd never see him again. The regret and sadness that hit me at that thought was unsettling. I was shocked to realize I had actual feelings for Dylan. I knew he'd be hurt when I disappeared tomorrow, and that bothered me. But I had to focus on why I was here. I hadn't gone to all this trouble to simply laze around and explore my newfound enjoyment of men. I'd come here to find out what happened to Dad and punish whoever was responsible. Tomorrow I'd grab Charles and make him tell me everything he knew. Then I'd probably have to kill him.

I had no time for warm and fuzzy feelings about missing Dylan. I'd enjoyed our time together, but as soon as the sun came up, whatever was between us had to end.

Chapter Nineteen

Dylan

I slept a few more hours and woke refreshed. I had no idea why I was so tired, but I was better now. Sex with Lex had been perfect. I wanted more, but I wasn't sure he did. He'd said the sex was great, and he'd definitely been into it at the time. That didn't mean he wanted to do it again though. He'd scratched his itch, and that was easily all he'd needed.

I showered and then joined Lex in the kitchen where he was busy chopping vegetables. "What are you making?"

He smiled at me and surprised me with a soft kiss. "Stir-fry."

"That sounds good." My pulse was quick, and my lips tingled as I leaned against the counter.

"Well, you were sleeping, and I didn't think I was allowed to go shopping. Wouldn't want Charles upset with me again," he muttered. "I decided to make something with what you already had here."

"I haven't had stir-fry in a year."

He widened his eyes. "What?"

My face warmed. "I told you I can't cook."

"Don't you have restaurants here?"

I laughed. "There's exactly two sort-of restaurants. They're really just a couple of omegas who like to cook for other people."

He shook his head. "I suppose next you'll tell me there's no Starbucks?"

"Nope."

"How do you survive?" His lips twitched.

"I make my own coffee. There's this new thing called a coffee maker."

"Sounds barbaric." He tossed broccoli into the large pan.

"Soon you'll be able to partake of whatever restaurants and coffee you want." I hoped I didn't sound as bummed as I felt. But the thought of him leaving was depressing. I really liked him, and I would have loved for him to be my roomie a little longer. But I wasn't about to say that because I didn't want to come off clingy.

He glanced over. "Will you remember me when I'm gone?"

"Will I remember you?" My voice was higher than I'd have liked. "You know I will."

He set the knife down and came up to me. He took hold of my chin, and he planted a gentle kiss on my mouth. "I'll remember you too."

"I would hope so." I smiled up at him. "You're supposed to always remember your first time." I hated the idea he'd go on to be with other people. Now that I'd had a taste of him, I felt possessive. Foolish, yes. But it was hard to control those feelings.

He wrinkled his brow, but he didn't speak.

"Looking forward to your meeting with Charles tomorrow?" I asked, knowing full well he wasn't.

"God, no. I'd rather stick needles in my eyes than talk to that guy." His voice was harsh, and he went back to chopping vegetables.

"But he might have good news for you. He might say the coast is clear, and you can go home."

"True."

"It will be weird to be here alone again. The cabin will seem so empty." I sighed.

"How long do you plan on staying here?" He sliced water chestnuts with a delicate hand. "Surely you could get a job anywhere you wanted to live."

"Probably. But the work I do here is important."

He frowned. "But you could deliver babies anywhere."

"I could." Naturally, he had no idea about the work I did in detail. Helping solar eclipse omegas deliver their babies was an honor. It wasn't easy getting qualified help up in the compound, and I wasn't going to abandon Dr. Peters. Maybe after I'd been here a few years, then I'd move on and try to live a more regular life. But for now, there was no reason to leave.

"But you won't leave the compound?"

"Why would I?"

He had a funny expression. "No reason."

"I'm glad I met you though," I said quietly. "You're the first alpha I've been with since... Jacob."

His gaze was intent. "How long ago since Jacob?"

I stiffened. "Eighteen months, two days, and six hours—but who's counting?"

He grimaced. "God. I can't even imagine what you've been through."

"Yeah, well, let's not go down that road." I pushed away from the counter and started unloading the dishwasher.

"I don't pity you, Dylan."

I glanced up at the seriousness of his tone. "Don't you?"

He shook his head. "I'm angry you went through that. I wish there was a way I could make Jacob pay for what he did, but I don't pity you."

"A lot of people do." I slammed a cupboard closed a bit too roughly. "They mean well, but I hate pity."

"Just the fact you were willing to... be with me... shows you're going to be okay. That's how I see it."

Frowning, I said, "Just one roll in the hay with you and suddenly I'm healed?"

"I didn't say that. I said it shows you're trying to heal."

"I've *been* trying," I grumbled. "It's not as easy as it looks."

He shrugged. "You're tough. You'll get there."

"Well, I'm not your problem. You'll be on your merry way before long, fucking every guy you meet, and I'll just be a faint memory." This time I knew I failed miserably at hiding the bitterness in my tone.

He gave a humorless laugh. "Is that what you really think? That I can't wait to go screw other guys now that I've had a taste?"

"Probably." It was frustrating liking him so much, knowing it could never go anywhere. I'd finally opened up to someone, and there was no possibility of a relationship.

He narrowed his eyes, and he put the knife down. Then he walked closer, a funny look in his eyes. "If you think that, you have no idea how attracted I am to you." His voice was husky as he slipped his fingers into the belt loops of my jeans. "You, Dylan. I'm not fantasizing about being with other men."

I shivered when he kissed the side of my mouth. "You're just saying that to spare my feelings."

"Bullshit." He leaned his weight on me, and his erection was obvious against my thigh. "Should I prove how much I want you?"

My heart began to pound. "Here?"

"Yeah. Right. Here." He moved his hands to his zipper, and he slowly lowered it. "Take your pants off."

Excitement soared through me. "Wh-what?"

His mouth found my ear. "Take your damn pants off so I can fuck you, Dylan."

I shuddered from arousal, but with trembling fingers, began to fumble with my jeans. When I had them around my ankles, I kicked one foot free. He didn't even wait for me to get my other foot loose; he yanked my briefs down to my knees, and he started kissing me. His hands roamed freely over my naked flesh, and his tongue searched my mouth. I moaned when he started rubbing my stiff cock, and I leaned into him.

"Oh, God, Lex."

His eyes were bright, and he watched me intently as he slid his hand up and down my length. "You have a beautiful cock. Never thought a guy's body or dick was sexy until you. I can't stop wanting to touch you, and be inside you."

My nipples beaded against my shirt as he rolled his cock against mine, smearing precum. He turned me to face the counter, and he kicked my feet open wider. His hands stroked my skin, his touch rougher than the first time. He seemed more confident now, and his breath was hot on the back of my neck. I arched my back, panting with anticipation.

"You want me?" I whispered.

He chuckled. "Oh, yeah." He sucked on his finger and then slid it along the crack of my ass, pausing to circle my hole. "You know I do."

"I thought maybe it was a onetime thing."

"Yeah. I thought so too. We were both wrong."

I gulped when he pushed his finger inside me. Pleasure radiated through my whole body when he hooked it and rubbed my prostate. I shuddered and humped the cupboard, but when he stopped moving his finger, I groaned my complaint.

"You're so sensitive there."

"Yeah," I moaned. "Give me more."

"What's it feel like?" he asked softly.

Blowing out a shaky breath, I said, "I don't know how to describe it. It just makes me want to come bad."

He rocked his hips, and his cock was rock hard against the small of my back. "And you actually like my cock inside you?"

"God, yes."

"It… it doesn't hurt?"

I frowned. "It can be rough if you have someone who doesn't know what they're doing."

"I didn't know what I was doing, but you still liked it. You fucking loved it."

"Yeah, you're a natural, I guess. If you don't mind, I'd love a repeat performance."

He laughed. "You're so impatient." He began to move his fingers again, teasing my insides in delicious, torturous strokes. "Don't you dare come yet."

I shivered, clenching my jaw as I tried to control myself. "Then fuck me."

Another husky laugh, and he pushed his fingers deeper. "I love the sounds you make." He nuzzled my hair. "So needy, and perfect."

I wanted to come bad. Prostate stimulation was intense. I wasn't a machine, and he had me too turned on to just wait and wait. If he wasn't going to fuck me, he at least needed to let me come. "Come on, Lex. You can't just leave me hanging," I grumbled. "Let me come."

He nipped the back of my neck. "But I want you to come with me inside you."

I rested my head on my arms, trying to contain my frustration. "Then do it. *Please.*"

He pulled his fingers from me and pried my ass cheeks apart. "I can't believe how much I want this," he murmured, rubbing the tip of his cock over my hole. "But I do. I can't stop thinking about it."

I reached back, tugging him closer. "Fuck me. *Fuck me.*"

Without another word, he pushed inside of me. He growled, and I saw stars. Fireworks flickered behind my lids as his thick shaft penetrated me deep. My cheek rubbed the tile counter, and I moaned with delight as he started thrusting slowly. The cabinet doors clicked and squeaked as he pounded me against the cupboards, locking and unlocking with every stroke into me.

Muscles at the base of my cock squeezed, preparing for release. I was so hard it hurt, and I stroked myself quickly, breathing jaggedly. "God, yeah. Yeah," I wheezed, praying my legs didn't give out.

His fingers dug into my hips as he held me in place, fucking me in beautifully perfect rhythm. He grunted and swore, mumbling how good it felt, and how he wanted to fill me with his seed. I shivered and clenched the muscles of my ass so it felt even better for him. He was so deep inside me, I could barely catch my breath. I'd never experienced the level of pleasure he gave me. His dick filled me so full, the friction was unspeakably good. It wasn't like we were just fucking; he was invading every inch of me, taking what he wanted, but also giving me so much more.

"Lex," I moaned, as my climax spiraled through me.

"Oh, fuck. So good," he whispered, his hips stuttering. "Oh *fuck*."

The warm flush of his seed sent me over the edge. My body jerked as my orgasm exploded inside me. My release spurted against the walnut cabinets, dripping down the dark wood. I couldn't even form words as pleasure ravaged me, zipping through my nerve endings and leaving me a weak, mumbling mess. As feared, my legs gave out, but he held me up, fucking me until his climax was done. Then he leaned on me, his hot breathing fanning across the nape of my neck. I could feel him trembling as he struggled to keep us both upright.

"Jesus. Fucking. Hell," he rasped. "You've ruined me."

I'd have loved to believe that was true. That'd he'd want to stay here and only be with me. But I wasn't naive. You couldn't hold alphas accountable for the things they said when they were dopey from an orgasm. I laughed gruffly and concentrated on catching my breath.

After a few minutes, he pulled out of me and stumbled to lean on the counters. His eyes were closed and his face a mask of contentment. I grabbed some paper towels and wiped myself and the cabinets clean. Once I had my clothes back in place, I glanced at him and found his eyes were open. He had a funny expression.

"Everything okay?" I asked.

His expression changed instantly, and he plastered on a pleasant smile. "Better than okay." He pulled his pants up, and he crossed the space to me. He took me in his arms, and his kiss was gentle, almost tender. When he lifted his head, his eyes were blue and enigmatic. "You're such a surprise to me."

"I am?"

He nodded and then released me. He glanced at the chopped vegetables and laughed. "Now… where was I?"

"You were cooking us a delicious dinner." I smoothed my hand over my shirt, feeling a little embarrassed about how we'd just gone at each other like wild animals. I couldn't remember my lust ever being so out of control before. He was the kind of alpha I could see spending the day in bed with. One time would never be enough. I'd have loved to forget about dinner and instead drag him to my room and just fuck until we couldn't move anymore.

He went back to slicing vegetables and chicken, and I watched him. We didn't speak for a few minutes, but then he said, "Have you really not been with anyone since Jacob?"

I hesitated. "I didn't want to be with anyone."

"But you do now?"

"Not necessarily."

He studied me. "I guess I'm not as charming as I thought."

I frowned. "You're not an option. You're leaving. You've made that crystal clear."

"True." He continued to watch me. "Would it surprise you to know I haven't been open to anyone either?"

"Yes. I had you pegged as a player. Breaking hearts left and right."

He winced. "I've broken a few hearts, sure. But I've felt detached. Disinterested in making a connection."

"Why?"

"Not sure. I actually understand your reasons more than mine. You suffered a trauma, and you pulled back into your shell. But I've just never had the drive to find an omega and settle down. It's expected of me, of course. But it's never been something I cared about."

"If you do give in to pressure, will you pick a female or male omega now?"

He looked nonplussed at the question. "I assume a female."

"Why?"

He blinked at me. "Well, as I told you, I've never felt attracted to a man until you."

"That will probably change… now."

He looked unconvinced. "Not sure that's true. But since I'm not seeking a mate just yet, I'll worry about that later."

I turned away so he couldn't see the distaste on my face. The idea of him settling down with some other omega bugged me. I knew it was stupid to let it get to me, but I couldn't seem to shake the possessive feelings he brought out in me. Even if he'd been at a stage in his life when he was ready to settle down, he'd never be content in a place like the compound. I couldn't really blame him either. The only reason I'd been so happy here was because I was hiding away from the world. Licking my wounds.

"Maybe we can make a silly pact, like in a movie." I spoke flippantly. "If in ten years, neither of us is claimed, we can agree to be together."

His lips curved in a smile. "Sure. Why not?"

"We actually get along fairly well."

"Yeah. We do." He twisted his lips. "Our sex life would be amazing."

"Of course, by then, you'd be an old man." I grinned. "You'd be pushing fifty."

He narrowed his eyes. "That still won't be a problem."

I sighed. "I guess I just have to wait a decade to find out."

He laughed roughly. "You keep giving me that challenging look and we may never eat dinner."

"Pfft. If you think that's a threat, you don't know me very well."

He blew out a shaky breath. "We're going to eat this food. I have plans for you tonight, and I'm going to need my strength."

Excitement shivered through me at the carnal look in his eyes. "Sure. We can eat and have an early night."

He went back to stirring the sizzling food. "Don't plan on sleeping, Dylan."

I laughed and went to set the table. As I moved around the table, performing the ritual of folding napkins and placing the salad fork next to the dinner fork, I realized that for the first time in forever, I was happy.

S.C. Wynne

Chapter Twenty

Lex

Dylan was like a drug I couldn't get enough of. We were both insatiable and spent the entire night enjoying each other's bodies, until the sky to the east turned pink and orange. Exhausted, Dylan drifted off eventually, tucked in my arms, but I couldn't sleep. I dreaded what the day would bring. Kidnapping Charles would be no easy task, and I was also faced with the fact that, after today, I'd never seen Dylan again. I couldn't understand why the thought of that was so fucking depressing. But it was.

I kissed his hair and inhaled his sweet scent, trying to imprint all the details of him on my memory. His smooth skin and beautiful mouth drove me crazy. I loved the little freckles that spread across his nose, and the birthmark on his hip. For whatever reason, Dylan meant something to me. I was frustrated that I'd met him under these circumstances. Perhaps out in the real world, we'd have been able to have something more than just a few nights together. But then, if not for these circumstances, I'd never have met him at all.

When the sun was fully up, I carefully slipped out of Dylan's room and showered in mine. I needed to get my head in the game. It was eight, and Gabriele and Hank would be waiting for me by nine. I took the license plate I'd found out of the picture frame and slipped it into my waistband.

Then I went into the kitchen and drank some coffee and forced a piece of toast down. I was nervous about having to handle Charles alone, until reinforcements arrived. He was a big guy. Big and tough. I wasn't a wimp by any means, but I also wasn't Charles's caliber of fierce. The guy probably ate nails for breakfast.

Dylan was still sleeping when I left the cabin. My heart hammered as I followed the street down toward the security building. The houses were dark, and I wasn't sure if that was because everyone still slept or if they were all still on lockdown because of me. As much as I resented Charles, the guy did have good instincts. A part of me looked forward to seeing him bloody and broken. If all went well, today I'd finally get some answers about Dad.

It was a quarter to nine when I knocked on the door to the security building. The door opened abruptly, and two uniformed alphas stood there. They looked surprised to see me, and I got the feeling they hadn't opened the door for me so much as they'd been about to exit the building.

"What do you want?" one of them asked gruffly. He was tall, skinny, and looked suspicious.

"I have a meeting with Charles." I noticed they both wore shoulder holsters, and my pulse sped up. "I believe he knows I'm coming."

The other alpha smirked. "Oh, yeah. You're the outsider."

I smiled pleasantly. "That's right."

They moved past me.

"He's expecting you," the skinny one said brusquely.

"Thanks." I grabbed the door before it closed and entered the cool building. It was quiet inside. I'd pictured more activity, but there didn't appear to be any other employees. That was good news for me. Charles alone would be hard to subdue, but if he had backup, I'd fail for sure.

There was one office with a light on, and I assumed that had to be Charles's. When I appeared in the doorway, Charles was on the phone, pacing back and forth. He was speaking loudly, and he looked annoyed.

"I'm not interested in your excuses. We ordered Demerol, not morphine." He had his back to me as he listened to the person on the other end of the line. "I know they both suppress pain, that's not the point. We don't use morphine."

I entered the office, but he still wasn't aware of my presence.

"I don't care if you usually deal with Dr. Peters, you're answering to me now." He listened again. "Bullshit. They are *not* the same. Morphine can depress the baby's ability to breathe. We aren't using it. You need to get us a shipment of Demerol today," he growled. "Don't fuck with me, Ned, or I'll have your ass fired."

I stayed near the door, not sure if I should leave and give him privacy, or if that didn't matter. He turned suddenly, and when he saw me, his face tensed. But the other person must have said something, because he turned his attention to the phone again.

"No. Not tomorrow. Today. We have several omegas scheduled *today*." He listened and then grunted. "Fine. That will work. But if you don't make it by noon, I'm finding another company." He hung up and faced me. "Huh. You actually showed."

I smirked and gave a cursory salute. "Reporting for my inquisition, sir!"

He didn't appear amused. "I thought maybe you'd have another bout of the flu."

"People get sick. Maybe you don't because you're perfect, but the rest of us do."

His eyes narrowed. "Even you must admit the timing was suspicious."

"Sorry. Shit happens."

He curled his lip. "Especially with you around."

God, I was going to enjoy wiping that arrogant look off his face. "Well, I'm here now."

"Yeah. You are." He gestured to a folding chair in front of his desk. "Have a seat."

"It's not going to electrocute me, right?" I sat as I spoke, crossing my arms.

His mouth was a grim line. "Is this all a big joke to you, Lex?"

"You kind of are."

He shook his head. "Why? Because I take protecting the residents seriously?"

I chuffed. "Something tells me you take everything seriously. I feel sorry for your omega, if you have one. You must be a ton of fun in bed."

Red spears appeared on his high cheekbones. "I don't have an omega."

"Yeah, cuz that was the point." I was purposely being antagonistic. I wanted him good and mad when I finally came clean. That way he'd be more likely to escort me from the premises personally.

"I can't imagine what the hell Dylan sees in you."

"Yeah, I don't know why he respects you either. I think you're a power-hungry blowhard."

He shook his head. "I care about these alphas and omegas. They're vulnerable and they need my protection."

"Whatever." I shrugged and glanced out into the other part of the building. "Where is everybody?"

"On patrol," he snapped.

I was stalling because I was a bit nervous about launching into my confession. He was already pretty worked up, and I wasn't looking forward to his fury. For all my bravado, he was an intimidating alpha.

He sat down behind his desk and shuffled some papers. "Let's start with your full name."

I felt breathless as I said, "Lex Osborn Sabine. Age thirty-nine. I'm six foot, one-hundred and seventy pounds of pure muscle."

He chuffed. "Right." He scribbled on a pad, but then he looked up sharply. "Wait… did you say *Sabine*? Lex Sabine?"

"That's right." I held his gaze. I'd expected it to take longer for him to recognize the name and react. But he looked immediately guarded.

"Corbin Sabine's son?"

"Yes." I watched him as various emotions flickered across his face. He almost looked… worried.

He set his pen down. "What are you doing in Yellow Springs?"

"Looking for my dad."

His gaze darkened. "You lied to Dylan. You said you were a medical supply salesman."

"I couldn't very well announce who I was, now could I?"

"Why not?" he asked softly.

"You know why."

"Do I?" A muscle worked in his cheek.

"Dylan wouldn't necessarily know who I am. But you would. If he'd said he wanted to bring Corbin Sabine's son inside the compound, I'd have never made it past you."

Color seemed to drain from his face. "Why?"

"Because you murdered my dad."

He didn't respond right away, and a thick silence fell. I found it interesting he didn't immediately deny the charge. Eventually, he said, "Why do you think that?"

"Because my guess is nothing happens in here without your okay, and the last time anyone heard from him, he was hanging around the compound."

"So you just have a hunch he was here."

"No. I have proof he was *inside* the compound." I kept my voice steady as I delivered that news, watching every tic and twitch of his features.

"What kind of proof?" he asked quietly.

"The personalized license from his car." I narrowed my eyes. "Care to explain how that would end up here if he wasn't also here?"

He held my gaze, his face impassive, but then he snarled, "I knew it was you who broke into the auto body shop."

"That's right." I smirked.

He looked like he wanted to strangle me. "You didn't just happen to meet Dylan, did you?"

Now it was my turn to look uncomfortable. "I did what I had to do."

"You're a piece of work. Did you... did you orchestrate Dylan's kidnapping?" He scowled, his face flushing red with anger. "God damn you if you did."

Guilt nudged me, but I pushed it away. I had to focus on getting Charles worked up. He needed to be so mad he wasn't thinking straight when he escorted me out of the gates. "An opportunity presented itself, and he was my ticket inside the compound."

He stood, scraping back his chair. "You're a fucking asshole, messing with that poor kid. I'd like to snap you in two for hurting him."

"I didn't hurt him," I hissed. "I *saved* him, remember?"

He came around the desk like a charging bull, and I rose and backed away. But he was too fast, and he grabbed me by the shirt and threw me across the room. I crashed into the wall and bounced off it, landing on my ass. I was stunned and not quick enough to escape him when he grabbed me again and hauled me to my feet.

"Dylan has been through *hell*. What he didn't need was someone toying with his emotions like that." He yanked me hard and pushed his furious face close to mine. "I should break your neck."

"Is that how you do shit around here? Kill people when you don't like them?" I rasped, tasting blood on my lip. "Is that what you did to my father?"

"I didn't touch a hair on your father's head," he growled.

"I don't believe you. Why hide his car, then?" I wiped at my mouth, seeing the scarlet smear on my skin.

"I'm not telling you shit, and your time here is done." He dragged me out of the room and toward the front door of the building. "It's going to break Dylan's heart when he finds out you've been using him. You're a fucking heartless monster."

"And you're a murderer," I hissed, struggling in his unyielding grasp. I prayed to God that Hank and Gabriele were on the other side of the gates. No way could I handle Charles on my own. The man was a beast, and I was like a rag doll in his hands.

He tugged me roughly out of the building, not even bothering to close the doors. There was a small gate cut into the walls of the compound so that people could come and go, without having to open the big gates. That was where Charles was dragging me. I pretended to struggle, just to keep him distracted, but my heart was pounding so hard I felt light-headed. If Hank and Gabriele weren't waiting for us, I'd have to start at the beginning again to figure out a way to grab Charles. I couldn't exactly go to the cops with the license plate. Odds were they'd be on Charles's side and arrest me for kidnapping Dylan.

We reached the smaller gate, and Charles unlocked it, his grip never loosening from me. This was the moment of truth. If my guys weren't waiting, I was screwed. He yanked open the door, and I was relieved when he didn't just shove me out, but he dragged me through. His attention was 100 percent focused on me. His gray eyes were filled with hatred, and I was almost afraid he might shoot me on the spot.

When I saw Hank behind him, pressed up against the wall, relief washed through me. Too late, Charles spotted him out of the corner of his eye, and he tried to retreat back into the compound. Hank was faster though, and he grabbed him from behind and smashed the butt of his gun against Charles's head. Charles immediately went slack, and for a second I was worried Hank had killed him.

Gabriele came screeching up with the car in a cloud of dust, as someone up above us started yelling over a speaker. I assumed that the voice was coming from the guard shed perched atop the wall. I prayed they'd be too worried about shooting Charles to open fire on us. I opened the car door, sweat running down my face as I helped Hank toss Charles in the back seat.

"What's going on?" a frightened, familiar voice came from behind me.

I stiffened in horror when I recognized Dylan's voice. *Fuck.* Turning, I found him running toward me, looking confused. When he reached me, his eyes widened in terror as he looked past me. I glanced behind me to find Hank advancing on him. Before I could say anything to stop him, Hank had Dylan by his scruff and was dragging him toward our getaway car. In shock, I followed, not sure what to do. Grabbing Dylan wasn't part of the equation, but security guys were now piling out of the gate and advancing toward us. I stood frozen next to the car, trying to think of what to do.

"Lex! For fuck's sake, get your ass in the damn car," yelled Gabriele, gunning the engine.

His voice jolted me out of my daze, and I dove into the front seat of the car. Gabriele revved the motor and threw the gear into drive, and we tore off in a giant cloud of dust and exhaust. I could hear Dylan yelling in the back seat and Hank swearing at him to shut up.

"Was I ever glad to see you two," I said, wiping perspiration from my face with shaking hands. "Anybody following us?" I did my best to block out the fact that Dylan was upset in the back of the car. I felt shell-shocked at the idea I might have to dispose of Dylan. I wasn't sure I had it in me to give that order. Much better not to think about that just yet.

"I think we caught them off guard," Lex shouted above the engine. "There's nobody behind us."

I prayed he was right. I was already uneasy about how fast he was driving. I didn't think my stomach could take a high-speed chase. I heard a choking sound, and I turned to find Hank with his arm around Dylan's throat. Dylan's eyes were wide with panic, and he was clawing at Hank's beefy arm.

"Hey! Let him go," I shouted, and Hank obeyed, releasing Dylan.

"He wouldn't shut up," rumbled Hank.

"Find another way to keep him quiet," I snapped.

Slumping, Dylan coughed roughly, clutching his neck. His breathing was more of a wheeze, and I was worried Hank had crushed his windpipe.

"Are you okay?" I asked, touching his leg.

Dylan jerked away, gasping for air. "Don't touch me."

"Dylan—" I started.

"What the hell are you doing? Why did you hurt Charles?" he growled, glancing at the still-unconscious Charles. "What the hell are you doing, Lex?"

Gabriele muttered, "He's a distraction we don't need, boss."

Hank gave a cruel smile. "I'm happy to shut him up."

I hesitated. I didn't want Hank touching Dylan, but it was important I didn't look sympathetic to Dylan either. Dylan would be safer if I treated him like I would anyone else. But that wasn't going to be easy because he wasn't anyone else.

"Shall I knock him out?" Hank asked, leering at Dylan.

Dylan cringed away and swallowed hard, looking like he was about to faint.

"Let's give him a minute to grasp the situation." I emphasized each word as I met Dylan's angry gaze. "You *need* to sit quietly." I gave him a cold, warning look. I didn't want him to miss my meaning; if he didn't shut up willingly, Hank would do it for him. He needed to understand that.

Dylan paled, and he sank back against the seat even more. He held his bruised neck, giving me a look of pure hatred.

My heart hurt as I held his loathsome gaze. But he had to hate me. There was no other way this could go now that he knew the truth about me. From here on out, it was only going to get worse too. When we started questioning Charles, Dylan was going to *really* hate me.

I turned back around and faced forward. In the rearview mirror, I could see Dylan watching me. He looked like he wanted to cry. I felt like the lowest asshole in the universe making him look like that. Just last night we'd held each other, and I'd had his complete trust.

Now, I was his worst nightmare.

S.C. Wynne

Chapter Twenty-One

Dylan

I couldn't believe what was happening. It had to be a terrible dream. It had to be. Lex wasn't a monster. Lex was the kindest, nicest alpha I'd ever known. I was falling in love with him. There was no way he was this hard, cold alpha calling all the shots. I couldn't be wrong again about an alpha.

Wake up. Wake up. Please let this be a dream.

I'd ended up in this situation because I'd gone down to the security building to lend moral support to Lex during his interview. Then I'd stumbled upon that horrible alpha Hank attacking Charles and Lex. At first, I'd thought Lex was trying to help Charles against the would-be attackers, but it had suddenly become clear, he was one of them. I couldn't wrap my head around that. Lex was a bad guy? *My Lex?*

All the way down the mountain, I kept hoping the security team would chase us. But they were nowhere in sight. It seemed Lex and his crew had caught them completely off guard, and without Charles telling them what to do, they'd fumbled the ball.

When we reached the bottom of the hill, the omega named Gabriele had another car waiting. We abandoned the first vehicle and continued into town in the new one. Charles was still out, and I was really worried for him. His breathing was jagged, and there was a big bump on his forehead where Hank had struck him. If he died, I'd never forgive Lex. I'd never forgive Lex anyway. I felt foolish for trusting him. He'd known that pig Hank this whole time? What kind of alpha was Lex if he was friends with a man like Hank?

My mind was spinning as I tried to put together what few pieces I had. Gabriele had the same build and sounded exactly like the man who'd fed me during my kidnapping. What did it mean that Lex knew my kidnapper and my would-be rapist? I didn't want to accept what that meant, but I had to. Lex had been pretending to be kidnapped. But why? Why had he wanted to befriend me? To get into the compound? For what reason? To grab Charles? That made no sense to me. Was this just some sort of personal grudge against Charles? I knew Lex and Charles hadn't gotten along, but if this was all about resenting Charles, why would Lex have faked a kidnapping? They could have just grabbed Charles if he went into town. They must have wanted to get into the compound, and Lex had used me to do that.

I'd hoped we'd stop somewhere in town, where there was a better chance of getting away. But that wasn't what happened. Instead they drove us way out of town to an old ranch house on acres of deserted land. Having a place ready to go reinforced how premeditated all of this was. As we pulled up in front of the big sprawling home, Charles groaned and started thrashing. Gabriele parked, and Hank dragged me out of the car, then went back for Charles.

Charles came out of the car throwing punches and swearing. I'd never seen Charles this angry. He was a terrifying sight, his eyes red-rimmed and his muscled shoulders bunched. He looked half out of it, but he was still trying to fight. I respected him even more, but I was afraid he was going to get himself killed. Hank seemed to enjoy hurting people, and he was smiling when he punched an already struggling Charles in the face. Charles landed in a heap on the dirt, and Gabriele surprised me when he moved in front of Charles, holding out a defensive hand.

"Hank, knock it off. We need him alive and conscious." Gabriele's blue eyes flashed a warning.

"Yeah, Jesus. Don't kill him." Lex shook his head, looking disgusted.

Hank spit on the dirt near Charles and stomped into the house. I moved forward, and Gabriele and I helped Charles to his feet. I was worried about Charles because his eyes were glassy. I knew the only reason he was even standing was pure stubbornness.

"Is there ice here?" I asked gruffly, giving Lex a cold look.

He didn't seem to notice my angry glance. "I have no idea. I was with you, remember?"

"Oh, yeah. I remember," I hissed.

His face was blank, but I didn't think I imagined the pink flush that washed over his face. He turned to Gabriele. "Is there ice?"

S.C. Wynne

"Yeah. I bought a bag to chill the beer."

Shaking his head, Lex moved toward the house. "I've been working my ass off, and you two have been sitting around drinking beer. Perfect."

"Hey, I got ice and beer in case *you* wanted that," Gabriele grumbled. "I figured you could use a drink after being cooped up in that nuthouse."

Lex grimaced. "Oh."

Charles scowled at Gabriele. "Get your hands off me, scumbag."

Gabriele rolled his eyes. "I let go of you and you'll fall."

Charles didn't seem convinced, and he jerked his arm from Gabriele's grasp. Gabriele scowled and watched the alpha, his hands on his hips. "Suit yourself, dumb-ass."

Once Gabriele was no longer helping to support Charles, that left only me. I tipped sideways and just about went down with Charles. Moving swiftly, Lex grabbed Charles's other arm just in time, or we'd have both hit the dirt. His reward was a string of obscenities from Charles.

It took a few minutes to get up the porch stairs because Charles was struggling against Lex, but eventually we had Charles inside the house. Hank tied him to a chair in the middle of the empty living room. I glanced around at the barnlike room, taking in cobwebs in the corners of the ceiling and peeling yellow wallpaper. I shivered, and stood near Charles, resting my hand on his broad shoulder. I didn't want to leave him because I was afraid of what they'd do to him.

"It's okay, Dylan. We'll be fine," Charles reassured me.

My eyes stung because he was trying to reassure me, but he was barely conscious. I gave Lex another hateful glance, and he looked away. I couldn't believe he was the same man I'd trusted. It seemed inconceivable to me that he could have concealed this horrible side of himself. What was wrong with me that I couldn't seem to see when an alpha was a piece of shit? Charles had tried to warn me, along with Dr. Peters. I hadn't listened; instead I'd been completely fooled once again.

Gabriele walked over with a ragged towel filled with ice. He held it up to the egg-sized bump on Charles's head, and the alpha grunted. Gabriele gave a funny smile as he watched Charles. "Does it hurt?" he asked with a smirk.

"No," growled Charles.

Gabriele shook his head. "I knew you'd say that."

"Takes more than some pussy hitting me with a gun to keep me down," Charles snapped.

Gabriele said, "Yeah, I can see that. You're a real tough guy."

"Yeah," Charles rumbled. "I am."

Gabriele met Lex's gaze. "Such a macho man. Whew, is it hot in here, or is it just me?"

Lex looked annoyed. "Knock it off, Gabriele. Stop yanking the guy's chain."

S.C. Wynne

"Why?" Gabriele laughed. "It's fun."

"I wouldn't touch you with a ten-foot pole," slurred Charles.

"Now you're just bragging." Gabriele snorted.

"You think this is funny?" I challenged Gabriele.

He narrowed his eyes. "Shut up, kid."

"Fuck off," I said, squeezing Charles's shoulder.

Gabriele leaned toward me, a menacing look on his face. "You think Lex will protect you? Think again. He used you, kid. You don't mean shit to him."

Heat filled my face, but I glared back. "Go to hell." How much had Lex told his goons? Shit, did they know everything?

When Gabriele started toward me, Lex moved between us. "Gabe, focus. We need to get the swelling down."

Gabriele didn't look too pleased, but he said, "You've got it, boss."

"What's it matter if the swelling goes down?" Hank complained. "We're just going to mess him up anyway."

"I need him to talk before he passes out." Lex frowned. "He looks like he's barely conscious."

"What he needs is to lie down," I said. I was trying not to notice the heat of Lex and the familiar scent of him. I'd allowed myself to really care about him, and now, seeing him as the enemy wasn't easy. But of course he was my enemy, and not accepting that could get me killed.

"I don't have time to coddle him," Lex muttered.

"If he wasn't tied to this chair, he'd be on the floor." I met Lex's gaze. "You know that's true."

Exhaling roughly, Lex nodded. "Probably." He addressed Gabriele. "Is there a bed in this place?"

"Yeah. Every room has a bed. The mattresses look like they're from the civil war era, but technically they're beds." Gabriele removed the ice from Charles's face. "You really want the guy to rest?"

"Yes." He addressed Hank. "You and Gabriele take him upstairs, and watch him. Tie his hands—he could be faking."

Hank untied Charles, and he and Gabriele held the alpha under the arms. Then they started toward the stairs. When I tried to follow, Lex stopped me.

"No. You stay here." His eyes were emotionless.

"Why?"

"Because I said so."

I watched the other two hobble up the rickety stairs with Charles. I didn't like splitting up. I was afraid of what they'd do to him if I wasn't there to watch over him. I turned my back on Lex and stared out the filmy windows at the barren acres that surrounded the house.

"Listen, I didn't want you to get mixed up in this," Lex said softly.

I faced him, feeling angry. He sounded like the Lex I knew, but this man wasn't the same. "I don't want your bullshit excuses. You used me. You fucking used me in every way possible, and I *hate* you."

He seemed to wince, but then he shrugged. "I couldn't tell you the truth."

"You mean that you're a thug who wanted to hurt Charles?"

"No. The full story about why I needed to get into the compound." He grimaced. "Why I had to trick you."

"Don't tell me. It's probably all bullshit anyway," I muttered.

He sighed, and I noticed lines under his eyes. "Charles murdered my dad."

"What?" I bugged my eyes. "No way."

"I found proof Dad was in the compound, and we all know Charles runs things." He reached under his shirt and tugged a metal vanity plate from his waistband.

"What's that?"

"My dad's license plate. Charles killed my dad and then had his car chopped up. Why would an innocent man do that, Dylan? Tell me that?"

I stared at the license plate, not knowing what to say. "That doesn't prove anything."

"It proves Dad was in the compound. No one has heard from him or his driver in over a month." He tossed the plate on the chair Charles had been sitting in. He looked exhausted, and he rubbed his eyes. "I can't just let him murder my dad and do nothing. That's not how it works in my world."

I scrunched my face. "Who the hell are you? Why do you have people calling you boss?"

"They work for me."

"Yeah, but why do you have hired henchmen working for you?" I eyed him suspiciously. "I know obviously you don't sell medical supplies. What do you do?"

He didn't respond right away, but then he said softly, "I run an art gallery."

I shook my head. "No. You must do more than that."

"Have you ever heard of the Sabine family?" His expression was wary.

"No."

"Well, Corbin Sabine ran a crime syndicate based out of Turbin. He's my dad." He pushed his hands into his pockets. "I'm the eldest son and the only living heir. It's my duty to step up and find out what happened to Dad. I've done that, and now the person who killed him has to pay."

"You really think Charles killed your father?"

"I do." He twisted his lips. "Once I have a chance to talk to him in depth, I'll know for sure."

"You mean torture, not talk."

"I need answers," he snapped. "I want my old life back, and I can't have that until this is settled."

"So you're just going to kill Charles, and then what? Am I next?" I hated that my voice wobbled, but I was scared. The more Lex talked, the more terrified I was.

His jaw hardened, but his eyes were filled with confusion. "I don't know what to do about you. You weren't supposed to be involved in this part of it." He scowled. "Why the fuck did you show up?"

My face warmed. "It doesn't matter."

"Yeah, it does. You were sleeping. Why did you hurry down there to the security building?" His gaze was intense, and he moved closer.

I blew out a shaky breath. "I had no idea you were a fucking *liar*," I growled. "I was coming down to lend you support because I knew Charles would be hard on you." My lower lip trembled. "I wish I'd never met you."

He closed his eyes, and his jaw hardened. When he opened his eyes, he looked like he was in pain. "I didn't want you to know any of this. I wanted you to be blissfully unaware, Dylan."

For one second I had a glimpse of the man I'd known. His tone was gentle, urgent, and my heart ached. But I shook it off and lifted my chin.

"It was all still a lie. You were working me. Playing me." I curled my lip. "And I fell for it. I can't believe I did, but I fucking believed you were my hero." I gave a harsh laugh. "What a fucking joke. You must have laughed your ass off at night at what a sucker I was."

"No." He shook his head. "I didn't find it funny in the least. I told you it was real. I told you that."

"Which part was real, Lex? How could *any* of it be real when I didn't know one fucking thing about you? Were you pretending to be straight? Was that just a big lie too? Were you manipulating me into sleeping with you?"

"God, no." He clenched his teeth. "That wasn't part of anything. That was just me being attracted to you."

"I don't believe you. I don't believe anything that comes out of your mouth anymore." I crossed my arms, glaring at him. "I want to go to Charles. I don't want to talk to you anymore."

His tone was bitter as he said, "So Charles can murder my dad, and you're still on his side?"

"He didn't. I would stake my life on that."

"By butting in, you very well may have done just that, Dylan. What the hell am I supposed to do with you now? If I let you go, you'll rat me out. Your loyalties lie with Charles. You've made that clear. This isn't just about me and you. If you turn me in, then Gabriele goes down too. He's like family. I can't just let that happen."

"No, much better you murder your ex-lover." I gave him a disgusted look.

His fists clenched. "I don't know what to do," he hissed. "Do you think this is easy for me?"

"Probably. If you're who you say you are, then murder and all of this crap is probably no big deal to you."

He shook his head. "I never wanted any part of Dad's business. I told you that. Maybe I lied about exactly who I was, but everything I told you about my family and my emotions was true."

"Jesus, do you not see how fucked-up that is? You're actually telling me, 'other than all the lies I told you, everything was true.'" I laughed humorlessly. "It doesn't work like that. I don't even know who you are. What I do know makes me think you're a monster."

His jaw hardened. "I guess you don't give a shit Charles killed my dad. That shows how fucking shallow you are too." He raked a hand through his hair. "And you wanted me too, so stop acting like I forced myself on you."

"I never once said you forced yourself on me," I snapped. "But you tricked me. If I'd known who you are, and what your intentions were, obviously I'd never have let you near me."

"I guess that's all water under the bridge now." His voice was flat.

Yeah." I sighed. "Can I please go be with Charles?"

"Go ahead."

I started toward the stairs.

"Hey, Dylan?" he called after me.

I stopped and faced him. "What?"

"Don't try to escape. If you do, I won't be able to protect you." His expression was grim.

"We both know I'm probably going to die along with Charles either way."

He didn't argue, just stared at me with his piercing blue eyes. A shiver went through me at that cold look, and I continued up the stairs toward Charles. Maybe we could figure a way out if we kept our heads. But there were three of them, and only two of us. They were professional thugs, and Charles was incapacitated, and I was way out of my element.

I couldn't believe I'd thought Lex was my hero. I felt foolish when I remembered how much I'd cared about him. He'd completely fooled me. I hadn't suspected him for even one minute. He'd played me perfectly, and now, because of me, Charles and I would die. Because while I did see regret in Lex's eyes, I didn't see mercy.

S.C. Wynne

Chapter Twenty-Two

Lex

"You hit him too fucking hard," I growled at Hank. "He probably has a concussion. How am I supposed to question him?"

Hank shrugged. "He's a big guy. I was just trying to subdue him."

"You subdued him all right. He's barely been awake for ten minutes straight the whole time." Gabriele met my gaze, looking pissed. "How long can we wait for him to come around?"

I grimaced. "If he doesn't wake up soon, we'll give him tonight to sleep. He's a tough bastard. He'll probably either be dead by morning or well enough to question."

Dylan was sitting beside Charles, listening to us silently. His surly gaze fell on me occasionally, and he'd look away quickly. I was trying hard to be unmoved by him, but it was almost impossible. That same drive to protect him I'd had from the beginning still gnawed at me. I didn't understand my instinct to shield him, but it was painful ignoring it. We'd only known each other a few weeks counting the cooking class, and yet, I felt like I'd always known him. His voice, even when angry, sent shivers through me. Even now, knowing he hated me, I wanted to go to him and hold him. Soothe him. What the hell was wrong with me?

When Charles suddenly opened his eyes, we all went on alert. But he didn't try and get up; instead his eyes immediately began to search the room, and he only relaxed when he found Dylan beside him. Dylan covered his hand with his and smiled weakly at him. Raw jealously clawed at me, and I wanted to yell at them to stop touching each other. Instead, I bit my tongue to silence those pathetic words. Gabriele would think I'd lost my mind if I showed how much I still cared about Dylan. Maybe I had lost my mind. I certainly wasn't behaving like myself.

"Could we have some water?" Dylan asked gruffly.

I nodded at Gabriele, and he went downstairs. Hank stood silently in the corner, giving Charles malicious glances. When he'd occasionally set his gaze on Dylan, I wanted to throat punch him. I knew he still wanted a taste of Dylan, and it was everything I could do not to fire his ass. But I needed him to help subdue Charles. Even wounded, Charles was a force to be reckoned with.

Gabriele returned and handed Dylan a bottle of water. He then went to Charles and held another bottle to Charles's lips. Charles eyed the bottle suspiciously.

"Sure this isn't poisoned?" Charles grumbled.

"It's not." Gabriele tipped the bottle, and some water went inside Charles's open lips, but more went down his chin. The alpha didn't even react as a water stain spread across his shirt. "We need you alive to question you."

Charles pulled his head away, signaling he'd had enough water. He coughed a few times and then struggled into a sitting position. His hands were tied in his lap, but I still kept my distance. I had no doubt he knew moves that could be dangerous if we got too close.

"Feeling better?" I asked. Regardless if I'd orchestrated this whole plan, I wasn't enjoying it. It would have been distasteful enough if Dylan hadn't been in the mix. I hated this violent side of things. But with Dylan here, it was worse. I just wanted to question Charles, figure out his responsibility in the equation, and put all of this behind me.

"I feel fantastic," rasped Charles. "Should we get this party started?"

"We were thinking of letting you rest until tomorrow," I said. "You seem out of it."

"Why wait? I'm looking forward to it." Charles smirked.

Gabriele laughed and shook his head. "Jesus, you're unreal."

Charles flicked his gaze to Gabriele. "I've been through way worse than this."

"Seriously?" Gabriele frowned. "You must have led an interesting life."

Charles didn't respond; he glanced at me instead. "You wanted to ask me questions. So ask."

I studied him; he did seem more alert. If he was willing to talk now, why wait? I pulled up a chair, making sure it was a safe distance from the bed. "So long as you talk, we won't need to take it to the next level. But if you clam up, it's Hank's turn. Got it?"

Twisting his lips, Charles gave a sharp nod.

I cleared my throat. "Let's start with the real reason I'm in Yellow Springs. What happened to my dad?"

Charles's gaze flickered. "I didn't kill him."

"That's not what I asked." I didn't actually believe him either.

Charles gave Hank and Gabriele a wary glance. "I'll talk, but not in front of those two."

Hank bristled. "Bullshit. You don't direct the show."

I hesitated. "Hank. Gabriele. Go downstairs. I'll call if I need you."

Hank scowled, and Gabriele looked insulted.

"Seriously?" Gabriele met my gaze. "Why are you letting him call the shots?"

"The point is to get him to talk. If we can do that without torturing him, why not try that first?" I held his gaze, making sure I sounded confident.

"He'll probably just make up shit." Hank gave Charles an angry look.

I moved my mouth in distaste. "We'll try this way first. If I think he's making shit up, you're up, Hank."

"Fine," snarled Hank, moving toward the doorway.

"This is fucking unreal." Gabriele had a stubborn set to his jaw, but he followed Hank out of the room.

Once it was just me, Charles, and Dylan, I relaxed a bit. I hadn't even realized how tense Hank made me until he was gone. He was unpredictable, and I hated how he looked at Dylan. "So, start talking," I said.

He glanced at Dylan. "You can't repeat anything you hear."

Dylan gave me a wary glance. "I'll probably be dead. I don't think it will be a problem."

My stomach clenched at the resolution in his voice, but I focused on Charles. "What happened to my dad?" I asked again.

"If you're Corbin's son, you know he was looking for Jack and Carter." Charles searched my face.

I nodded. "Yes."

Dylan looked confused. "He was?"

Charles met his gaze. "Yes. He wanted to kill them."

Giving me a hard look, Dylan said, "Your father wanted to kill Jack?"

"He had his reasons."

"Jack's a good alpha. Why the hell would your dad want to hurt him?" Dylan looked angry.

The respect toward Jack in Dylan's voice annoyed me. Had he had a crush on Jack? I wasn't prepared for the anger that raced through me at that thought. "There's a lot you don't know, Dylan."

He curled his lip. "Ain't that the truth."

Charles said, "Your father was outside the compound, Lex. He was never inside."

"Bullshit. I found the license *inside* the compound."

Charles shook his head. "He bribed a guard to bring Jack and Carter outside the gates. That's where everything happened."

I studied him. He didn't look like he was lying, but then why had the license been inside the fortress? "That isn't making sense."

"I can't tell you everything, but I can confirm that your dad and his driver are dead." His voice was almost apologetic, which was a surprise.

When he confirmed my dad was dead, I'd expected to feel something. But mostly I was just numb, and still needing details. "You don't get to pick and choose what you're going to tell me. I need to know everything."

His jaw hardened. "I can't tell you certain things."

Dylan looked at him bewildered. "You knew this whole time Lex's dad was dead?"

Charles nodded. "Yes."

"Why didn't you tell him? He... he deserved to know that."

"Dylan, I didn't know who Lex was."

"Oh, yeah." Dylan gave me a resentful look. "That's right. He was lying."

"I had to lie to get answers, Dylan. Maybe you haven't noticed, but nobody likes to talk about what happens in the compound. I couldn't get anything out of anybody in town. I needed to know what happened. I deserved closure."

Dylan dropped his gaze, a line between his brows. "I'm sure if you'd been honest, Charles would have told you stuff."

I laughed harshly. "You're wrong. You actually think if I'd admitted who I was and asked Charles nicely, he'd have told me?"

Charles glanced at Dylan. "He's right, Dylan. I wouldn't have told him anything."

Dylan looked shocked. "But... why?"

Sounding impatient, Charles said, "As I've said already, there are things I can't talk about. I've said too much as it is."

I pinned my gaze on Charles. "You say you didn't hurt my dad... so who did?"

He pressed his lips tight. "I've told you all I can."

A mean smile touched my lips. "If you think that is going to pacify me, you're wrong. You've admitted Dad and Sal are dead. His license was inside the compound. You run the compound, that means the buck stops with you."

Charles swallowed hard but then lifted his chin. "That's fine. But I've said all I'm going to."

Dylan didn't look any more pleased with his response that I was. "That's not fair, Charles. If you know what happened to his dad, why can't you tell him? Not telling him makes you look guilty."

"Then I look guilty."

Dylan met my gaze, and for once he looked less angry with me. "But… it was his *dad*."

"You know there are things we can't talk about, that happen inside the compound." He gave Dylan a pointed look. "Don't push this."

Dropping his gaze, Dylan looked conflicted. "I know… but…"

"What happened to their bodies?" I asked gruffly, switching gears. "Did you dispose of them as ruthlessly as you did the car?"

"There were no bodies," Charles said quietly.

"What?" I scowled. "Then how do you know they're dead?"

Sighing, Charles said, "Jack and Carter witnessed their deaths. There was blood evidence and ripped clothing supporting their story."

Dylan widened his eyes. "Wait… is this all connected to the animal attack?"

Charles avoided his gaze.

"There was no animal attack, was there?" I asked.

"You're not getting any more details, so drop it," growled Charles, his eyes guarded.

"Drop it?" I laughed humorlessly. "Drop the fact you're at the center of my dad's murder?"

"It wasn't murder. It was self-defense." Charles frowned. "It was to protect Carter and Jack."

"I don't give a fuck about protecting Jack and Carter," I hissed. "Someone has to pay for Dad's death. That's how it is, and there's just no changing that."

"So make me pay. But let Dylan go. He had nothing to do with any of this." Charles gave Dylan a worried glance.

"I'm not just going to sit quietly while they… kill you, or whatever they have planned," Dylan said softly.

Ignoring Dylan, Charles addressed me. "He's an innocent in this. Let him go."

I pushed away the urge to give in and get Dylan to safety. I couldn't focus on him right now. "I'll figure out what to do with Dylan later. Right now, I need all the details, Charles. If you won't willingly tell me, it's time to go downstairs and let Hank do his magic."

"God, no." Dylan looked like he felt nauseous. "Charles, please just tell him what he wants."

Charles shook his head and then blinked as if the movement made him dizzy. "I can handle whatever they dish out."

"You can't," I said coldly. "Trust me."

"Please, Charles. Don't be stupid." Dylan watched me, fear plain on his face.

"Your dad is dead. That's all I can tell you. How he died isn't important."

"It is to me," I growled. "If you didn't kill him, it makes no sense why you won't tell me who did." I half admired Charles's reckless bravery and pitied him for being a fool. Hank wasn't going to go easy on him. He'd wish he were dead halfway through. Hank was a brutal, disgusting person, but he always got the job done.

"You wouldn't be able to punish those who killed your father anyway. It's impossible." Charles avoided my gaze. "If someone has to pay, then I'll do that."

"I wouldn't be able to punish them?" I frowned.

"No."

"How is that possible?" I asked.

"It just is."

Dylan frowned. "Was it the Ancients who killed them?"

Charles glared at Dylan. "Enough. Stop talking."

Red appeared in Dylan's cheeks. "You just want me to watch you die?"

"I believe in the greater good." Charles's jaw tensed. "I'm willing to sacrifice myself."

"I can't figure out if you're brave, nuts, or both." I scowled.

Dylan clamped his hand on Charles's arm. "You're be bravest alpha I've ever known."

My gut churned at the look Dylan gave Charles. I still remembered how Dylan had looked at me like that before. Now most of his glances were filled with disgust. Losing Dylan's respect hurt way more than I'd expected. A part of me wanted to abandon this entire mess and beg Dylan to forgive me. But how could I do that with Gabriele and all the others looking to me to make things right?

"I take no pleasure in what comes next," I said gruffly. "But you leave me no choice, Charles."

"I understand." He met my gaze full-on.

For the first time since we'd met, we seemed to understand each other. We were both two alphas with no choice. Our destinies were guided by the needs of others. It was frustrating being in power. I didn't like these types of decisions. I wasn't a brutal person by nature, and this type of thing made me sick. But if I backed down or showed weakness, I could very well find myself in Charles's seat instead.

I stood and moved toward him. Dylan stood too, his face flushed with fear and anger.

"Don't do this, Lex. Please," he whispered.

"I'm sorry." I grabbed hold of Charles and pulled him off the bed. The alpha didn't fight me. He now seemed more resigned than rebellious. Maybe he felt guilt at what had happened to my dad. He said he hadn't killed him, but maybe holding the secret of who did was tiring. Secrets were exhausting. I'd hated having to trick Dylan, so I got it.

Dylan ran around the bed and started hitting me. I let him land his blows at first, but then I shoved him away and he fell against the wall. But instead of staying back, he came at me again. "Hank, come here," I yelled.

There was the sound of boots pounding up the stairs, and Hank appeared on the landing, looking excited. "It's about time." He grabbed Charles's arm and dragged him down the stairs.

I turned to Dylan and caught his flying fists easily. Then I backed him back into the room and pressed him against the wall. He was breathing hard, his eyes glittering with hate. But there were other emotions too—lust? Confusion. I leaned my weight on him, and he went still. I could feel his arousal against my leg, and I found myself also turned on. This was a fucked-up situation. I wanted to kiss him. Quiet him, and tell him I'd protect him. But the words were stuck in my throat. I couldn't promise him that because I had no idea if it was true.

"Let me go," he said softly.

"You don't understand." My voice was plaintive. "I don't want any of this. I don't want you to hate me."

He blinked at me, his confusion palpable. "But I do hate you. I've never hated anyone more."

That hurt. I didn't even think he meant it because surely he hated Jacob more. But still, the words sank into me like knives. "You weren't supposed to ever know what I am."

"But I do know." His warm breath fluttered against my lips. "I can't believe I ever let you touch me."

His words said one thing, but his body told me another. "Oh, really?"

"Yes," he spat out. "You disgust me."

Stupidly, I gave in to my needs and kissed the side of his full mouth. Wanting to prove him wrong. "Liar."

He turned his head away, and I brushed my lips beneath his ear. He shivered and pulled in a sharp breath. I licked down his throat to kiss the sensitive skin where his neck joined his shoulder.

"Stop," he whispered.

His cock was hard, and mine was too. I wanted to undo his pants and take him right there, against the wall. Prove that he still wanted me like I wanted him. I didn't even care if everyone heard us. I just wanted to bury myself in his warm body and go back to how it had been. I wanted him to hold my gaze while I entered him and have him tell me how much he needed me, like before.

"I don't want you anymore." He sounded panicked.

I smoothed my hand between our bodies, stroking his full cock through his jeans. "Yeah, you do."

"My body does." His blue eyes were hard. "*I* don't."

I stilled and pulled my hand away. It was true the body could be stimulated against its will. I was no rapist. If he said he didn't want me, I had to listen. I let him go, and he slumped. My mouth was dry, my heart aching. This was a fucking nightmare of my own making. "You should get some rest," I said.

As I finished speaking, Charles gave an anguished groan from downstairs. Dylan immediately tried to push past me, and I stopped him. He struggled, swearing and trying to punch me, but I held him tight. "Calm down, you can't help him," I hissed.

"Fuck you," he yelled, still fighting me.

I didn't have time to be distracted by Dylan. I needed to get downstairs. The entire point of letting Hank at Charles was so I could get answers. I dragged Dylan to the bed, and I shoved him down on it. Gabriele had been kind enough to leave extra tie wraps on the nightstand, and I grabbed one for Dylan's wrists and one for his feet. He fought hard, but I was way stronger than him. Eventually he gave in, and breathing hard, allowed me to bind his hands and feet.

"If you hurt him, I swear," he shouted, his frustration obvious. He knew there was nothing he could do to help Charles.

"I have a right to avenge my dad." I glared at him.

"Charles is no murderer. You know he's taking the bullet for someone else." His voice was urgent. "I'm sure it's the Ancients who killed your dad. It's not Charles."

"The Ancients." I sneered. "I can't believe you buy that weak-ass story."

"They're real. There are a lot of things you don't know, Lex. I'm telling you, there are amazing things you don't know about." His eyes glittered, and he definitely believed what he said.

"Like what?"

He frowned. "You wouldn't believe me if I told you."

"Try me."

"No. Not yet." He looked away. "God knows what an alpha like you would do with that information."

"An alpha like me?" I scowled. "What do you really even know about who I am?"

"I think I've seen enough in the last twenty-four hours to tell me all I need to know."

I jabbed my finger at his face. "I didn't ask for *any* of this. What am I supposed to do, let someone murder my dad and just say, 'oh well'?"

He had no answer to that. He scowled and rolled onto his side, facing away from me. "Go away. You make me sick just looking at you."

I moved to the door, angry and frustrated. I slammed out of the room and took the stairs two at a time. I arrived in the living room in time to see Hank slicing a knife down Charles's bare stomach. Blood dribbled from the wound, and Charles cried out, but his expression was still obstinate.

I stood over him. "Who killed my dad?" I demanded, still shaking from my encounter with Dylan.

Pressing his lips tight, Charles avoided my gaze.

Gabriele stood off to the side, his expression muddled. I got the distinct impression he wasn't enjoying Hank torturing Charles. He was no more into this side of things than I was, but he had a more hardened attitude than me usually. He respected Charles, I could tell. Maybe that was why he found this so unpleasant.

"Why would you take the fall for something you didn't do?" I tried to sound reasonable.

"You wouldn't understand."

"If I can't punish whoever did this, why not tell me?" I leaned toward him. "Are you still trying to pretend the Ancients killed Dad? Why would they?"

He clamped his mouth closed again.

Hank had switched out his knife for a cattle prod. When Charles refused to speak, Hank jabbed the tip against the other alpha's ribs, and Charles jerked and shouted in agony. Breathing hard, he gave Hank a look that said he'd kill him if he could just get his hands on him. Hank laughed and went again, and Charles yelled and swore, sweat slicking his body as he struggled against his restraints.

"Fucking asshole," Charles screamed, standing, taking the chair with him. He advanced on Hank, only to get another jolt in the stomach. Charles fell on the ground, still strapped to the chair.

"That's enough," Gabriele shouted, moving to kneel beside Charles. He studied the moaning alpha, a strange look on his face.

"Get the hell away, Gabriele. What are you doing?" Hank looked pissed.

Gabriele's expression was confused, and he stood. I wasn't sure exactly what was going on with him, but it seemed obvious he was hating watching Charles being tortured. "Just tell them what they want, you moron," Gabriele said to Charles, his voice harsh. "What's the point of letting Hank do this to you?"

Charles held Gabriele's gaze, his body trembling. "There are those who need protecting."

Gabriele shook his head and moved away. "Stupid, stubborn fool."

Hank went at Charles again, jolting the alpha until he was nearly unconscious. I couldn't take it anymore, and I stopped Hank. "Wait. Give him a minute to breathe."

"If you two can't handle this part, you need to not be here," Hank grumbled. "I can't be effective if you keep stopping me."

He was right. I knew he was spot-on. Gabriele and I had no stomach for torture, and we were doing more harm than good. But I didn't want to kill Charles; I just wanted a name. Someone I could punish. I sank onto my haunches next to the quivering, groaning alpha. He didn't want to tell me who killed Dad, but maybe he'd tell me why they'd been killed. "Charles, why did my dad have to die?"

"He wouldn't stop," he wheezed. "He just wouldn't stop coming after Jack and Carter."

I knew that to be true. Dad had been obsessed with those two. "Were you there when Dad died?"

"No," he whispered.

Gabriele raked a shaky hand through his dark hair. "If he wasn't even there, come on, Lex. Why would we kill him?"

"I'm not trying to kill him," I said softly. "I'm looking for answers."

Giving Hank an uneasy glance, Gabriele said, "He's already weak. If you keep shocking him, he's probably going to die of a heart attack."

"So what?" Hank's face was flushed and angry.

Charles's color was kind of gray and his breathing uneven. I could hear Dylan swearing and yelling upstairs, and my natural disgust for Hank's techniques took over. "Let's take a break."

"I'm sorry?" Hank looked about ready to murder. "That isn't how this works. You don't get fucking lunch breaks during an interrogation."

Gabriele had left the room, and when he returned, he knelt beside Charles with a damp washcloth. He smoothed it over the alpha's slack features, a worried line between his dark brows. "I believe him when he says he didn't kill Corbin."

"That's not the point," Hank snapped. "He's supposed to tell us who did kill Corbin."

"If you kill him, he can't talk." I met Hank's resentful gaze. "We're taking a break until tomorrow. He'll be stronger then."

"Un-fucking-believable." Hank strode from the room, his expression grim. The front door slammed.

Gabriele and I looked at each other.

"Do you have it in you to kill Charles and Dylan?" Gabriele looked bewildered. "I don't think Charles killed your dad, and I know Dylan didn't."

I rubbed my face roughly, my gut churning. "If I let them go, they'll go straight to the cops."

"But we'd be long gone by then, and they couldn't prove shit. Do you really have it in you to... *kill* Dylan?" He didn't look convinced. "You seem to have a soft spot for him."

"When the hell did this get so complicated?" I shouted in frustration, feeling bad when he winced. I sucked in a deep breath and said more calmly, "Do you believe in the Ancients?"

He frowned. "I do in theory."

"But do you believe they would come and kill my dad because he was hunting Jack and Carter? Why would they even care about Jack and Carter that much?"

"Special," mumbled Charles.

We both looked at him in surprise. Charles was semiconscious, but he'd responded to my question. I met Gabriele's startled gaze, and he widened his eyes. "Ask him something else," he mouthed at me.

I addressed Charles, "Special how?"

Charles groaned, and his lips moved a few times before he whispered, "Babies. Have to protect them and the babies."

I frowned at Gabriele, and he looked equally confused. "What babies?" he asked softly.

"S.E.O. babies." Charles opened his eyes suddenly, and he looked confused. He sat up, his expression dazed. "What's happening?"

I didn't know what to say.

"Where's Dylan?" Charles tried to stand, but he was too weak, and he slumped to the ground again. "Have to protect Dylan."

"He's fine. He's upstairs," I said, resenting how much the other alpha seemed connected to Dylan. I wanted to be the only alpha Dylan wanted and respected, but that was a joke. He hated me now.

Charles closed his eyes again. "Fuck. What's wrong with me?"

"Oh, just a probable concussion and a couple thousand volts going through your body, no biggie." Gabriele stood and put his arms under Charles, dragging him to his feet. "You need sleep."

Charles looked like he wanted to argue, but he still seemed muddled. I helped Gabriele get him up the stairs to one of the other rooms. Once he was securely tied up, I went to check on Dylan, leaving Gabriele to watch over Charles. Dylan was sitting up in bed, his face flushed an angry red and his eyes dripping hate as I entered.

"If you've killed Charles…" His blue eyes were cold.

"He's sleeping," I said.

I moved closer to Dylan. I knew the best thing for me would be to avoid him as much as possible. He could play with my emotions so easily. But I found it impossible to stay away. Even though he hated me, I wanted to be near him. That desire wasn't logical, I knew that. My need to be around him was no doubt some alpha instinct gone horribly awry.

"I heard you torturing him."

"If he'd talk, we wouldn't have to hurt him at all."

"That would probably disappoint Hank. I get the impression he likes hurting people." He gave me a searching look. "You know what he wanted to do to me, right? That day at the Purple Pooch?"

I swallowed. "Yes. But I stopped him."

"My hero," he hissed.

My face warmed. "I'm sorry this is where we've ended up, Dylan. I really do care about you."

To say he looked angry didn't do his murderous expression justice. "Are you out of your mind? You don't treat people you care about like this. Don't you know that?"

I blinked at him. "I'll admit this has spiraled out of control, but my original intent was simply to find out what happened to my dad and make whoever killed him pay."

He squinted at me. "You say that as casually as you might if you were talking about getting a haircut. Normal people don't do that, Lex. Normal people don't pretend to befriend others or kidnap people."

"I know that isn't normal to you, Dylan. But it's the world I was raised in. It was what was expected of me when Dad went missing. The Sabines don't go to the police and hope for the best. We take matters into our own hands."

"It's barbaric," he said angrily. "You said you didn't want to take over your dad's business. Were you talking about this kind of thing?"

I nodded. "But I'm the last of the Sabine line. In this instance, I have no choice."

"There's always a choice."

I shook my head. "No. If I didn't handle this, I'd have probably been assassinated by a rival mob. My men wouldn't have protected me because I didn't protect them. I had to do this to prove I'm loyal."

"So, even though you don't want to, you're just going to become the head of the Sabine mob?" He stared at me like I had two heads.

"That isn't my plan. I'm hoping that once I bring my dad's murderer to justice, I can appoint someone else to take the helm. I don't want the job. I'll have done my duty by my men, and I should be able to move on."

"But… you said you're the last Sabine."

"The name will change. When my father first began working in this world, it was for the Cancio family. He took over from the last Cancio member, and it became the Sabine family running things."

He looked confused. "And you couldn't just walk away without all of this violence?"

"No. I *had* to handle things."

He fell silent, but after a few minutes, he said, "Are you going to kill me?"

I couldn't admit I'd rather take a bullet for him than see one hair on his head harmed. That would put me in a position of weakness. Dylan had to at least suspect I would kill him to keep him in line. If he thought he could manipulate me, that would be bad.

Without answering him, I stood and moved to the door. "You should rest. Tomorrow is going to be a horrible day for all of us."

As I closed the door, I caught a glimpse of him. His eyes simmered with hostility. After the intense connection we'd shared together in the compound, it was gut-wrenching to see the contempt he now had for me. But I had no choice but to continue on this demoralizing path.

Chapter Twenty-Three

Dylan

I woke to the realization I was about to puke. I jumped from the bed and hobbled to the door, almost falling on my face because my ankles were tied. The door was locked, and I willed my stomach to calm as I pounded frantically on the door. "I need to use the bathroom," I called. "Please. I'm sick."

It took a few moments, but the door opened and Lex stood there looking exhausted. I must have looked convincingly ill because he immediately helped me down the hall to the restroom. He cut the ties around my wrists quickly, and I stumbled to my knees, reaching the toilet just in time.

It felt like an hour passed with me dry heaving into the porcelain bowl. I was covered in sweat when I finally slid to the floor, lying with my hot cheek against the cool tile. I groaned and trembled, feeling like I was about to die. I couldn't even think straight I felt so sick. I had no idea if Lex was still in the room or not. Eventually, my breathing slowed, and I heard the scrape of a shoe behind me. I lifted my head and found Lex sitting on the floor next to the tub.

His eyes were dark with worry. "Feel better?"

I didn't respond; I simply groaned and dropped my head again. I was so weak. I couldn't even contemplate getting to my feet. If he wanted me to go back to my room, he was going to have to carry me. Slowly, the nausea began to fade. The perspiration dried on my skin, and the trembling stopped. I was still very weak, but I managed to sit up.

"You didn't have to stay," I mumbled, pulling myself to my feet by hanging on to the sink counter. I rinsed my mouth with water and leaned on the vanity.

"You had me worried."

I met his gaze in the mirror. "Go to hell."

His jaw tensed, and he rose. "I'm just concerned."

My laugh was harsh. "Right." I wiped my face and stumbled toward the door.

He caught me, or I'd have gone face-first into the wall. I wasn't about to thank him; instead I jerked away. His familiar scent made my heart ache. It was like the Lex I knew had died, but his memory lingered on in this stranger.

He surprised me when he cut the ties around my ankles. "I don't want you to fall," he said gruffly.

I thought he'd lead me back to my room, but he didn't. He took me downstairs and into the kitchen. Gabriele was there cooking a giant pan of eggs. There was also a big frying pan with country-style potatoes sizzling on another burner. It was a bizarrely domestic scene. Unfortunately, the smell of food immediately made my stomach roll, and I gagged and turned quickly to leave the kitchen.

Since Lex was right behind me, I bumped into him. When his big hands descended on my shoulders to steady me, I yanked away.

He scowled but didn't speak. I pushed past him, and he followed. I had no idea where to go, or even if I was allowed to roam. But since he wasn't stopping me, I headed toward the front door. I needed fresh air, and the entire house smelled of food. I stepped out onto the porch and inhaled. The scent of ragweed and hay filled my nose, helping to calm my swirling stomach.

I sank onto the porch steps, and when Lex sat next to me, I gave him a dirty look. He didn't react; his face was an emotionless mask. I hugged my legs, resting my chin on my knees, and I closed my eyes. Meadowlarks sang a lilting tune in the big oaks that surrounded the house. If I pretended hard enough, I could almost make myself believe I wasn't in one of the worst nightmares of my life. I had no idea where Charles was, and I was afraid to ask. It worried me that Hank also didn't seem to be around. Was he torturing Charles as I sat here feeling sorry for myself?

I didn't want to talk to Lex, but I really wanted to know where Charles was. So I cleared my throat and asked, "Where's Charles?"

"Sleeping." His voice was equally gruff.

"You wouldn't lie about that?"

"No." He sounded insulted.

I stared across the yard of the old farmhouse. There was a tire swing hanging from one of the largest oaks, but my guess was you'd be taking your life in your hands to use it. This had probably been a pretty nice spread at one time, before years of neglect had allowed the golden weeds to strangle away all signs of civilization.

I was extremely annoyed at how aware I was of Lex next to me. I wanted to hate him so much, and a part of me did. But talking to him last night had almost made it harder to truly loathe him. Being mad at him was kind of like being angry at a shark for being a shark. He seemed to live in an alternate reality. It was obvious he didn't really see his behavior as that strange. I suppose growing up how he had, his twisted concept of loyalty and honor had been drilled into him. He truly seemed to think how he'd handled everything was the right way. Although, I did occasionally see glimpses of regret in his blue eyes. But I didn't see actual remorse.

"What if Charles still won't talk to you today?" I asked.

He sighed. "Someone has to pay."

"But, by now, you must know that Charles didn't kill your dad."

"Yes."

"Then why would *he* pay?" I gave him an impatient glance.

"Because he's protecting the real murderer."

I shook my head. "This is all very clear-cut for you, isn't it?"

He didn't respond immediately, but when he did, he seemed to pick his words with care. "Parts of it are; the parts with you are not."

"Why are the parts with me not clear?" I turned to study him.

He didn't look at me. "Because what I felt... feel... for you, Dylan, was never an act."

Against my will, my pulse sped up with excitement, but I squashed it. "What you feel is lust."

He grimaced. "Oh, yes. That is most definitely true." He met my gaze finally. "But that's not all I feel. You think because I had to still follow through with my plan that my feelings for you weren't legitimate. But they were. To be honest, I've never experienced what I did with you. I don't even know what to call it. But it wasn't just lust."

My heart wanted to respond to his heartfelt words, but my pride refused. "You used me to get into the compound. You never really cared about me. It was an act."

"No." His voice was firm. "The first time I met you, I felt something. Mostly I thought you were an unfriendly punk, but there was something about you that drew me in. The more I was around you, the more I couldn't stop thinking about you."

"I don't know what you want me to say to that."

"Nothing. I don't expect you to say anything. I know that you hate me. I can see it on your face every time you look at me. I'm just trying to tell you that the reason you didn't figure out I was fake was because my feelings *weren't* fake."

"Lies. It's all fucking lies."

He grunted. "Maybe it's best you feel that way. Because the hard stuff is still to come. It's best if you hate me."

I didn't like the sound of that. "What if I can convince Charles to tell you who murdered your dad? Will you let us live?"

"I'd like to. My fear is Charles wouldn't let it lie. He'd want to come after me, and that doesn't work for me."

"So, whether he talks or not, we die?"

He wrinkled his brow. "Tell me how I can release you and not become hunted myself?"

"Charles is a fair alpha."

"He might not feel so magnanimous after his balls have been zapped with a cattle prod." He studied me. "Besides, I don't think he'll talk."

"Then why aren't we dead already?"

He chewed his bottom lip, his eyes impossible to read. "You must know the answer to that."

"No, I don't."

He looked disbelieving. "Dylan, you're the reason."

"Me?" I frowned.

He reached out and brushed my cheek with his fingers. I flinched but didn't pull away. His mouth turned down slightly. "I would do anything to have you look at me the way you did before." His voice was husky.

"Anything?" I gave a harsh laugh. "Then let us go, unharmed."

His expression was melancholy. "Then you'd like me again? No. I don't think so. It's too late."

"Then just get it over with," I snapped. "You're talking in circles. You know Charles won't talk, and yet you plan on torturing him. Why, if you know he won't talk? You don't want to kill me, and yet you think you might have to. Jesus, Lex, make up your fucking mind." I stood and moved to go back in the house, but he grabbed my wrist and tugged me back down.

His fingers were hard and his eyes bright. He leaned in to me, eyes pinned on my mouth. "I didn't plan on falling for you. Don't you get it?" he whispered. "You've got me all muddled."

"You didn't fall for me. I don't believe you." I was breathless as I held his heated gaze.

"I didn't want to believe it either." He clenched his jaw. "But the decisions I've made, they're not logical. I'm not thinking like a survivor. I'm think like a man in love. All I worry about is something happening to *you*." He sounded resentful. "By telling you all of this, I give you power. That's foolish. Every fucking thing I do is stupid because all I can think about is keeping you safe." His fingers dug into my skin.

"Ouch." I winced. "You're hurting me."

He let go of me immediately, and he hung his head. "Realistically, I should have executed you and Charles last night. I should already be halfway home by now. Instead, I'm in a stalemate with Charles. That's insane. I should never have allowed that to happen. Every minute that ticks by makes me look weaker and weaker."

"You're many things—weak is not one of them."

He shook his head. "My men judge me differently than you would."

"Judge you? How?"

"Hank and Gabriele can see I'm being wishy-washy with you and Charles," he murmured. "I'm not worried so much about Gabriele, but I'm definitely worried about Hank."

"You mean… he might turn on you?"

"Yes." He swallowed hard. "I think he'd love to take my place. He's never respected me. Now that he knows Dad is dead, he'll make a move. It's just a matter of when. My guess is he'll try to take me out, just to show how tough he is."

My anger toward Lex seemed to evaporate at the idea of him dying. It made everything feel very different. "What happened to loyalty?"

"It's a kind of gray area when there's a power grab."

"Gabriele wouldn't turn on you, right?" Inexplicably, I now felt more worried for Lex than anything else.

"I don't think so." He frowned. "But stranger things have happened."

Without thinking, I touched his hand. He smiled tentatively at me, and the warmth of it seeped into me, calming the panic growing inside. My feelings for him hadn't disappeared overnight, but I was still hurt and confused by all the lies. A part of me suspected, even now, all he might be doing was playing on my sympathies. Maybe he just wanted me to convince Charles to talk to him, so he was sweet-talking me. I didn't trust him after all I'd discovered about him. But I also knew I had a better chance of survival if he was in charge, rather than Hank.

"I don't want you to hurt Charles, but I… I can't make him talk. However, I can tell you the things I do know about the day of the animal attack." I met his curious gaze.

"What kind of things?"

I grimaced. "I don't know exactly what happened with your dad, but something really spooked Jack and Carter. And Jack isn't an alpha easily spooked. He's the same breed as Charles, tough as nails."

"When was this?"

"The same day the guard was bribed." I frowned. "Do you think it was your dad who bribed the guard?"

"Sounds like Dad."

"Okay." I narrowed my eyes, trying to remember what I knew about that day. "Something happened that shook Jack, and I don't think it was just that an attempt was made on him and Carter either. Jack was used to that shit. No, something scared him. He was deeply shaken. But he wouldn't give me any details."

"Just how close were you to Jack?" he asked, looking annoyed.

"We were just friends. He was completely smitten with Carter."

Some tension left Lex's shoulders. "Yeah, that's how Jack got into a problem with Dad—protecting Carter."

"Really?"

He nodded and said softly, "He killed my brother, Nick."

I widened my eyes. "What?"

He stared out across the yard. "He killed Nick, and then my dad was hell-bent on revenge. That's why Dad was up here. Blood for blood."

"Jesus." It took a minute for me to absorb his words. "When does this crap end? One person gets killed, and then the other person gets killed avenging him? Pretty soon everybody is just fucking dead."

He sighed. "Pretty much. That's one reason I hate that goddamned world."

I grimaced. "If he hadn't come seeking revenge, he'd still be alive."

"Probably," he said tiredly. "And I'd never have had to do any of this shit."

I met his blank stare. "But he did come here seeking retribution, and now he's missing."

"And I can't get any answers because of all the secrets that surround the compound." His tone was bitter.

"I'm telling you what I know, which, unfortunately, isn't much."

"I find it hard to believe my dad and his driver were attacked by some wild animal." Lex's tone was derisive.

"It seems far-fetched, but something happened because there was blood and ripped clothing."

He frowned. "But no bodies." He shot me a curious look. "What's a S.E.O. baby?"

Shocked at his reference to the solar eclipse omegas, I dropped my gaze. He obviously had no idea what they were, but the fact he'd just used the term we used at the compound was startling. "Uhh… where did you hear that?"

"From Charles."

Charles had let slip about the solar eclipse omega babies? That was hard to believe. He'd have to be completely out of it to blurt something like that out. "Oh, that's just a name for the babies at the compound," I said nonchalantly. He didn't need to know that the only babies delivered at the compound were those of solar eclipse omegas.

"He was going on about protecting the S.E.O. babies." Lex frowned. "That they were special."

I stiffened. "Well, he was being beaten and tortured. He was probably confused."

"True." He watched me intently. "Are the babies connected to the Ancients or something?"

My gut clenched as I struggled to keep my face blank. "From what I understand, the Ancients don't have babies."

He rubbed his chin. "It's weird he started talking about babies when I was asking about the Ancients protecting Carter and Jack. Makes me think they're connected somehow."

I didn't respond.

"I don't understand why Charles won't just say who killed Dad," he grumbled. "This all could have been avoided."

I scowled. "It never should have come to this. Period."

He shrugged. "You'll never understand my world."

"No. I never will."

He rubbed his face roughly. "Which is why I'm fucking stupid for caring what you think about me."

His words were so heartfelt, I found myself unwillingly moved. "I don't think you're all bad."

He chuffed. "Just mostly?"

"I couldn't live like you do," I said quietly, holding his gaze.

"No." His eyes glittered. "I know."

I thought for a second he was going to kiss me. His gaze was on my mouth and his breathing quick. Would I let him? How could I want his mouth on mine after all he'd done to me? But I did. I still wanted him.

Gabriele's brusque voice came from behind us. "Food's ready."

We both jumped, and Lex stood abruptly. "We'll be right in." His face was flushed, and he looked embarrassed.

I followed him into the house, wondering what came next. I knew that just because I'd shared a moment with Lex, nothing had changed. He was still determined to find out the name of the person who'd killed his dad. It was heartbreaking because I could tell he knew this wouldn't end well for any of us, but he was still pushing onward. Driven by some strange sense of duty, to a father he didn't even seem to care about.

S.C. Wynne

Chapter Twenty-Four

Lex

It was amazing how affected I was by those few moments on the porch with Dylan. For one moment there, he'd looked at me with less hatred and more pity. While I didn't enjoy his pity, I preferred it to him loathing me.

Regardless of the mounds of food Gabriele had made, Dylan ate nothing. He said his stomach was still upset. Hank did though; he ate enough for all of us. I guess being an asshole really worked up his appetite. He was actually enjoying this situation, while the rest of us just wanted it to end.

I went up to Charles's room midmorning with a plate of food. He was awake, looking angry, but his color was much better.

"Where's Dylan?" he demanded, ignoring the food on the nightstand.

"He's fine. He's in his room." I studied him. "Feel like talking yet?"

"Not particularly."

I shook my head. "You're being stupid. This could all be over if you'd just talk."

"We both know you're not going to let me walk, no matter what. I doubt you'll let Dylan walk, and I think you actually care about the kid."

My face warmed. Was it that obvious I had feelings for Dylan? "I haven't decided what to do with either of you. But both your odds are better if you give me what I want."

"You always get what you want, Lex? Is that why you're such a smug asshole?"

I exhaled tiredly. "I have a right to know who killed my father. Whether you like me personally or not isn't the point. Wouldn't you want to know this information, if you were me?"

"Probably. I'd go about it differently though."

"Roses and boxes of candy?" I sneered. "You wouldn't have told me shit no matter how I approached you. You've made that clear already."

His expression was funny. "I'm not keeping the information from you because I don't like you."

"I know. You're protecting someone."

"Yes."

"A murderer."

He grimaced. "It's not as simple as that. I can't say certain things without saying too much."

I moved closer, glaring. "I'm tired of your riddles. Your stubbornness is going to get you and Dylan killed."

He laughed humorlessly. "You actually want to pretend that would be my fault?"

I clenched my jaw, anger and frustration rippling through me. "Of course it is. Just tell me the fucking name, and I can *try* to save your ass," I hissed. "Otherwise, we're going downstairs now to visit with Hank. You remember him, right? The guy with the cattle prod?"

His face twitched, and I knew he was afraid. He'd have been a fool not to be. But he shook his head. "I can't."

I rubbed my face and snarled, "*Fuck.*" I dropped my hands at my side. "Then you leave me no choice."

He leaned toward me, his gaze imploring. "Please, Lex, let Dylan live. *Please.* I don't care what you do to me, but leave him alone."

The door opened behind me, and Hank stood there with a gloating expression. "Sorry for eavesdropping, but I think I just figured out how to get him to talk, boss." His smile was ugly. "How about Dylan takes your place today, Charles? You can have a front-row seat to the festivities."

The color drained from Charles's face instantly, and he looked like he wanted to murder Hank. I knew exactly how he felt because I had the identical visceral reaction to Hank's words. The difference was, I had to hide my repulsion.

"That wasn't the plan," I said softly, hoping I didn't look as horrified as I felt.

Hank narrowed his eyes. "No. It wasn't. But I can guarantee, the second Dylan screams in pain, this prick will spill his guts."

The image of Dylan being tortured was like a punch to the gut. I almost couldn't draw in a breath. I could pretend to be objective about him all I wanted, but I wasn't going to be able to let

Hank touch him. I couldn't do it. I'd rather die than let that happen, and no way could I say any of that out loud. I kept my mouth clamped tight so none of my feelings came out, but I nodded as if I was fine with his idea.

I met Charles's furious gaze, and I said, "See what you've done, Charles?"

"What I've done? What *I've* done?" he raged.

Through gritted teeth, I said, "Give me the name now and Dylan won't have to go through anything bad." I wanted to leap across the bed and strangle the stubborn son of a bitch.

"I can't," he yelled, veins bulging in his face. "God damn it, Lex. I can't tell you. You're the *enemy*."

Hank's laugh set my teeth on edge. "I'm going to enjoy this."

I faced him, trying to think of a way out of this nightmare. But nothing came to me. If I protected Dylan, Hank would lose his shit. He was right—the best way to get Charles to talk was to torture Dylan. I'd known that all along, but I'd refused to accept that truth. I couldn't allow that to happen. I couldn't. But how the hell was I going to prevent it? I had to stall somehow until I could figure out how to get Dylan out of here. He had to escape this nightmare alive. He had to. I didn't have enough control right now to keep him safe. I could see Hank was already teetering on rebellion. Was Gabriele on his side?

"Lex." There was a desperation in Charles's voice. He was hoping I'd save Dylan because he couldn't. His eyes were frantic, and he seemed to be trying to send me a message telepathically. "Please."

"Go get Dylan," I barked at Hank.

He gave a gloating smile and left the room. I turned immediately to Charles. "I'm going to untie your hands. You have to pretend you're still tied. Do you understand?"

He looked shocked, and he stared at me in silence.

"Do you fucking understand?" I snapped.

He jerked. "Yes. Yes. I understand."

My heart hammered in my chest. "Don't do anything until we're downstairs. We have to surprise them. I don't know if Gabriele is on my side or not. If he's on Hank's side, we're fucked."

He nodded. "What's your plan?"

I laughed harshly. "I have no fucking plan. When an opportunity presents itself, make a move. Get Dylan out of here. Get him to safety. I'll back you up as best I can." I grabbed his hands and sliced through the ties with my pocket knife. "We're all probably going to die."

"No." He shook his head. "We're not."

I didn't have his faith. Maybe because I wasn't as tough as him, or maybe because I was so scared for Dylan, I couldn't think straight. What the hell was I doing? I was betraying my own plan for Dylan. I felt nuts. Completely out of my mind.

I prayed Gabriele would take my side. I loved him like a brother. I wouldn't be able to hurt him either, and that was a problem. He wasn't going to understand what was happening. Odds were, he'd fight with Hank.

I led Charles down the stairs, feeling as if I was heading to the guillotine. Dylan was already downstairs, gagged and sitting in the chair Charles had occupied yesterday. He looked terrified, white as a sheet of paper and his blue eyes huge. When I entered the room, he locked eyes with me. He didn't look relieved to see me. I knew that was because he thought I didn't care what happened to him. He was wrong. So fucking wrong.

Gabriele stood behind Dylan, looking uneasy. He didn't know exactly what was happening, or why Dylan was now in the hot seat. I made Charles sit in a chair across from Dylan, under the pretense I wanted him to see everything that happened to Dylan. Truth was, in that position, Hank couldn't see that Charles's hands were free.

I felt light-headed with anticipation, or was it terror? I met Gabriele's gaze, and maybe he saw something in my expression, because he narrowed his eyes. Was that look suspicion? Reassurance? I had no idea. All I knew was my world had turned upside down the second Hank suggested we needed to brutalize Dylan to get Charles to talk.

Hank held the cattle prod, looking gleeful. "We decided since Charles doesn't feel like talking, maybe we could give him some incentive." He pressed a button and a blue spark arced between the electrodes, accompanied by a loud clicking sound. Hank put the prod near Dylan's face, and Dylan began to struggle wildly, desperately trying to get out of his restraints.

My heart hurt watching him. His struggle was futile. He wasn't going anywhere unless we helped him. I met Charles's hard gaze and he gave a tiny nod. I inched closer to Gabriele, needing to be near him in case he tried to jump Charles. Of course he'd try to jump Charles. What else would he do? He had no idea what was coming, and he still thought it was us against Charles.

Hank lowered the cattle prod to Dylan's chest, and it took everything in me not to kick it away. "Such a pretty face," rasped Hank. "Can't wait to see what you look like when you're in agony."

Once Hank's back was completely turned toward Charles, the other alpha leapt up and charged him like a bull. He moved so quickly, it took even me by surprise. Hank and Charles went down with a loud crash, and Hank started swearing and punching.

Gabriele lunged toward the two men, and I said sharply, "Gabriele. Stop."

He froze, but his face was a canvas of completely bewilderment. "Boss?"

I held out my hand. "It's okay."

"But…" He glanced at the two men rolling around on the ground, trying to kill each other.

"It's okay, Gabriele," I repeated breathlessly, jumping forward to stomp on Hank's wrist. He yelled in pain, and he dropped the cattle prod.

Gabriele watched, muscles bunched, his face angry and confused. I knew he wanted to join in, but he stayed where he was, obeying my command.

I moved to Dylan, who sat in stunned silence. I tugged the gag down, cut through the ties on his wrists and ankles, and pulled him up into my arms. It was stupid to take time for sentimental nonsense, but I had to touch him. I had to feel him against me so I could calm down. Once I knew he was okay, I released him. He looked shell-shocked, and while he hadn't returned my hug, he also hadn't fought me.

"What's happening?" he whispered.

I didn't respond. I needed to be sure Hank wasn't getting the upper hand with Charles. I joined in the wrestling match, and after a few minutes, we had Hank hog-tied. His face was red, and even gagged, he screamed obscenities at us, but he wasn't a threat at the moment.

Gabriele came up to me, looking furious. "What are you *doing*?"

"This has gone too far." My breathing was ragged. "I can't let him use Dylan to make Charles talk."

"Why the hell not?"

I shook my head. "I just can't."

He narrowed his eyes as if he thought I had lost my mind. "But… you can't just let them go. They'll go to the cops. What are you thinking? You can't trust outsiders. For fuck's sake, Lex. Are you nuts?"

"We won't go to the cops." Charles wiped at his bloody lip, seeming unimpressed by the scarlet smear on his hand.

"Bullshit," Gabriele snapped. "Why wouldn't you?"

Charles put his arm around Dylan. "I'm telling you, if you let us leave unharmed, we won't go to the cops."

Gabriele turned back to me. "This was your plan. I don't understand why you'd betray your own plan."

I blew out a tired breath. "What the hell is the point of this? Dad's dead. There's no bringing him back. What good would torturing Dylan do?"

Gabriele's expression hardened. "Since when are you in the business of doing good?"

"Gabe," I said softly. "You weren't enjoying this any more than I was."

"Like that's the fucking point?" His eyes flashed angrily.

"I don't have the stomach for this kind of thing. I never have."

He looked like he wanted to punch me. "You're choosing some omega you barely know over us?"

Shame washed through me. "I'm sorry."

"You're really not fit to lead. Your dad was right," growled Gabriele.

I winced but grumbled, "I never wanted to lead."

"Good. Because you're a fucking disgrace," he snarled. "If I don't agree with this, are you going to tie me up too? Beat me into submission?"

"Do we have to?" Charles answered for me.

Gabriele shot him a warning look. "Come near me and I'll put a bullet between your eyes."

"Is that right?" Charles rumbled.

"We don't need to tie him up," I said gruffly. "Right, Gabriele?"

Fuming, he didn't respond. But he also made no aggressive move toward us.

"What do we do with him?" Charles gestured toward Hank.

I sat on the chair Dylan had been in and slumped. "Hell if I know."

Dylan spoke up finally. "He tried to rape me. He probably has raped other people. I say we shoot him and bury his body on this farm. No one would ever find him."

Hank started cursing again, and Charles kicked him. "Shut up."

Hank grunted and gave Charles a surly look.

Gabriele curled his lip. "Is that how this goes now? You save outsiders and murder your own men?"

I met his gaze. "I'd prefer no one dies."

Gabriele didn't look convinced.

Somehow, Hank had worked his gag down enough to talk. "You should kill us. You're toast, Lex. The second I get back to Turbin, I'm gathering some men and we're coming after you. You won't survive the fucking week."

"You're sick. You get off on hurting people, don't you?" I scowled.

"Yeah, I do," hissed Hank. "And I'm going to enjoy making you scream. I know all kinds of way to make you suffer. Ways you'd never let me use on anyone else." His smile was malignant. "I can't wait to watch you piss yourself when I peel the skin off your face."

A shiver ran through me at the obvious hatred in his eyes.

"Jesus," Dylan said, looking repulsed. "You're disgusting."

Even Gabriele looked troubled at Hank's outburst. He moved to the other man, and he tugged the gag back into place. Hank gave an indignant growl and tried kicking him. Charles seemed to have had enough, because he strode over and punched Hank hard in the face. Hank went limp, and Charles straightened with a smug expression.

"Asshole," he said, breathing hard. "Don't suppose you guys will let me use the cattle prod on him?"

"No." Gabriele's voice was stiff, and he faced me. "You realize you ruined your life, right?"

"I know." I hadn't really thought much past saving Dylan. He was safe now, but I wasn't. Well, at least I'd done one good thing in my life.

"If you go home, you're dead." Gabriele studied me coldly.

"Yes."

Dylan gave a sharp intake of breath. "Your own men would kill you?"

I met his worried gaze. "I've betrayed them. Of course they'll turn on me now."

"Goddamned right," Gabriele spat out. "We have every right to do that too."

"He needs to come back to the compound with us," Dylan addressed Charles. "He'll be safe there."

"What?" Charles didn't look thrilled with that idea. "No way."

"He saved us." Dylan's expression was stubborn.

"Dylan," Charles groaned. "You know he can't come with us."

"Why not?"

I sighed. "Dylan, it's okay. I know I can't go with you."

"So we just leave you vulnerable after you saved our lives?" Dylan looked angry, and he gave Charles a resentful glance. "That's not fair."

Charles leaned toward him. "He created this whole nightmare. We wouldn't have needed saving if it wasn't for him."

Pink touched Dylan's cheeks. "I... I know... but what's done is done. We can't just let him die."

Eying me, Charles didn't look like he agreed.

"I'll be fine, Dylan. Don't worry about me." I forced a smile. "I'm tougher than I look."

"Besides, knowing him, this is all just part of his plan to get back inside the compound," muttered Charles.

"No." I scowled. "I was already inside the compound. Why would I do that?"

"Who knows with you."

Anger prickled me. "The only reason I had to do any of this shit was because you wouldn't tell me stuff I have a right to know. I have a right to know who killed my dad. If you'd been up-front with me, none of this would have happened."

"So this is all my fault?" Charles huffed. "You're delusional."

"It's not unreasonable he'd want to know what happened to his dad," Gabriele said gruffly.

Surprised he'd defended me, I met his emotionless gaze. "Exactly."

Charles clenched his jaw and said nothing.

I met Dylan's worried gaze. "You and Charles take the car out front to the compound. Gabriele and I will figure out other transportation."

"I don't want to just leave you." Dylan's mouth was an obstinate line.

My heart squeezed at his obvious concern for me. "Dylan," I said roughly, "don't let this all be for nothing. I want you safely tucked away in the compound."

"Where will you go?" Dylan asked softly.

"Don't worry about me. I'll be fine." So long as I kept ahead of Hank and anyone else he convinced to come after me. Financially, I'd be good. One thing about growing up a Sabine, I'd always feared this day would come. I'd thought I'd be running from the cops, not my own organization, but regardless, I had money stashed all over the country in various banks. I wouldn't go hungry, not by a long shot.

Gabriele met my gaze. "Lex, can we talk outside?"

"Sure." Giving Hank a wary glance, I followed him out front.

Once we were on the porch, I sighed. "Look, I know you're mad. But I didn't have time to tell you what was happening."

He scowled. "That's bullshit."

"I swear. Hank came up with the idea of torturing Dylan to make Charles talk on the spur of the moment. I had no way of telling you anything."

"You didn't trust me."

"That's not true." I frowned.

"I have you alone right now. If I wanted to shoot you, I could." His voice was emotionless.

"If I thought you were going to do that, I wouldn't have followed you outside. Obviously, I trust you."

He narrowed his eyes. "Admit it, you weren't sure I'd take your side."

I grimaced. "Well, okay. I had a moment's doubt. But only because I knew you'd be confused about what the hell was happening."

"How the hell could you think I wouldn't have your back? Even for one second?"

"Gabe—"

"I've *always* had your back," he interrupted. "No matter how fucked-up things got, I've always had your back, Lex." His face flushed, and hurt crept into his voice.

I felt like shit because I could see I'd wounded him. "All I can say is, I'm not myself. I don't know what I'm doing, Gabe. I just cut my own throat to save Dylan. I don't understand what's happening with me."

Maybe the agitation in my voice got through to him because his expression softened. "You've got it bad for that kid."

"But why?" I met his gaze, feeling bewildered. "I don't understand my own actions."

"Don't ask me. I've never been in love."

I frowned. "Love? But how can I be in love?"

He laughed gruffly. "Jesus, Lex. I'd hope you're in love if you're pulling the shit you just pulled."

I exhaled as if in pain. Truth was, the emotions I felt for Dylan were kind of painful. "You don't think it's weird that I have feelings for a guy?"

He shrugged. "You're attracted to who you're attracted to. I don't see the problem."

I hadn't realized until that moment how much I needed his approval about my feelings toward Dylan. Subconsciously, I'd been embarrassed to be attracted to a man. I'd hoped I was more enlightened than that. I'd always accepted Gabriele's attraction to guys; I guess it was different when it was me. I knew that probably came from how negatively my dad had viewed homosexuality. "Well, I'll probably be dead by the end of the week, so none of this will matter."

He scowled. "Don't say that shit."

"You know Hank means every word he says. He's going to come for me."

His mouth tensed. "He can try."

I smiled at him. "You're going to protect me?"

"Hell, yes, brother. To my last dying breath."

I was embarrassed when my eyes stung. "Keep saying that shit and Hank's going to be after you too."

"If you don't know I'm already on his list, you're blind. He knows my loyalty will always be with you. Always."

I frowned. "Then you can't go back either." It wasn't a question. Of course he was right; he was my best friend. No way would Hank let him live, if only to hurt me more.

He cleared his throat. "Uh… I know you won't want to hear this because you're a prideful son of a bitch, but I think we need to go to the compound for a bit. If only so we have somewhere safe to formulate a plan of action." He rubbed his jaw. "This was pretty fucking spontaneous. I have no idea where we'd go, and I think that's pretty important if we want to stay alive."

I laughed harshly. "You saw how Charles was. He won't let us in."

He smirked. "I also saw how Charles is where Dylan is concerned. If Dylan really wants you inside the compound, Charles will give in. I'd bet a hundred bucks I'm right."

"You think so?"

"Oh, yeah." He sighed. "He's almost as devoted to that kid as you are." He sounded almost annoyed about that fact.

"And that bothers you?"

His cheeks tinted pink. "Let's just say watching Charles in action was a turn-on. But if he's in love with Dylan, he might not be open to other things."

I narrowed my eyes. "He's fond of Dylan, but I don't think it's anything sexual. From what I've gathered from Dylan, Charles is straight."

He arched one dark brow. "Oh, really? Hmmm."

I laughed. "Why do I get the feeling that just made you more interested?"

His lips twitched. "I like a challenge."

I widened my eyes. "If you've set your sights on Charles, you'll definitely have that."

"The chase is most of the fun anyway." He grinned.

I put my arm around his shoulders as we headed back into the house. "Better start training soon, Gabe, because if you plan on chasing that son of a bitch, that's gonna be a marathon."

Chapter Twenty-Five

Dylan

Once Lex went outside with Gabriele, I was able to turn my full attention on Charles. If he thought the conversation about bringing Lex into the compound was over, he was dead wrong. He sat in a chair, holding ice to his head, wincing every now and then as if he were in pain. The bump on his head had gone down overnight, but the skin was tinged purple.

"Can I get you anything?" I asked, giving Hank an uneasy glance. He was unconscious, but he still made me nervous. Even tied up he was a malevolent presence.

As expected, Charles responded, "No."

I couldn't help but smile. He was one of the proudest alphas I knew. I had the feeling his entire leg could be chopped off and he wouldn't admit he was in pain. "You sure?"

"Yes."

I cleared my throat. "Are you up to talking?"

He slid his slate eyes to mine, and there was a hint of suspicion. "What about?"

I pushed down the nervousness I felt. "I still say Lex should come to the compound with us."

He sighed wearily. "Come on, Dylan. Stop."

I forced myself not to shrink from his disapproving stare. "Just for a while."

He shook his head. "No."

Irritation prickled the back of my neck. "Charles, you're being short-sighted."

"In what way?"

"Lex is the only reason I wasn't tortured." I shivered.

He scowled. "Dylan, it's his fault you were ever even vulnerable."

"I... I know... but he could have just stuck to the plan. It would have been easier for him to do that." I met his gaze full-on. "But he didn't. He stood up for me. He protected me."

He took a deep breath, and I knew he was going to try and pacify me.

"No, don't do that," I snapped. "Don't pat me on the head and ignore what I'm saying. I'm not a child. I want Lex to be brought into the compound."

"You don't say who enters. I do." His tone was patient.

"I should have some say in this."

"Why?"

I frowned. "Because I'm a huge reason for why Lex is now in danger."

"You're too emotionally involved to be logical about this."

"You're not being logical either. You're being spiteful."

He laughed harshly. "What?"

"You're being unfair because you also are too emotionally involved."

"Pfft. You're wrong."

"No. You're allowing your dislike of him to overshadow what is the right thing to do."

"Dylan, you're *wrong*."

I lifted my chin. "You'd never be this hard-nosed about anyone else in this situation. You're being like this because you don't like him."

He gave me a pointed look. "I was right not to like him. He turned out to be the bad guy."

"I know his intentions weren't pure in the beginning. But after all he's done, how can you deny him our protection? By sending him away, you're signing his death sentence."

"You're being dramatic."

I widened my eyes. "You've seen Hank. Do you have any doubt he'll murder Lex if he can?"

He didn't respond to my question, but a muscle worked in his cheek. "He doesn't even want to come inside the walls."

Is that a good sign that he said that?

"He's saying that because he knows you don't want him there," I said.

"I don't think that's true."

I gritted my teeth. "Charles, I know him better than you. Lex and I have a connection."

"Meaning what?"

My cheeks warmed. "We… we got very close when he was inside the compound."

He narrowed his eyes. "How close?"

I knew my face was red, but I held his gaze. "I'm an adult, not a child."

He flinched. "Wait… are you saying you *slept* with him?"

The heat of my face increased. "Yes."

"Oh, for God's sake, Dylan. How could you do that?" He stood and began to pace. "Did he seduce you?"

"What?" I laughed. "No. Of course not."

"But you barely know him. Why would you sleep with him?"

I shrugged. "We're drawn to each other. I don't know any other way to put it."

He shook his head. "I don't know what to say."

"Say he can come inside the walls."

His jaw was hard. "Dylan, he's still dangerous."

"What?" I frowned. "No he's not."

"He still wants to know the details of what happened to his father. Details I can't give him. For all you know this whole thing was just part of his plan to get more information."

I looked at him like he was insane. "There's no way."

"Maybe he and Gabriele are plotting outside right now. We aren't home yet." He watched me. "This could just be part two of his plan."

"No. I don't believe that."

"What if he decides someone still has to pay for his dad's death? What then? What if he decides *you* should pay?"

"Me?" I asked, startled. "He wouldn't do that. Why save me if that was his plan?"

"Who knows? I don't think like a criminal."

"He wouldn't hurt me." I shook my head, positive I was right. After today, I knew beyond a doubt Lex would never hurt me. "He's turned his back on his family. What would be the point of harming me?"

"Pride?"

"Look, I agree, he might still try to get you to tell him who killed his dad, simply because he wants to know. He has a right to know. But it wouldn't be for revenge. Not anymore."

He twisted his lips. "It's a moot point anyway because he doesn't want to come with us."

I smiled. "Trust me, I can convince him."

He shook his head. "I've never seen you like this, Dylan."

"No, you haven't. The entire time you've known me, I've been grieving." I winced. "But Lex woke me up again. I'm still young, and I want to live my life. I... I think Lex loves me. After what he did today, I can't turn my back on him."

"You're so sure he actually has feelings for you?"

I nodded. "Yes."

He sighed, watching me with a frown. When he finally spoke, he sounded resigned. "I hope this doesn't bite me in the ass."

I brightened. "You'll let him inside?"

His expression was grim. "If you can convince him to come to the compound, I'll let him in. You do realize everyone will hate him, right? After the stunt he pulled, no one will trust him."

"I trust him."

"God, you're so young."

I bristled. "This has nothing to do with my age."

He didn't argue, but I knew he didn't agree. When Lex and Gabriele appeared in the doorway, Charles tensed. It was obvious he was still very much on edge around the other two.

"You two should take the car and go now." Lex met my gaze. "Gabriele and I will wait here with Hank. When we think you've had time to reach the compound, we'll take off and leave Hank here."

"You're leaving him here?" Charles looked puzzled.

"Can't very well take him to the cops without getting locked up ourselves," Gabriele said.

"But if we take the car, how will you guys get to town?" I asked.

"Don't worry about us." Lex gave me a tentative smile.

"But I do worry," I said softly.

"You shouldn't." Lex avoided my gaze.

I glanced at the unconscious Hank. "Will he die? If you just leave him here?"

Gabriele snorted. "Unfortunately, no. He'll get free. It will take him a while, but he'll get free." He glanced at Lex. "Then the fun begins."

"You mean he'll start hunting you?" I grimaced.

"He'll go home first to get some backup." Gabriele shrugged. "But Lex and I are smart. We'll be fine."

Lex nodded but didn't speak.

"You're staying with Lex?" Charles sounded surprised.

"Yes." Gabriele met Charles's gaze. "Where Lex goes, I go."

Curling his lip, Charles said, "My, my. Who knew Lex could inspire such blind loyalty?"

"He has mine too," I said.

Red spears appeared on Charles's cheeks. "You're too forgiving, Dylan. For me, 'Betrayal is the only truth that sticks.'"

"Hard-ass," mumbled Gabriele.

Charles gave him a surly glance.

I met Lex's gaze. "Hey, Lex, can we talk for a minute?"

He looked wary, but he nodded. "Okay."

I led him into the kitchen and closed the door. I faced him, feeling short of breath. "I wanted to let you know I convinced Charles to let you come with us."

He frowned. "What?"

"To the compound."

Instead of looking pleased, he looked suspicious. "Why?"

"Why?" I laughed. "Because you'll be safe there."

He still looked like I was trying to trick him. "I don't understand."

I tilted my head, studying him. "I want you safe. What's so hard to understand?"

His jaw clenched. "Dylan, I used you. You should hate me."

I sighed. "Maybe I should. Maybe a part of me does hate you."

His gaze flickered.

I moved closer to him, and he stiffened. I looked up at him, taking in the aristocratic line of his nose and the thick dark lashes that framed his sky-blue eyes. He was so familiar to me and yet such a mystery. "Yes, you lied to me. But you also protected me."

"I know… but…" His eyes held mine. "I'm not a good man, Dylan. Just because I did something right for once, that doesn't make me good. I have my father's blood in me."

"If you weren't at least a little good, you'd have let Hank torture me. Then you'd have had your answers."

He winced and surprised me when he reached out for me. He pulled me close, kissing my hair. "I couldn't let him hurt you," he whispered. "I just couldn't."

I slipped my arms around his waist, pressing closer. God, what was it about his touch? Being in his arms was like coming home after a long, tiring trip. I felt safe, and like nothing could ever hurt me so long as Lex was beside me. And yet the danger had come from Lex, so why did I trust him? I lifted my face, and he kissed me. His kisses were needy, and desperate, as if he feared he'd never taste me again. He pressed me back against the stove, and the pans rattled as we rocked against each other. He groaned and explored my mouth with his seeking tongue.

"Dylan," he whispered, kissing my eyes and cheeks as if I was precious to him.

I rested my head on his chest, listening to his racing heart. He wasn't faking his attraction to me. This was real. Our connection, while unconventional, was real. "I want you to come with me," I whispered.

He stiffened. "Charles would probably have me court-marshaled the minute I showed up."

"That's not true. He said he'd let you in."

He narrowed his eyes. "Why would he?"

"To protect you. Like you protected me." I kissed the side of his neck, inhaling his clean scent mixed with sweat. "I want you there."

His mouth still had a stubborn tilt, but his eyes flickered at my words. "I don't think I should."

"Please," I whimpered. "I *need* you there."

His nostril flared, and he shivered. "What the hell are you doing to me?" he murmured. "Why am I so fucking spineless around you?"

"I'm the same with you."

"You should hate me." His voice was tinged with guilt.

"Maybe I should."

He licked his lips and lowered his head, capturing my mouth again. This time the kiss was deep and slow, and his hands roamed over my body. I had little doubt of what he wanted, and I yearned to give it to him. "I should say no," he murmured against my mouth.

I smiled against his full lips. "Ignore the voice of reason. That's what I'm doing."

He gave a gruff a laugh. "Promise this isn't a trap and Charles won't have the cops waiting for me?"

"This isn't a trap."

He sighed. "All right."

Excitement rolled through me. "You'll do it?"

"I can't seem to say no to you."

"Good."

He straightened. "But Gabriele has to be allowed in too. Otherwise, I'm not coming."

I grimaced. "Charles is probably going to blow a gasket at that."

His expression was serious. "I mean it. Gabriele comes, or I'm out."

"Charles will just think you want Gabriele there so you have someone to help you do your dirty deeds. He doesn't trust you. He thinks you're still playing me."

"What do you think?"

I let go of him and took a step back. "I want you. I want you with me. But I'd be lying if I didn't admit a part of me worries. You saved me, but you also used me. And you were convincing too. I really believed you cared about me, and now I struggle with what was real and what was an act." I frowned. "But you were so kind to me about Jacob and Ayden. I can't believe those moments were fake."

"They weren't." His eyes were darker than usual. "I swear they weren't."

"I feel like I need you with me. But I worry. I worry that you seem confused about why you saved me. You don't seem to understand your own actions. That makes me nervous. Perhaps you'll regret your decision to protect me, and that could endanger people I care about, not just me."

"No. I won't turn on you."

"But you don't really think you did anything wrong, do you?"

He hesitated. "I... I honestly don't know how to answer that. I needed closure, and no one would willingly give me that. I had other people looking to me to act. It seemed right to do what I did." He swallowed, his eyes apologetic. "But when I look at myself through your eyes, I don't like what I see."

"I like a lot of what I see." I dropped my gaze. "And parts I don't understand."

He sighed. "I have no idea what happens next. I've never been without a plan. I'm scared that I've fucked up my life and Gabriele's." His frustration was obvious, but his gaze gentled as it settled on mine. "What I don't have any doubt about is protecting you. I don't regret it. I'll never regret that. I'd do it again without hesitation, and fuck the consequences."

My heart ached, and I hugged him. "Okay. That's a good place to start."

Chapter Twenty-Six

Lex

Dylan convinced Charles to let Gabriele accompany me into the compound. His capitulation wasn't graceful though, not by a long shot. It was obvious he didn't think either of us belonged, and he didn't care if we knew that. When we arrived at the compound, the looks his men gave us was intimidating. I knew they'd have loved to knock us around because we'd made fools of them. I felt vulnerable because our weapons were confiscated, but his men all still carried. Gabriele's grim expression mirrored my own as we were led from the building.

"What the hell is this place?" he whispered as we were led from the security building by Charles.

"It's not Disneyland, trust me."

"Gives me the creeps." He squinted up at the sun. "At least you get to room with Dylan. I'm stuck rooming with Charles." He scowled. "Asshole is just trying to keep his eyes on me, and not in a good way."

"He thinks we're planning a coup." I smirked, watching Charles as he strode ahead of us with his back stiff.

"You sure we wouldn't just be better taking our chances out in the real world, boss?"

I wasn't sure of anything. I simply needed to be near Dylan. But I didn't want to tell Gabriele that because it made me sound pathetic. "This is only temporary."

"Good. I just hope Charles doesn't slit my throat in the night and pretend it was suicide." He grinned at me. "Promise me you won't buy that story."

"No way."

Charles stopped walking, and he held up his hand. "Lex, this is you."

Dylan came out of the cabin, and as he approached, my pulse sped up. I couldn't wait to be alone with him, and I hoped he felt the same.

"Welcome home," he said softly.

"Home?" Charles chuffed. "Remember, Lex, you're still not allowed to wander freely."

"Got it." I nodded, trying not to show how much his bossy tone annoyed me.

"You're only here because of Dylan." He slid his gaze to Gabriele. "That goes for you too."

"Didn't think I was here because you wanted me," Gabriele said with a smirk.

I moved toward Dylan, giving Gabriele a sympathetic grimace.

Gabriele rubbed his hands together briskly. "Okay, show me my new home. I'm sure it's as warm and cozy as you are, Charles."

Charles scowled and started walking up the hill again. Gabriele shook his head and waved at us, then trotted after the alpha.

I followed Dylan inside his little home. He seemed a bit nervous as he faced me, and his smile was shy. "Are you hungry?" he asked.

"Not for food."

His cheeks flushed and he laughed.

"I'm just teasing," I said so he'd relax. I wanted him, but I didn't want to rush things. I understood if he needed some time.

He sighed. "This is weird, right?"

I nodded. "Yeah. But at least we have no secrets from each other now."

His smile slipped. "Yeah." He grimaced. "I uh, I bought you some clothes."

"You did?"

"It took them so long to process you guys. I had plenty of time to kill."

I frowned. "You didn't have to do that."

He shrugged. "I know. Unfortunately, Jim wasn't as willing to lend his clothing this time around."

"Ahh, yes. My reputation has taken a nosedive."

"He had horrible taste in clothing anyway."

I moved closer to him, and his breathing picked up. I hoped this awkwardness between us would go away. We were being so careful with each other. Polite. It made me feel like we were strangers, and that wasn't what I wanted with Dylan.

"Are you sure you're okay with me staying with you?" I asked.

"Yes. I want you here." He twisted his hands. "It's just a lot has happened. It's hard to see you the same way."

I winced inwardly. "I understand."

"I just need a few days. I'll get there." His expression was apologetic.

"Take all the time you need." I gave him a reassuring smile.

"Thanks." He sighed and led me to the guest room.

I was disappointed he wanted me to still stay in there, but I understood. I moved into the room and sat on the bed, bouncing up and down. He laughed, which made me happy.

"Thank you for not being mad." He grimaced.

"It's fine. Don't worry about it. You're too tempting. I'll get more sleep staying in the guest room."

"That's true." His eyes were heated, but he turned away. "I'm supposed to go talk to Charles. Will you be all right alone?"

"Yes. I'll be fine."

He nodded. "It won't take long. I'm not even sure why he needs to see me."

"Probably wants to fit you with a chastity belt."

His face reddened. "Geez, Lex. Don't say shit like that."

"What? You know he disapproves of how we feel about each other."

"Still." He frowned.

"Fine. I won't mock him. I can see you don't like it."

He flicked his gaze to mine. "He's a good alpha. You saw that yourself firsthand. You saw how protective he was of me."

Jealously spiked through me. "Yep." I forced myself to say, "I'll try and be more respectful."

He gave a quick nod. "Okay. Well, I'll be back." He left the room, and I heard the front door close.

I lay back on the bed, kicking off my shoes. I stared at the ceiling, finding the familiar patterns in the stucco from when I'd stayed here before. It felt like a million years ago since I'd been here, when in truth it had only been a few days. I knew I was bothered by how stilted Dylan was with me now. We'd had such an easy friendship before, and it had blossomed so naturally into more. Now he was guarded. He watched me intently, as if waiting for me to change right in front of him. I suppose it made sense. He'd thought I was this perfect alpha, and I'd transformed into a monster right before his eyes. Sometimes I worried he might never see me the same way again.

I closed my lids, intending only to rest my eyes, but the next thing I knew it was dark. I sat up, temporarily confused about where I was. For one horrible minute, I thought we were still at the ranch house. Relief washed through me when I realized where I was. I glanced at the clock on the nightstand: 10:00 p.m.

I'd slept six hours? I got off the bed and went to splash water on my face and brush my teeth. Then I went out into the main part of the cabin. There was a lamp on in the corner of the room, and Dylan was on the couch, sound asleep. I perched on the arm of the sofa, and a smile curved my lips as I watched him sleep. His delicate features were relaxed, and he looked like an angel. His auburn hair was tousled and his cheeks pink. My stomach tensed at the sight of him. I'd never had such a visceral reaction to another person in my life. Just the sight of him made my nerve endings tingle.

He suddenly opened his eyes, and when he saw me he smiled. I'd been afraid there might be fear in his eyes, but there wasn't. He simply looked happy to see me. "You're awake," he said softly.

"So are you." I smiled.

He laughed and stretched, causing his shirt to ride up. My mouth went dry at the sight of his smooth white stomach, and it took all of my control not to try and kiss him. I stood and moved away so that he'd be less tempting.

"We missed dinner. Would you like me to cook us a late-night snack?" I asked.

He got off the couch and approached, still looking a bit sleepy. "What would you make?"

"Grilled cheese?"

His eyes brightened. "Yes, please."

I grinned. "That was easy."

"I love your cooking." He moved closer.

I love you.

I squelched that response and said instead, "I'm glad." I went into the kitchen and opened the fridge. "It's so weird to be back here."

"Is it?" He frowned.

"Good weird."

He leaned against the sink, arms crossed, watching me. I moved around the kitchen, aware he was staring intently. Just being in the same room with him felt nice. Especially since his energy was warm and open. He wasn't afraid of me anymore, and that meant everything.

Once the sandwiches were ready, we sat on the couch and ate them. He lay lengthwise facing one direction, and I did the same in the other direction. Our legs were intertwined, and it felt intimate. Perfect. I couldn't believe he'd given me another chance. I didn't really deserve one, but I was so grateful he wanted to try.

He licked his fingers and sighed. "That was the best grilled cheese I ever had."

"That's flattering."

"It's true. You shouldn't have been taking a cooking class. You should be teaching one." He laughed.

"I'd probably be a terrible teacher." I wrinkled my nose. "I'm not very patient."

"You seem patient."

I shrugged. "That's because I am, with you." I smirked. "Ask Gabriele how patient I usually am. I'm sure you'll get an earful."

He laughed. "I will. He can tell me all your deep dark secrets."

I frowned. "There aren't any that you don't know."

Wincing, he said, "That was just a joke."

"Oh."

He picked at a loose thread on the seam of his jeans. "My meeting with Charles went well."

I tensed. "Did it? I didn't want to pry. I thought I'd let you talk about it if you wanted to."

"How very considerate of you," he smirked. "More like you don't want to hear about Charles, so you didn't bring it up."

"Well, I don't want to think about him, but that wasn't the reason. I'm trying to give you your space. I know I put you through hell."

He frowned. "I feel better already just being back here with you."

My heart lifted. "Really?"

He smiled. "Yeah."

I sighed. "I'm so glad."

His gaze was affectionate. "Me too."

We fell silent, and then he said, "Do you think Hank is free yet?"

Anxiety jolted through me. "Yes."

His eyes widened. "Really?"

"I would be."

He scowled. "I think we both know I wouldn't be free."

Guilt washed through me. "You weren't brought up preparing for the worse things that can happen to you. We were."

"How do you prepare for that?" He looked mystified.

I shrugged. "My dad was all about making me tough. He'd tie me up and leave me in abandoned buildings to see if I could escape. I got pretty good at getting out of handcuffs and zip ties." I finished speaking and realized he was looking at me horrified. My face warmed. "Sorry. That's probably weird to you."

"Of course that's weird to me. What kind of father does that?"

"He was… different."

"God."

"He wanted me to be prepared in case I got grabbed. It was a real possibility being his kid." I gave a hard laugh. "But I also think he kind of enjoyed it. He changed a lot as the years went by. To be honest, I barely knew the man who disappeared up here. He was a stranger to me."

"And yet you came to find out what happened."

"I had to."

"I guess." He studied me. "What will happen to your art gallery?"

I didn't want to think about that, but it was a fair question. "It'll shut down. Too bad, too, because it was a cool place."

"Is art your passion?"

"Not really. I like art, and I like to paint. But mostly I was just trying to distance myself from Dad. I didn't want to follow in his footsteps, so I picked something he wasn't interested in. He had zero artistic taste. He judged art based on price. If it was expensive, he liked it."

"That's an interesting approach." He stifled a yawn. "God. Sorry."

"It's fine. We should go to bed."

He nodded, but he avoided my gaze.

I could sense his uneasiness, so I decided to let him off the hook. "I don't want to sleep with you tonight."

He looked surprised. "What?"

I laughed. "I mean, I want to, but I don't expect to. In fact, I don't think we should."

"Why?" he asked quietly.

"You need time. I said I'd give you that, and I will." I grinned. "Even if it means I'll suffer from blue balls."

He sighed and kicked my foot. "And you say you're not a patient man."

S.C. Wynne

Chapter Twenty-Seven

Dylan

"What the fuck is wrong with me?" I muttered, holding on to the toilet bowl as another bout of nausea washed over me. I heaved for a few more minutes, and then eventually the sickness faded. I stood on shaky legs to splash my face with cold water. I brushed my teeth and rinsed. Then I stared at my pale reflection, confused and uneasy.

Four days in a row. I've been sick in the morning four days in a row.

I let myself out of the bathroom, and I went into the kitchen to make myself some tea. My stomach couldn't handle coffee lately; it instantly gave me indigestion. The teakettle was whistling by the time Lex came into the kitchen. My pulse picked up at the sight of him, and I couldn't wipe my happy grin from my face. Seeing him each morning was like the warm sun peeking through six straight days of rain.

He made a beeline to me, and he kissed me softly. I pushed closer, winding my arms around his neck and opening my mouth to his seeking tongue. God the feel of his warm lips on mine was perfect. Fucking perfect. I wanted him so bad, it was hard not to blurt that out. But we'd been taking it slow. Really. Really. Really. Slooooooooow. So slow, I was beginning to be annoyed, even though I was the one who'd insisted we sleep in separate rooms. I'd expected him to push harder to be in my room, but he'd been a complete gentleman. He'd respected my wishes, and so I was horny and wound up so tight I could have come with just a few strokes.

"Morning." His voice was husky from sleep.

"Good morning, Mr. Sabine." I smirked. "Would you like some mint tea?"

He gave a gentle recoil and said politely, "No, thank you."

I laughed. "I made coffee too."

"Aww." He kissed the top of my head. "That was sweet of you."

I shrugged and sat at the table. I watched him stir cream into his coffee, admiring his pert ass, accentuated by the thin cotton of his pajama bottoms. I needed to let him know I was ready to move forward. I couldn't take another week of no sex.

He sat across from me, and he sipped his coffee for a few minutes. Then he set the beverage down, his expression serious. "Did I hear you getting sick again?"

Embarrassed, I avoided his gaze. "God, you heard me?"

"I've heard you every morning."

I glanced up, and he looked concerned. "I think it's just a bug."

A line formed between his smooth brows. "But you're always fine the rest of the day."

"Yeah." I nodded. "Maybe it's stress."

"That only hits you in the morning?"

"I wouldn't worry about it. I'm sure it will pass." I stood. "I have to get to work. Will you be okay alone today?"

He smiled and stood too. "You ask me that every day. I'll be fine today alone, just like I was fine yesterday, and the day before that."

"Sorry. I just feel guilty leaving you alone."

"I can tell."

I moved to the door, and he followed. "I'll try to come home for lunch if I can."

"Really?" He looked pleased. "That would be great."

"What will you do while I'm gone?"

"Probably visit with Gabriele. He needs a shoulder to cry on. Charles is driving him nuts. I think those two are either going to kill each other or end up fucking. There's a lot of tension in that house."

I laughed gruffly. "I told you, Charles is straight."

He cocked a brow. "So was I. The mountain air does strange things."

I snorted. "Those two hate each other. There's no way."

"You're probably right." He trailed his hand down my back.

I shivered with pleasure at his touch. "Maybe you can sleep in my room tonight." I felt breathless as I said that. I wasn't sure why. I knew he wanted to. But I felt a bit shy for whatever reason.

His eyes immediately lit with interest. "Yeah?"

"Yeah."

He blew out a shaky breath. "Shit. Now that's all I'll be able to think about."

"Me too." I kissed him, and our mouths locked hungrily. I was tempted to call Dr. Peters to tell him I was going to be late, but I instead pulled back. Licking my lips, I laughed. "Hold that thought. Maybe we can skip lunch and take a nap." I made air quotes on the word nap.

"I'm all for that idea." His eyes buzzed with lust.

I straightened my shirt collar. "Okay, I'm really going now."

He smacked my butt. "Hurry home, dear."

I laughed and set off down the road to the clinic. Things were going so well with Lex, it almost made me nervous. It was hard to shake the feeling something might ruin our happiness. Life seemed to have a way of throwing a wrench in things. It worried me a lot that Lex still had no idea about the solar eclipse omegas, or that I was one. It made me feel guilty when I'd insisted he have no secrets from me, but I held a huge secret. I wanted to tell him the truth, but Charles wouldn't let me. He said it wasn't fair to all the other solar eclipse omegas, that I could be endangering them by telling the truth to a man like Lex. While I didn't agree with his reasons, I was afraid Lex would be repulsed by me if he knew what a freak of nature I was.

When I got to the clinic, Dr. Peters had one solar eclipse omega already prepped for surgery. I washed up and got into my gown, and I joined him in the operating room. The omega had opted to be unconscious for the delivery, which was unusual. Usually the omegas loved to be awake, but maybe this guy was too nervous. I'd want to be awake if I gave birth. Not something I ever saw happening since only my fated mate could get me pregnant. The odds of meeting that mate were very slim. Especially when you'd spent the last year hiding in the mountains.

I shook off those thoughts because I was happy with Lex. I didn't care if I ever had another child. I wasn't even sure I'd want that because I'd loved Ayden so much. It occurred to me that for the first time in a long time, I was able to think about Ayden without feeling overwhelmed with grief. The realization of that shook me but made me happy too. I loved the idea of being able to remember Ayden in a happy context. For too long his sweet memory had been overshadowed by the tragedy.

Dr. Peters and I delivered two more babies, and as lunchtime neared, excitement ramped in my gut. I couldn't wait to see Lex. As Dr. Peters and I washed up at the sink in the surgery, I suddenly felt light-headed, and I tipped slightly, catching myself on the sink.

Dr. Peters grabbed my arm. "Are you okay?"

I nodded, leaning on the sink. "God, sorry. I just got so dizzy."

He looked worried, and he led me over to a folding chair. He felt my head and sat down next to me. "Are you eating properly?"

"Yeah. I'm probably eating better than ever because Lex is such a good cook." I gave a weak smile.

"You're so pale. Maybe you're low on iron."

I blew out a shaky breath. "Maybe. Could that cause nausea?"

"Nausea?"

I nodded. "Yeah. Four days straight I've been sick in the morning."

"Four days—" He scowled. "Dylan, why wouldn't you have me check you over? Four days is a long time to be actively throwing up."

"I kept thinking it would pass."

His mouth was a grim line. "You're probably dehydrated."

"Yeah. That's probably true."

He stood. "Just to be sure, we need to take some blood. God knows what you might have caught hanging around that old farmhouse."

"Yeah." I stood, still feeling drained. "Maybe it is low iron. I'm really tired."

"Sit. I'll take your blood here." He went to the cupboard and pulled out a syringe and everything he'd need. Then he returned to me. He tied a band around my elbow and inserted the needle into a vein. Once he had enough blood, he walked it personally to the lab.

I found it sweet he was so concerned, but I kept checking the clock because I didn't want to keep Lex waiting. Dr. Peters came back, looking annoyed. "The technician is at lunch. We'll have to wait till he gets back for the results."

"That's okay." I stood. "I was going home for lunch anyway."

He smiled. "Is that right?"

I nodded.

"I remember not so long ago you always worked through your lunch break."

"Yeah." I frowned. "I did do that, didn't I?"

"You and Lex seem to be getting along well."

I felt myself blushing. "Yeah, we're a good fit. Regardless of what Charles thinks, Lex is good for me."

"Charles has his mind made up."

I met his gaze. "Lex is so good to me. Yes, he screwed up in the beginning, but he treats me like gold."

His smile was kind. "I don't really know Lex, but I can see a difference in you."

"Can you?"

"Yeah. Charles will come around when he sees that Lex is a changed man."

"I hope so. I live in fear Lex will want to leave because Charles is such an asshole to him."

Chuckling, Dr. Peters said, "Lex doesn't strike me as an alpha who runs easily."

"I hope not." I grimaced. "I'll be back after lunch."

"I'll see you then." He waved and headed to the cafeteria.

I made my way out of the building, inhaling the crisp air. I felt better now that I was out in the sunshine. The breeze hissed through the pines, and I sighed, feeling content. When I reached the cabin, Lex was in the kitchen. It smelled delicious in the house. "I only have a half hour," I called out. "I don't have time to eat and do... other things."

He came toward me, and the minute he saw me, he frowned. "Are you feeling okay?"

"Yeah." I hesitated. "Why?"

"You look pale." He led me over to the couch. "Sit."

I obeyed, and he sat beside me.

"I was light-headed earlier at work. Dr. Peters is doing some tests on me." I laughed. "He thinks I might be anemic."

"Really?" He looked worried.

I smiled. "It's okay. I'll just take some iron and I'll be fine."

"I don't like it when you're sick." He sounded so put out, I had to laugh.

"Well, I don't like it either." I touched his face. "I don't want to just talk about me."

"Yeah?" He licked his lips. "What do you want to do instead?"

I smirked. "I'm not sure. Do you have any ideas?"

"Yeah. I have a few." He pushed me gently down on the couch. "Since you're so weak, I'm going to take care of you."

My heart pounded. "Take care of me how?"

He slowly unzipped my jeans and tugged them down roughly to my knees. "I'm going to suck you."

"Really?" He'd never done that to me before, and since I was the only guy he'd been with, that meant he'd never given head. "You sure you want to do that?"

His eyes gleamed salaciously. "Oh, yeah. I want to taste you. I've been thinking about it for days."

Excitement zipped through me. "I had no idea."

"Just lie back and enjoy." He knelt between my legs and bent down. His warm breath wafted over my swollen cock, and I moaned when he nibbled the base. He pushed his face into my auburn pubic hairs, and he inhaled. "God, I love your scent," he growled, cupping my balls in his palm.

When he took the tip of my cock into his mouth, I hissed. It felt so good to finally be intimate with him again. I'd missed it. Missed everything about this. He took me deeper, and even though he struggled to get my length down his throat, just the fact that it was his mouth made it ten times sexier. I tangled my fingers in his silky hair and rolled my hips slowly.

He groaned around my length and increased his suction. I heard the sound of a zipper and noticed he had his cock out and he was stroking himself. I was so turned on, I had to pump into his mouth. I couldn't hold back. I tried to be gentle, but it had been too long since we'd fucked.

"Oh, shit, Lex." I shivered when he fingered my hole. "Yeah. Touch me there."

He did just that, pushing his finger inside me as he bobbed his head up and down my length. The wet heat of his mouth brought me to the edge, over and over, but he'd always back off right before I came. I was frustrated from coming so close but never actually climaxing. I felt like a stretched rubber band, ready to snap any second.

"Let me come," I begged, fucking his mouth harder. "Please, Lex."

His suction increased, and my eyes rolled up in my head it was so good. I arched my back as he took me deeper, and all at once the rubber band let loose. With a guttural cry, I came in hard, long pulses. He swallowed my warm cream as if it was mother's milk, never once backing off. My body trembled and I lay there weak and satiated.

He pulled his mouth off me and started jacking himself roughly. "I'm gonna come. Fuck. I'm gonna come."

I tugged at him. "In my mouth. Come in my mouth, Lex."

Lust roared through his eyes, and he moved closer, straddling my chest. He pushed the ruddy tip of his dick against my lips. I opened my mouth, sticking my tongue out. That turned him on even more, and he started groaning. "So hot. So fucking hot."

I suckled his tip, and he gasped and shot thick, hot streams over my tongue. He tasted tangy and perfect, and I sucked the cum from his cock as he growled with pleasure. He slumped, shudders still raking his body. But then he moved off me, as if afraid he was too heavy. He collapsed beside me on the couch, and we held each other, kissing softly.

"Best lunch ever," I said, laughing against his shoulder.

"I missed being close like this." He tightened his arms. "I know I hurt you by hiding shit. I'm truly sorry."

Guilt nipped at me like always because of my secrets. "It's okay. I swear."

He kissed me again. "I'll never keep things from you, promise. Even if it's bad. I'll tell you."

I couldn't speak. I just stroked his back, feeling awful.

Eventually it was time to go back to work, so we got up, and I straightened my clothing. Wrinkled clothing or not, it had been worth it. I kissed Lex and went back to the clinic feeling much better than before. I was still feeling run-down, but my entire body was warm and relaxed now.

When I walked into the clinic, Dr. Peters was waiting for me in the surgery. I could tell immediately that something was wrong. I frowned at him, and he grimaced.

"Your test results are in," he said cheerfully, but he had a line between his brows.

"Low iron?" I asked uneasily.

He hesitated. "Uh…"

Fear went through me. "Something worse?"

He put his arm around me. "Let's go to my office to talk."

I widened my eyes, real fear setting in. "Is it really bad?"

We reached his office, and he had me sit. He went around to the other side of his desk. He clasped his hands, and he leaned forward. "I have some surprising news for you, Dylan."

"Surprising?" Well, that was better than bad news.

"I'm not going to beat around the bush." He laughed nervously.

"Okay."

"It would seem you're pregnant."

I squinted at him. "What?"

"You're pregnant. That's why you're having morning sickness."

Shock rolled through me, and I searched his face for signs he was kidding. It wasn't a very funny joke if he was kidding. "You can't be serious."

"As an aside, you are *also* low on iron."

I touched my stomach, disbelief settling on me. "But… I don't understand."

He shook his head. "As insane as it sounds… Lex must be your fated mate."

My mouth moved, but no sound came.

"Of course, he's going to be extremely surprised." He winced. "Maybe even freaked-out."

"My God." I blinked at him.

"The odds of you meeting your mate the way you did." He looked like he had no idea what else to say.

I stood, feeling light-headed. "I'm afraid if I tell him the truth, he'll reject me."

"Well, there's no question he will be blindsided."

"I would have told him about myself already." I scowled. "But Charles didn't want me to. He didn't think he had the right to know."

"He certainly does now."

"Things are so good right now." I met his gaze. "I'm scared this will ruin everything."

"But you're having a baby. That's a great thing." He sounded chipper, but I could see he wasn't sure how Lex would take the news either. "Do you love each other?"

"Yes." I winced. "But I've been lying to him about myself. I was mad at him for doing that, and now I'm the liar."

"What's done is done. He has to know the truth now."

"I know… I just don't know the best way to tell him."

Dr. Peter's gaze softened. "He came here the first time seeking answers. Charles wouldn't tell him certain things because doing so would tell him about the solar eclipse omegas." He laughed. "There is now no reason for Charles to not tell him the truth about what happened to his father. This could end up being a good thing for Lex. He'll have his closure."

I swallowed hard. "Yes. But it could very well be the end of our relationship too."

"But if you love each other, what could be better than also having a child?"

"He won't understand any of this. He doesn't even believe in the Ancients."

"Ahhh. A skeptic."

"Yes. He thinks I'm gullible."

He shrugged. "That, my boy, is because he didn't know any of the truths. He's about to get a very large dose of it from you. Go home. Talk to Lex."

I met his gaze, anxiety eating at me. "We just reconnected. We're in such a good place. This could destroy that."

"What is the alternative?"

I lowered my head. "There isn't one."

"Now there will be no more secrets between you. That's a good thing."

"Yes. I only hope our fragile relationship can handle this much honesty." I moved to the door.

"Good luck, Dylan. The Ancients wouldn't have matched you if they didn't want you together. Remember that. Lex might falter, but I think he will step up. He hasn't been perfect, but he's done the right thing when it really mattered. I'm hoping he will do that this time too."

"I wish I could speak to the Ancients. I'd love to ask them why we have to have so many secrets. It just makes this all so much harder for my kind."

"It's to protect you."

I gave him a sullen look. "Or is it to protect them? To make them feel important?"

He looked shocked. "Dylan, that isn't true. Protecting the solar eclipse omegas is one of their greatest chores."

"Where were they when Lex had me captive? No one came to save me."

He looked disappointed in me. "Dylan, that's because you were with your fated mate. They trusted he would protect you. And he did."

Shame filtered in at his heartfelt words. He had a point. Lex had always been in control, and because of his love for me, I'd probably never been in any actual danger. "Well, it was pretty terrifying for me since I had no idea he was my fated mate."

He laughed. "I know. I do wish there was a better way. But things change. Perhaps the Ancients will modernize one day. There are more and more solar eclipse omegas being born. They might have to change because of that."

"I won't hold my breath."

He sighed. "Go home to Lex. Tell him the news. Perhaps he will surprise you."

I nodded and left the clinic. Earlier I'd been so excited to get home to see Lex; now I was dreading it. Dreading the look of repulsion I feared I'd see on his face when I told him I was carrying his child.

Chapter Twenty-Eight

Lex

The minute Dylan entered the cabin, I knew something was wrong. He wouldn't look at me, and he went straight into his room. Worry attacked me as I waited patiently in the living room, but when he didn't come out, I went to knock on his door.

"Dylan?" I called softly. "Are you okay?"

He didn't respond, and I started to walk away. But then I decided that was silly. We'd had a wonderful day together, and if something was wrong, it couldn't be my fault. For all intents and purposes, I was his alpha. It was my role to comfort him. I opened the door slowly and found him sitting on the edge of the bed.

He looked surprised when I opened the door.

"I knocked," I said. "But I guess you didn't hear me."

"I heard you."

That wasn't the response I wanted. "Is something wrong?"

He shrugged.

"Why are you hiding in your room?"

"I'm trying to think of how to tell you something."

My heart sank at his glum tone. Had he decided he didn't want to be with me anymore?

Shock rattled through me, leaving me panicked. What could have changed between now and lunchtime? I struggled to keep my breathing calm, and I entered the room more fully. "Just tell me. You don't need to sugarcoat things."

He glanced at me, and his eyes were filled with fear. That confused me, and I moved closer, instinctively wanting to comfort him. But before I could reach him, he stood and moved across the room. I clenched my jaw, frustrated that he wouldn't tell me what was going on.

"Dylan," I said brusquely, "Tell me what's bothering you."

"You're going to be upset."

God. What could this be about? I felt sick with fear. "You know I love you, right? I'm not good at saying it, but I do love you. More than anything."

His face wrinkled as if in pain. "Don't say that. That only makes it worse when you take it back."

I was mystified by what he could mean. "I'm not taking it back."

"You're only saying that because you don't understand. You don't know the truth about me."

I tilted my head, feeling confused. "What truth?"

"You've come clean with me, but I've been hiding something from you." He rubbed his face roughly. "God, why can't I ever just be happy?"

"I want you happy. I want to make you happy." I met his gaze. "Tell me what's wrong."

He groaned and sat on the edge of the bed again. I went to stand in front of him.

"Let me ask you this: Do you have any interest in having a child with me?"

The question came out of left field. "Children?"

"Yes."

I scowled. "What could that possibly have to do with why you're upset?"

"It's important."

Was this about Ayden? Did he want a child because of that loss, or did he not want a child because of that loss? I studied him, trying to guess his reasons for asking such a strange question. Since I couldn't read him, I decided to try and actually answer the question truthfully. I thought about having a child with him, and the truth was it excited me. He'd be a great father, and while I would suck at it, perhaps he could help me be a better dad than mine had been to me.

I met his wary gaze. "I'd love to have a baby with you, Dylan."

His eyes seemed to tear, and he shook his head. "Don't just say that to be nice."

"I'm not." I smiled at him hesitantly. "I swear."

He sighed and stared at his clasped hands. "I have to tell you something that might change your opinion of me. But I was born this way, and I had no choice in the matter. I'm no different than any other omega, unless I meet my fated mate."

"Fated mate?" My lips twitched. "You know I don't believe in that."

"Well, you might have to change your mind on that, Lex."

I gave a confused laugh. "I'll do whatever you want. I just want you to stop looking so sad."

"I can't do that until I know how you're going to react."

I squinted at him. "I'll be honest, I'm really confused."

"I know. That's why I came in here. I don't know how to put into words what I have to tell you."

"Well, I have no idea what this big secret is... but I love you, and I want you to be honest with me." I moved closer. "Just tell me what it is."

He exhaled roughly. "This compound is a safe place for a special type of omega."

"Okay."

"We're called solar eclipse omegas." He paused. "S.E.O. is the other term we use here inside the walls."

I nodded. "Yes, I remember Charles mentioned them."

"We're different. Special."

"Special how?"

He groaned. "This is where it gets hard."

"Just keep talking. Don't stop and go off track."

"You're going to think I'm nuts. But I'm not."

"Dylan," I said impatiently. "Tell me what you need to tell me. I don't understand what's happening. Everything was fine, and now you're talking in riddles."

He clenched his jaw. "Solar eclipse omegas can have babies."

"Okay." I frowned. "Lots of omegas have babies."

He sighed. "Solar eclipse omegas are only male."

A thick silence followed his statement while I struggled to understand his meaning. At first I thought I must have heard him wrong. I frowned at him, and he looked away. The only thing I could get from his face was that he was scared. "You said that you're a solar eclipse omega."

"Yes."

I squinted. "And you're saying that these male omegas can have… can have babies?"

He nodded, looking even paler than before.

I swallowed. "Are you…" I laughed gruffly. "Are you saying that *you* can have babies?"

He looked like he was about to be ill, but he nodded slowly.

My mouth dropped open. I wanted to laugh, but he didn't look like this was a joke. He looked like he was at a funeral. "I… I don't know what to say."

"It gets worse."

I stared in confusion. "It does?"

"I'm pregnant." He gulped. "With your baby."

This had to be a joke. It had to be. But he most certainly was not laughing. "Men don't have babies."

"Usually that's true."

"But you don't have the equipment to have a baby. You don't have a uterus or a vagina." Blood was draining from my head, as I began to face the realization that the man I loved must be mentally ill. "Dylan, have you talked to anyone about these feelings of yours?"

He did laugh then, although it wasn't a pleasant sound. "The entire compound is filled with these solar eclipse omegas, Lex. I'm not crazy. I can show you two pregnant male omegas in the clinic right now."

Was he delusional? Psychotic? Just damaged from losing a child? So damaged he'd made up this story, so that he could have another child?

"I can see the wheels turning in your head." His voice was bitter. "I knew you'd think I was crazy."

"What you're saying sounds crazy. It defies science."

"Yes. I know. I'm a fucking freak of nature," he snapped. "But I didn't ask for this. I was simply born this way."

I shook my head in silent rejection of his words.

"We're fated mates. You were only able to get me pregnant because of that."

"Fated mates?" I scowled. "Dylan, that is just a wives' tale."

"No. You're wrong. It's true, and you and me are fated to be together. We were paired by the Ancients."

My laugh was hard. "I refuse to believe I had no say in being with you."

"You could have rejected me. Some fated pairs don't work out."

"No. This is crazy."

You're crazy.

"You can deny it all you want, but we're fated mates, or you couldn't have gotten me pregnant. We're going to have a baby. That's the honest truth."

I felt heartbroken, but I didn't want him to see that. I didn't want him to see that I thought he was deranged.

"I... I need some air." I moved to the door.

"You can't run from this."

"I..." I shook my head and left the room.

If he called after me, I didn't hear him. In a daze I left the cabin and started walking in the direction of Gabriele. I didn't know who else to turn to. My stride was long, my breathing hard. I felt sick. Brokenhearted. I loved Dylan so much, it hurt. I'd stand by him no matter what; even crazy, I'd still love him. But the future I'd hoped for with him was gone. Shattered the minute he'd started babbling like a crazy person about being pregnant and fated mates.

When I got to the cabin Gabriele shared with Charles, I knocked on the door. I'd expected to see Gabriele, but instead Charles answered the door. "Gabriele," I said harshly. "I need to talk to Gabriele."

Charles started to say something, but he hesitated. His gaze became more intent. "What's wrong?"

"I just need to talk to Gabriele," I rasped.

He glanced behind me, and when I turned, Dylan was walking up the path. I closed my eyes, not sure what to do.

"I had to tell him the truth, Charles." Dylan's voice shook. "He thinks I'm crazy now."

"You did what?" Charles sounded angry. "Why would you be so reckless?"

"I had to tell him."

Shaking his head, Charles said, "Come inside. Both of you." He stepped aside.

I moved into the house, acutely aware of Dylan behind me. But he moved to the other side of the room, avoiding my gaze. I was relieved when Gabriele wandered into the room, looking surprised to see me. He smiled, but it soon faded into a frown.

"Are you okay?" he asked me.

I shook my head.

He squeezed my arm. "What's wrong?"

"Let's all sit," Charles said before I could respond. Once we were seated, he pinned his frustrated gaze on Dylan. "What exactly did you tell Lex?"

Dylan's lips moved, but no words came out.

"He says he's pregnant with my child," I said gruffly.

Charles looked horrified. "God, no."

"That's what he said," I whispered.

Gabriele's head snapped toward me. "What?"

I sighed. "He says he's pregnant."

Gabriele shot Dylan a funny look. "Pregnant?"

Charles cleared his throat. "How is this possible that Lex would be your mate, Dylan?"

"How would I know?" Dylan frowned.

Looking at Charles, I was struck by the fact he didn't seem surprised about the idea of male pregnancy; he seemed more upset that I would be the father of Dylan's child.

"You know he can't be pregnant, right?" I stared Charles down.

His gaze flickered, and he once more shot Dylan an impatient look. "Of all the people to spill the truth to, Dylan, did it have to be him?"

"He's the father," snapped Dylan. "I couldn't keep it a secret from him."

Gabriele laughed. "Well, it can't be true."

Charles looked at him but didn't respond.

"Men don't have babies," Gabriele said.

"That's what I said," I muttered.

Dylan glared at us. "I know perfectly well you think I'm nuts. I'm not."

Charles put his hands together like an umpire. "Time out." He addressed Dylan. "Are you sure you're pregnant?"

"Yes. Dr. Peters did a blood test because I've been having morning sickness."

Gabriele gave another one of those nervous laughs. "Guys, what the fuck is going on? This isn't funny. You've got Lex pretty worked up."

"This isn't a joke," snapped Charles.

"Well, it's certainly not a good joke," Gabriele said.

Charles stood. "I know this is all very confusing for you two. I… I trust you will keep you mouths shut about what you've learned."

"What we've learned?" I frowned. "Men can't have babies, that is what I already know. That's what everybody knows."

Sighing, Charles faced me. "There are many things that are not known outside of this compound."

"You're saying male pregnancy is one of those things?" I asked.

"Yes. That's why we have this compound, to protect the S.E.O's from the same kind of hostility and ridicule you two are showing Dylan."

I frowned. "I'm not ridiculing Dylan. I'm worried for him. I love him."

Charles looked surprised at my response. "You seemed more angry than concerned."

"I'm confused. Both you and Dylan seem like rational people, and yet what you're saying is not logical."

"The truth isn't always logical." Charles gave Dylan a compassionate glance. "We're not lying. I know you find this impossible to believe, but if Dylan says he's pregnant, he's pregnant."

"But how?" Gabriele looked mystified.

"Those are details you don't need to know." The set of Charles's chin was stubborn.

Dylan's eyes were wounded as he addressed me. "Do you seriously think I'd make up something this embarrassing? Why would I?"

His plaintive tone hurt my heart. "Maybe it's a result of what happened with... Jacob."

Anger replaced the pain in his gaze. "That's bullshit. I'm not mentally or emotionally ill. I'm pregnant."

"It's no use, Dylan. He's close-minded. I knew he wasn't worthy of being your alpha. I've told you that from the beginning." Charles looked smug.

I scowled. "You know what? Fuck you, Charles. I've never heard of solar eclipse omegas before today. Excuse me if it takes me a second to grasp that everything I've been taught might be wrong."

"If this is true, that's pretty fucking mind-blowing." Gabriele nodded.

"It is true." Dylan held my gaze. "Like I said before, I never asked for this."

"But why would you exist?" I frowned. "We have female omegas already to bear our offspring."

Charles answered first. "Long ago the females of our kind got sick, and there were no live births. We faced extinction, but then the solar eclipse omegas appeared. They saved our species."

I studied Dylan. He didn't look crazy. He looked angry. Hurt. I knew there were things in the world beyond my comprehension—was this one of those things? "This is difficult to accept."

"I know." Dylan's mouth drooped. "That's why I was afraid to tell you. I knew you wouldn't believe me."

"I want to believe you," I said softly.

"Do you?"

"My mind tells me this isn't possible, but my heart says to trust you." I held his worried gaze.

"Which will you listen to?" he asked.

I gave a husky laugh. "When it comes to you, my heart always seems to win out."

He looked on the verge of tears, but he pressed his lips together as if refusing to give in to his emotions. "I'm going home. I'm tired and I've said all I can say. If you don't believe me, I can't change that."

"I'm coming too." I stood.

He gave me a wary look, but he didn't argue.

I nodded a good night to Gabriele and trailed Dylan out into the cool evening. Dylan had nothing to say to me, and I wasn't sure what to say to him either. I knew we needed to talk, but I didn't know where to begin. When we got to his house, once inside, he started to go to his room. Instinctively, I knew that would be a mistake. We needed to iron this out now and not let the hurt feelings fester. I didn't want to lose him.

"Dylan, wait."

He stopped and glanced at me over his shoulder.

"We need to talk."

"I'm tired."

"Then we can talk in bed."

He narrowed his eyes. "You're not sleeping in my room."

"Yeah. I am."

Anger sent a flush across his cheeks. "Says who?"

"I'm your alpha. I sleep where you sleep."

He chuffed. "Now you're my alpha?"

"We're fated mates. I don't have much choice, do I?"

"You suddenly believe in fated mates?"

"I believe in you. I believe in my love for you."

He chewed his bottom lip, looking uneasy. "I don't want you around if you're going to make me feel bad. This pregnancy will be tough enough without that."

I winced. "I don't want to be the thing that upsets you. I want to be your comfort."

"But how can you do that if you think I'm crazy or lying?"

I clenched my jaw and moved toward him. "I told you I'm following my heart. I believe you. If you say you're carrying my child, I believe you."

"No you don't," he said, sounding on the verge of tears.

My heart ached, and I approached him, feeling calmer than earlier. I loved him so much. What could be worse than losing him? Nothing. Absolutely nothing. If he truly carried my child, that would be just one more wonderful thing we would share. Because I wasn't ever leaving his side. Even if he sent me away, I'd find a way to stay close. Dylan was the end of the road for me.

I wrapped him in my arms, and he stiffened. "I love you. I'm sorry I hurt you." I kissed his hair and continued to hold him. "You can be mad at me if you want. You can even yell at me, but I'm not leaving. I'll never leave you. I wasn't abandoning you earlier. I just needed to talk to Gabriele."

"You think I'm a freak."

"Never."

He lifted his face to mine, and his eyes were filled with pain. "I can't help what I am."

"Stop apologizing. I'm the one who is sorry." I tightened my arms around him. "I overreacted. If I'm honest, I'm a little scared about being a dad. I had a terrible role model, but the idea of you carrying my baby is actually kind of a turn-on."

"You didn't look turned on, you looked horrified."

I winced. "I'm sorry. I was just stunned."

"I knew you'd be upset."

I sighed. "Dylan, this won't be the last time I overreact or let you down. I'm not perfect. But I know I fucked up, and I'm trying to say I'll do better. Okay?"

"This might be too hard for you. If you're going to go, it's best you do it now."

"I don't want to go." I sighed. "I need to be here. With my omega."

"Don't call me that just to be nice."

I smiled weakly. "You know me. I'm not nice just to be nice."

"True."

"Please, Dylan. Let me love you." I closed my eyes, worried he might try and send me away. What would I do if he did? There would be a gaping hole in my heart without him. I wouldn't be able to move on, not now. I loved him too much.

When he slipped his arms around my waist, I could have cried with happiness. "I don't want you to go."

A lump rose in my throat. "I'll be a good alpha. I swear."

He nodded and then leaned into me as if exhausted.

"Come on. Let's get you to bed." I led him to his room, and I was relieved he no longer seemed mad.

I helped him undress, and I crawled in beside him. He stayed on his side, but when I scooted over, he curled into me as if he craved my touch. I held him, listening to his soft breathing. I really was worried about what kind of dad I'd be. Could you be a good parent if you had no idea how to do it? Would it come naturally? It hadn't to my dad. But Dylan would be a natural. Of that I was certain. He'd make up the slack for me, hopefully.

I put my hand gently on his stomach. He tensed, but then he relaxed. "I love you, Dylan," I whispered. "Please don't give up on me."

There was a slight hesitation, and then his hand covered mine. "I won't," he said softly. "I couldn't if I wanted to."

S.C. Wynne

Chapter Twenty-Nine

Dylan

After our blowup, things were even better between Lex and me. If he doubted I was pregnant, he kept that to himself. He made sure I ate all my meals and took my prenatal vitamins. He forced me to go for walks even when I grumbled about it. He was the perfect alpha—attentive, affectionate.

By the end of the first month, it would have been impossible for Lex to deny I was pregnant. My stomach was visibly rounded, and my cravings increased. He made me anything I wanted, no matter what time of day or night. I felt kind of bad because I wasn't sure what I brought to the table. But he seemed content simply to be with me. His hunger for me seemed insatiable, and I felt the same toward him.

The solar eclipse omega pregnancy was only a three-month cycle. Nothing much happened the first two months, but during the third month I'd get huge. I worried a bit that my big stomach would turn him off, but there was nothing I could do about that.

Today was my two-month checkup, and Dr. Peters had promised us an ultrasound. Lex seemed excited as he dressed, and he kept kissing me and watching me.

"The ultrasound won't hurt, right?" he asked, running his fingers through his hair.

"No. Not at all. They just put gel on my stomach and move the paddle around." I laughed. "At most, it tickles."

"Okay. Good." He frowned. "What's the test with a needle?"

Surprised he knew about that test, I said, "The amniocentesis?"

"That's it." He hesitated. "Do you have to have that?"

"No. Only human have that."

"I see."

I smiled. "Where did you hear about that test?"

"I've been reading up. Gabriele and I have been researching on the web."

"Seriously?"

"Yep. We have nothing else to do. Charles still won't let us work in the compound." He scowled. "When will he relax?"

"I don't think he ever relaxes."

"Gabriele approached him about us running a restaurant, but he said no."

"You would want to do that?"

"Just for lunchtime meals maybe?" He sighed. "I need something to do. I'm going stir-crazy. It's fine when you're home, but you go off to work, and I feel weird being home alone."

"When the baby comes, there will be plenty to do."

That didn't seem to help; if anything, his face got even more tense. "I don't know anything about babies. I don't want to be left alone with the kid. I might accidentally kill it."

"No." I laughed. "Besides, I'll be home for three months after the baby is born."

He brightened. "Really?"

"Yeah."

He seemed visibly relieved. "Oh, thank God."

"Did you think I'd just toddle off to work after popping out a baby and leave you in charge?"

"What the hell do I know about this stuff?" He raised his brows.

"I wouldn't do that to you. Alphas aren't the ones who usually stay home with the babies."

"Exactly. But because Charles is being such a dick, our roles are reversed right now. I don't like it. I want to work."

"Gabriele can't convince Charles to change his mind?"

He chuffed. "They barely speak. Charles tries never to be home."

"Poor Gabriele. He must be lonely."

"He is. But as you know, there aren't a lot of available alphas in the compound."

I smiled. "No. That's how I met you. I went looking. Well, Dr. Peters made me go looking."

"If Charles doesn't let Gabriele leave the compound for a day trip soon, Gabriele might try and make a break for it. The poor guy needs to get laid."

I grinned. "I could try talking to Charles."

"About the restaurant idea or Gabriele's sex life?"

"Both?"

He chuckled and hugged me. "You ready? We're going to be late for our appointment."

"I'm ready." We left the cabin and made our way down the street toward the clinic. Now that Gabriele and Lex knew about the solar eclipse omegas, the lockdown had been lifted. Children played in the yards, and pregnant omegas didn't hide inside their houses anymore. I was relieved because it made Lex feel like less of an outsider.

Once we reached the clinic, one of my coworkers weighed me and then led us to an examination room. Dr. Peters joined us after a short wait.

"How are you two today?" he asked cheerfully.

"Good," I said."

"Excited to see the baby," Lex announced.

He had no idea how happy I was to hear him say that. It was obvious from his happy expression that he wasn't secretly harboring suspicions that the pregnancy wasn't real. That was the first time it really hit me Lex was 100 percent on board. I hadn't realized how much I'd feared he was just going along with everything to pacify me.

Dr. Peters pulled the sonogram machine over to the examination table. "You know the drill, Dylan."

"Yep." I climbed on the table and lay down. I lifted my shirt and smiled at Lex. "I've seen a hundred of these. Never really thought I'd be the one lying on the table."

His expression was gentle. "I'm glad it's you I'm experiencing this with."

Chuckling, Dr. Peters spread gel on my stomach. "You two are adorable. I'd never have thought of matching you and Lex, Dylan. I guess the Ancients know what they're doing after all."

"I hope so. They're supposedly running everything."

Lex's expression changed, but when he saw me looking at him, he forced a smile. Dr. Peters fired up the machine, and soon we were looking at a black-and-gray image on the screen.

"All the arms and legs are present and accounted for." Dr. Peters squinted at the screen. "Heartbeat is strong, lungs look great." He smiled. "This baby is going to be a good size."

"It's all the food Lex makes for me." I laughed.

"You're not fat though," Dr. Peters said. "Everything looks perfect. You and the baby."

I met Lex's gaze, and I felt a bit choked up. "We're having a baby. An actual baby."

He nodded, and his eyes seemed glassy too. He wasn't a hugely emotional person, so it touched me even more to know he felt what I felt.

Dr. Peters printed the image and then turned off the machine. He handed Lex the picture, and Lex stared at it with an expression of wonder. "It really looks like a baby."

"That's because it is." Dr. Peters smirked. "Funny how that works."

Lex laughed.

"Okay, well, whatever you're doing, just keep doing it. Everything is phenomenal."

I wiped the gel off my stomach with the paper towels Dr. Peters handed me. "When do you need to see me next?"

"You're going on paternity leave this week, right?" he asked.

"Yes." I was looking forward to that too. A whole month of just me and Lex home together. I couldn't wait. Once the baby came, things would get a lot harder.

"Unless you experience bleeding or actual contractions, I shouldn't need to see you until your scheduled C-section in four weeks."

"Great." I slid off the table.

"I'll keep him well fed until then," Lex said. He hesitated. "Uh… I wanted to ask you some things about how this all goes. I mean the delivery. I know you're going to do a C-section, but how will I know when it's time to bring him in? What if he goes into early labor? Will I know that?"

Dr. Peters grinned. "When it's real labor, you'll know. There will be no mistaking the pain he's in." His smile faded. "But remember, he has to get in here within thirty minutes. That leaves no time for anything like showers or scenic drives. When real labor starts, you get him here. The earlier the better."

"Okay." Lex's jaw was tense. "I can't believe the solar eclipse omegas have no way to birth the child other than a C-section. That seems like such an obvious oversight."

Dr. Peters nodded. "Ours is not to reason why…"

"I'm just glad I don't have to deal with being pregnant *and* having a period." I scowled. "It's weird enough being a man who can get pregnant."

Lex laughed. "You do have to go through a lot. But I suppose in a way, you should feel honored."

"I should?" I frowned.

"Yeah, you were chosen. Without your kind, none of us would be here. From what Charles said, you saved our species. You're not just special to me; you're special to our entire kind."

My heart warmed at his heartfelt words. "Thanks, Lex."

"Don't thank me. I'm just happy to be with you."

I grinned. "So you're a romantic after all."

He twisted his lips. "I wasn't. Not even a little."

"But then you met me." I smirked.

He shrugged. "Yeah, then I met you."

Chapter Thirty

Lex

Dylan and I were enjoying a lazy morning on the sun-drenched porch, when Charles came striding up the driveway. My gut immediately tensed, just like it always did when he appeared. He stopped in front of us, unsmiling as usual. Well, to be fair, he smiled at Dylan, but it faded as soon as he faced me.

"Morning, Lex." His voice was gruff.

"To what do we owe this pleasure?" I asked sardonically.

Dylan laughed softly.

"Since Dylan is ready to pop out the baby tomorrow, I figured it was time you got the closure you wanted." He shifted uneasily. "If you've hung in with him this long, I have to assume your intentions are pure."

I sat up, staring at him intently. "Of course my intentions are pure, and what do you mean you're going to give me closure?"

"About your dad." He looked uncomfortable. "I don't think you should have to forever wonder about how your dad died."

My heart picked up speed. "Okay."

"It's about time," Dylan grumbled. "You should have told him months ago." He rubbed his big belly. "He obviously wasn't going anywhere."

"I couldn't be sure." He grimaced. "But Gabriele convinced me that it's time you knew the truth."

"Gabriele convinced you?" I laughed. "I didn't think you two talked."

He shrugged. "Can't avoid him all the time. Occasionally he says something worth listening to."

"How can you give me closure?"

He leaned against the porch pillar. "I didn't kill your dad, which I think you already know."

"Yes." I frowned.

"But I know who… or should I say what did."

I squinted at him, not sure how to respond.

He crossed his arms in front of his broad chest. "Your dad wouldn't stop coming after Jack and Carter. He was relentless."

"I know." His tenacity had shocked even me. He'd refused to let Jack be happy with Carter.

Charles cleared his throat. "Dylan already knows this, but Carter was a solar eclipse omega."

I widened my eyes. "He was?"

"Yes. That was why they were here. Carter was with child." Charles studied me. "They should have been safe here, but your father bribed a guard to get Jack and Carter outside of the back gates. There, your dad was planning on murdering them. But he didn't get the chance."

"Did Jack kill him first?" I asked.

"No. According to Jack, both he and Carter would have died if… if agents from the Ancients hadn't interfered.

"Agents from the Ancients?" Dylan looked as confused as me.

"The Ancients have… others… who can do their bidding. The Ancients themselves never come here, but they do keep watch, and they do intervene when they must. In the case of Carter and your father, they had to intervene or Carter and his baby would have died."

"You said who or what killed my father." I narrowed my eyes.

"Jack said something came from the woods." Charles wrinkled his brow. "Creatures. Half wolf, half man."

I blinked at him, not sure if he was joking. He didn't look like he was joking.

"These creatures killed your father and his driver to protect Carter." He grimaced. "I work with the Ancients, but I've never actually seen creatures such as the ones Jack described. But I believe I know what they were."

"What were they?" Dylan asked.

Charles hesitated. "Harlotz. They are guardians of old. They hunt in wolf form, but attack in a more human shape. They're brutal, and terrifying. It's strange that they would be sent. They're not a good choice to set loose on this world. They're ruthless and hard to control. I can only guess the Ancients truly believed there was no other way to stop Corbin."

I shuddered. "My God." It was horrible to think of Dad dying in that way, but I also knew he'd never have stopped until both Jack and Carter were dead.

"I couldn't tell you the details because I'd have had to explain about the solar eclipse omegas too. It's because Carter was a solar eclipse omega that the Ancients protected him. I wasn't prepared to tell you about him or the others. I couldn't do that just to give you closure. My job is to protect the solar eclipse omegas, and you were... not to be trusted." He frowned. "I like to think that has changed."

"I have changed."

"Yes." He nodded somewhat grudgingly.

I frowned. "If my father was killed outside the gates, why bring his car inside?"

Charles sighed. "I had it dismantled to hide the evidence that he'd been here. If the cops had found the car and gotten involved, well, knowing what you know now, I'm sure you see why I couldn't let that happen."

A chill went down my spine. "What happened to the bodies?"

"According to Jack, there wasn't much left." His mouth was a grim line. "What was left, the creatures carried off into the woods."

Dylan shifted beside me. "Jesus."

I took his hand, and he squeezed my fingers. "I guess if you'd told me this in the beginning, I wouldn't have believed you. I'm finding it hard to swallow even now."

Charles studied me, his gaze assessing. "I understand. You, of course, realize this story can never be shared. I know you'll probably tell Gabriele, but other than that, no one on the outside can hear about any of this."

"Who would I tell?" I frowned and looked at Dylan. "The only people I care about are inside the compound."

Charles straightened. "Well, now you have your answers. Hopefully you have the closure you wanted."

"Thank you."

Dylan grunted. "Oh, God."

Charles and I both looked at him and found him clutching his stomach. "Shit." He groaned. "Oh, that fucking hurts."

I stood, panic jolting through me. "Is it… is it the baby?"

He gritted his teeth. "I hope so, otherwise something is really wrong with me."

I started to take his arm, but his face contorted, and he pushed me away. He was flushed and panting when he finally opened his eyes. "Get the bag. We need to go."

Charles stood watching, looking flustered. "Lex, just go to the clinic. I'll get the bag and bring it to you. Where is it?"

"Bedroom," I yelled, helping Dylan down the steps to the car. Even though it was only about a ten-minute trip on foot, no way would we be able to walk. He was in too much pain, and it would probably take an hour. We only had thirty minutes.

I got him in the car, and he leaned against the door, cursing and writhing. My hands shook so hard I almost dropped the keys, but I managed to start the engine. "It's okay. It won't be long now." I kept my voice calm, even though inside I was definitely panicking.

He kicked and groaned. "This is fucking unreal," he hissed. "I didn't expect it to hurt so much."

I gritted my teeth and backed carefully out of the driveway. "Two minutes and we'll be at the clinic."

"Fuck," he rasped, throwing his head back.

I drove slowly because I was afraid of getting into an accident if I wasn't super careful. Even so, we were there with plenty of time to spare. I helped Dylan from the car and up the stairs.

Dr. Peters greeted us at the doorway to the clinic. "Charles called me to tell me you were on the way." He sounded breathless.

"Oh, yeah. I didn't think to do that." I frowned.

"Of course you didn't." He smiled. "The alphas never remember. They're too busy tending to their omega."

Dylan groaned. "This has given me a new appreciation for our patients."

Dr. Peters chuckled and led the way to the surgery. "Lex, do you want to be in here, or do you want to wait outside?"

"I want to be here." I didn't even hesitate.

A slight blonde walked up. She smiled and handed me a gown and mask. "Put these on."

"Thanks." I gave her a nervous smile.

"I'm Priscilla. I'm filling in for Dylan while he's out on paternity leave."

"Could you two maybe get acquainted later? I'm having a fucking baby here," Dylan grumbled.

I grimaced.

She laughed, looking unfazed. "All omegas are grumpy when they get here. Sometimes they even hit their alphas and yell. Dylan's being pretty nice right now."

I slipped into the gown, while Dr. Peters helped Dylan up on the operating table. Priscilla rubbed iodine over Dylan's rounded belly, and Dr. Peters administered gas to help Dylan relax. Then he gave him a shot to block all pain during the surgery.

I stood beside Dylan, holding his hand. His grip was so tight, my fingers felt like they were about to crack under the pressure. "You're doing great," I said softly.

He nodded, looking nervous. "At least the pain is gone."

I smiled. "Now we just let Dr. Peters do his thing."

"It's so weird being on this side of it all." He sighed. "I'm glad you're here with me."

"Me too."

"Sometimes the alphas prefer to stay outside." He held my gaze. "You… you can do that if you want."

I scowled. "No. I want to be here with you."

Tension seemed to leave his face. "I didn't want you to feel obligated."

"Stop." I kissed his forehead. "No place I'd rather be."

He sighed. "We're having a baby, Lex."

"Yep." I smiled, excitement buzzing inside of me.

Dr. Peters was calm and precise as he made his incision. I looked away during a lot of it because, while I wasn't a squeamish type, I didn't like the idea of anything slicing into Dylan. I spent most of my time talking to Dylan, and soon there was the squawk of a newborn baby, and Dr. Peters held up a wiggling child.

"Congratulations, you have a beautiful baby boy." He grinned.

I met Dylan's tearful gaze, my eyes stinging. I kissed him and he laughed against my lips.

"We did it," he said.

I nodded because the lump in my throat made it hard to talk.

"Lex, you want to cut the umbilical cord?" Dr. Peters looked at me expectantly.

"Sure." I moved down to where the baby was. He was pink and chubby, and his eyes were a soft blue. I fell in love the second I saw him. I snipped the cord, finding it way tougher to cut through than expected.

Priscilla took the baby, weighed him, and wiped him clean. Then she swaddled him in a blue blanket, and she brought him over to us. He was still fussing but not actively crying. The expression on Dylan's face almost made me start crying. I'd never seen such love as when he looked at our son. He kissed the baby's little head, and he sniffed.

"He's so perfect," he whispered.

I nodded. "He is."

"I already love him." He met my eyes, and there was a flash of guilt and confusion. I knew instantly he was thinking of Ayden, and my heart almost broke.

I leaned down and said against his ear, "Loving him doesn't take away from how much you loved Ayden."

Tears spilled onto his cheeks, but he nodded. "I'll do better this time. I'll protect him."

I almost started to cry too because his pain was so raw. "We *both* will always protect him. I'll never hurt him, and I'll never hurt you."

He kissed the baby's bald head. "I know you'll protect us. This time I got it right."

"You never got it wrong. Jacob did."

He sighed, gazing down at our son. "After all you and I went through together, Lex, how is it possible this is where we ended up?"

"True love?" I smiled.

"You don't believe in true love. Remember? It's too fantastical."

I took his chin and kissed his pretty mouth. When I lifted my head, I said, "You've made me a believer."

Epilogue

(Three months after the birth of the baby)

Dylan

"Charles agreed to let me open the restaurant." Lex's gaze was bright. "He finally gave in."

I widened my eyes. "Seriously?"

We were outside on the front porch, and our son, Will, sat on my lap. He was gnawing on my finger with his gums and squealing every few minutes. "Why did he change his mind?"

Lex grinned. "Gabriele wouldn't let up. He's going stir-crazy. I have you to keep me happy. Poor Gabriele is bored out of his mind."

"Has Charles still refused to let Gabriele go into town?"

"Yes. He says an alpha matching Hank's description was spotted lurking, and it's too risky to let Gabriele venture from the compound. He knows if Hank can't get me, he'll be only too happy to grab Gabriele in my place."

I shivered at the reference to Hank. I prayed that asshole alpha would just go away, but feared he was just waiting for his chance at revenge. I almost worried more about Gabriele than Lex because he was more vocal about wanting to venture into town. He was lonely, and there weren't many available alphas to socialize with inside the compound.

"Charles can't keep Gabriele behind these walls forever."

"I know. Gabriele is mostly happy here, but he does need... other things too." Lex grimaced.

"Yeah. It's a lot to expect him to be celibate the rest of his life."

"Especially an omega like Gabriele. He had a very active love life before."

"Poor guy."

Lex frowned. "How come Charles doesn't seem to need anyone in his life?"

"There aren't many female omegas here that are single. Besides, he's married to his job."

"God, yes. Gabriele says he never takes days off."

I grinned. "But you two get to do your restaurant! That's wonderful."

He nodded, looking ecstatic. "I don't want you to worry. We're only going to do lunch. That way I'm here to help with Will most of the time."

"Lex, you have every right to do something you enjoy. Besides, I told Dr. Peters I want less hours when I go back next week. I need to be home with Will. That's what makes me happiest, being home with you two."

He leaned over and kissed me. "Thank you for being supportive."

"The compound is going to love your food. I just know it."

He sighed. "Well, it's not as prestigious as running a fancy art gallery, or being the head of a mob. But it will give me some self-respect to contribute something."

"You contribute constantly."

"I'm an alpha. I need to work."

"I understand your macho needs. You do you."

"I'd rather do you."

My face warmed, and I covered Will's ears, grinning. "Shhh. You'll traumatize our child talking like that."

He smiled. "I'll wait until he's down for his nap to talk dirty to you."

"It's a date."

He leaned back in his rocking chair. "I have a few recipes I'm going to try out on you."

"Can't wait."

Will started fussing a little, and without a word, Lex took him from me and started bouncing him on his knee. "I need to pick up some milk and cheese later. Oh, and diapers. God, don't want to run out of those," he murmured.

My heart squeezed watching him. He wore a white fitted shirt and jeans, and he looked so sophisticated with his high cheekbones and perfect sable hair. He'd taken to fatherhood beautifully. He'd been worried he wouldn't know how to be a dad, but he was a natural.

He glanced over and caught me watching him. "What?" He smiled.

"I was just wondering how I got so lucky."

His expression instantly became serious. "I'm the lucky one."

"Maybe we're both lucky."

He pursed his lips. "Actually, luck has nothing to do with this. We were fated. Meant to be."

"What if we'd never taken that cooking class. Would we have still met? Not all fated mates find each other."

"I don't want to think about that." His voice was surprisingly hard.

"I'm just theorizing."

He scowled. "I can't even entertain the thought of not being with you."

"Calm down. Don't get upset."

He clamped his jaw and then gave a jagged laugh. "Sorry." He hung his head. "It's just sometimes I'm afraid that this is too good to be true, and that the Ancients will send Charles to tell me there's been a mistake."

I scrunched my face. "You're holding our son. You couldn't have gotten me pregnant if we weren't fated."

"I know what you're saying logically, but my greatest fear is losing you."

"You're not going to lose me. Ever. Remember, I'm the gullible guy who believes in a love that transcends even death."

"Yeah, that's right." His eyes were very blue.

"I'm not sure what loser came up with that whole *till death do us part* crap, but you're not getting away from me that easy." I grinned.

He laughed, and the tension left him. "God, I love you, Dylan."

"I love you too," I whispered. "How about we put Will down for his nap?"

"And I can talk dirty to you?"

"You can do anything you want to me."

He grinned. "Why are we still on the porch?"

"Hell if I know."

We went into the house and put Will to bed.

Then Lex taught me a few new dirty words.

JOIN MY MAILING LIST
Get a free book!
https://dl.bookfunnel.com/zz
ayvv4ka7

Other Books by S.C. Wynne

Hard-Ass is Here
Christmas Crush
Hard-Ass Vacation
The New Boss
Guarding My Heart
The Cowboy and the Barista
Up in Flames
Until the Morning
Falling into Love
The Fire Underneath
Kiss and Tell
Secrets from the Edge-Rerelease coming
soon!
Hiding Things-Rerelease coming soon!
Home to Danger-Rerelease coming soon!
Assassins Are People Too #1-Rerelease
coming soon!
Painful Lessons-Rerelease coming soon!
Assassins Love People Too #2-Rerelease
coming soon!
Believing Rory-Rerelease coming soon!
Unleashing Love

More Books Continued

Starting New

The Cowboy and the Pencil-Pusher

Memories Follow

Shadow's Edge Book #1

Shadow's Return Book #2

My Omega's Baby (Bodyguard & Babies Book #1)

Rockstar Baby (Bodyguard & Babies Book #2)

Manny's Surprise Baby (Bodyguard & Babies Book#3)

Strange Medicine (Dr. Maxwell Thornton Mysteries Book #1)

Doctor in the Desert

Redemption

Married to Murder

Crashing Upwards

Single Omegas Only

Footsteps in the Dark Anthology

Omega Kidnapped Book One

Copyright (c) 2019 by S.C. Wynne

Omega Tricked-Book Two
 (Bad Guys and Babies Series)

This is a work of fiction. Any resemblance to persons living or dead is entirely coincidental.

Made in the USA
Lexington, KY
13 September 2019